EDUARDO FERNANDO VARELA

# PATAGONIA
## ROUTE 203

*Translated from the Spanish by*
*Peter Bush*

MLP

Originally published by Casa de Las Américas, La Havane
and Editions Métailié, Paris.

First published in the English language in 2024 by
Mountain Leopard Press
an imprint of HEADLINE PUBLISHING GROUP

1

Cataloguing in Publication Data is available from the British Library

Hardback ISBN 978-1-914495-48-9
Trade paperback ISBN 978-1-80069-915-1

Designed and typeset by EM&EN
Printed and bound in Great Britain by Clays Ltd, Elcograf S.p.A.

Headline's policy is to use papers that are natural, renewable and recyclable
products and made from wood grown in well-managed forests and other
controlled sources. The logging and manufacturing processes are expected
to conform to the environmental regulations of the country of origin.

HEADLINE PUBLISHING GROUP
An Hachette UK Company
Carmelite House
50 Victoria Embankment
London EC4Y 0DZ

www.headline.co.uk
www.hachette.co.uk

*For restless Laura*

*For luminous Persia*

The road cut across the steppe, twisted between hills and valleys, then up and over slopes that bent the horizon's line into a position it held for kilometres, as if it were floating in the air. Towards the cordillera the continent arched its back like a cat preparing to pounce; towards the ocean, a huge plain fought the sky over the horizon. The wind blew down from eternal glaciers, nervously caressing pasture lands and seeming to ruffle the earth. When its gusts combined with the sea breeze, huge, languid whirlwinds of dust spiralled into the sky. A distant dot on the landscape, the truck went on its way, swaying from side to side, pursuing a rhythm that surged from the depths of the planet. The undulating terrain slowed its progress to the slither of a lethargic snake, and rather than motor, the truck seemed to slip along in a liquid stream.

Parker drove keeping his eye on the road, never blinking, resting one hand on the steering wheel and the other on the back of the seat, as if embracing a would-be companion. After hours of isolation in that emptiness, he travelled along hypnotised by the slow, constant movement, his mind a blank, cradled by the to-and-fro. He was surrounded by a vast desert that at some point met up with the rest of the planet, but there, in the midst of that solitude reinforced by remoteness, it imposed boundaries set by its own capricious rules.

1

Parker was transporting cargos of fruit on behalf of a mysterious enterprise from fertile valleys to remote Atlantic ports visited by the farthest-flung maritime routes in the southern hemisphere that communicated with the east. Ships under exotic flags that seemed alien to the territory unloaded cheap goods and filled their holds with fruit and frozen meat for the return journey. Parker spent hours and days in his drab den, driving that vehicle and imagining it was a space capsule. He was enclosed in his cabin amid a plethora of clothes, books, beer bottles, a coffee thermos, music cassettes and dog-eared scraps of maps he had to piece together like a puzzle in order to identify his route, photographs stuck to the sides and items of handicraft that hung from the ceiling as if gravity did not exist. The black case of his gleaming saxophone was propped beside him, one of the few elements he had saved from his previous life, his only company on those lonely journeys, though he never succeeded in coaxing out a single note. Every once in a while he shifted in his seat and surveyed the passing land-scape to detect the minimal changes in the terrain from one kilometre to the next: the changing shades of the steppe, the shadow of a cloud resting on a hillside, or a fleet-of-foot animal escaping over the scrublands. Parker navigated rather than drove, and when the straightness of the road allowed, he closed his eyes and cruised for a few seconds, challenging his sense of direction. Sometimes the languid hum of the engine would fade almost to the point of becoming a distant vibration, then nothing at all: absolute silence, were it not for the whispering wind brushing against the cabin. A flock of ostriches might rush from nowhere, running alongside for a good stretch, listening to the engine before they melted into the bushes on the low hills. When that emptiness enveloped him, the truck's wheels made a gentle lift-off from the asphalt and rose above the yellow contours of the desert. From that moment on, the air thickened, weight dissolved in the atmosphere and the road became a hesitant line vanishing into the distance. As Parker gained height and the sky turned a deep blue, he saw dry river-beds like scars on the planet's gnarled surface. The detail of things was lost, the past was shrouded, the future seemed a transparent halo, and all that remained was a vaporous, mysterious present, home to gentle stimuli, a sweet languor allowing him to wander through infinite space and time. Night and day, he could meander for hours; he had no timetable, only rendezvous that depended on the imprecise departures or arrivals of the vessels awaiting their cargo. Sometimes he endured lengthy, lifeless days before reaching his destination, otherwise he drove on, stopping only to fill up the tank or shower in the bathrooms of a service station lost in the middle of nowhere. When sunrise or sunset signalled the end of his shift, Parker prepared his vessel to land at the side of the road, reduced speed and looked for the perfect spot to establish his encampment, one without slopes or obstacles. The truck juddered to a halt in clouds of dust, Parker leapt from his cabin as if reaching dry land after months on the high seas and checked that the terrain was suitable, with firewood nearby. He used a lazy, rotating arm with a pulley fixed to his vehicle to unload what had once been his home. His trailer disgorged a wooden table, a battered leather sofa, an old icebox, a standard lamp, a large carpet, a wardrobe, a bed and mattress, and a side table with lamp. It took him less than an hour to unroll the carpet and arrange his furniture, creating a perfect homely lounge beneath the immense sky of the steppe, lit up at night by various cables connected to the battery. From afar Parker's encampment looked like a miniature city silhouetted against the frenzied red of twilight clouds that at night challenged the Milky Way with its twinkling lights. The desolate plain was his favourite habitat, the last homeland surviving of the many he had lost throughout his life, the only place in the world where he felt relaxed and secure. It was bliss in such a space, an inner exile sheltering him from all the evils on this earth, and he spent days on end camping out on those empty, anonymous expanses. He sometimes eked out his journeys, choosing secondary roads to extend the magical time that existed like a state of grace between his departure point and his destination. Those late arrivals infuriated his boss, old Constanzo, the owner of several trucks and a modest transport firm that operated between the cordillera and sea ports, for whom Parker worked more out of ease of habit than convenience. They had met years before in a tavern at the beginning of the huge steppe that extended to the fjords of the Strait of Magellan and Tierra del Fuego.

Parker came from Buenos Aires, fleeing a turbulent past, searching for solitude and anonymity at the continent's southern tip. The driver of the small removals van who was transporting him and his few belongings had abandoned him outside that tavern because he hadn't been paid. The few belongings Parker had salvaged from his last shipwreck were heaped by the roadside. Old Constanzo and Parker had met at a table in the restaurant when the latter was looking for a way to continue his journey southwards. After a brief conversation, his future boss, a sharp observer of human fauna, realised he could put unreserved trust in that taciturn, prickly misanthrope. He brought Parker and his belongings aboard and employed him to help load and

4

unload merchandise in ports. In exchange, he gave him food, a few pesos and lodging in the trailer of the truck he was now driving. Constanzo was too old and ailing to persevere in that life, and needed only a couple of weeks to feel he could entrust his vehicle to his new employee, who seemed honest and responsible, and retire to lead a sedentary life after an existence shackled to the rigours of the road. Parker was the ideal employee: he asked few questions, came cheap and had one ambition: to commit to that peaceful wandering life. Their initial relationship was hassle free, but old Constanzo had become addicted to drink and gambling, and began to mismanage his enterprise. For his part, Parker could not wholeheartedly trust a man who hobnobbed with smugglers and dealt in goods that were for the most part illegal. It was for that reason Constanzo insisted his trucker use secondary roads, patrolled by local police who were easier to corrupt, and avoid main roads that were under the jurisdiction of the national gendarmerie. Sometimes in the early hours Parker had to load and unload in abandoned sheds mysterious boxes full of what purported to be plastic baubles. He knew he might run into problems at any moment, but enjoyed an unstable, anonymous life that verged on the clandestine. He floated over vast expanses of desert that absorbed his existence in their remoteness, atomising his past in wind and dust, that left it hollowed out and unidentifiable. Parker drove for days along inhospitable roads that shot like arrows towards the immense steppe, and stopped in the last settlements to stock up on food and petrol, as if he too were setting sail from some remote harbour. He exchanged a few words with service-station workers and then let himself be meekly guided by the road. He spent his days on the asphalt talking to himself, listening to music or inventing solitary distractions that helped lighten the passage of time. His favourite diversion was a kind of lottery that involved filling bits of cardboard with the final digits of the registration numbers of passing vehicles, an activity that could last for weeks on roads where only two or three drove by each day, one of them being his own.

After living for several years in those far-off places, Parker learned to distinguish subtle shifts in the terrain. Sometimes it needed only a curve to vary the colour of the land, or a slope for the shrubs to change the way their branches bent according to the direction of the wind. Or a change in the vegetation, as now, when, prompted by a whim of nature, yellow thickets of thorn bushes that he was seeing for the first time made a sudden appearance. "Keep straight on that way, turn left on Thursday and at night turn left again, and sooner or later you'll reach the sea," he had been told by road menders, but it was already Friday, the sun was setting amid dense dark clouds and the road he was driving along snaked between monotonous bends and hills. The setting sun's warm light lengthened the shadows of his truck against the contours of high ridges, and he was yet to find a single side road, a minimal change in the route ahead, a sign heralding the proximity of the sea. And by now it was almost Saturday. Leaning back in his seat, staring at the asphalt, Parker lifted a cigarette to his lips. While his fingers tapped the steering wheel to the rhythm of the music, he watched the sunset through the side window, took one long drag and hummed the tune, his eyes half-closed. A herd of wild guanacos and their young crossed the road in front and forced him to reduce speed. They were a graceful enough sight, necks erect, stopping now and then on a little mound to observe the intruder invading their territory before leaping over the barbed-wire fences along the roadside in elegant, time-honoured fashion and vanishing into the distance. Parker reduced his speed to the minimum, and watched the herd with a mixture of delight and anxiety: he knew only too well what might happen if an inexpert foal mistimed its leap, he had seen that happen dozens of times. His gaze lingered on one of the last animals running towards terrain unsuitable for jumping, and felt alarmed. The guanaco spurted and readied itself to jump, but at the last moment realised its error and stopped. It retreated hesitantly while the rest of the herd ran across the steppe, then it resumed its run. Parker knew it was about to make a fatal mistake, and shut his eyes. The animal made a second attempt at jumping. Part of its body made it over, but its back legs caught on the wire, and the post supporting the wire lodged under its rear and suspended it there like a dummy. While it kicked and shook trying to free itself, Parker stopped his truck on the roadside, although there was little he could do: the animal would suffer a slow death, and eagles would circle lower and lower until their feast could begin. That barbed wire was littered with dry bones and carcasses, eviscerated by birds and foxes, though their hides and bones remained intact, blanched by the Patagonian sun. At the last moment, in an act bordering on the miraculous, the guanaco freed itself with one violent shake, reached the other side and trotted off towards its herd as if nothing had happened. Parker gave a sigh of relief at what he believed to be a good omen and drove off, but his relief soon reverted to gloom: the hazy light that came after sunset before darkness descended created an opaque melancholy that invaded his body and gripped his innards.

The line of the horizon, which had been a huge space full of promise a moment before, now sloped downwards as if following the curve of the planet: it was the way pitch-black night was heralded in those latitudes. The smoke from his cigarette coiled for a second in the cabin, then escaped through the window. Parker wondered if the force dragging him into certain areas of his mind derived from the time of day, the slow beat of the music or his unstable psychological state. He knew what the answer was but couldn't turn back: the hands of the clock were nailed into that cosmic quadrant, staking him in that present and that landscape. His only option was to change the music; he had learned in hours and kilometres on the road that it was better not to quarrel with his whimsical spirit. He stretched a hand out to the chaotic, littered territory at his side and fumbled among old music cassettes, granting chance the privilege of choosing the next rhythms. He extracted one, the words on which were almost illegible, slotted it in and waited for the first notes to ring out.

As the music spread around the cabin, his thoughts realigned and something was born anew inside him. Distant happiness buried in the crannies of his memory suffused his gaze like an inner caress, blending with the melody and extracting the stake imprisoning him in that quadrant of time and landscape: such sudden, inexplicable epiphanies were the back door to something resembling happiness. He smiled, because he was about to exert his control over his capricious mind in that ambiguous glow that mediated between the last light of day and the darkness of the desert. In a moment he would feel better, and, after a while, better still. That instant was a temporary boundary post marking a turn in the day, a fissure in the frozen surface of time that called out to be greeted with a drink. He took a bottle of beer from his icebox, and was about to use the opener dangling from the dashboard when he was shaken by a hellish screech. Something had happened in his cassette player. His sudden twist of the wheel hit the truck and made it judder and go into a gentle skid. Parker threw his cigarette out of the window and tried to remove the cassette, but was stalled by the loops of tape hanging down like a bunch of intestines. He tugged, the skein tangled round his fingers, yielded in the end, and he used a pencil to rewind the tape and reinsert it. The rhythms flowed again, clear and light, but were drowned once again inside the device with an agonising rattle that augured disaster. Parker cursed under his breath as he hurled the gutted tape out of the window. Within seconds the wind wrapped the brown tape around bushes on the plain, but Parker's mood also snagged on one of his inner thickets, and there would be no way to rewind it before nightfall. His days were like that, exposed to the numerous avatars that lay in wait as he drove along. He would have loved to believe in a mischievous deity of the road, lurking in that solitude to play practical jokes on him, but he couldn't. He tried to surrender to the popular myths and legends that proliferated along the highways of Patagonia, to yield to an ingenuous magical gaze upon the world as a way of being at one with the landscape, but his absolute rationalism intervened.

When he met locals, he listened to their talk of the fantastic creatures and strange phenomena that surfaced in those desert wastes, imaginings that served to enliven the barren heaths. Such stories were told at night, around campfires, in the middle of the road, to strumming guitars, singing and alcohol. That was how Parker had first heard

9

tell of the Trinitarians, cannibals who lived in the salt flats, of mysterious submarines that appeared on the Atlantic coast, of spaceships with bases in the craters of the cordillera and of phantoms in abandoned mines. However, nights of crossing those dark, solitary fastnesses and seeing no apparitions, extra-terrestrial beings or cannibals confirmed him in his scepticism. The fable of the Trinitarians was the one he found most attractive: it was rumoured that in the era of the conquest a Spanish galleon had been swept along by storms and wrecked on those coasts. The few survivors had been devoured by Indians, more from hunger than any evil inclinations. From that moment onward a curse lay on the descendants of those barbarians, who were born with the features of men from Asturias or Extremadura and used words uttered in a strange accent very few could recognise as ancient Spanish. Moreover, they retained peninsular memories and customs, such as the taste of meals, certain dances and songs foreign to their rites, and a strange nostalgia for the unknown land of the devoured. It was said that the Indians themselves attributed such outlandish traits to divine punishment, and, fearing contagion, they confined those so possessed to the dark galleries of the mines, although some claimed they had used the white expanses of the salt flats. Several centuries later, few remained of those Spaniards reincarnated in Indians, or Indians possessed by Spaniards, in their mimetic forms. They starved to death in the desert, or died from horrible illnesses, having preserved intact their savage longing for human flesh.

Whoever was to blame, there would be no more music that night, so Parker decided to speak to himself. Hearing his own voice, after so many days without conversing with anyone, produced a strange feeling of companionship, as if it were a sudden encounter with a childhood friend. At first he found little to say, but after a time, as he became more confident, scattered words transformed into sentences and then long speeches. Song or soliloquy were the zenith of closeness to the self, a form of intimacy that laid bare matters of the soul. On this occasion he was not at all talkative, and, after a brief conversation, he changed tack and preferred to sing. He closed his eyes and reviewed his mental repertory to find the song best suited to that moment. The most diverse rhythms and melodies passed through his mind, from school songs to those that had been the musical soundtrack to subsequent years, but he did not linger on a single one: they were too sad, or laden with sombre omens. He let the radio decide; that was why it was there. The device began to search for the few frequencies that reached those far-flung haunts. First it was the hum of short and long waves fighting over the territory in the ether, then metallic noises that stopped with a jolt as if they had run into an obstacle. Parker was annoyed to find that everything, from his jokes to radio frequencies, kept snagging on the thorny scrub by the road, together with bits of paper and plastic bags blown along by the wind. Parker hated those treacherous, cunning thickets; he might not believe in the goblins of the road, but he had no doubts about the deceitful malice of those bushes, and at night enjoyed burning them on lofty bonfires that crackled and sparked in the half-dark. After all his attempts failed, he was forced to re-engage with technology: steadying the steering wheel between his knees, he half leaned out of the window and connected the radio to a wire aerial attached to the cabin roof. The device went silent, then there was a rush of radio stations with announcers who chatted about the day's horoscope and the benefits of believing in God, with messages and greetings, sales offers, folkloric ditties, meaningless conversations and dialogues, stations from bordering countries that somehow reached there, anonymous music, sport and weather forecasts.

Parker allowed that universe of sounds to parade past several times, but never stopped at any station in particular. When the radio finished its search, the voices disappeared at one end of the dial, as if turning a corner, then reappeared at the other, always following the same order. He let that round circulate a couple of times, before impatiently switching the radio off and consulting his oracle: the cabin's mirror to which he only resorted in moments of stress. He did not abuse it, he did not like to appeal to it for any trifling reason, but this time he had no choice.

"Little mirror, little mirror," he said, looking at himself askance, seeing days-old stubble, long wisps of faded red hair clustering over a face furrowed by premature wrinkles, and eyes sore from so many hours at the wheel. He repeated his invocation, but the oracle still did not respond, perhaps occupied by more important matters, so he preferred not to trouble it. He picked up his bottle of beer, cut a few slices of cheese and salami on the dashboard and, with a yawn, resumed his drive until the endless steppe was immersed in the dense midnight sky.

"I think we are lost," a sudden voice declared from the mirror. Parker reduced speed and stopped by the roadside, the truck's flashing sidelights dotting the darkness. He gathered together his navigational tools and jumped out of the cabin. The silence was what first caught his attention: for the first time in weeks there were only two or three gusts of wind, and that absence created a tranquillity that allowed him to hear the twinkling stars. He searched the nocturnal vault for the constellations where the reference points he used to find his bearings hung like baubles: the lonely Betelgeuse, the inevitable Southern Cross, the Milky Way whose silvery fingers caressed both hemispheres, Orion's belt touching Aldebaran. That night, however, the horizon was hidden behind huge dense clouds and the stars weren't helping. He had to consult his compass and circle his becalmed vehicle, looking for an axis where he could focus his existence, but the cardinal points were not helping either, and his instinct and senses were all he could use to discover where the ocean was on that devilish night. Standing still on the road, he raised his head and tried to catch the breeze coming from the mountains, crystalline as the floor of lakes and perfumed with the scent of woods and pristine glaciers. That was enough to confirm the way he should be going: as long as the cordillera was on that side, he could drive for several days without worrying, until he met the strong, penetrating aroma of saltwater.

○  ○

Parker reached his port of destination a few days late, mere hours before the ship's captain, who had been waiting impatiently, had decided to set sail. He delivered his cargo of fruit and turned his prow towards the north-east, on his way back to the central valleys. Old Constanzo was waiting for him there with another consignment and an advance on his wages that was in fact four months' back pay. Days later his crammed truck was once more heading across desolate plains towards the east coast of the southern cone, but before he crossed that far end of South America, he was expecting an important rendezvous, one of the few obligations Parker respected as if it were part of the cycle of nature, inexorable and impossible to predict, but one that frequently occurred. A vague date, the closeness of which Parker divined enigmatically, was to take place around that time, in those barren wastes. All he could do was wait, so he stopped on the verge, lingered, inspected his surroundings, guessed it would be a long wait and began the complicated operation of setting up camp before nightfall. Using that pulley system he himself had designed, a mechanical arm extracted his furniture from the trailer, one piece at a time, and lowered them to the ground. Parker arranged them in a circle, against the bulk of the vehicle, and organised the remaining items as neatly as any housewife would: in one corner, a pantry cupboard, next door, the kitchen range, and shelves with a few books, notebooks and motley items. Then he sorted the double bed, tugging the sheets and blankets to flatten out the faintest wrinkle, and installed the bedside table. He unrolled the carpet in the middle and placed on it chairs and a table on which he laid a tablecloth, a vase of plastic flowers and an ashtray. For his finishing touch he scattered around various lamps connected to the truck's battery. If the rigours of the climate demanded it, he covered his encampment with tarpaulins and plastic sheeting, otherwise the intense depths of night on the steppe were all there was overhead. Parker lived that life for the part of the year when the season of benign luminosity allowed him to exist in the open. In the dark, freezing part of the year, when everything became icy and threatening, Parker did what nature itself suggested: he enclosed himself in his cabin and hibernated like a mammal in its cave, slept for days on end, only getting up now and then to cook himself a hot meal. He made the most of the few hours of daylight to take a walk, wrapped in his sheepskin poncho that made him look like a troglodyte, peering at the sky and checking his truck had not been buried under copious snowdrifts or downpours of ash spat out by a nearby volcano. Once he had verified that the world and universe outside still existed, he immersed himself in sleep for several more days. His mind as well as his body sank into that lethargy, while his thoughts congealed for hours around a single becalmed image that a weary, mysterious hand kept changing as if in a slide show.

When he had finished setting up camp and had collected firewood and lit a fire, Parker arranged several strips of meat on the grill, let them cook slowly, then set the table for two. As he sank back in his armchair to smoke and leaf through a yellowing newspaper, he heard a distant sound coming along the road. He raised his head and looked round like a bloodhound pricking up its ears. Something was moving in the desert; the breeze tore through the dense silence of dusk and an engine's hum approached from the west. He stood up and walked to the road, still holding that daily paper, like someone going to his front door to see who is coming along the street. He halted in the middle of the asphalt ribbon and gazed at the horizon, where a couple of lights seemed to have stopped in the distance: in those vast empty spaces the movement of objects diminished to the point of invisibility. When the headlights were almost upon him, a vehicle rushed past, slicing the air with a muted whine. He looked at the car moving away until it became a distant murmur once again, and out of habit consulted a watch whose haphazard timekeeping rendered it useless. He would have to wait that night, and many more, before the man he was expecting

15

actually arrived. He walked back to the table, opened a bottle of wine, lit the candles on a candelabra, although daylight was still glimmering, and chewed silently on a chunk of cold, dry meat. His last encounter with a human being had occurred four days earlier, or maybe six, or a week; nor did he remember who it had been. Later on he took his sax from its case, sank back in his armchair and tried to play a note, but only produced a random series of out-of-tune chords that floated in the air. He chased them away like flies with a wave of his hand, as the shadow from his truck, lengthened by the sun's last rays, swathed the encampment in a gentle haze, continuing on its way along the floor of the desert until it disappeared. Without a single cloud to mar the vast expanse of sky, night's black shroud descended on cue. Parker picked up his notebook and began writing his diary by candlelight. He did not know why, but something hadn't been working properly over recent days, there had been a subtle disruption to the order of things. The mechanism he ignited every minute and every hour seemed to have jammed, its parts and cogs grinding with a series of faint squeaks. He got up and walked away from the vehicle enjoying its drowsy sleep like a good-natured pet, then looked up and sought an explanation from the firmament. His gaze vanished into the dark vault of the universe; the clouds had gone, but everything seemed serene up above: Pegasus was resting, indifferent and self-absorbed, his long tail resting on Andromeda while Bellatrix was seeking shelter in the arms of the Perseids. He returned to his armchair and fell asleep swaddled in blankets that made him look like an obese scarecrow. He tried to dream, his last resort in such circumstances, but dreams at the end of the continent did not come automatically and he had to employ strategies to invoke them. The few that did reach those remote parts scurried into their burrows the moment the sun rose, like nocturnal animals, until daylight dragged them from their hiding places and dissolved them. Below the fortieth parallel they were mean and basic like the terrain; born contorted by gale-force winds, like the scrub on the steppe, they evolved in parallel to a reality the tips of their branches occasionally touched: in that barren land, where even carrion was scarce, dreams could not feed on desires or remnants of daytime unless they chanced upon a forgotten memory caught on a barbed-wire fence like a dying animal, nothing more than a paltry illusion.

That land was an avaricious whirlpool swallowing everything and hollowing out the consciousness of everyone that crossed it, which was why Parker tossed and turned in the night, grasping at straws so as not to disappear. His sterilised memory was a barrier that prevented him from seeing beyond the day when he had assembled the small sums available to him and departed the capital city never to return. A dark abyss lurked behind, where a woman and a child wandered like ghostly spectres, a zone where he was now an intruder, because it belonged to someone Parker had long since ceased to be.

The following week, one morning when the first rays of sun lit up his truck, the camp was suffused by a golden hue, the table was set and the fire still smoking. As he read his book, wrapped in blankets, Parker suddenly looked up and around, trying to catch what it was: another muffled sound was approaching from the south-east. He glanced at his watch to distract his eyes, then headed towards the double yellow line on the asphalt and stood there like a potentate. A mirage, a blurred, vaporous shape, mutated into a car caked in earth and mud, laden with luggage, leaving a dust cloud in its wake. The vehicle slowed down, reached Parker with its last gasp, almost at walking pace. It was about to stop, but there was a slight incline and the vehicle gathered speed and drove on. A tall, thin man with dishevelled, greying hair, wearing a long overcoat and faded scarf, got out of the car, and ran and stood in front of it, trying to stop it with his body.

"Why do you take so long when I need help?" the new-comer said.

Parker observed the scene as if he had seen a ghost, picked up a rock from the verge and ran to place it under a wheel. The car juddered to a halt, and the man fixed the other wheels with more stones, then smiled and headed towards Parker with open arms. Their hug lasted the time it took the dust cloud to disappear.

"What happened, journo?"

"It's the brakes, I have to anchor the car whenever I stop. They stopped working one morning."

"I didn't mean that. We agreed to meet last week, if I'm not mistaken," Parker observed, taking offence. The meetings between Parker and his journalist friend did not have any particular purpose, they happened out of the blue, were unpredictable, however much they agreed specific dates at specific locations on the road. It was impossible to respect any fixed points of space and time in territory that changed like the ocean, the currents of which could pull them out to sea or towards land, like all the creatures that lived there. They were haphazard alignments of bodies that collided once in a while and followed mysterious paths.

"I needed to stop to catch up on my sleep, I've been driving for three days. You know what these roads are like," the journalist said. "Nothing beats sleeping in the middle of the countryside," he added as he sat down at the table, yawning and gazing into the limpid, morning sky.

"Tell me about it," Parker said after he'd poured two cups of tea.

"That's last year's news!" the journalist exclaimed when he picked up the newspaper from the table and looked at the date.

"I bought it the last time I was in a city, and I've still not finished reading it."

"You're crazy. What world are you living in, Parker?"

Parker's eyes circled the empty landscape. He waved his index finger upwards.

"Time and dates don't exist here, that's why one sleeps so well."

"I need dates, my work depends on them."

"How's your research going? Any new discoveries?"

"I found the place where they disembarked."

"'They' being who?"

"What do you mean 'who'? Have you forgotten what I told you last time?"

"Practically. Something to do with the war, I believe?"

The journalist went back to his car and returned with a dusty, leather case. He took out a map, spread it on the table and pointed at a location.

"Here, in this bay. That's where they disembarked."

Parker leaned forward and looked at that place on the map, pretending to be interested.

"So how did you find out? I mean, weren't they secret operations?"

"Top secret, but that was sixty years ago. I've spoken to eyewitnesses, I've consulted books and documents," the journalist said, pointing to other places on the map.

"Several submarines were seen here. Many surrendered, others were lost forever, without trace."

"So why did they decide to come here, where there was nothing?"

"That was why, precisely because there was nothing. And no-one to see them. They unloaded gold and documents and took everything to their hideouts in the cordillera. I've almost finished my next book, impressive, what do you reckon?"

The journalist took out a bulky folder packed with hand-written pages, and thumped it down on the table.

"Look how fat that is, I might even win the Pulitzer."

Parker took the folder and weighed it in both hands.

"If weight counts, you might even get a Nobel. So Nazi booty reached this neck of the woods?"

"Right! They say even Hitler was in these parts, I'm searching for proof."

"Do you think anyone is going to publish that claptrap?"

"How would you know? You don't inhabit this world."

"You're not so familiar with it either."

The journalist ignored him and pointed at the map again.

"There could be remains of a shipwreck in this bay, maybe the U-745. I've been chasing it for years."

"The U-745? And what's that, the local bus service?"

"Don't be stupid. 'U' stands for '*Unterseeboot*' – a submarine."

"So did Hitler arrive here in one of these U things?"

"Very possibly, they were secret missions to land fugitives and money. Then they sank them, to get rid of any evidence."

"They didn't get rid of it, they left it there. They can't have been so clever to do that."

"At the end of the war the U-530 and the U-977 surfaced opposite Mar de Lobos and surrendered to the authorities, but there were other sightings. One of them might have been the U-1206, which was reported missing in the North Sea in April 1945."

Parker yawned and focused his attention on all around him. While the other man talked, he calculated his next routes and days on the road, how he would recover the lost week he'd spent waiting, but the journalist kept piling on detail, with increasing enthusiasm.

". . . over a few days periscopes and turrets were seen opposite San Alfonso, perhaps the U-326 or the U-398, which were thought to have been lost in Scottish waters. But the one I'm looking for is the U-745, seen for the last time in the Gulf of Finland, and which might have surfaced here, in Puerto Médanos, several months later," the journalist said in a tense voice. He shut up for a moment to take a breather, then stared hard at Parker.

"What do you reckon? Isn't it fascinating?"

Parker sipped his coffee and shook his head in disbelief.

"You're too old to be playing battleships, you'd do better playing 745 on the lottery, you might win something that way."

"As well as being stupid, you're a sceptic. I can tell you, lots of people have investigated this . . ."

"It takes all sorts . . ."

"You're not kidding," the journalist said, casting his eyes over the encampment and truck and lingering on Parker, who hadn't grasped that remark was aimed at him. They stayed silent for a while, silhouetted against the flatlands and the sky, drinking coffee and smoking.

"You're a strange bird. You're not from these parts, are you?" the journalist asked.

Parker's lofty gaze was lost in the distance, as the other man pointed at his saxophone case on the armchair and stared at him while waiting for his reply.

"Nobody is, everyone is from the other side. The people from here don't exist anymore."

"And you're as much a trucker as my grandma, real truckers don't play trumpets."

"It's a sax, not a trumpet."

"That's even worse."

The journalist ruminated for a second.

"Do they call you Parker because you play the sax?"

"No, that comes from a pen I won in a school raffle when I became an instant celebrity."

"What's your coming and going all about?"

"I take fruit from the valleys to the port, avoiding the human species, I've told you a thousand times."

"In other words, you don't consider me to be part of the human species. I am flattered."

"You are an exception. I still don't know why. Nobody can beat you at being boring."

"Don't be fooled by appearances, I'm much worse than I seem."

The journalist tried to catch Parker's elusive gaze, which was still surveying the horizon, then he put his cup on the table and leaned over.

"Don't tell me *you* are running away from something?"

Parker nodded in the direction of the folder.

"I'm probably a grandson of Hitler, include that if you want. We'll split the proceeds when it's published."

The journalist looked back at Parker who was still smoking, ignoring him, muffled by a weeks-old beard, his prominent paunch barely hidden by layers of blankets.

"If your grandfather Adolf saw you now, he'd say it was all futile," he retorted. Parker returned his glance, gesturing like an interrogator, then looked himself up and down.

"What do you mean?"

"The master race, that is."

Parker scrutinised himself once again, at a loss.

"Do you have an issue with my race?"

"Not at all, I was only saying . . ."

"Don't be duped by appearances."

"You're right, you too must be worse than you seem."

They exchanged glances that entwined like invisible threads.

"We must have something in common."

"I don't know whether to be pleased or shout for help."

"You better be pleased, nobody's going to help you here."

Parker and the journalist said nothing for another long interlude, then they dragged themselves to their feet and ambled around.

"I sometimes envy you, you can only appreciate true freedom in the midst of this solitude," the journalist declared, staring at the horizon. Parker paused before replying.

"Yes, it's not half bad."

"You don't seem at all sure."

"At this stage in life, I'm not sure about anything."

"You don't seem to be suffering so much."

"No, but the pay is poor and, what's more, the firm is a

disaster, my boss is on the run, my papers are a mess and I don't know how long this truck can hold up."

"These are minor details. You come from the city, that's obvious. How do you manage to survive here?"

"I've got used to fresh air. I couldn't live with traffic and noise now, or tolerate a routine, a house, seeing the neighbours' faces every day. That would be like prison."

"Are you going to live the rest of your life like this? Watch out, this can be worse than prison."

"Why shouldn't I? It's a life like any other. I can get another firm, another truck and . . ."

The journalist interrupted him with the gentle dig of an elbow that sank into the wall of rags around Parker's midriff.

". . . and another identity."

Parker stopped, then walked on.

"You really do like spinning yarns! I hope they pay you well."

"It's called having a nose. You must be in trouble with the law."

A riled Parker halted again.

"What business of yours is that?"

"Don't get me wrong. If you want new papers, I can get them at a good price. That's how I finance my research."

"My problems are with criminals rather than the law."

"That's tricky. It's harder to bribe mafia than a judge."

When they were back at the table, the journalist rummaged in his bag and took out a fistful of ID papers he displayed like playing cards on his hand.

"Look how many personalities I've got, I must be multi-schizophrenic."

"Don't use them all at once."

"Do you want me to lend you one?"

"I like the Nazi-hunter profile, but that's been taken."

"You got there late, choose another."

"Were you always into hunting down submarines?"

"No, it was UFOs before that."

"Well, I could use *that* identity, if you can lend it me."

"Not a good idea, there aren't as many as there used to be. Flying saucers land in Siberia nowadays."

"That's unfriendly territory, far from everywhere and going nowhere unless you're off to the Antarctic," declared Parker glumly.

"Geography is no joking matter," the journalist said, thinking he was voicing a great truth, as he kept foraging in his bag.

Parker frowned at him as he produced more and more documents.

"You're forever chasing some madcap idea."

"Luckily, I'm not. They are all links in the same chain."

After lunch Parker got into bed to take a nap and the journalist slouched back on the settee. When the shadow of the truck threatened to lengthen once again, the latter jumped to his feet, collected his things from the table, took a calendar from his overcoat and placed it next to the map.

"I must get back on the road. We can meet in thirty days, here at kilometre 207 on route 26. La Cuesta del Huemul."

Parker turned over in bed and spoke without opening his eyes.

"That's good, but don't keep me waiting again."

"I'll be punctual, but don't you take the wrong road again."

The journalist took a red velvet box from his bag and extracted a gleaming, golden, ancient instrument.

"That must be an astrolabe?"

"Don't be an ignoramus. It's a sextant."

"That's not as stupid as mistaking a sax for a trumpet."

"This might save your life, a trumpet never will. I'll lend it to you so you don't lose your way in these remote parts, and while you're at it, you might find your place in life."

"I've already got a compass."

"You can't compare a compass to a sextant. It locates you in space, not just on the map."

An ecstatic Parker took the instrument and examined it.

"I've always wanted one of these."

"Use it. See you in thirty days on La Cuesta del Huemul. Have the fire ready. I'll bring the meat and wine."

Parker and the journalist looked at each other for a few seconds, exchanging half-smiles and total complicity. Lit by the sun, their silhouettes stood out against the dark clouds on the horizon as they hugged each other goodbye on the empty road's double yellow line. The journalist freed up his car by removing the stones from the wheels and sat behind the steering wheel.

"That submarine stuff is a secret, don't tell anyone, and inform me if you come across anything odd," he said, sticking his head out of the window.

"I'll let you know if I see any Nazis."

The journalist drove off in another cloud of dust, Parker watched the car disappear into the distance, then went back to his encampment. He doused the fire, gathered up and organised his belongings and put them back using the usual system. A while later his vehicle's wheels crunched over the pebbly ground as it drove slowly off and climbed back onto the road like a snake coiling round the branch of a tree.

O  O

Parker drove with a bottle of beer in one hand and a cigarette between his lips, while beyond his cabin windows the calm, limpid desert sped by. Spare, sober music was the ideal accompaniment to that landscape. The lazy chords of a cello drifted across the tundra and provided his movement with a suitable rhythm, a sensual cadence that touched Parker's innermost strings and immersed him in a state of sublime serenity. He had a couple of weeks to reach another port with his new cargo, more than enough time to let himself be swept along by those hidden currents, by the dry riverbeds that seemed to scar the continent. He imagined the dawns that awaited him on the road, those happening right then, beyond his reach, between the waves of the sea and the peaks of the cordillera and felt they were all his, cosmic events in his honour, offerings placed before his eyes. The universe presented itself on a scale that was born in the truck's cabin, passed over the line of the horizon, and was transformed into dawn or dusk and then the starry sky. That was the frontier to his vision, and as far as his mystic side went, he had no way to cross it and he wasn't interested in what might exist beyond, or nearer, that kind of boundary. Nevertheless, closer to home, there was another universe, equally populated by enigmas and mysteries: a system of devices that were like planets turning in their orbit, cogs, pistons, cables, nuts and bolts that followed the master plan of the mechanics of his engine. To open the bonnet was a defiant insult to Pandora, a challenge to the powers behind creation, and that was why he gave another start, when, in the course of a gear change, an unusual noise from that recondite system sounded out like a warning from the great beyond. Something had begun to screech in that microworld beneath his feet, a disturbing development his hands could feel through the gear lever. His senses stiffened and went on the defensive, he extinguished his cigarette and threw the bottle of beer out of the window; it rolled down the side of the road and died intact. He changed gears several times, and every time the engine screeched, a worrying judder got louder, a shudder that was immediately transmitted to his body. He kept moving the gear lever until the engine emitted a horrible crunch and began to suffer spasms. Like a rider on a wilful horse, his body shook with each jolt. Parker switched from cajoling to threatening to set it on fire, but the truck would not see reason. The convulsing and screeching from the cogs biting into each other turned into a wail that reached to the ends of the desert.

Several hours later, Parker and his agonising truck came to a village that, according to the map, went by the name of Jardín Espinoso, on the banks of a dry riverbed that on a couple of days every three or four years flowed with muddy water, an occasion celebrated with big angling competitions. There were no signposts, he had to ask a pedestrian to confirm where he was, an elderly man who was smoking and gazing at the horizon from a rock on the village outskirts. Parker greeted him affably.

"Is this Jardín Espinoso?"

"No, señor, this is El Suculento."

"Can you tell me where I might find Jardín Espinoso?"

"Yes, señor, it was right here."

Parker asked him to repeat what he had just said, but still couldn't fathom what the man was saying.

"Jardín Espinoso used to be here, but isn't anymore, now it's called El Suculento."

Parker looked around for someone in his right mind to consult, although he had by now lost all interest in finding

28

out. How can thorns turn into something tasty, he wondered. There was nobody else, and he had to persist, more out of curiosity than anything else.

"How do I get to Jardín Espinoso?"

"That's impossible, señor. Nobody can ever again go to Jardín Espinoso, not even those of us who were born there."

A long pause followed when the men stared at each other with a mixture of curiosity and pride. Parker understood that he must pander to the man's whims if he wanted any clarity.

"So where did Jardín Espinoso go then? What on earth happened?"

The man looked away from him and back at the surrounding landscape with a serious and solemn air.

"What happened was that they changed its name. Now it's called El Suculento."

Then the man went on, puffing his chest out:

"It was an electoral promise made by our mayor, and one he kept. We are now a fertile, prosperous town. Jardín Espinoso was poor and dry."

Parker thanked him for that information and drove to the town entrance. He stopped at the first service station. He climbed out of his cabin and onto the roof to study the solitary island where he had just been marooned, afraid he might spend the rest of his days there. He had driven through the place several times, but it was the first time he had ever stopped. He had nothing but contempt for that kind of crossroads stop-off, with its bonhomie of a village-hall get-together. The brethren of the highways assembled there, before or after long days behind the wheel: truckers, tourists, bus drivers, passengers and commercial reps celebrated goodbyes and re-encounters. He realised he should go in and greet acquaintances, inform them of his plight, ask for help, explain things to the polite and respond to the inquisitive. But that was all too much. After he had taken a quick look around, his body felt riven with anxiety and he longed for the ever more remote possibility of a lonely death on a deserted heath. Several lorries were parked on the huge esplanade that was bounded by flatlands, forming a square that gave protection against the elements, like the caravans or carts of trail-blazing settlers. Inside, truckers were eating and drinking around a big fire where they roasted meat, spun yarns and played their guitars until dawn. Parker detested the way those people in transit sought human contact, invented futile conversations, amused themselves with over-wrought belly laughs and corny jokes they all lapped up as if hearing them for the first time. That wandering fraternity zealously enforced its rituals for encounters and gatherings, requiring each of its adepts to submit to the group or be condemned to derision. He had been involved several times in such rendezvous where actors and scenarios might change but the liturgy never. Parker fled that camaraderie like the plague, and constructed his own artful solitude, the only place where he felt safe from that madding crowd, but he also knew how to sidestep his neighbours without wounding their susceptibilities: he had learned that nobody could freewheel in that random life on the road. He decided to make his escape before he was spotted and was forced to accept their invitation, yet he *did* need help, and that constituted a greater danger. Mechanical mishaps were great opportunities to fire up merciless trucker solidarity and impose a duty to help your neighbour whatever the cost, which was often an excuse to pry into his life. He imagined them discussing his bad luck, feigning concern and seizing the opportunity to give advice, consolidate friendships, voice opinions and make indiscreet enquiries. They would congregate around his truck, one would bring tools, another firewater and fake know-how, all pretending to be interested. He needed a mechanic, not smirking "friends" or colleagues who would overwhelm him with affability he was in no state to reciprocate.

Parker slipped off the roof and through the window back into the cabin and manoeuvred his vehicle until it was out of sight, though the clatter from the engine turned it into a noisy tin can on wheels. He managed to park without being seen, far away, in a space littered with eviscerated cars, tyres and spare parts like a huge open-air museum. He crossed that battlefield to his possible salvation: an old caravan, adrift among a tangle of scrap metal, with a dirty, dead, neon sign that said MECHANIC. He clapped his hands, then knocked on the door several times at the end of his tether, but got no response. After a while a middle-aged individual with a days-old beard, looking as if he had just got up, wiping his hands on a rag and zipping up his grease-stained trousers, appeared in the opening to a cardboard and tinplate lavatory at one side of the caravan. The two men squared up to each other, separated by a pregnant silence, waiting for the other to speak first. There was an element of truculence in that wait, and Parker realised those moments were establishing the norms for an accord they would reach a few seconds later: if he did not manage to get the upper hand, the fellow would win the contest and impose his rules of engagement. That was the nature of human relationships in these wastelands, inhabited by uppity folk unaccustomed to being polite. They assessed each other in that duel of gazes, until the other man made the first move.

"Did you want me?"

Parker looked around and waited a moment before answering. Huge black clouds were furrowing the sky, the wind's sudden violence was burying the landscape in dust, shrouding it for several seconds. A gust shook him, another blew sandy dust up his leg. He noticed that the onslaught seemed to attack only him, because the other man's hair was almost unruffled. He looked in vain for shelter.

"Is this a repair shop?"

"No, it's a doggy hairdresser's."

Parker realised he had lost the first round.

"You people here are so witty . . ."

"I wouldn't know, I'm not from these parts," the mechanic said, shrugging, still untouched by the gale, pointing to a dot in the distance.

"I'm from there, from Mula Muerta."

Parker looked in the direction indicated, using his hand to shield his eyes against the sun, and saw a cluster of five squat, adobe houses with tinplate roofs that stuck out on the plain. Endless plastic bags flapped in the wind, hooked on the weary barbed wire that surrounded the houses like a crown of thorns.

"So those houses are the infamous Mula Muerta? Today is my lucky day," Parker counter-attacked. The mechanic snarled.

"You've got it wrong, that's Mula Vieja. Mula Muerta is the one after that, you can't see it from here."

"It all looks the same to me, how do you expect me to know?"

"It's about common sense, not what you can see. What comes first, Mula Muerta or Mula Vieja? Come on, you're a city man, what do you reckon?"

Parker stared at the other man thinking he spoke another language, and could not find a response.

"First the mule ages, soon after it dies. Or is it the other way round in Buenos Aires?" the man went on.

Parker appealed to the stars for patience and looked around again. He glanced back at the fellow, submitting him to close scrutiny for a few seconds. He could not think what to say, and when he could, it only made things worse.

"It depends where you're coming from," he declared exultantly.

"You can only come from here, there's nothing past Mula Muerta, no towns, no roads, no mules. Everything ends there," the mechanic spelt out with almost metaphysical resignation.

"Everything ends and nothingness begins," Parker reflected, following his thread, infected by his spontaneous, plain speaking. The mechanic stopped pondering and turned to Parker who was still using his hands to protect himself from the gusts.

"What nonsense are you spouting, guy?" he snarled, suspecting he was talking to a madman, before grinning morosely and adding: "Are you drunk, or has the wind got to your brain?"

Parker ignored him and switched sides, but he could not fox the wind, and changed sides again. It was his turn, and his response had to be immediate, for he was losing the contest. He preferred to go straight to the point.

"Can you check my gearbox? It's making a peculiar noise."

The mechanic said: "I'm sorry, we're closed for the holidays."

Parker turned serious and upped his tone of voice.

"And when do the holidays end around here?"

The man looked at his watch for an age, as if deep in thought.

"That depends."

"You're having me on!"

"I'm having you on? I work all year and on top of that you want me to interrupt my holidays on your say so?"

Parker gave up, lowered his arms, patted the mechanic's shoulders, faked a smile and tried to seal an honourable surrender.

"All you *porteños* are the same. You think you're the centre of the universe," the mechanic snorted.

"I'm not from Buenos Aires."

"So where *do* you come from?"

Parker waved vaguely at a spot on the horizon.

"I'm from over that way . . . from Indio Malo," he lied, preening himself.

The mechanic looked at the spot indicated and peered into the distance, but found nothing. He had fallen into the trap, Indio Malo didn't exist; he now exchanged glances with Parker and shook hands. He had earned his respect with the evil Indian.

"Pleased to meet you. Let's see what's up. From your face, I'd say you're in real trouble," he said, rolling up his sleeves.

The two men inspected the engine for an age, their bodies hidden under the bonnet, until the mechanic stood up and wiped his hands on a rag. Parker emerged a moment later.

"A couple of cogs need changing, it will be ready in a few days, if you're lucky."

Parker jumped to the ground and walked edgily between

the truck and the mechanic, talking to himself and invoking the heavens.

"And if I'm not lucky, what's likely?"

"That you can't get a spare, you'll have to order it from the capital and wait a week."

"Don't fuck me about, mechanic, I'm not in the mood."

"Or the roads might flood and you'll have a two-week wait."

"I'll pay you double if you sort it today," Parker said, dismayed.

"Do you think I'd be living in this shithole if I could work miracles?"

"Try my engine, perhaps it will work a mini-miracle."

"I don't think it would be enough to get me out of here," the man said, resigned.

"What am I going to do in this dump for two days?"

"What do you think I've been doing these past thirty years?"

"That's your business, not mine."

"I could say the same."

The mechanic saw Parker was desperate and took pity on him for a moment.

"Go to the amusement park, chill out a bit, that's what you need to do."

"Do you think I'm in the mood for a merry-go-round?" Parker barked.

"Go on, you'll enjoy it," the mechanic assured him, then turned around and went back to his caravan.

"*Porteños!*" he muttered, swaying his head.

"Provincials!" Parker fired back. As the mechanic vanished beyond the door to his home, he seized his head with both hands and walked round in circles, cursing his luck.

After a while, the mechanic's head reappeared through a window.

"Do you have anywhere to sleep?"

Parker signalled that he did and walked to the tavern, swearing under his breath. He noticed a group of drivers in the parking lot singing and laughing to the rhythm of a guitar. He hid behind a pillar and spied on them. An hour later, his stooping silhouette walked down the streets of the town; he was still using his hands to shield himself against the gusts that were blowing scrub and litter everywhere. He stopped to light a cigarette, but couldn't, he had to use his body as a shield, but that didn't work either; he leaned back on a wall and kept trying until he gave up for good. An impish blast blew the dead cigarette from his lips, another carried it off into the distance. At the end of his tether, he threw his lighter into the air, kicked it as it flew off and walked several blocks between whirlwinds of sand that got into his eyes. He reached one end of the settlement where the dirt streets ended and the flatlands began without noticing that he had gone from one end to the other. These places had no familiar pattern, they were a scattered hotch-potch of unplanned houses and wasteland where you could get lost like in a big city; they lacked a centre, a square, a point where main roads crossed. He stood still opposite an empty expanse opening up before him, then turned around and walked back to a street corner. He kept looking at his watch, wanting to hurry along the hands that seemed glued to its face: time stood still among these strings of houses. The mechanical fault, the loathsome individual his fate now depended on, the nearby presence of truckers and now that town in the back of beyond appealed to his worst side. And to cap it all, these damned blasts of wind kept upsetting everything he had been making an effort to settle hour after hour, day after day. Such was the impact of perpetual gusts over time: they created inner turmoil, the feeling that nothing was in its proper place, that everything in this life was precarious or futile and all that mattered was to find a spot to hunker down. There was one kind of solitude that had the consistency of moss and stuck to objects and individuals like a persistent stain, that grew in those inhabited backwaters, between low-built houses and alleyways dotted with potholes and puddles, and there was another kind, which was the wild, wilful wind blowing across vast spaces where the human figure had never been factored in. One had an infinity of faces and plunged Parker into moods of sterile melancholy that didn't produce a single worthwhile emotion, while the other was nature in a pure state, larded with sensations, images and musical notes that left a deep mark that did finally lodge somewhere in his body.

Parker was relieved to see a group of youngsters walking towards him from a street corner, pushing, shoving and laughing. He needed to exchange a few words with them to rid his mouth of the bitter aftertaste left by his conversation with the mechanic. They were children, unpolluted, innocent lives, safe from adults and their platitudes, and he could enjoy spontaneous, sincere conversation with them. He leaned back on a wall and waited for them to come closer. There were five or six of them, ten years old or less, and all were sucking big, brightly coloured lollipops that seemed like masks over their faces. They were also carrying bunches of balloons with painted faces that the wind blew forwards till they almost touched the ground as if bowing reverentially. They walked by without even giving him a glance, and Parker imagined they were soldiers on parade

37

commemorating a patriotic date on the calendar. Parker went over to the one who looked the oldest, and said a few words. The group halted and seemed to register his presence. Parker said hello, but the wind blew his words away and they stayed silent for a few seconds, waiting for another gust to blow them back, although they had been lost forever. Without breaking rank, the boys crossed the street to a sheltered spot so the balloons would stop thudding down and regain their vertical position. Parker followed them, delighted in that respite, and waved again, but they looked at him, expressionless and dismissive. The experience of meeting a human was of no interest, and they could not wait to get round that intruder and back to their own business.

"Where's the circus, kid?" Parker asked the one who seemed the liveliest, and once again his words were swept off to the outskirts of town.

The boy looked at him absentmindedly, put his lollipop in a pocket and started eating popcorn he cradled in his hand. It didn't blow away, which annoyed Parker even more. He stared in awe at the balloons becalmed above their heads, while he turned round in a futile quest for a windshield, wondering why the climate affected him alone. He imagined the breeze hit only what possessed a surface and created resistance, and that he was the single person in that land of unsubstantial beings made of actual matter. Nothing could erode those intangible, identical individuals, without features of their own, tiny figures cut out by the same scissors: clothes, gestures, the way they sucked the lollipops they held in one hand while the other held the strings of their balloons, teeth eaten away by the colourants staining their tongues with artificial pigments.

The boy half signalled to Parker to move aside, but Parker didn't cotton on and kept talking to thin air.

"I'm just asking you where the circus is, kid. Or are you deaf?"

The boy kept staring at him, hypnotised, a tad cross-eyed, his mind a blank.

"What circus?" he blurted, as if he'd been considering his response all that time.

"Where did you find that?" he insisted, pointing to the balloon.

"I didn't find it," replied the boy, still sucking his lolli-pop.

"Where did they give it to you?"

"They didn't give it to me."

Parker wasn't just annoyed; he felt the anger in his words starting to shift to the palm of his hand that was shaping up to deliver a wallop.

"So where did you find it?"

"I didn't."

Parker raised his voice even more loudly, but none of the others, who looked like figures painted on the landscape, flinched.

"Kid, I'm asking you who gave you that balloon."

"Nobody gave it to me . . ."

Parker closed his eyes, anticipating the moment he would leave the place for good.

". . . I won it at the amusement park," the boy conceded at last, between two licks of his lollipop.

". . . that way," he followed up, pointing to a vague spot between the houses and the steppe.

Parker put his arms akimbo.

"So you're another joker, are you? I suppose you too come from Mula Muerta."

"No, señor, I was born here," the boy said, while the faces painted on the balloons stirred themselves and nodded.

"I can't wait for the day I leave El Suculento, never to come back," Parker replied, as his parting shot.

The boys laughed in unison, their guffaws echoing down the street.

"Señor, this is Jardín Espinoso, not El Suculento. Whoever told you that?" one asked.

"A man sitting on a boulder at the entrance to the town."

The boys guffawed again, with even more gusto.

"Sure, that's mad Bermúdez. He wanted to be elected mayor in the last elections so he could change the town's name, but nobody voted for him."

Parker threw up his hands, turned around and walked towards the place they'd pointed out, a string of curses hurtling from his mouth. He looked back from every street corner, and saw the group of boys in the same spot, their becalmed balloons peering into the distance like extensions of their bodies.

○ ○

Parker walked once more through that cluster of houses and reached the other end without finding what he was looking for. He decided to go back and give that boy the slap he'd not given him before, but when he turned one of the many identical street corners, something akin to a square popped up like a mirage. He wondered why he'd not seen it before, since he had crossed the town two or three times. That anonymous esplanade was surrounded by the usual low-built houses, a church, a town hall, an eatery, a bank, various empty plots and a general store. All kinds of rubbish the wind piled high in every corner at different times of day: in the morning litter heaped up between houses on the north side, in the afternoon it whirled around the flagpole in the middle, and at night accumulated on the south side, although that logic was sometimes reversed in step with the seasons of the year. A mixture of fairground and amusement park had been set up in the square, surrounded by a wall of caravans, vans and lorries all decorated with circus motifs. The entrance was down one side, under a metal arch with a welcoming sign. The fairground was contained in that square like an embryo in its uterus, the same way that the square was in the town, and the town in the flatlands, like a set of self-contained matryoshkas. Parker reviewed the outer walls of what appeared to be a fortress, then went in by way of the main entrance and walked to the centre. There he found numerous kiosks, shooting galleries and games with prizes of every kind, colour and size. He was shocked he had not noticed that the capricious gusts had stopped, not only for the locals but for him too. A little further on, past the Hammer and Wriggly Worm, he came to a motionless Big Wheel that looked like a clock waiting for time to go by. Past that was a Flying Chair, then a merry-go-round with fire engines, military tanks, ambulances, patrol cars, flying saucers, a horse-driven chariot and a rocket, and at the end he found a large dodgems where the cars were gyrating like drunkards. The ghost train loomed behind various kiosks and a Bear Hunt, a large metal structure emblazoned with drawings of ghosts, skeletons and a huge sign written in letters dripping with blood that proclaimed WELCOME TO THE HORROR TRAIN. Two large openings with monstrous

41

jaws were the entrance and exit into and out of a dark labyrinth of tunnels and passageways where cars decorated with skulls, vampires and werewolves trundled by. In the entrance, a hooded executioner waved a bloody axe in one hand and a decapitated head in the other as he welcomed and tore the tickets of the intrepid travellers venturing into that tenth circle of hell in exchange for a pittance.

Parker felt himself to be in seventh heaven as he sat at one of the tables in the bar, where a Bolivian-looking employee swept and tidied tables, chairs and crates of beer. Other employees and fairground traders were beginning to take up position and ready themselves for the customers who were about to arrive. He inspected every detail of that fairground, and thought it was a place of sadness rather than amusement, and spotted several empty lots between one booth and the next, suggesting that a number of attractions hadn't yet arrived or had thrown in the towel. Parker decided that the best way to end that wretched day would be to take a ride on the Big Wheel; the view of the sunset from those heights was another way to foil those flatlands; a few metres were enough to plunder hundreds of kilometres from the horizon. He bought his ticket from the ticket office, while groups of people appeared from nowhere and slowly circulated between the attractions. He observed the weathered faces of coal miners, ranch hands, road menders and oil-well workers strolling with their families after shifts that took them from one end to the other of that territory. The fairground was livening up by the minute; small lamps and luminous signs flashed against the last moments of daylight sky, lit up as if by magic. Parker went up and down, leaning back in his seat, swayed by the haphazard movement of the wheel, from the highest point of which he could see the first, timid stars. Down below, the fair was a blotch of light that night-time impaled against the flatlands, square roofs and streets that disappeared past the town boundaries. Beyond that the tavern stood out, where his truck rested in a corner like an animal on its side. Whenever the gyrating wheel plucked him from the silent heights and returned him to the level of mere mortals, he was hit by a rabid chorus of voices and laughter, between fumes from grills and the aroma of roasted meat. He felt an ecstasy in that orbit that in seconds flew him from the detail of individuals to a vast, panoramic expanse and back again. Everything seemed like a premeditated sequence returning with each whirl of the wheel, until all of a sudden, while he was careering above the Bear Hunt, where customers were trying to knock down a row of teddy bears with rag-balls, he spotted something that caught his attention: on one side, amid the prizes hanging from the ceiling, wearing a tight blouse that emphasised her curves, the young woman in charge of the stall appeared in his sights, a fleeting, startling apparition that vanished the second the wheel returned Parker to the solitary heights. Whenever he circled above the stall, Parker strained to observe the girl arranging teddy bears on shelves and collecting up the rag-balls. A second later, unused to being so topsy-turvy, he felt something turn in his stomach, in the opposite direction to the wheel, provoking inner queasiness. When the wheel juddered to a halt, he walked towards the Bear Hunt, impelled by an unusual fervour that almost took his mind off the queasiness knotting his guts. He shivered when he saw the girl from the right angle, close up and at ground level, her clothes emphasising her svelte lines, surrounded by plastic dolls, bouquets of artificial flowers, carnival masks, footballs, statues of the Virgin, jugs, photo albums with Alpine

43

landscapes, rings, necklaces, phosphorescent bracelets and wristbands that transmuted her into a venerated oriental goddess on her altar. There was a contrast between her pale white face and dark tresses, like two elements fighting over her intense dark eyes, a face that was also home to another conflict between indigenous features and ones that had travelled from the other side of the ocean. Parker was totally engrossed in that spectacle, then slipped through the crowd until he stood opposite her as she gave out prizes, smiling broadly and inviting passers-by to try their luck. A feeling that had lain peaceful stirred whenever she retrieved a ball and her low neckline opened invitingly. Parker stayed in the front row training his gaze on her, afraid the vision might vanish at any moment, until the other people drifted off to other attractions.

"Want to have a go, caballero?" the girl asked. In a voice that shut out the noise from the fairground, she offered him three rag-balls and a smile Parker was incapable of returning.

"It can't be that easy," he said, taking the balls; then he took aim, shut one eye and threw several times, missing each time.

"I'll show you how," she said, descending from her altar. She stood at his side and threw three balls with such a good aim that five teddy bears fell backwards, lethally wounded, one after another, knocked down, as if by magic.

"What do you reckon?"

"My congratulations, you're quite an expert when it comes to knocking down . . ."

Parker broke off a moment before saying "dummies", and stammered a couple of times, looking for a word that would avoid that unfortunate phrase, but he was left groping in the dark. The woman looked at him in a way that rendered him defenceless, smiled with a pout and came to his rescue, just when he was about to walk away, shamefaced, his insides still in the grip of that gyrating wheel.

". . . to knocking down furry toys?" she asked, returning to her stall, and with three dead-accurate throws, she downed another row of teddy bears that dropped as if they were obeying an order.

"You have to watch out with a girl like you," Parker replied, as nothing else came to mind. She gave him a cheeky nod and a shy smile, then returned to her altar and attended to her other customers.

"How much do I owe you?" Parker asked, putting his hand in his pocket.

"It's on the house," she responded, carrying on with her trade.

A delighted Parker thanked her and walked away from the stall, head down and lost in thought. Every so often he glanced back at the girl who was getting smaller and smaller against her altarpiece, until he came to the dodgems circuit, where small cars were circling around, colliding, scraping and crashing head on, like bored animals. It was an excellent observation point from which to try to fix on his retina the vision he had just witnessed. He bought a ticket, eased himself into a car and drove off, weaving and swerving, drawing a perfect figure of eight while moving his head so the girl almost always remained in the frame. Parker soon went into a trance similar to a state of intoxication, and with each swerve his hand caressed that body. He described several figures of eight and circles, swerving calmly from side to side, enchanted by a vision that made him dizzy, until a sudden collision shattered his daydreams:

Parker's head lurched forward, impelled by a head-on crash with another car that had just invaded his orbit. Shocked by that collision, he massaged his neck with both hands and looked to see who was responsible, but another crash, this time from behind, flung his head backwards, even more dramatically. A moment later he confronted the car that had just hit him, driven by the same kid from town who had looked at him squint-eyed while licking his fuschia-tinted lollipop. Now tied to the steering wheel, his balloon bobbed from side to side, and tried to hide a smile.

"Not you again," Parker muttered between gritted teeth, clenching a fist and fuming with rage. He turned his steering wheel, reversed to build up speed and pointed at the car of the boy who was still attached to his lollipop, determined to give him his just desserts. He gripped the steering wheel in both hands, put his foot down on the accelerator, and leaned forward, ready for the definitive collision that would wipe from the face of the earth that runt who was souring his day, but a second before, another of the boys hit him on one side and sent him spinning to the edge of the circuit, where Parker's car juddered to a halt. The boys lined up and threw themselves at Parker's car in rapid succession, before reorganising with military discipline to repeat their attacks. Parker was like a boxer on the ropes, on his last legs, and he reflected that the journalist was right, these devils must be the offspring of a Nazi leader. By the time he had reacted and prepared his counter-attack, his time was up and the cars stopped in their tracks as if they had run out of petrol. The Bolivian bar employee crossed the floor and asked him if he was alright.

"You've always got to look in front, bro, you weren't on

the ball," he declared in a strong accent, while Parker felt his temples.

"Give me another round, and I'll slaughter them," he threatened, holding out a note and glaring at the boys who were waiting for the next ride, holding their lollipops, their balloons tied to their steering wheels. The Bolivian gave him a wary glance.

"No, señor, this is about having a good time, not hurting anyone, you know, better you get off."

Parker squeezed himself out of his car and headed towards the gang, swearing at them, but when he was half-way, the cars restarted and he was forced to run off to avoid being hit. He decided to seek some light relief, and looked for an excuse to talk to the girl, but when he reached her sideshow he found that an unfriendly-looking brawny guy covered in tattoos had taken over from her. He needed a drink to recover and say a few words to that employee who had dared deny him. He sat at one of the tables and waited for him to come back, but the fellow who appeared shortly was the ghost train's hooded executioner who sat beside him, rested his decapitated head and axe on the table and looked him up and down.

"What's wrong with you?" an uneasy Parker asked eventually.

"Nothing, bro, my problem is being here, and that's not yours," the executioner said in an offended tone, observing him from the eyeholes in his hood.

"Do you really have to sit at my table?" Parker said, shocked by his forward manner.

"Did you reserve it? It's not your table until you order a drink. Besides, I'm working, can't you see that?" the executioner replied, pointing to his axe, before holding out his hand as if to say hello.

"Fredy Mamani Camacho, pleased to make your acquaintance." He took off his hood to reveal a face similar to the previous one, but Parker, who was livid by now, was not in the mood for play-acting and preferred to go back to his truck. He left the fairground and crossed the drab streets as the first drops of rain began to fall. Whatever the season, a storm was an opportunity he couldn't miss in those arid flatlands, so he decided to sleep out in the open that night. He set up his encampment following the usual routine and added a metal structure he covered with a roof of tarpaulins and plastic sheeting. He settled down on his sofa with a good supply of cigarettes and beer, and began to watch the few vehicles driving down the road and sending up clouds of water, but the events of a day that had been intense from the early hours were what filled his thoughts. First he had been beset by the plight of his truck marooned in this ghastly town, then the conversation with that despicable mechanic, then the group of diabolical kids and the lippy Bolivians, but what most obsessed him was the vision of that deity attending to her attraction, surrounded by offerings, while he went up and down on the Big Wheel. Something about her drew him with extraordinary force and it wasn't only her physical attractiveness, but the aura of sensuality she radiated. You had to watch her a while to capture the essence that was suggested by the way she moved, looked and addressed everyone else. When it was pitch-black, he switched on his portable lamp, wrote in his diary, turned the radio on and fell asleep on the sofa with an aching neck. During the night, the image of the woman sharpened and assumed the consistency of a creature of the night. He dreamed of her several times, each time a dream with different storylines and situations, but the heroine was always the same. As he twisted on the sofa looking for a position that did not exist, Parker's face was lit up by the streams of light and coloured reflections from the service station's neon signs. The noise of cars on the wet asphalt fused with the crackles from the radio, jolting from wave-length to wavelength in what seemed an endless quest, until the first rays of dawn, limpid after the night rain, projected long shadows all around. Parker woke up to the rhythms of nearby hammering that echoed in the depths of his brain and merged with his dreams; he yawned. His eyes were still shut as he moved his head, trying to throw off the pain from his sore neck, and he began to massage himself, taking deep breaths and exhaling. He soon realised the hammering was coming from the bonnet of his truck. The mechanic, his body half under its hood, was delivering one blow after another to that solid block of metal. Parker walked over and the fellow emerged into the daylight, holding a couple of cogs between his oily fingers.

"How did El Suculento go down? Did you like it?"

Parker was on the point of saying he did, but then recalled his conversation with the kids.

"Suculento my eye, this place is Jardín Espinoso!"

The defiant mechanic stared at him.

"Are *you* now going to tell *me* what the name of this town is?"

Parker jumped into his cabin and came back with an unfolded map he stuck under the other man's nose.

"Tell me what it says here, that is, if you know how to read," Parker said, sounding triumphant.

The scornful mechanic looked at the spot indicated.

49

"It says Jardín Espinoso," he admitted.

"So I'm right then?"

"No, because Jardín Espinoso is another town about six hundred kilometres further west. This is El Suculento, however much you may dislike that fact. Either your map is wrong, or you are, and I reckon that's more than likely."

Parker was bemused and started studying the map again, unable to understand where the error was, and before developing an ulcer, he threw the map in the air, but a gust of wind blew it back in his face. Once freed from there, the map continued its trajectory and caught on some barbed wire.

"Did you like the amusement park?" the mechanic said with a knowing glance, but Parker was in no mood for small talk, he just wanted to find out when he could leave that place.

"Have you finished the job?"

"I've only just started, right? But it's time for a bite to eat. You could invite me to breakfast," he suggested, as he walked to the encampment, sat on the sofa and began reading the newspaper.

Parker boiled up coffee on his camper stove and prepared an omelette he divided between the two plates. They ate in silence.

"Don't you have a more recent paper? This news is no news to me."

"Read it all the same. It'll be topical again in a couple of days."

"It's not nearly as fresh as these eggs," the mechanic joked, savouring a mouthful, "but the omelette is really tasty. I've got good news, no need to order a new cog, I ought to have one similar over there."

"And where might 'over there' be?"

The guy swivelled his fork and pointed at several mounds of rusty spare parts and a mountain of old engines next to his caravan.

"I reckon I saw an identical part last year, and I don't think anyone has touched it."

"You 'reckon'? You're not even sure!"

The mechanic half closed an eye and tried to think back.

"You're right, it wasn't last year: it was two years ago."

"And you've got to find it in that mess?"

"*We* have to. If señor makes the effort to help me, he might be able to leave earlier."

"There must be more than a hundred scrap engines scattered 'over there'."

"It's up to you if you want to look elsewhere, but it's more likely here."

Parker and the mechanic spent the rest of the day searching the piles of parts and spares for something like the faulty cog. Parker wandered around that abandoned cemetery at a ghostly pace, gripping the original item like a magic charm, as he mentally revisited time and again the altar where that goddess would be performing her ritual surrounded by dolls and plastic baubles. Head down, his gaze hopping from one pile of rusty metal and chassis to the next, he dissected word by word every sentence he had exchanged with that young woman to be sure he'd not made a fool of himself. He needed to see himself through her eyes, to discover the image he had projected on the mirror of her gaze, even if it did him no favours. By the time dusk fell and the shadows began to elongate they'd collected twenty parts similar to the original. They were exhausted when they returned to the caravan, like two peasants with a poor harvest. After so much crouching, it was not only Parker's neck that hurt, his back and lumbar muscles also felt sore.

"We've done our bit for today. Tomorrow we'll check whether or not they work," the mechanic said, looking pleased with himself.

"Can't you work a bit longer?"

"I've got guests coming tonight and I'd like to get supper ready," he replied as he cleaned his hands.

"Oh, for a moment I assumed you had a concert to go to," Parker said.

The affronted mechanic looked at him, quite taken aback.

"I broke off my holidays for you, and now you want me to lose all my friends?"

Parker did not have the energy to retaliate. He turned and walked towards his camp, chuntering, ready to accept anything in exchange for a little rest.

"Wait! OK, I'll do it just for you, you're a nice guy. Go and rest, and I'll let you know," the mechanic said.

Parker stopped and stared, not knowing whether to thank him or tell him to go to hell; he shrugged and continued walking.

"These *porteños*!" the mechanic mumbled as he searched for a tool.

Parker slumped in a disconsolate heap on his sofa. Another day had gone by and he was still trapped in that wretched hole. As he poured himself a drink, the memory of the girl brought on another rush of blood and he decided to relax for a few hours, shower, change clothes, then go back to the fairground and start a conversation with her. While he was thinking of the best way to approach her, his eyes soon closed, reality melded into his dreams and he enjoyed a deep sleep until he was woken up by the mechanic's voice. But that was another day.

○  ○

The mechanic stopped opposite the encampment and clapped several times as he called out to Parker, who jumped to his feet, hoping for news, good or bad: he suspected following the drift of the last few days, that it would be bad.

"Sorry to say we didn't strike it lucky," the mechanic explained, sitting at the table, fishing for an invitation to breakfast.

"Is there omelette today?"

"Would you like to see the menu?" Parker asked sarcastically.

"No, I like surprises."

"How was supper with your friends?" he asked after a while, finding it hard to believe the man had any friends, let alone ones who came to dine in that miserable backwater, but the fellow pretended not to hear.

"My advice is that you go to a tyre place run by a friend of mine and ask for a replacement. His name is Iribarne, Goyo to his friends. You can call him whatever you want, but don't be too casual, he has a short fuse."

"So where do I have to go now?" Parker said, panicking. The mechanic pointed to a dot on the horizon. Parker stood next to him to see where he was pointing, but distance had already swallowed the spot and the mechanic was forced to show him again.

"There, there!" he indicated, gesticulating frantically.

"I can't see anything that looks like a tyre place, or anything of the kind."

"I'm not indicating the place, but the route. That's the way to go."

Parker spotted the faint trace of a track disappearing into the scrub.

"Nobody uses that track. Take my bike and get going, you must get back before nightfall. Go straight, always easterly, until you see a dead fox by the roadside, that's where my friend's tyre store is, it'll take you two or three hours at most. But get a move on, before the wind changes direction."

"Three hours! That's six, if you include the return ride," Parker protested.

"You're an ace at maths."

Parker abandoned all idea of breakfast, went out, and began to ruminate as he walked in circles. The mere idea of riding a bike for six hours alarmed him. As far as he was concerned, a bike was a childhood thing he'd put behind him centuries ago, together with his parlous timidity and countless complexes the names of which he had already forgotten. But he didn't need to meditate too long: as with everything else that had happened over recent years, his decisions were irrelevant: there were never better alternatives. He wanted to go back to the fairground, but had to resign himself and seek consolation in the idea that he would return in time to go that night. Once again the memory of the young woman raised his spirits; after all, fate had grounded him in that wasteland, the same fate now not allowing him to leave. There had to be a good omen there, who could tell what the future held? If they'd repaired his truck that first day, he'd never have met her, he pondered as he put on an overcoat, grabbed the rickety bicycle and rode off in the direction he'd been told to go.

"If Iribarne doesn't put in an appearance, don't waste time looking for him, he will have died. In that case, listen to me, go to the ditch near the barbed-wire fence, and under some half-rotten tarpaulins you'll find an oil can, near an engine that's been stripped down. A couple of years ago there was a cog similar to yours around there, I don't think anyone will have taken it." So advised the mechanic from his caravan door.

Parker stopped and looked at the guy for a second, trying to discern a double meaning in his words, but he found none.

"Why don't *you* go?"

"I swear I would, but I've bought tickets to the theatre."

"Fuck off, mechanic."

"Don't be spiteful, *porteño*. Besides, a little exercise will do you good."

"You'll pay for this one day," Parker threatened, before cycling off.

A short pedal was enough to get him going; the wind drove him on with supernatural might and he crossed the steppe effortlessly, without ruffling a single hair. He travelled so fast he soon regained his good mood: a quick calculation told him that if he found the blasted cog in a jiffy, he'd be back in time to see the girl at the amusement park. He derived huge pleasure from the idea of sitting at the bar and drinking a beer without being interrupted. The smooth, silent pace at which he cycled across those flatlands gave him renewed optimism, auguring that things would soon start going his way.

An hour later he reached his destination, or that's what he thought: at a crossroads of minor roads that could have been dirt tracks, or worse, he came to a battered hut surrounded by piles of old tyres that looked like trench parapets. Its roof comprised loose sheets of metal that clattered against each other in a constant hammer-beat that gave it a life of its own. He could not believe it had once been a tyre shop; it was impossible to imagine what it was now. Parker braked, afraid he might sail past, and then he felt the impact of the wind, a faithful companion that had remained a tailwind. There was no sign of Iribarne, nor were there any other signs of life in that abandoned wasteland, although some form of intelligence *had* existed there not long ago: two hundred metres away lay the skeletal remains of what had been a big shed. A downcast Parker imagined a civilisation destroyed by a catastrophe. He looked for his treasure, inspecting every bit of that expanse of dry pastureland littered with animal bones, stripped chassis and abandoned engines. There was no trace of the ditch and barbed wire mentioned by the mechanic, even less of an oil can under rotting tarpaulins. He sat down on the carcass of an engine, lit a cigarette and began wringing his hands, desperate to invoke a pleasant memory to keep him company. But all his good omens disappeared in a second, as dusk began to weigh down, and a familiar unease spread through his system, far too akin to anguish. When total solitude and the lack of comfortable shelter joined forces they turned Parker into a hobo, a homeless pariah wandering the planet like a soul in limbo. Such a state of mind hit him without warning, treacherously, depending on how his thoughts reacted to the climate, and his state of mind to certain kinds of landscape. He missed the comfort of his truck and its welcoming warmth. When he surveyed the horizon, the memories he'd revisited in recent days were tinged by the pastel colours of the clouds, touching the deepest chords within him and leaving an aftertaste of sadness. He thought destiny must be playing a practical joke by leading him to that depressing spot, as he smoked, exposed to the elements, sitting on a dead carcass, while that young woman, surrounded by lights and people, ran her Bear Hunt. The image of her appeared different now and he felt something had matured since the last time. From a distance, he now intuited a form of innocence in her determined behaviour, an ingenuous fragility in her bright gaze that contrasted with her self-confident manner.

The clatter of corrugated metal turned into shouting, music and partying. He had constructed his dwelling among solitary peaks, far from any neighbours, living at ease, doing without the human species, but was experiencing a sudden longing for crowds and bustle. That was the worst joke fate could play on a creature of the steppes, although those symptoms heralded changes that were gestating deep within. Now, however, he was faced by a different task; he put aside his tribulations and concentrated on the search for that spare part among the heaps of scrap metal.

Several hours later, after an arduous, fruitless search, while he rested on that same chassis, his state of mind was like a weather vane turning and pointing to dark clouds. He fretted as he smoked, producing clouds of smoke that disappeared in moments, blown away by a wind that was still tolerable. After a short pause for thought he changed his mind and decided that the only person to blame for his situation was that avatar who had appeared out of nowhere to undermine his existence. She had shifted the axis of his existence, making him take wrong turns, upsetting his reading of precise, navigational instruments and blurring his itinerary. Several times he muttered that it would be better to forget her, focus on the best way to resume his journey and simplify his life. He should dismiss that tempting siren from his mind and get back on schedule, as soon as his truck was repaired. Right then a familiar shape hit his eyes as they roamed inanely over the clutter of spare parts littering the pasturelands: a cog similar to the one he was looking for leapt out of the void from among the skeins of dry grass where his melancholy gaze had lingered. Parker jumped up, afraid the part might escape. He immobilised it, trapped it with his foot. Fascinated by his miraculous find, he turned it over and over, wiping off the dust and the rust and comparing it to the original part. At times they seemed identical, at times they did not, depending on how he held them and turned them over. You could know nothing for sure in those barren heaths, where the only certainties were the clouds that suddenly loomed with a promise of rain only to disperse in thin columns behind a hill. He put one part on top of the other so they matched, eyed them for ages so there could be no doubt, because he knew the mechanic was an expert at manufacturing mishaps, and the part's suitability would depend on the conviction with which Parker himself presented it. When he was certain they were identical, he headed towards the abandoned hovel where he'd parked his bicycle. He jumped on as if it were a surly mount, and waited for the wind to hit his back. He had to hurry, before the weather changed, or worse still, before the dark desert night engulfed him. He would be back in time to replace the part, he would be back on schedule that same night and would leave behind forever the fairground and the mischievous goblin that had upset his routine and caused him so much extra stress. He unbuttoned his overcoat and spread it like a sail until the wind billowed it out and did the pedalling for him. He progressed several metres, but suddenly felt his wheels sink into the sand, his route was an uphill struggle and the bicycle weighed a ton. He stood erect on the pedals, pressed down with all his might, advanced a few metres, but then had to stop to gather strength again. A while later, after progressing several kilometres pressing his chest on the handlebars to reduce resistance, he halted exhausted at the side of the track, acknowledging he was never going to reach his destination. He had lost the support of the wind that was to carry him home, and was now engaged in single combat against another wind that was holding him back, and who could say when a third would replace it? He glanced at his watch and looked around for any sign of a dust cloud thrown up by a vehicle travelling through the area, but the only thing moving was the entire landscape, blasted by the gusts. When would the hellish weather in that forsaken spot change, Parker wondered. That wily mechanic must have known what was coming, you bet he'd sent him on purpose to drive his life further off kilter; those guys knew nature's whims as if they were their own, and they were many and treacherous. Whenever he surveyed the scene, the gloom was like a bird of prey circling overhead, and, to cap it all, the ocean gales had become icy gusts that attacked from every angle, and invariably into his face. The cold started to penetrate his clothes, scouring his body with icy hands, and he had no choice but to stretch out on the ground, light another cigarette, and look up at the sky. Before finishing his smoke, Parker had already taken another decision: he pulled up his coat collar, jumped on the bike and let himself be blown back towards the abandoned hovel, the only haven in those parts where he could spend the night in the company of old Iribarne's ghost. As he picked up speed, the tailwind drove him along and the whistling onslaught on his face and eyes stopped, communicating a feeling of calm. He would have let it blow him along for the rest of the day and the night too, as long as that sense of comfort and ease could be sustained, but how would he know where it might drag him, and how would he engineer his return? He felt he was being swept along by the benign current of a river flowing into the open sea, although he might end up wrecked on the first reefs of the cordillera, or, worse still, be flung into the unforgiving waters cascading down from glaciers. He reached the hovel by the old tyre store and tried to work out the best way to spend the night. Inside was a down-at-heel bed, several dusty animal skins and pieces of cardboard sealing off the gaps through which the wind whistled like sharp-edged steel. Parker made himself as comfortable as he could and cleared his head so that no thoughts would clutter his mind until the wind changed direction. Although he was exhausted, he struggled to drop off and his sleep came in jagged spells that kept time with the constant clatter of the hovel's metal sheeting and wooden planks. He found it impossible to keep the vision of the girl at bay in such circumstances; she was the only creature in the universe who could offer him any mental shelter, and he had to surrender to it. His absurd situation altered his perception of events: he recalled how he had discovered the spare part by chance at the precise moment he was deciding to forget her. Was that some kind of message? He imagined that only an obtuse mind could deny that the two facts were related. In other areas of the planet that logic might seem absurd, but not in that elemental void powered by its own rules that modified cause and effect. Everything that happened in those limitless spaces related to a logic that was enigmatic. It was obvious to Parker that evoking the young woman in the midst of desolation and finding the spare part were two sides of the same coin. He changed his mind for the third time that day, and, contradicting his previous resolve, decided to return to her and the fairground. After reaching that conclusion, he managed to forget the weather and the clatter of metal and wood, and fell asleep with his mind at peace.

The following day the wind conditions had not changed: he made a couple of attempts to ride back, but couldn't overcome the invisible barrier blocking his way. He sat on the same bereft chassis and waited all morning for a vehicle to drive by, chain-smoking, shivering, until a gang of labourers passed on horseback. He didn't bother to consult them and they didn't bother to stop: just an exchange of polite nods. What could he ask them that he didn't already know? They would have responded in the devious, oblique manner people had in that area; it seemed like another language. His spirit was still resisting, but he could not say for how long, and those people might drive him crazy, so he looked away and let them gallop off. One of the men, with a leathery face and a hat tied down with a neckerchief, stopped abruptly, turned his horse round and cantered over to Parker.

"Do you want to go to town?" he asked, nodding towards the dirt track.

Parker wasn't expecting such an offer, weighed up the possibility and accepted with a wave of the hand. He stood up, grabbed the bike, hid it in the hovel, then steadied himself to leap on the horse's haunch. The labourer gave him a surprised glance, bewildered by what he was doing.

"What are you doing? We're going in the other direction, towards Loma Chata. If you want to go to town, wait a while, the wind will change at midday," he said, consulting his watch, then looking at the horizon. "Unless you're in a rush, which I don't reckon you are."

Parker thanked him with a sense of resignation and went back to the chassis, quite despondent. The man shrugged, at a loss, and caught up with the others, not even bidding him farewell. They soon vanished into the hills.

"Loma Chata," he repeated in the tone of a litany, shaking his head in disbelief. He would never get used to those contradictory place names. "Flat Hill, I ask you!"

The midday breeze that was going to blow him back to his truck arrived on cue. The thorn bushes stopped their nervous jittering, birds in the sky changed the way they soared, the scent in the air made a sudden swerve, and a light warm shadow began to tint the western side of the rocks. First a warm crosswind caressed him, followed by a strong wind that freewheeled him along, as it had powered him there, along the deserted track to where his truck awaited him, its bonnet raised. He made a long detour to avoid the other drivers still camped in the vicinity. The mechanic was sitting on his sofa waiting for him, reading a magazine.

"I know what happened, no need to tell me. It does happen, it's like that around here. Did you find it?"

Parker handed him the spare without saying a word; he was starving and headed straight into the kitchen to cook something. Then he looked at himself in the mirror, and saw the aftermath of a bad night in the bags under his eyes.

"Are you sure they *are* the same?" the guy said, weighing up the two parts in his hands and looking at them with one eye then the other.

"What do *you* reckon?" Parker retorted. He had anticipated that comment.

"They might be, but appearances can deceive."

Parker snatched the parts from him and put one over the other, showing him they were a perfect match.

"Don't try to be clever, they are identical," he said, waving them a few inches from the other man's face.

"Did you count both sets of teeth? They have to be identical."

A nervous Parker counted the teeth on both cogs, and lost count several times before abandoning his attempts.

"They are the same, whatever you say. Now change it, before your teeth are the ones you have to count."

"Fine, but don't claim victory, because neither you nor I will have the last word, that's the truck's privilege. It will decide whether the spare fits or not," declared the mechanic.

Parker finished eating, pulled out some clean clothes and cut a furtive path to the service-station showers, hiding every now and then to avoid meeting anyone. A little later – his hair smartened and in his best clothes – he returned to his encampment.

"Don't tell me you're going back to the amusement park . . ." the mechanic said, seeing him turn towards town as he peered out from under the truck.

"Mind your own business, I'm not paying you to give me advice," Parker rasped, and walked off without further ado.

o  o

Parker strode down the muddy streets to the town square, but ground to a halt on a street corner. His heart missed a beat and something sank in his chest: a deserted esplanade covered in sacks of rubbish, ripped cardboard boxes, broken plastic chairs and litter comprised the space the fairground had occupied. Several half-dismantled structures survived, as if a tornado had devastated the place, alongside mud-spattered, clown-faced panels that had collapsed and metal supports and trailers waiting to be towed away. The two Bolivian handymen emerged from one corner, dragging rolls of cables and wooden boxes they loaded into a van parked in the middle of the square. A melancholy Parker observed the panorama and wandered among the debris, at a loss, trying to identify the spot where the Bear Hunt had been located. He retrieved a muddy teddy bear that looked like a wounded animal begging for help, then walked over to one of the Bolivians, the one he'd met in executioner garb who was now wearing civilian clothes, although the difference was negligible.

"Where's the fair gone?" he asked. The Bolivian didn't register he was there and he had no choice but to repeat his question twice in a louder voice, aware he wasn't listening.

"It went that way," the Bolivian said half-heartedly, not even looking him in the face, and pointing to one of the streets leading from the square to the steppe.

"What do you mean 'that way'?" Parker bellowed, flourishing the muddy teddy bear. The handyman stopped and responded with a sarcastic wave of his hands:

"That way, I said. I mean, where do you expect people to go, if the entrance and exit to this town are one and the same?"

"I'm not asking which way it went, but where it was going."

"They only left a short while ago."

"I didn't ask you when they left, but where they were heading, to which town," Parker persisted, adopting the other man's sarcastic attitude.

"Oh, if you wanted to know where they were off to, I mean, spell it out. They gone south, making the most of the downwind."

The other handyman joined in, standing opposite Parker as he rolled a skein of cables round his arm.

"Some went to Lago Negro, and others to La Trocha. Nobody wants to stick at it, very few are left, everyone's going his own way."

"What will we do, Señor, what will we do if the fair shuts down, I mean, where will *we* go, Señor?" wailed the first man, keeping his head down.

"I couldn't tell you," Parker commiserated.

The Bolivian stared at him.

"I'm not asking you, señor, but our Señor."

Parker continued firing questions.

"Where's the Bear Hunt? In Lago Negro or La Trocha?'

"I mean, we'll end up unemployed if people keep leaving," the ex-executioner griped again.

"Neither, they went to Teniente López, that's where the boss drove the truck, the big trailer and his missus, and that's where we're heading as soon as we've taken down the stand," the second Bolivian said, the cable now rolled over his arm.

Parker stood there deep in thought, while the Bolivians peered at him askance.

"You fancied his missus, right?" one said.

Parker stared at them, at a loss.

"Don't act dumb. Did you or didn't you fancy his missus, Maytén? She's the wife of Bruno our boss and he's a dangerous, evil guy," warned the other.

While he thought of a suitable response, Parker sensed he had been caught red-handed, and blushed bright crimson.

Humiliation increased his rage, but he needed to know more about her, so he held back. In any case, he now had a couple of useful facts: her name, Maytén, and the name of the town they were heading towards. He corrected himself. Three facts: Bruno, her dangerous husband.

"I hope the señor will help us," said one of the workers, reacting to the trucker's blank expression. Then he added, holding out his hand:

"I mean *you*, the señor with the small 's'. Will you give us a hand?"

Parker let them get on with their work and walked back, the girl's name now constantly in his thoughts. He kept repeating "Maytén" under his breath, so the name became familiar before it was lost to oblivion forever. He had scant experience of dealing with women, having had just a couple of girlfriends whose names he'd forgotten, and an ex-wife whose name he couldn't find a way to forget. The presence of that young woman, whom he could now refer to as if they'd known each other for a long time, had rattled him. She stopped him sleeping at nights, and never left his thoughts during the day. He knew he must forget her before it was too late and he got involved in big trouble; he didn't need any new manias; he already had enough of his own to idle his time away. He could lose his mind, follow her to the ends of the tundra and declare his love to her, letting his work slip and plunging his life into fresh chaos, which might end in fisticuffs with Bruno. One of them would emerge black and blue – himself, he expected, since his peaceful nature was no virtue in such contests. After a lengthy battle with his emotions, he changed plans for a fourth time, deciding that once his vehicle was repaired, he would continue his journey to the coast until he had forgotten an affair

66

that had only ever kickstarted in his neurotic ramblings. He would never see her again; it would take him time to shed all his memories of her on the endless roads he would drive down and spend ages in his armchair drinking himself silly, on lonesome twilights; he might even extract a few sad notes from his saxophone, the desert would turn a shade yellower and things would slow down. Better that way, he repeated, feeling he had broken off a relationship that had lasted years. No desire was more stubborn than one that ran only half the course, no nostalgia more potent than nostalgia for something that had never happened, but after a good few days, without him realising, that open sore would heal like so many others, his peace of mind and sleep patterns would be restored, everything would be back on track and the only trace of that young woman would be a mud-spattered teddy bear. But Parker did not realise that Maytén, with whom he had exchanged barely twenty words, was no longer simply a woman he'd glimpsed from afar; her name was riveted in his memory and echoed round his mind. Unknown to himself, an affair had begun to be woven that already possessed a plot and a bevy of possible outcomes. He was so overwhelmed by waves of excitement, as if he needed to take a key decision and couldn't find the courage, that he could hear his heart thudding. He unfolded his map and retraced the route he had abandoned because of his breakdown, then he walked back to the outskirts looking for the mechanic. He reached his caravan, clapped his hands several times and waited to be attended. Minutes later, he saw the guy observing him out of the window.

"Were you looking for me?"

"Did you think that was a round of applause?"

The mechanic came out of the caravan and looked Parker in the eye.

"I deserve some applause, there's your dear little truck, and it's all ready for the off. It drives better than ever."

"Why didn't you tell me the fair had upped and left?" Parker said.

"I was going to tell you, but you told me not to interfere and to mind my own business, so don't bellyache now."

"Which way did the trucks go?"

"I don't know, some went this way, others went that."

"Whereabouts is Teniente López?"

The guy looked him up and down and reacted as if he understood what was at stake.

"So you like that girl? Watch out, not everyone survives in Patagonia; fools pay a dear price."

"Thanks for that. Do you know Teniente López?"

"No town by that name exists around here. Whoever told you it did?"

"One of the Bolivians . . ."

The mechanic managed a hollow laugh.

"The ones who work on the ghost train? Don't believe them, that pair are more clueless than you."

"Keep your opinions to yourself, mechanic," Parker said, taking his wallet from his pocket and handing him a wad of notes.

"Fools pay a dear price in these parts, but you got off cheaply, I gave you a good price, you can't complain," the mechanic muttered as he counted the money.

Parker did not lambast him, because a mechanic, even such an impertinent one, was always useful on those southern roads, which came and went following their own instincts. He might need him again at any time, so he gave him a farewell handshake.

"I don't intend going after the fairground, I was only asking out of curiosity," he explained unnecessarily.

"Have a good trip, I'm sure we'll meet again."

"I sincerely hope we don't."

"Don't be such an optimist," the other man retorted, walking back to his caravan.

Parker struck camp, changed his clothes and consulted the map again, now more closely. He discovered that the place the Bolivians mentioned did in fact exist, much farther south, and assumed the mechanic had lied to him, not wanting him to catch up with the fair for some mysterious reason. Now he didn't feel like swearing at him but giving him a good hiding. He could stomach humiliating banter, that was part of the local folklore, but not the lies, so he decided to ask him to explain himself. Map in hand, he went back to the caravan and confronted him as he tidied away his tools.

"So Teniente López doesn't exist?" he snarled.

The mechanic looked at him, at a loss, and said in a surprisingly off-hand manner:

"It doesn't exist, I swear on my mother."

Parker stuck the map under his nose.

"It doesn't? Take a good look, then tell me it doesn't exist! Have a read!"

The mechanic took the map and studied it for a while.

"Here it says Teniente Primero López, and that town does exist, it's over there," he replied, nodding in that direction, continuing to put his tools away.

"Isn't it the same place?" Parker shouted.

"No way. You call a first lieutenant 'lieutenant' and just see how insulted he is."

"I'm sick of the lot of you!" Parker screamed, on the point of grabbing the mechanic by his overalls. He stopped himself at the last moment, when another truck driving past greeted him with a honk of its horn.

"Why are you getting so worked up? I can see you're very angry with yourself."

"I can get angry with whoever I want to," Parker gasped, calming down; later he thought there might be something in what the guy had said and felt even angrier.

Several hours later his truck was making swift, silent progress along a straight, dusty line through an immense expanse of oil wells. The extraction towers, scattered over the whole plain, rose and lowered their metal beaks, like birds pecking at an animal carcass. Then it drove by several clusters of hovels and half-finished bare-bricked houses, surrounded by rubbish and plastic that storm winds heaped against any mounds on the terrain.

"Nobody is going to tell me who I can get angry with, let alone a mechanic," an irritated Parker told his reflection in the side mirror, an indispensable item for the occasional check that he existed and was regaining awareness of himself, which he sometimes lost in those vast, empty spaces. He was clear his annoyance was rooted in the events of the last few days, and, especially, in Maytén. Although they had exchanged very few words, they had been intense and charged. Parker and his reflection suddenly looked each other in the eye and agreed, without saying a word, that on behalf of reconciliation and future harmony, he must head straight to Teniente Primero López and face the risks. "What do I do? Do I or don't I?" he asked the mirror, and waited for a reply. The mirror peered into his eyes, not knowing what to reply, then he looked out at the immense landscape rushing past, waiting on an answer.

After several hours on the road the truck drove through a group of caravans, home to road-repair workers, dotted among road-mending machines and fuel tanks, the dark petrol stains from which had stained the light desert soil. In the distance, on the horizon and against the light, oil derricks continued to dip their beaks into the earth's cortex, searching for the dark sap circulating in subterranean rivers. A few kilometres further on, Parker reduced speed and drove almost at walking pace through a gypsy camp formed by large canvas tents, surrounded by cars, more caravans and vans. Every so often, on any road corner, you might meet clans on the move, rehearsing the ancient itineraries of their lands of origin imprinted in their blood. The stormy winds of the tundra were the ideal habitat for the people of the wind and their tribes. Several men recognised his vehicle and shouted greetings from inside the tents. Parker waved out of the window and honked his horn in reply. Boys playing football in the middle of the road ran alongside, laughing and shouting, right up against his wheels, engulfed by the thick clouds of dust the truck threw up. Parker stopped and jumped out of his cabin with bags of sweets he had no time to hand around before they were snatched from his hands. That was one of the few moments when he descended of his own volition from his tower to mix with human fauna he considered to be his next of kin.

"Did an amusement park drive by?" he asked the boys, who were so busy sharing their spoils they paid him hardly any attention: some pointed randomly one way, others indicated the opposite direction; most shrugged their shoulders, totally indifferent.

Parker took the opportunity to stretch his legs and kick the ball about, but on this occasion anxiety and uncertainty led him to abandon the game before it was finished and return to the road. Hours later he halted in front of an abandoned train station, where dozens of out-of-use carriages were lined up along dead railway tracks the desert was covering with sand and scrub till they were erased from the landscape. The families of oil-well workers had transformed the carriages into dwellings, and over time created an extensive village with its own streets and square, where the old water tank had become a kind of central monument. Forgotten in time and space, old train engines rested at one end of the village. Youngsters played hide-and-seek behind the rusty doors of boilers and ran along the tops of trains and chimneys; at the other end lay carriages that preserved intact old cargoes of minerals extracted from the Sierra Vieja and La Conquistada mines dozens of years ago.

Parker walked over to a set of carriages that had been converted into chicken coops and animal pens, where there was a butcher's. He bought a few hunks of meat. Then he went to the bakery carriage and selected loaves an old woman was kneading with wrinkled, calloused hands.

"Doña Encarnación!"

"Parkercito, you're back! What are you after now?" the old woman greeted him with a smile, flashing her few remaining teeth. Whenever Parker drove through there, he stopped and bought supplies from her, even if he didn't need any; the pleasure of exchanging a few words with her justified the diversion and the things he bought, which he would give to someone else on another day.

72

"I come and go, like the breeze. I'm after an amusement park. Have you seen one pass by?"

"Some trucks drove by only yesterday, they must be the ones. They were heading south," answered the old woman, pointing to one end of the road.

"Is Teniente Primero López very far?"

"A couple of days, if there's no wind. Keep straight on, turn left tomorrow, drive over the hill, and then take another left for half a day, more or less."

The next morning after a quick breakfast, he got back on the road, ready to make up the advantage the fairground lorries had. He leaned back in his seat and drove, cigarette in hand, pulse and thoughts racing anxiously. That same afternoon, as the sun disappeared behind the clouds on the horizon, he met up with another group of trucks on the roadside and several men gathered around who were crucifying a sheep over a fire. They seemed friendly enough, so he asked from his cabin whether anyone had news of an amusement park moving south.

"Yes, they drove past yesterday, but I don't think they're going to Teniente Primero," said one of the drivers, a fat fellow with Mapuche features wrapped in a dark-coloured poncho. They looked like courteous folk, so Parker got out of his truck.

"Why so?" he said. That's what the Bolivians had told him and they'd no reason to lie to him, or so he believed.

"Because it's dead there. I'd go as far as Capitán Sosa, westwards, past Río Manso, that's where they'll be," answered Fatso, keeping his hands under his poncho. Parker was not so sure.

"Do you really think Capitán Sosa has much to offer?"

"You bet, a cousin of my wife lives there!"

73

Here we go again, thought Parker, as he readied himself to exchange banter with them too.

"He hadn't worked for years, but found a job there in the end," Fatso said, looking serious.

"Oh . . ." Parker said, feigning interest.

"But the pay is poor," Fatso continued, resignedly.

"Oh . . ." Parker said, fed up, regretting he'd ever asked.

The man turned to his colleagues and asked them if anyone had a clue. That sparked a long debate about the best places to set up an amusement park, depending on personal whim and conviction. It was as if they'd been waiting for an opportunity to engage in dialogue.

"Patagonia's Andean climate isn't suited to amusement parks, supermarkets are a better bet," said one man with a vague accent, as he seasoned the roast by applying long strips of an unidentifiable sauce with a brush.

"They're all stingy sourpusses in Capitán Sosa, but there's a profit to be made from setting up a brothel in Puerto Hondo," another said, a tall, lean man with a stoop, holding a maté in his hand, and pointing to nowhere in particular on the horizon.

Parker felt something simmering there, and that it would be best to leave; he knew how arguments and fights kicked off. He tried to explain it wasn't that important, but he had left it too late: they'd set out a chair for him and someone was looking for a plate and glass. The first driver had taken offence and was now shouting to clarify his position: "My wife's cousin lives in Capitán Sosa and he's a generous, cheerful guy, and there's no need to put any brothels in Puerto Hondo because all the women there are whores anyway."

Another of those present who until that point had been

74

stirring the fire with a stick, came over, waved a sooty finger in that man's face and demanded he withdrew his remark.

"My sister lives in Puerto Hondo and she's a decent woman. I won't allow anyone to say she is a whore; if it's real whores you want, then you'll find them in Punta Norte."

The man seasoning the sheep came over, flourishing a brush dripping with thick oil, and proclaimed: "It's true! The best women, whores or not, are in Punta Norte, people there know how to enjoy themselves, whether you're setting up a brothel, circus or a store."

Tempers flared by the side of the sheep turning on the spit, and the truckers got embroiled in an argument quite unconnected to Parker's original question; old quarrels and squabbles over money surfaced. Parker made one last effort to calm them down, but nobody was listening to him anymore. In the midst of the mêlée, the fat Mapuche lifted up his poncho and took out a bundle they all thought was a weapon, and after a tense silence, the group, Parker included, shuffled backwards. The driver rushed over to the man with the brush he had been arguing with a moment earlier. Red with rage he insulted him while extracting a fistful of notes from his bundle, which he rubbed in his face, then threw at the other man's feet.

"There's the cash I owe you! You know where you can stuff it!" he shouted.

"You bastard." The man he had offended threw such an off-target punch he himself fell to the ground. They started shoving each other and grabbing the other's shoulders or sleeves, a prelude to the next clout that could land at any moment. While that was happening, the man with sooty hands, ignoring everything but the glowing embers, walked over to Parker and said in a low voice: "It's not true what they say about Capitán Sosa, very good people live there. I had a very pretty girlfriend there by the name of . . ."

"I need to go to Teniente Primero López!" Parker said.

"Then keep on eastwards and take the main road."

"I prefer local roads. If there are police controls, I don't have the papers for my cargo."

"In that case take the 74 to Montefeo, and turn off there. It will take two days more, but it's safer," the other man assured him with a wink, ignoring the way his colleagues were pushing and shoving him.

"Right or left?"

"It makes no odds, you either take a turning or go straight on. If you turn off and don't find the town, the town will find you."

Parker backed away from the fracas, convinced that bottles and chairs were about to start flying. He climbed into his truck and continued his journey. Soon the huge, empty flatlands swamped the road again.

○  ○

That night the trucker slept in his cabin and in order to save time didn't set up camp; he had felt in a rush from the moment he decided to see that girl again. His head kept repeating "Maytén", trying to assimilate the name in all its possible forms. The sound of it evoked the terrain and the landscape, the blue lakes of the cordillera, the warm spring breeze caressing bodies. "Maytén" echoed, fragile and crystalline, with an accent and vowel-less end that endowed a subtle, airy grace. The more Parker repeated that name in the half-shadows of his truck parked beneath the stars, the more meanings it evoked, to a magical point that perfumed the early morning. He switched on the cabin light and wrote it on a blank sheet of paper he leaned on the dashboard. Seeing the name in writing added nuances: initially, it was just another name, one that seemed quite unpromising, but halfway a doubt or shadow appeared, something that might be an "i" or a "y", auguring something special, and then the accentuated ending that tinkled like a bell. What kind of name was that? Was it for real? And what if the girl was called something else, and the Bolivians had played a joke on him. That pair had the vice, or habit, of playing pranks, like so many people he met on the road. They might be part of a conspiracy against him, perhaps she was really a Juana or a María, and it was their fault he had frittered his time away giving shape to a rebellious, awkward sound that was fake into the bargain. He went on muttering "Maytén" for a while, but his doubts about how to spell the name meant it never curdled, nor did his sleep: snow was turning to sleet, then water, till it vanished into nothingness. His final resort, on such a spectral night when the universe lost its shape, was numbers, the infallible logic that gave things order and a specific location. He needed to count something, anything, imagine sheep jumping over a fence, as he'd been taught as a child to vanquish sleeplessness. They could be sheep, guanacos or stars, any set of material objects that could be encompassed by a round number: it seemed the only way for the universe to reclaim its lost dimensions. And what if one of the imaginary animals he was counting snagged on barbed wire by the road, as it jumped? An incident like that might ruin his night even more, so he desisted. That's what his wakeful nights were often like, permeated by the disturbing vertigo he felt when suspended between earth and sky; at peculiar times he seemed to carry on his

77

shoulders the entire weight of a nocturnal universe criss-crossed by meridians, tropics and parallels. Parker teetered backwards and forwards along those lines like an acrobat on a high wire.

During the day, his hands gripped the steering wheel, his eyes fixed on the road, and his mind focused on the task of driving and harmonising an imprecise number of parts, valves, levers and devices; he became part of the engine, the tower from which his hands controlled tons of metal. At night, when his mind was released from that task, the idea of losing control over his life terrified him, and, at a stroke, his wandering existence seemed absurd. He had been stupid to live so many years between heaven and the horizon, imprisoned by that ersatz scenario from a lousy cowboy film, but he had had no choice. He repeated "Maytén" for the nth time and at last achieved what he was after. That name which had seemed contrived and remote now shed its exoticism and became familiar. That woman could be called by no other name, and that supposed a specific kind of mutual trust, like two lovers meeting up again after years and years apart. If he decided to pursue her, the time spent would no longer be a blind chase into the unknown, but the engineering of a rendezvous that had been long in the planning, Parker reflected, as a black curtain descended, smothering his consciousness and making him at one with all that was sleeping around him.

○ ○

It took the brothers Eber and Fredy, Bruno's Bolivian handymen, several days on the road to reach Teniente Primero López, the fairground's new location, bringing the last things they had left in the previous town. Their boss was waiting for them in order to finish installing the fair. They had driven along the main road and arrived some time before Parker, who'd wasted precious days meandering on local byways. A few hours of intense labour and the structures of the ghost train and the Bear Hunt were up and ready next to the rest of the attractions.

Bruno walked round the fairground seeing to final details, while Maytén busied herself with domestic chores in their caravan. She had washed the previous night's dishes and their dirty clothes in a bowl. In a kitchen apron, a scarf round her head, she was now putting the final touches to a stew in a blackened pot on their camping stove and was about to give the caravan a sweep and air the sheets and blankets. After squeezing the clothes with her sinewy young arms, she pegged them on a line strung up between two posts to stop the fierce wind from blowing them away. As she was finishing, one of the posts began to keel over until it collapsed, spreading the clean clothes over the bare ground. Maytén watched the scene, gesturing in despair, and turned furious and foul-tempered. Quiet for a moment, then enraged, she began to look around, spitting at the first person she encountered. Fury magnified the wild beauty of her face.

"It was your job to fix the post, it wasn't that hard! I'm tired of the lot of you!" she shouted, as she paced backwards and forwards, arms akimbo, in the direction of Eber who was sweeping up dust and pebbles in front of the caravan he shared with his brother.

"You didn't say a word to me, my dear, it must have been the other fellow. God is my witness, I'll sort it right now," said sleepy-eyed Eber as he retrieved the muddy clothes

79

and put them back in the bowl. Maytén waved him away, grabbed a mallet and was all set to knock the post back in place. She was stopped dead by the grating voice of her stubble-cheeked husband, wearing a sleeveless T-shirt and smoking a cigar, as he peered out of a caravan window.

"Will we eat soon?"

Maytén threw the mallet angrily at Eber. She did not know which one she was annoyed with, and that infuriated her even more; she was sure the Bolivians swapped identities to dodge responsibility.

"You all think I'm Wonder Woman," she declared, as she stormed into the caravan and set the table for lunch.

Bruno smoked and drank wine as he eyed the pieces on the chessboard. He leaned his elbows on the table, held his head between his hands and glared at them. At times he shifted the board from side to side as if setting a compass, at others he turned it round and scrutinised the pieces again, thinking they had moved themselves in those few seconds. Maytén watched him out of the corner of her eye, as intently as he surveyed the pieces, waiting for the opportune moment to say what she had decided to say.

"I can't cope with all this work, we need another helper, those two don't even do the work of one," she erupted, but Bruno kept his eyes on the chessboard, sucking on his cigar, then sipping his wine.

"Shush, I can't concentrate on the tokens, that's why you always beat me. You women are always up to your tricks."

"Pieces, not tokens. *Pieces*," she insisted as she served out two plates of stew and sat down wearily at the table, leafing through a magazine opposite her husband who was still hypnotised by the board. Out of the blue, as if he had received a message from the great beyond, Bruno made his move, taking a queen with a pawn that was in the adjacent square, then glowered at his wife.

"What do you reckon? I just snaffled your queen . . ." he announced, pleased as Punch by his brilliant move. Maytén ignored him and concentrated on what she was reading, but something inside her rebelled.

"When will you ever learn? You can't move like that in chess," she parried, continuing to skim the pages of her magazine. Bruno studied the chessboard trying to spot his mistake, thinking that women never liked anything, that they always complained. You can't make a move like that? Why not? Who said so? I'd bet anything a woman invented this game, he thought to himself. But he wouldn't be ordered around by Maytén, the simple fact that she got her own way and imposed her own whims blew him. He tried to be philosophical and persuade his wife with his logic.

"It's harder with tokens that move in every direction. I like it that way."

Maytén held a hand out, moved a rook following the rules of the game and took a knight. Bruno observed her move, and before she could remove the knight from the board, he returned the pieces to their positions.

"See how you like to cheat? You can't stand losing."

Maytén put her magazine aside and repeated the exact same move, in her turn challenging Bruno, but Bruno was hungry and didn't want to waste any more time arguing. Piqued, he pushed the board away and tucked a napkin around his neck.

"Move them as it takes your fancy, I've got too much else on my plate to argue with a rude, moody female."

They ate in a painful silence that only tolerated the monotone sound of cutlery drifting from mouths to plates.

When they finished, Maytén piled the dishes in the kitchen sink while Bruno drank one glass of wine after another, deep in thought. He downed several more before he answered the question that still hung in the air.

"We can't afford another helper, there's almost no work, and the fair is getting smaller and smaller. The Space Ships left last month, Formula One broke down a couple of weeks ago, nobody can fix it, so they'll have to sell it as scrap."

Maytén finished drying the dishes, not saying a word, her eyes staring out of the caravan windows. Bruno waited for her to say something, then carried on explaining the fairground's plight as she remained silent.

"El Turco told me he's off to the coast with the Barbecue, he's found a fairground that stays in one place. We're dwindling by the week, and must make do with Eber and Fredy; they're not wonderful, but they come cheap and eat next to nothing," said Bruno as he staggered to his feet, holding on to the caravan ceiling with both hands to keep his balance. Maytén looked out of the window and watched the Bolivians digging a pit in the stony ground, expending a lot of effort to achieve very little.

"That pair work less than one man, and give us more work than if they weren't around."

"If it wasn't for them, we'd have had to abandon the fair too. We're losing an attraction in every town, and if we go on like this, you'll have to start dancing in the nude," he said, raising his voice and celebrating his witticism with a guffaw.

Maytén picked up a tea towel, rolled it into a ball and launched it at his face, though he ducked and dodged it, and kept laughing between bouts of coughing and throat-clearing.

"So why don't we change direction? We keep going farther south, it gets colder and the people get sadder and poorer. Why can't we try a big city with a bit more life?"

"The shearing season starts soon and there'll be work for everyone. Hands are paid at the weekend and they like going out to have fun with their families. So we need to go even farther south," Bruno said, staring at the chessboard to find inspiration for his next move. Elated, he took a white queen with a black pawn.

"Mate," he declared, tugging his wife's arm. She gave him a withering look.

"That's exactly what you said last year, and it was a dead loss. No hands came, let alone their families."

"How was I to know a volcano was going to spew out ash?"

"So now it's the volcano's fault. Next year it will be an eclipse," Maytén rasped, trying to provoke him.

Bruno started to lose patience.

"Lots of animals died. People lost their jobs. But this year we'll rake it in hand over fist. Then we'll go to the coast when the fleet gets back and the fishermen will land, not having spent a cent of their wages. We'll have work galore."

Maytén whirled round.

"To the coast, even farther south? You promised we'd go up country when the shearing was over!" she came back at him in a fury.

Bruno stood up and pursued her as she moved around the caravan's narrow confines, then stood behind her, leaned his body into hers, swaying his hips, and started to kiss her neck.

"What about a change of game? Let's see who'll win now. This pawn is about to carry off his queen," he said, grabbing her breasts from behind. Maytén threw him off and turned round on the offensive.

"I set the rules in this game. You can forget me, until we get another helper. I have to work in the fair, cook and wash."

"We can't afford one, but I'll help you on the stall," Bruno conceded, as he softened his tone, making it sickly sweet, and leaned into her body again. "I'm up for that, my love."

"So I'm your love now, am I? I knew this fairground wouldn't work out, we ought to have stayed in town," she said, holding him off with both hands.

Maytén had long since stopped being afraid of her husband and giving him what he wanted. With every day that went by, her patience shortened, but she knew what Bruno was like when he was angry and didn't want to trigger another fight. She'd promised to make the effort needed to salvage their marriage, but love like in their first days together had gone. She knew how frail her state of mind was, and that she must decide when and how to move on. For the moment she could not, she lacked the means and the inner strength to abandon the fair and the security a house gave, or at least that caravan, her only abode in the world. Beyond that were volcanoes that cast shadows over the steppe for weeks, rivers that burst their banks and cut off roads, gales, droughts and floods that pushed flocks all ways, driving them to any of the cardinal points, heavy snowfalls, harsh winters and mean summers, and *she* was part and parcel of all that. Water and winds swept down from western peaks, accompanying the slow descent of the glaciers; in the east the sea ruled with its fishing seasons and unpredictable tides, its deserted beaches populated by the bones of whales and sea lions. Whichever way you turned, the same spectacle came back to haunt you after it had circulated the world across waves and roaring ocean, without ever touching an inch of land. That was how remote the planet was down there, in those extreme latitudes locals were happy to call "the land at the end of the world", as if it was a source of pride. Maytén vaguely intuited that she was just one more creature populating that world; she'd been born and had grown up there. She was subject to the same rules as the rest of the fauna and flora, but couldn't resign herself to that fate. She was crushed by the endless steppe; those expanses caused her soul to disintegrate. She could imagine another existence, or at least other places to lead the same life, but needed something to advance her piece on the chessboard, a push from some external force to take her away from the fairground and Bruno. She consoled herself by thinking that that moment must be nigh, even though this sad day heralded another of Bruno's violent outbursts.

"Would you rather we'd stayed in town? We'd have starved to death after the gym shut down! Who was I going to give boxing lessons to? I was left punching fresh air," Bruno said.

"No, more like getting sozzled, feeling sorry for yourself the whole day long and losing your temper. And it's not only air you've punched," Maytén said, lifting a sleeve and showing a bruise near her shoulder.

"I work day in day out, sunrise to sunset. I have a right to a drink."

"I can't stand this life any longer, Bruno. It's not even a life; we barely have enough to buy food."

Her husband let out a deep sigh, seized his head with both hands and started shouting.

"Are you sure we'd have been better off in Buenos Aires? What would you have done apart from wash dishes and make beds?"

"Anything would be an improvement on this!"

Bruno grunted and smashed a cupboard door with his fist. Pieces of wood flew around. Maytén raised her arms, she knew she would be next. She strode past her husband and out of the caravan, throwing her apron at his feet; she went to the back and hurried through the wings of the fair on her way to the exit. Eber and Fredy, who were at work on the ghost train, had taken out all the mannequins and monsters to give them an airing in the light of day. Maytén walked past the long line of Draculas, mummies and werewolves standing to attention like soldiers, while the Bolivians tidied and dusted their clothes. Bruno had built those monsters himself to boost the little train's terror levels, using old window dummies, rags, masks and remains of materials from the gym; they were now his children. Maytén left the fairground and crossed the town, but soon came to a halt. She was confronted by the vast space of the steppe, and something inside her shuddered. She felt dizzy and had to find something to hold on to so she didn't fall. She was enveloped by a dark shadow that contrasted with the bright light over the steppe, and her mind was filled by childhood images of herself playing with her sisters in the backyard of the house where she was born, a brick cube in an anonymous cluster of houses the name of which neither said nor suggested anything. She had struggled to survive there with her mother and sisters for years, until the flatlands consumed them one by one. She recalled the constant wind and cold, the sand in her eyes, the dry, cracked hands they used to swing the rope over which they laughed, sang and skipped.

While she tried to divert those memories to other areas of her mind, Maytén had to repress the impulse to go back to the caravan and protect herself from the neglect she had suffered from childhood. She tried to exorcise her panic by defying it: she walked in a straight, if hesitant line towards the flatlands that began a few blocks away, until she'd put the town behind her and crossed the parched terrain, gripping her shoulders with her hands to comfort herself. She surveyed the space around her and perceived the infinite vastness of the cage imprisoning her, without doors, bars or windows. A cell where she could move at will, but from which she could never escape. The most horrible of prisons that extended its walls as far as her eyes could see and even beyond that. She wondered where her hopes and dreams had gone, the ambition she had once cherished to leave that emptiness forever and live in a city with decent streets and buildings, with people who walked along pavements not needing to hide their bodies from gales or always be on the lookout for shelter. Her sisters had left to seek out new horizons, and she'd stayed behind waiting for her opportunity. When she met Bruno, she thought the moment had come to abandon that spartan existence forever, but she soon understood that she was wrong. The glow of city lights had receded farther and farther; once again her fate was solitude.

Maytén pinched her face and cheeks several times, but her fingers were as dry and cracked as the land she was treading. Standing before that immense void, crossing her arms and gripping her shoulders, she looked beyond that remoteness and travelled back in time. She vaguely sensed that the origin of her struggles began when her forebears arrived in those parts. She wondered why they hadn't stayed in Europe rather than end up in those miserable wastes. She knew nothing about that continent, or the hunger that drove them to seek their fortunes anywhere on the planet, even *there*. She knew from stories her family told that Ciro, her paternal grandfather, had left Naples at the beginning of the twentieth century and joined in the escapades of a famous pirate from the town of his birth by the name of Pasquale the Pirate, a smuggler dealing in goods and people the length of the Strait of Magellan, on the southern tip. He had belonged to those gangs for years, until the governments of both countries decided to put an end to their trafficking. After several years in prison, Ciro transformed himself into a gold prospector on Tierra del Fuego, taking with him his young son Pasquale, Maytén's future father, named in honour of his pirate friend. Ciro went mad soon after, screwed up by the elements, the follies of wealth, syphilis and alcohol, and he yielded to his chimeras by mingling with Indian tribes that still survived on the shores of the strait. No more was heard of Ciro, executed perhaps by a chieftain who discovered the role he had played in the massacres of Indians. Little Pasquale was taken hostage in a remote encampment and stayed in captivity for years until he was purchased by Italian missionaries who reared and fed him until he came of age. From then on Pasquale spent most of his time visiting ranches and pioneer settlements with a cart pulled by oxen, dealing in food, furniture and other goods. His trading took him from one end of Patagonia to the other, and in an anonymous hamlet he met Maytén's mother, a young mestizo Indian woman who worked as a cook in a miners' camp. Maytén and her two older sisters were born and grew up there, wandering from settlements to ranches where they started doing domestic chores from an early age. Her sisters managed to marry and give up that life and Maytén finished her classes in a rural school. When she met Bruno, a likeable young man, exemplary worker and promising boxer, she imagined she might at last free herself from the stigma of her blood. Bruno had promised her a better life and represented a tangible opportunity to escape from those existential quicksands where her relatives had been trapped and to break at last the chain of poverty-stricken lives ruined by adversity. But that ambition proved to be another failure, the waters of destiny resumed their rebellious flow time after time, sweeping away anyone who resisted. Maytén's hopes turned into more dreams and utopias. The factories moved to another part of the country. Bruno lost his job and used his compensation to build a gymnasium in a prosperous Atlantic fishing port. Bruno's boxing classes were not appreciated by locals who were of the opinion that imposing rules on fights eliminated what made them interesting. Besides, what sense was there in paying for physical exercise if they already got enough loading sacks and boxes on wharves or shearing sheep, something a lot like single combat, like bar-room fisti-cuffs. Bruno's business soon went bankrupt, and took with it his passion for boxing and wrestling: he had succumbed to the treacherous dunes of the tundra, dragging Maytén with him. The couple invested the small savings they salvaged in two elements of an amusement park – the Bear Hunt and the ghost train – that plied the roads between the coast and the settlements on the steppe. The fair had begun to leak water several months before, but blinded by frustration and drink Bruno refused to accept reality. Maytén warned they should abandon ship before it sank again, without a lifeboat this time, and that was an affront to Bruno's self-esteem: her often merciless words ripped his pride to tatters, threw failure in his face, and aroused violence he'd struggled to repress for years. Bruno lowered his arms and surrendered, prepared to go down with his boat, driven by elemental virility. He did not have the courage to do it by himself, he had lost even that strength, and needed her, the only love of his life, the source of the few caresses and affectionate words he had enjoyed in his harsh life, to accompany him on his road to disaster.

Standing before that vast plain, hugging her shoulders, Maytén surveyed the emptiness around her. She could hear the distant threatening curses and wails Bruno was directing to the four points of the compass. She waited a moment and retraced her steps to the fairground where Eber and Fredy had joined the considerable row of dummies lined up as if on a parade ground, standing to attention, arms by their sides. Maytén observed Bruno, who looked like a general issuing orders, while his subordinates listened, motionless and silent. The Bolivian handymen, heads down, glanced at each other askance, waiting for the moment when their chief finished his harangue and action began.

"Stupid idiots! It's your fault we're going under! You'll all end up on the street!" Bruno bellowed as he reviewed his troops.

"It must have been God's will, boss," Eber said.

". . . who lights up every step we make," added Fredy, eyes glued to the ground.

"The only will that matters here is mine, and I light up my own footsteps, helped by nobody," Bruno thundered.

"Come to church with us one of these days, boss, and see Him and know His light," Eber insisted.

Bruno resumed his tirade with renewed energy, threatening his employees with sudden violent death whenever they regurgitated their religious nonsense. If anything put him in a bad mood, apart from his wife's whinging, it was the Bolivians' attempts to convert him. When he stopped clamouring, Eber and Fredy knew what was coming and moved away from the formation. Brutal Bruno started to kick and punch his dummies, most of which turned their heads around and fell apart: the skeletons' bones rattled, Dracula's cape fluttered with each attack, and Frankenstein's unhitched body swung backwards and forwards after each blow.

"You damned fools ruined my life, you frighten nobody, we're a laughing stock!" Bruno shouted and raved as he fell to the ground and picked himself up.

Maytén walked to the back of the caravan, rolled up her coat and went back to washing the mud-smeared clothes. Eber and Freddy stood to attention, watched her from afar, looked at each other, happy they didn't have to fight such an irreverent woman, and felt pity for their boss.

○ ○

Parker kept on turning over the name of "Maytén" while steering his tons of truck with aplomb. From the day he had first encountered that name, he had been trying to extract every possible meaning, shape and nuance from it. The features of her face, of which he retained only a fleeting memory, thus acquired new expressions, enriched by other perspectives. His reverie was interrupted when he drove past a service station and realised he should have warned old Constanzo long ago of the days he had missed on the road and justified the turnings he had taken. He stopped and called the office from a telephone booth; it was late, but

Constanzo worked, ate and slept in the same place. The telephone rang several times before the gruff old man replied as if afraid someone wanted to inform him of problems and ruin the football game on television and his daily intake of empanadas.

"My vehicle is holed up in Teniente Primero López, and they've still not sent me the spare part, so I've no choice but to wait here," Parker lied, sounding concerned.

His boss responded with a stream of reproaches and complaints that forced Parker to hold the phone away from his ear and repeat his explanation several times. Constanzo's voice was distorted by alcohol, as if he were speaking from inside a cellophane bag.

"That truck must be in port before the end of the week, the boat sails on Monday!" the old man snarled, sniffing his food. Parker let him talk; that meant leaving that night, renouncing Maytén, perhaps risking losing all trace of her forever. They argued for several minutes, not allowing the other to finish his sentences. The source of conflict soon surfaced: delayed pay and broken promises.

"How long are you going to be stuck there?" the old man said when he calmed down, chewing an empanada.

"If I were a fortune teller, do you think I'd be driving a truck up the backside of the world?" Parker said, echoing the mechanic's turn of phrase.

"Don't play the smart-ass with me, you must deliver your cargo on time. If the spare doesn't arrive, make one."

"Why don't *you* bring me one?" Parker asked, knowing the old man only shifted from his office if there was an earthquake, and his part of the country was not considered a seismic area.

"You forget who pays your wages," Constanzo said, changing his tone.

"If I forget, maybe it's because you haven't paid me for four months."

Constanzo wiped his mouth with a piece of paper, pondered a few seconds and went on chomping.

"Is it four months? Doesn't time fly?" he joked, spluttering and laughing.

"If you think it's such a laughing matter, I'll tip your truck into the first gulch I find," Parker said. Constanzo emptied his glass of wine and changed tone again. He knew Parker was incapable of carrying out his threat, but he was the only employee he had left, and he needed to hold on to him.

"I was only joking, man, you've got such a poor sense of humour! I'll see to all that next month."

Parker had stopped believing in his promises, just as Constanzo did not believe Parker's story. He suspected his delay was intentional, knowing, like an old habitué of those byways, that such situations usually involved a woman.

"Sure you didn't pick up a little roadside chickadee?" he said in a honeyed voice, licking his greasy fingers.

Parker was so convinced of his own lies that he was sorely offended by his boss's allegations. He concluded with some home truths about him and his firm, and at the end of the conversation was left holding a silent receiver, looking at it and imagining sentences must have got trapped inside. Constanzo had not been there for some time. He clattered the phone down, and, after paying for his call, headed towards his vehicle, all set to reach the amusement park the following day. He decided he would stay as long as he wanted, if he had the chance, even if the boat had to leave without its cargo. At that point he could not have cared less.

On the following morning, Parker passed a sign indicating that he was crossing the forty-eighth parallel, and half a day later he reached his destination. He drove under a rusty metal arch emblazoned with the town's name and covered with flapping flags and red pennants. Rough-and-ready sanctuaries rose up on each side of the road, packed with little huts built from planks, tins and bricks where people worshipped the pagan deities that truckers scattered throughout the land: miraculous gauchos, figurines and images of the Santa Muerta, robin hoods, rural bandits and flaky saints who had found refuge in popular beliefs. Bottles of water and all kinds of offerings were piled up to venerate some saint who had died of thirst in the desert and now offered miraculous cures from the life hereafter. Those wind-blasted huts housed statuettes and red candles whose molten wax stained the earth. Walls were covered with plaques and ex-votos, photographs, aerosol-sprayed names, plastic flowers and handwritten letters giving thanks, or asking for a wish to be granted. The offerings and bottles of water, piles of tyres, oil drums transformed into spits, wooden crosses and sculptures proliferated from chapel to chapel. Every available surface was covered by hundreds of old car number plates, the figures of which created a single, huge number, an infinite number that seemed to contain the mysteries of the Kabbala. That improvised pantheon attracted large crowds of the faithful who appeared out of nowhere every morning on carts, horseback or foot to venerate their deities, and then returned at dusk to nowhere until they were swallowed up by the plain. Passing vehicles stopped to pay homage, people meandered, devotedly touching images, making signs of the cross and lighting torches. Entire families visited the area on mystic quests, tidying offerings, cleaning chapels and decorating sanctuaries, then sat down to drink maté and light fires under spits. Those who did not stop greeted the saints and hooted to apologise for their disrespect.

A municipal sign stood between the entrance arch and place of worship, tied firmly to the ground by lengths of barbed wire: "Welcome to Teniente Primero López – Hotel Service-Infirmary-Telephone-Police-Fuel-Burials and Tyre Supplier". Someone had written on one side of the sign in thick brush strokes "the hotel is rubbish", and someone else had riposted in smaller letters "it's not true". Parker drove straight to the centre without greeting the deities, crossed a long, empty boulevard and parked in a small square in the middle of which stood a flagpole and a dry fountain crammed with earth around an equestrian statue of the town's first lieutenant namesake, swathed in a poncho and flourishing a rifle. He had been a minor hero in the conquest of the desert, a man who had earned his reputation thanks to massacres of Indians disguised as battles fought on behalf of progress, and who in his turn had been ambushed and killed by Indians. A plaque commemorated his feats and called on future generations to follow the example of such an upstanding citizen, but in a gesture of national reconciliation the local authorities had added by his horse's feet the statue of a long-haired Indian in a loincloth, who walked beside him, obedient and inappropriate, like a faithful squire.

Parker steered his truck down the streets of Teniente Primero López, and reached the wasteland where the fairground was lodged. He parked in the vicinity and began to spy on every movement through his binoculars, searching for Maytén. It all seemed very quiet, the fair was much smaller, several stalls and attractions had evidently deserted, including the Hammer and the Barbecue. Various individuals were adding the finishing touches to the few attractions that still gave life to the fairground, while Bruno was sorting the last details for the imminent opening. Opposite the entrance to the ghost train the Bolivians were repairing the injured bodies of dummies with bandages and ropes, smearing paint to heighten the horrible expressions on their emaciated faces before repositioning them in the labyrinthine tunnels, crouching in the shadows between and on the bends. Parker's gaze visited every corner of the fairground, looking for his objective around caravans and kiosks. After a while he spotted a hazy silhouette emerging from a caravan, adjusted the focus of his binoculars and that silhouette soon became Maytén pulling a shopping trolley. He decided to follow her – at a prudent distance – between the low, white-washed houses to the fruit store. He took the opportunity to study the goddess outside her temple, stripped of the offerings that adorned her gallery altar, so he could enjoy a more commonplace, everyday take on Maytén. When she stood in the queue next to other women, he appeared out of the blue, greeting her with an expression of surprise. This flesh-and-blood Maytén seemed like any other house-wife out with her shopping trolley, but proximity enhanced rather than cheapened her image. Which did he prefer, the reality or the largely imaginary vision? He couldn't say yet, and wouldn't find out in the days to come either, though he would only have access to one.

They looked at each other, at a loss for words; Maytén had no reason to pretend she was surprised, because that meeting meant nothing. It took her a few seconds to recognise

Parker's face, which sparked no associations. She smiled politely and sought out some detail to help her. She kept smiling and dug deep in her memory. Parker took several seconds to react.

"We met in El Suculento," he said.

"Where? I've never heard that name before," she said, dumbfounded.

"It used to be called Jardín Espinoso, the last town the fairground visited."

Maytén frowned.

"Are you sure? I've never heard the name."

Parker could not think what to say, but he bridled at the thought that he was about to have one of those meaningless conversations with her too. Maytén dithered, had a vague, blurry idea, then remembered. That guy in the Bear Hunt, she thought and blushed.

"Ah, yes," she exclaimed, as casually as she could.

Who was that stranger who'd turned up at the fair, coming from God knows where? Her first impression, now confirmed, was that he was a peculiar, scheming individual.

"I too have come to buy bread," Parker explained, not waiting to be asked, simply to break the silence, while his swirling hair seemed about to take flight.

"This is a greengrocer's, they don't sell bread," she said.

He must be one of the many truckers who passed that way, although he did not resemble any she had known: they were taciturn, grizzly and coarse.

How idiotic, Parker thought, covering his face with the back of his hand to ward off the breeze, convinced that also helped him not to seem ridiculous. He eyed her intriguing body silhouetted against that liquid void around them. She too seemed immune to the gusts. He changed position several times, searching for that invisible shelter; he failed, but she deftly eluded their reach.

"This climate garbles words and makes for confusion," he said, as she took his arm and moved him a couple of metres to one side, where the wind granted him a truce.

Maytén believed it was a chance encounter, which often happened with people in transit in those parts, but this time there was something odd about their meeting. She sensed that Parker was the most interesting man of all those she had ever met in her itinerant life along byways and in remote outposts. She tried to sketch in his character with the few elements she had to hand. Was he an outlaw, some-one who had dropped from the sky, a parachutist, a figment of her imagination, a phantom, an inexplicable aberration among the motley human crowd that engaged in long hauls over those flatlands? He did not correspond to anything she knew, and even less to anything her mind could con-jure up, so accustomed was it to a banal perception of the everyday. She was intrigued by his old-fashioned courtesy, his old-style gestures, the way he moved and spoke, typical of a person who doesn't really know where he is or why he is there. Behind a shield of apparent self-confidence, she glimpsed that fragility she felt in her own flesh, and that was why he stood out. Although she could not use any of her usual markers to locate him, he represented a break-point in the monotonous flow of her lacklustre life.

Soon after, she and Parker left the shop and walked down the streets in animated conversation, coming to a halt at a street corner. The sudden silence told Parker it was the moment to make the next move while he had the oppor-tunity. He looked for the right words, but once again the wind swirled around his feet and made him stumble. Hair unruffled, her clothes undisturbed, Maytén grabbed his shoulder and shifted him half a metre to the right. Parker's shirt and hair settled down.

"Anyone can see you're not from these parts," she said with a smile, and, not giving him time to respond, she indicated a spot behind Parker and sighed, "I have to go that way."

Now, he thought, biting the inside of his lip.

"Wouldn't you like to go for a drink?"

"No, thanks, I'm not thirsty," she said politely, sensing what was behind his invitation. She could not stifle a laugh, but then made up for it. It was the first time she had experienced anything like that.

"Go for a drink around here? There are no bars. It's not Buenos Aires."

Parker was in no doubt the girl was from the area, that is, from some point on a radius of at least two to three thousand kilometres.

"I know a place where they sell the best Coca Cola in the south, it's really bubbly."

Maytén hesitated for a second, smiled, then smiled again.

"You mean, drink a Coca Cola sitting on the edge of the pavement?"

"We could get a bag of crisps while we're at it."

"The salty sort, I suppose."

"Yes, although you've already got plenty of tang."

Now Maytén's smile wasn't so broad. She was shocked and stared at Parker, waiting for him to follow up.

"That was a compliment, although you may not think so."

"Is that what 'tang' is? A compliment? First I heard of it. Thanks very much, but I must go."

Parker started sweating, and for the first time he missed the breeze.

"It means the opposite of tasteless."

"Yes, I'd got that, I'm not stupid," she replied, holding out a hand.

"Will we meet again?"

"I told you there's a teddy bear down there."

"I've got a good aim."

"I don't think it will be good enough."

"I do have other virtues."

Maytén walked past Parker, and just as she was crossing the barrier dividing past from present, the moment after which he would disappear forever from her life, she cheekily glanced over her shoulder.

"See you at the fairground later?"

"Oh, I don't know about that, I'll have to consult my diary," he joked.

Maytén seemed put out; the words they exchanged were from different registers.

"I mean I will," Parker added, afraid of a misunderstanding, but she had already crossed the road and was pushing her trolley towards the square. His gaze lingered on her, then he looked for a kiosk, bought a bottle of fizzy water and sat on the edge of the pavement to celebrate their meeting.

It was a gleeful Maytén who crossed the settlement; the mere fact she'd swapped those innocent words with someone who wasn't her husband infused her with an optimism she hadn't experienced in a long while. She felt desired and seduced, the object of someone else's gaze. It dispelled the despondent image she held of herself: a sad, down-at-heel woman wasting her youth and the best years of her life in pathetic squabbles and domestic chores. When she reached the square and was confronted again by that colourful encampment surrounded by caravans and lorries decorated with circus motifs, she felt a sinking feeling in her chest. She had never before harboured such loathing for the fair. Between the amusements she could see the double silhouette of Eber and Fredy who were preparing the attractions, sweeping the ground with palm leaves and sitting down to discuss pages of the Bible. She turned round to go back to the town centre, pretending she had forgotten to buy something, and walked several blocks, hoping in her heart of hearts to find Parker again, though the very idea seemed absurd. She felt like a silly, ingenuous adolescent, while her cheeks blushed again, as if she had been caught thinking of something sinful. What could that man offer her, except to make her sad fate even sadder and turn it into a hell? She hesitated for a second, then decided she would not see him again. After walking around for a while, she spotted Parker still sitting on the pavement edge and staring into space. She found it funny to see him like that and thought about approaching him, had second thoughts and returned to the fairground that had been home to her for the last few years.

She walked past the empty attractions, still dragging the shopping trolley. If there was one thing that depressed her even more than the amusement park, it was that same park when it was closed and deserted, when walking between those empty booths was like crossing a cemetery. As she strolled between gravestones and sepulchres, Fredy and Eber looked like gravediggers wandering between tombs with their spades and brooms.

"Goodbye, boss, we've fixed your post, now you can hang out all the washing you want," Fredy told her from a pile of empty beer-bottle crates.

More standoffish than ever, Maytén nodded her thanks and grimaced. She walked to her caravan where Bruno would, of course, be gripping a bottle, his body slumped over the table, focusing on that absurd game of chess he insisted on playing according to the wrong rules, pretending it was draughts.

o o

Parker walked through the fairground tracing the footsteps of his deity and reached the hallowed precinct, the gallery where Eber, or Fredy – who could tell? – was arranging teddy bears on a shelf. He was wearing the same clothes he wore for big occasions, dark, baggy trousers and a crumpled shirt barely hidden by a striped jacket. The ticket office was shut, and a man in the kiosk, the bear by the name of Bruno Maytén had been referring to, was dealing with clients and making candyfloss. He made a detour so as not to arouse suspicions.

"Fancy your chances?" asked a ruddy-faced old lady with watery eyes, wrapped in a poncho, as she offered him a fishing rod and pointed to a pond where different-sized and -coloured plastic goldfish were floating. Parker thought it would be a good way to kill time until Maytén showed up, and he took the rod, leaned on the counter, and unsuccessfully tried to hook the biggest fish. He tried others, which were just as elusive: they slipped along the sides of the pond as if they were alive, and every time his rod was left dangling and empty. Now and then he looked around to check for any sign of movement: the ticket office was still empty, the shrine's bodyguard was still transforming grains of sugar into strips of white floss, while one of his handymen was still slotting passengers into the ghost train. Maytén put in a sudden appearance without betraying her celestial nature, went into the ticket booth and started selling tickets with an absent, melancholy air. Parker tried to catch her attention several times, but she concentrated on her work and did not even look up. Put out, he continued to try his luck as an angler, until the situation provided him with the means to approach her. He was becoming more adept with the rod; he landed several fish and earned congratulations from the old lady who applauded and encouraged him to persevere. He counted up the points he had won and realised his tally was not enough to claim the top prize: for that, he had to catch the biggest, trickiest, most slippery fish. Parker grasped his opportunity when the old lady was distracted for a moment; he leaned half his body over the counter, grabbed the fish with one hand, put it on the hook, then landed it, exultant. The old lady turned round, and suspected he had cheated the second she saw Parker exhibiting his trophy with a victorious flourish.

"You been cheating, young man? Nobody has been lucky enough to catch that fish in all my years in fairs," she declared, half closing her rheumy eyes. Parker said nothing.

"You're not from these parts, are you? You must be from Indio Tramposo."

Maytén caught snatches of their conversation, looked up from her books of tickets and saw Parker. Her eyes were sad and bloodshot and her makeup had run. She tidied her hair and clothes and tried to smile, to rid herself of the gloom around her.

"How could you even associate me with Cheating Indian, señora?" Parker said, failing to hide a smile.

"You *porteños* think you're so smart," she rasped.

103

"I'm not from Buenos Aires."

"That's what they all say, trying to act all innocent."

Silence descended for a few seconds, until the old lady's stern expression melted into one of complicity.

"You must be a good person, even though you're *porteño*. We will assume you caught that fish fair and square."

"Can I choose a prize?"

"Yes, you can, but make a wise choice," she answered with a wink.

Parker looked at her, but didn't catch the drift of what she had said, then opted for a tap that hung in the air and spurted water. The old lady looked at him pitifully and shook her head.

"You didn't get me. Choose something better."

Parker looked at her intrigued and she smiled back. He glanced at the other prizes hanging from the ceiling and selected a plastic sword with a brightly sequined hilt.

"Don't be silly, better than that."

Parker fingered the prizes, but couldn't make up his mind.

"I'm assuming you want a present for someone special?"

Parker was about to choose a jug full of luminous flowers, but the old lady huffed, took a makeup case from the shelf and plopped it down.

"You men are so obtuse! Take this, it will go down very, very well."

Parker studied his prize and gave the old lady a grateful kiss, and she used his closeness to whisper in his ear.

"Take care, this neck of the woods is no place for fools," she muttered.

Parker was bewildered, then registered what she was insinuating, and, case in hand, walked off, eying the ticket counter. He had a free run: her husband had gone and the Bolivians were working, their minds elsewhere. He went over, half hiding the prize against his body; she saw him coming and looked down.

"Can I have a ride in the ghost train?" he asked point-blank.

"How many tickets would you like?"

"Ten thousand, please."

"Ten thousand pesos?"

"No, ten thousand tickets."

Maytén laughed. Her face brightened for a moment, then turned serious.

"I don't have that many. You know, the ghost train can stir really strong emotions."

Parker surveyed the fairground again and realised that, apart from the old lady with her fish pond, who was now smiling enigmatically in his direction, he still had a free run.

"I like strong emotions, give me all you have."

Maytén tore one off and gave it to him.

"Did you mean emotions or tickets?"

"Both," he replied, sliding the makeup case under the window. "I've brought you a present," he explained, though he didn't need to.

She gave it a nervous glance, then looked around the fairground again. Nobody could hear them except for the old lady, but she didn't seem to mind her. Flattered, she thanked him in a faint voice.

"I can't," she said, head down, pretending to count money and ticket stubs. She returned the case, as if she'd just taken a big decision. "Let's meet in half an hour at the entrance to the train."

Parker pocketed the case and ticket. He realised his faux

pas, apologised and mingled with the few passers-by now entering the amusement park. He waited a while, and when the moment came, he walked over to the front of that small station of horrors with its décor of mummies, skulls, cobwebs and blood-drenched letters. One of the Bolivians, now sporting a vampire's incisors and wearing a shabby, blood-stained uniform, was announcing the train's immediate departure through a loudspeaker. Parker, the only passenger at that time, hoped he wouldn't recognise him, but the other guy identified him right away. He took his ticket, and said nothing as he inspected it like a frontier policeman staring at a passport.

"When's the train departing?" Parker asked uneasily.

"Any moment now, from here," replied Fredy, or Eber.

"I didn't ask you from where, but when, at what time," Parker retorted, recalling that he'd been there before.

"Right now, or maybe later, it all depends," the buoyant Bolivian replied. Parker pondered his reply, sensing that the employee was trying to read his thoughts.

"How did you get this far?" the other guy asked, giving him a funny look.

"Where do I come from, you mean?" Parker replied, bemused.

"No, how did you get this far, was what I said."

Parker stared at him for a second, not understanding his question, but even if he had, he wouldn't have answered, because that was prying. The Bolivian's peculiar way of speaking was the only thing that persuaded him to persevere with such a ridiculous conversation.

"I'm asking which way you came, or are you deaf?" the attendant said, sighing, then reworded his question.

"Was it easy finding your way to Teniente López, or was it a struggle?"

Once again Parker was puzzled, wondering what the Bolivian was getting at.

"Teniente Primero López is somewhere else. Call a first lieutenant a lieutenant and you'll soon see how insulted he is," he corrected him, repeating what the mechanic had previously told him.

"Whether you say it first, or later, he'll always be a lieutenant," the Bolivian declared sententiously. "Now get on, you're the only passenger, and don't be awkward, bro," he added, pointing to one of the cars.

Parker climbed nimbly into a car adorned with Frankenstein's face, drawn in such a way you could not tell if it was trying to scare or amuse. He gripped the bar with both hands, ready for anything, and let himself be driven off, surrendering to his fate. "Welcome to the train of death," proclaimed a cavernous voice from the depths, prompting an echo that ended in a loud guffaw. Parker shuddered, not because of a voice that wouldn't have frightened a child, but because he suspected that something unexpected awaited him within. The Bolivian looked at him, hoping for a reaction, but Parker sat there expressionless.

"What do you fancy, young man? An exciting ride or one for little girls? You're the only passenger, so it's your call."

Parker eyed him suspiciously, and kept gripping the bar.

"Halfway, not too much, not too little. Get me?" he boomed, looking back into the black maw opening before him.

The Bolivian glanced at him scornfully, one hand hovering on the key controlling the train's speed and another on a metal lever worn by use.

"Not too much, not too little? They're not the words of a man. You should have stuck to teddy bears, you know."

"Get the thing started, and don't try any tricks, I don't want any surprises," Parker retorted between gritted teeth. He'd have liked to give that impertinent fellow a drubbing, the other one, too, just in case he'd mixed them up.

"So why take the ghost train if you don't want surprises? You know, there's a merry-go-round for sissies, if you're that frit."

Parker voiced a clear death threat, the man in charge shrugged, he wasn't sure why, turned the key as far as it would go, and activated the lever.

"That's what you get for not trusting in Our Saviour."

The train juddered off and jolted Parker's head back as it whizzed through a frayed burlap curtain and disappeared into the tunnel's entrails, juddering down dark labyrinths to blood-curdling shouts and screams. Parker lost all notion of space, and was choked by a feeling of claustrophobia. He panted breathlessly and his body shook as if he were descending into the worst of hells. Each bend was a jolt that forced him to grab the handrail to stop himself being hurled out, and in under a minute, the car was spewed out into the daylight by the monster. The curtain opened wide and the whole train exited to a clatter of tins between its painted jaws. He looked for the attendant to stop that hell, but he had gone. He tried to see whether Maytén had returned to the ticket counter, but, blinded by the sudden daylight, and confused by turning this way and that, his gaze wandered across the fair without locating her. Seconds later the mouth of the tunnel swallowed him up again, and with each swerve his head and limbs felt more like a broken mannequin's. Another thirty seconds of jolts and howls, and Parker re-emerged, more bemused than ever. Maytén was the only person who could stop that torture, but there was no sign of her on his second exit either. He looked for the friendly old lady, his last chance, before he was devoured again by that lunatic device. Emptier than ever, the fairground was a desolate, hostile space, a deserted stage. The train continued to run, but Parker noted that a merciful hand had reduced its speed. It braked to a sudden halt halfway round, and stood motionless in the gloom. Parker's eyes surveyed the shadows and silhouettes against a backcloth of scythes, axes and knives. The only sound he could hear in that dense silence was the creaking of the whole structure, like a deep sigh. He was startled when he spotted the hooded figure of the Grim Reaper a few feet away and when a human shape appeared at one side and gestured to him to leap out. His first instinct was to throw himself on the floor of the car, but he recognised Maytén's silhouette in the dim lamplight. Her miraculous apparition curbed his anxiety, although he could not fathom the reason behind her summons. What did it mean? Had he fallen into the clutches of a lunatic; was he at her mercy? He jumped out and advanced a couple of metres along the rails towards her; she was waiting for him, wrapped in a poncho and behind a mummy. Parker approached tentatively, she activated a lever and the halted cars began to process through the tunnel's innards. The second he was next to her, he gripped her shoulders gently, she yielded, their bodies touched and they kissed passionately to a chorus of howls augmented by the metallic clatter of the cars trundling by.

"Watch out, don't go near the dummies," she said, breathless and excited. Parker gripped her waist and asked in a seductive tone, "Why? Do they bite like you?"

"No, they are filthy, people spit and throw things at them."

They kissed and caressed again, until Maytén held Parker's face in both hands and stared at him. "You do know what we are doing?"

Parker couldn't think what to say, but just as he was about to come up with something, she moved away with a start, looked around and stammered: "I must go, quick, get in a car. Our next town is Colonia Desesperación, I'll expect you there next week."

A second later Maytén disappeared between the silhouettes in the tunnel. Parker ran along the rails, dodging the decapitated heads hanging from the roof, and jumped on the first car that sidled by. He grabbed the bar at the exact moment the train accelerated, and after hitting his head again, he gyrated through the labyrinth. The burlap curtains opened at a stroke, and he was back in the kingdom of the living, his eyes bulging out of their sockets. He was surprised by how normal the fairground now seemed: the Bolivians were tidying scattered cars, Maytén was working at the ticket window as if nothing had happened, and at the far end of the fairground her husband was walking between the caravans bent double by the rolls of cables on his back.

Parker was still in a state of shock, wondering if what had happened had been a product of his imagination, or if the tunnel of terror was populated by spiteful creatures who liked playing practical jokes on the train's unwary passengers.

"Enjoy your ride?" the Bolivian asked, as he went to help him alight.

Parker rebuffed his helping hand and jumped out.

"Yes, Eber, it was very nice, thanks so much," he said, still nonplussed, still not really knowing what he was saying.

"Eber's the other guy, I'm Fredy."

Parker ignored his remark, right then he couldn't care less which of them it was, it could be either and life on the planet would carry on as before. He tottered off, his body tingling from head to toe. He was not worried whether what happened was imagined: it had happened at one of those enigmatic levels that make up reality. He was filled by a sense of ecstasy; the way he saw the world had changed in a few minutes. He strode towards the exit like a man advancing towards a new world full of promise, and barely heard the sinister guffaw issuing from the tunnel's dark twists and turns.

○  ○

Half-naked and washed out, Bruno was drinking wine at the table in their caravan, surrounded by a pile of balance sheets and a calculator. Maytén caught a whiff of sweat, alcohol and the hot spicy meal she had cooked the previous night in the vain hope that a sore mouth would mellow his tongue and mood. His fingers nervily keyed in numbers, then broke off and started the same calculation a third or fourth time, convinced that repetition would change the result. The same figure kept coming back, although Bruno would not resign himself and changed the order of factors as much as he could. But the maths was unerring in its verdict, and there was no disputing its conclusions. That was what he was doing when Maytén walked in, draped her coat on the armchair, greeted him blankly and started organising the chaos reigning in the caravan's slim cupboards.

"I waited for you. Why did you take so long?" he asked, his eyes glued to the numbers.

"I had to wait an hour for them to see me in the bank," Maytén sighed.

Bruno did not even hear what she said; he turned round, stretched his hand out towards the armchair and grabbed his wife's handbag. He pulled it open and took out a wad of notes. He counted the money, divided it into several heaps, and put them alongside his calculations. He did a couple more, pushed away the mounds of paperwork and leaned back in his chair, shaking his head, resigned.

"Why didn't you take more money out?" he asked, looking through the window, though he already knew what her answer would be. She finished tidying souvenirs, figurines, dolls, plastic flowers, photographs and frames on the shelves, and said: "I don't need to tell you, you know better than I do."

Bruno poured more wine, swept everything off the table and slid the chessboard nearer with the pieces in their positions from the previous game. He held his head in his hands, leaned his elbows on the table, stared and concentrated on the game. When a wary Maytén had entered the fairground, scrutinising every detail on its outer rim, she'd sensed that something different and nasty was haunting the becalmed attractions and empty sideshows. The fairground folk's routine seemed like a libretto that had been rewritten dozens of times before, but she felt the ill omens floating in the caravan she shared with Bruno. She assumed that something untoward had happened in her absence, another member of the fair had deserted, or there was a new bill to pay, but soon realised it was the same everyday slide towards the abyss. She felt no remorse at deceiving Bruno, only fear, fear he might discover her infidelity. She had been faithful to her word and her companion for a long time, but was starting to think it was time to be faithful to herself. Sacrificing her youth and her whole life for nothing might be the worst betrayal she could ever commit. She wasn't prepared to go down tamely in the same ship as Bruno, and had made up her mind to jump at the first sight of an escape route. Seeing her husband immersed in numbers, she thought balance sheets and invoices would now convince him of what she had been trying to tell him day in day out: they needed to change. He might not wish to listen to her, but the numbers spoke for themselves and he couldn't argue with them or bawl them out.

Maytén looked askance at her husband, waiting for him to react. Meanwhile she dusted the furniture with a damp cloth, trying to engage her mind elsewhere and pass the time in useful, orderly tasks.

"I asked why you didn't take more money out of the bank," Bruno insisted. She was about to repeat her answer, but there was no need; her husband's questions were a reflex reaction, answers went in one ear and out the other. She put the cloth down and sat down opposite him.

"I told you, because that's all there is."

"So what about the money you kept back in the caravan?"

"That's all that's left from my savings and it's there in case of an emergency."

"This *is* an emergency, and you could lend it me until better times come."

"That money stays where it is, I've already put a lot into buying bits of this fair that are now worth less than half what they were."

Bruno reflected for a second, stretched out a hand and shifted a white rook to the next square, took a black knight and concentrated on that contest. He saw the mechanism that moved the world in the way those pieces were arranged, and needed Maytén to move the pieces too so the mechanism was validated and functioned as it was supposed to.

"It's your turn," Bruno said, between one gulp of wine and the next, while she set the table.

"I'm worn out from washing and cooking all day and working on the stall, I've told you a thousand times, but you make no changes."

"Make *your* move, stop whining, and let's see if we can finish this game once and for all. Women!" Bruno said, staring up at the ceiling.

"If we can't afford more workers, let's do something else. I'm not going on working like a slave," she said. She had never used that tone since they had been together, and Bruno noticed the change.

"I'm not going on working like a slave . . ." he repeated, mocking her intonation.

"I mean it."

"You don't want to make a move because I'm winning. Women are such poor losers."

Maytén responded to his challenge and in an absurd move took a white queen with a pawn that was adrift on one side of the board. Bruno studied her move for a second, then moved his knight to the adjacent square.

"Check," he exclaimed, convinced his was a brilliant move.

Maytén sighed, resigned, and waited a few moments until she'd calmed down, then threw her apron on the bed and wagged her index finger at the board.

"Don't you realise this isn't chess or anything like?"

"I play the way I want to."

"Then you're going to have to play by yourself."

"I set the rules here. If you don't like it . . ."

Maytén flared up again.

"I'm finished with this idiotic game! What are you going to do, hit me again?" she asked, crossing her arms. Bruno took his eyes from the table and focused on his wife's face, on an expression he had never seen before. A horrible thought flitted across his temples, halting between his eyebrows. What if Maytén did leave him, and he had to manage the fairground by himself as well as feed the Bolivians? Where would he go without her, and what would that caravan be like in her absence on endless winter nights? A long-forgotten tenderness mellowed Bruno's mood, prompted by the possibility he might lose her, something he had never before contemplated: he sensed his life was hurtling beyond a point of no return.

"Maytén," he pleaded, whispering, "we don't have to do that much. Let's be patient until things improve. We can't take on more workers, at least we've got those two, who we pay as if they were only one."

"They don't even add up to that," she replied and then regretted saying that, because the issue was the life they led, and not their handymen.

"We must keep heading down south at least until winter time. Then we'll see."

"See what?"

"It's a surprise, I didn't want to tell you, but as you keep on . . ."

Maytén opened her eyes and held her breath. She had always considered a Bruno surprise as something positive, until yesterday, but now she had lost all hope. What if he was trying to trick her? For years she'd been desperate to leave that wretched life, wandering from town to town, among spectres that roamed at the ends of the map. A faint flame flickered and raised her hopes, but she knew her husband too well, she knew he didn't like surprises, and that a surprise in that situation could only damage her.

"Don't now tell me we're going to leave our fair!" she shouted, implying that, if they weren't, he could forget any other new schemes. Bruno abandoned his rough manner and harsh tone, and caressed her arm with his thick, calloused fingers, smiling and meekly bowing his head.

"I've spoken to a friend who works in the port."

"Are we going to start a city restaurant?"

"Something much better. We can join a fishing boat till next summer, they need an electrician and a cook, and that would be just right for us. Initially four months, though it could pan out for longer."

Maytén dropped the cutlery on the table and looked Bruno in the eye to check he was being serious, not that she ever remembered him cracking a joke. She tried to react, but felt the world weighing on her shoulders once again. Bruno added with renewed glee: "It's all about saving, because you can't spend aboard ship."

"So I'm going to be peeling potatoes on the high seas for four months?"

"Didn't you want a change?"

"A change for the better, not for the worse."

"You can go ashore for a few hours, depending on the weather."

"Really? And where do you do that in the Antarctic?"

"Nothing new ever fires you up, we always have to do *exactly* what you want," Bruno said.

Maytén sat down and put her head in her hands. They said nothing, waiting for the other to take the next step. They had never reached that stage before. Such conversations were always resolved by a slammed door, by bawls and blows, but never that kind of grim silence enveloping them both. Both could hear the sound of something falling apart, but only she knew nothing would ever be the same again, and that filled her with deep uncertainty and secret hopes.

Maytén gripped a black pawn, and took a castle, a bishop and two knights, jumping from one end of the board to the other, then set the pieces down the side. Bruno studied her moves for a few seconds and returned the pieces to where they had been.

"Cheating again. Make a different move," he ordered.

Maytén made the exact same move.

"I don't play well, but at least I play cleanly," he said in a threatening tone.

"You'll not impose your rules on me."

Bruno reversed her move again, but when she stretched out an arm to repeat the move, he sprang to his feet like a jack-in-the-box. Glasses and bottles fell on the floor, the whole caravan shook and the suspension creaked. Maytén instinctively covered her face, but Bruno's hand followed a different path and descended on the board, scattering the pieces around the caravan, which swayed as its rusted suspension squealed.

"It's all pointless, we can't go on like this," Maytén sobbed, her face contracting and tears streaming down that she wiped away with the back of her hand.

"It's all your fault!" Bruno shouted.

Maytén recovered and confronted him. While he shook her shoulder, she knocked off the few pieces still on the board. Bruno's free arm swung backwards, gathering momentum, but his elbow smashed into a piece of wooden furniture behind him, shattering it. He grimaced in pain as he stared at his numb arm, which he brought down on Maytén, who was struggling to free herself. She leaned on the kitchen counter to stop herself from falling and grabbed a huge knife. That stopped Bruno in his tracks as he readied himself to lash out again. Maytén flourished her weapon in her husband's face, then dropped it, feeling it was burning her hands. She watched it fall and disappear, lost among the other objects littering the floor. Both were paralysed as they looked into each other's eyes, then she ran out and vanished among the fair's sideshows. Bruno tottered after her, calling out, pleading with her, but his voice hung in the air. Rubbing his injured arm and swearing, he wandered between attractions until he emerged opposite the ghost train. Eber and Fredy had heard them quarrelling and lined up the mannequins in a row so their general would find someone to unleash his fury on.

"What are you two doing? I'm the only person who ever does any work on this fairground."

"No, boss, the dummies were damp and smelly and we're giving them an airing," Eber pointed out, waving a rag he was using to clean Dracula's face.

Bruno started to review each dummy, as if he were selecting his victim, then started punching and insulting them.

When he had calmed down, he sat on a barrel, panting, shut his eyes and meditated for a while. Then he took out a cigar and lit it, but had to take several draws before it glowed.

"Lads, we can't go on like this, Maytén's right."

"They don't scare anyone anymore, boss. You're scarier to the punters when you're angry," Fredy said, slotting a monster's loose arm back into place. Eber flourished a ghost's yellow sheet, exposing the life-size mannequin underneath.

"You're a ghost too, a decent man beneath the sheet. It's time you saw the light and removed the sheet, boss. You must learn to look at God," he proclaimed.

Fredy went over, holding out several magazines.

"He speaks in our ear, here is His word," he added.

"What fucking light!" Bruno roared, sending the magazines flying. He leaned on a tree from which a figure hung, tongue dangling, and warned them: "Enough of that nonsense. I don't need to see any lights, don't bother me again . . ."

The three men shut up, heads down, and waited for something to happen.

"I'm afraid Maytén will leave me for good. What can I do? None of this is going anywhere," a pitiful Bruno confessed.

"Women are all the same. They don't know what they want, they talk and talk, but do nothing. Pick up the reins, keep them on a short lead, as God ordained," Fredy advised.

"Females will be females," Eber chimed in, and the trio remained silent for a while. Bruno felt recharged by that exchange, his faith in the fairground was rekindled and he wanted to do things and take initiatives. No, Maytén would never put a brake on his aspirations. He stood up, walked past the line of troops and reviewed them yet again.

119

This time he tidied their hair, inspected their clothes and checked that their jaded features still inspired terror. Eber and Fredy stood to attention and awaited their orders at the end of the row.

"Get ready, we're leaving this town."

"But we only just got here!" his employees answered as one.

"Maytén's right. It makes no sense going down to Colonia Desesperación. We'll try our luck in Tambo Seco."

"What if the other attractions don't want to?" Fredy said.

Bruno turned in the direction of his caravan and replied over his shoulder.

"No matter, we'll go on by ourselves," he resolved, searching for his wife among the sideshows.

"Maytén, I've got news for you, I promise we won't go any farther south!" he shouted, although his words echoed and disappeared in the deserted fairground.

Far off, dark clouds ran amok over the foothills of the cordillera and the wind shook the bushes on the plain.

o  o

Parker opted for a well-tried method to fend off sleep in the hours he spent driving in a slow, monotonous, straight line: he drove blind, counting the seconds he could do it without losing his nerve or leaving the road. His record was thirteen seconds, from which point the tension became so unbearable he had to open his eyes, like someone surfacing with a desperate need for an intake of oxygen. Then his blood began to circulate again and his mind was imbued with an extraordinary lucidity that saw off any drowsiness and encouraged reflection.

As he went in pursuit of the fairground attractions, immersed in the music coming and going around his cabin, Parker let himself be seduced by a sweet lethargy that helped him deceive time and consciousness. The engine's purr was a distant murmur and the gentle breeze seemed to lift the wheels over the hills and dissolve the truck into the air around the peaks, while below the road disappeared into the distance, following their contours. As Parker levitated, nearby detail faded and time zones fused, the past touched the future, and the present was limited to those musical notes, inner caresses penetrating his innermost fibres.

On this occasion, however, Parker sensed a subtle breach opening up, a dissonant note; a strange chord echoed in the cabin, mutated into a projection of his brain. He felt he was not alone, that other notes and chords had invaded his space and were trying to mingle there. First, it was a numbed sensation stirring within him, like the rustle of cellophane, then unease, a shudder bringing him back to earth and the horizontal part of his existence. Something was on the prowl, threatening to change a routine that had been established with the utmost care. The stave keeping him in that cosmic quadrant suddenly yielded, and at the precise moment when something died within him, something else was reborn. For the rest of that drive he thought somebody was occupying his place, a feeling that accompanied him into the early hours when he stopped at a service station that loomed like a spaceship lighting up the darkness. Several food stalls and a night club, illuminated by neon signs, tinged the shadows of the tundra with their metallic glimmer. Parker tried to avoid the small crowd in that area and parked at the other end, near the bathrooms. One of the women hawking herself at the roadside, her lurid clothes and makeup heightened by

121

the neon's artificial hues, recognised him and walked over. She was young, exuberant, with girlish features.

"Who'd have thought it, Parker, you back in these parts! Shall we meet tonight, my love?" she asked with a wink, prompting comments and laughter from the other women.

"Are you getting ready for me?" she said flirtatiously as he jumped down, carrying clean clothes and items of personal hygiene. Parker greeted her with a hug and a couple of kisses.

"I can't today, we'll have to leave it to next time."

"You're not cheating on me, are you? You promised you'd take me with you," the girl said, pouting in disappointment.

"Did I really?" he said, as someone who had stopped making promises at least a decade ago.

"Promises of a driver, worse than a sailor's," the woman added, sashaying.

Whenever Parker met these girls of the road, he stopped to have a drink and chat, but he couldn't waste any more time now, or he would lose track of the amusement park.

"Seen any fairground attractions lately?" he asked casually, hoping for a lead.

"We're the only attractions you'll see around here," she replied, cupping her breasts in her hands and flashing her thighs. "Take a look, I'm better than any clown."

"Much better, but it's not clowns I'm after," he said, admiring her magnificent body.

"You cheating on me with a trapeze artiste?"

"I'm looking for a fairground, not a circus. A ghost train," Parker explained.

The girl frowned.

"You cheating on me with a ghost?" she asked.

Parker thought for a second, then nodded several times.

122

"Too right I am, with a ghost . . ."

"Everyone finds their better half eventually," the young woman said, walking back to her friends.

Parker washed in the service station's showers, first with lots of hot water. While he was shaving in front of a mirror, wrapped in a towel, two drivers walked past and smiled at him.

"Parker, what can you be up to, getting all prettied up? Some little darling or other?" one greeted him, a corpulent guy wearing a leather fringed jacket, earrings, rings and long hair tied in a ponytail. It was the fat Juan he sometimes bumped into on the road in one of his few reluctant encounters with colleagues. He tried to avoid him, but it was not always possible.

Parker looked at the men in the misty mirror, his face lathered in foam, and did not have the time or the inclination to reply. The other guy burbled on.

"Julio, let me introduce you to my friend Parker, driver and musician," Fat Juan said to his mate, a gaunt man with a scarred face and a tattoo wrapped round his neck like a scarf.

"How are you, man? I've heard a lot about you," Julio said, trying to please, but Parker still did not give him a glance. He rinsed his face and began putting his things in the bag, refusing to join in the banter. Fat Juan, whose threadbare jacket stank of wine and cheap fry-ups, winked and gabbled on, forcing his laughter.

"Driver, musician, and much else besides. Perhaps rather than a frump, he's got a slice of fruitcake. He's a strange guy, you know?"

A contemptuous Parker looked him up and down as he dried his hair.

"Look at yourself in the mirror, and tell me which of us is the stranger," he said.

The man in the leather jacket thought that was a hoot and celebrated his comment, finding it flattering; he doubled his belly laughs and squeezed Parker tight, slapping him on the back.

"This Parker guy is hilarious, the things he comes out with," he said, glancing at a highly amused Julio, who kept nodding. Parker looked over his shoulder as they headed to the urinals and started peeing, rocking back and forth with laughter at each other's jokes.

"My dear Parker, we've got a roast on the go outside with the lads. We'll be expecting you. Julio cracks the greatest jokes," Fat Juan said.

Parker feigned a smile as he accepted their invitation, gathered up his belongings and walked out of the bathroom promising to see them later. He took a few steps and stopped, as if dazzled by a revelation. Seeing the key in the door, he hesitated a couple of seconds, turned it twice to lock it, then jumped into his truck with a feeling of deep satisfaction, started up and drove off. After he turned the first bend, he hurled the key out of the window.

Days later Parker drove through the entrance arch to Colonia Desesperación and didn't need to reach the main square to realise that Maytén's fair wasn't in town. He drove repeatedly around the area but only found a sleepy cluster of houses on the bare slopes of a foothill that petered out over the steppe. The metal skeleton towering above what had once been a sand quarry overshadowed the houses, its trembling bulk threatening to take to the air. Parker thought it must be the wind but then spotted silhouettes of men clambering up and dismantling beams and struts. He drew closer and saw a long, prolix line of gypsies coming and going with their loads at an ant's pace on their way back to their carts. He forgot the fair for a moment and stared a while, fascinated by their minute insect toiling. He asked if they had had any news of the amusement park, but nobody had. He returned to the town centre and asked other locals, but they didn't have much to offer either: some reckoned an amusement park had passed through the previous year, and remembered the ghost train perfectly, but had no recent news; others assured him it could appear any moment since it was the time of year for fairs. The people he asked were affable to begin with, warm after the first exchanges, and friendly in the end. A small group surrounded him and a debate was begun over the fair's possible location and its estimated arrival date. One faction affirmed the caravan must surely be crossing the Quilquihue gullies, and would take more than a week to arrive: others imagined the likeliest way it would come would be along the river until it joined route 245, although one guy was sure the 245 had been closed for years and it was a disgrace the authorities hadn't got round to repairing it. The conversations about the amusement park's potential itinerary continued that same night in the bar in the town square. A large gathering of deadbeats and layabouts drew maps and conjectured as if they were plotting a complex military manoeuvre. Close on daybreak, the majority decided to defer the debate to the following day, when the twice-weekly bus would arrive from the provincial capital, and its passengers would know about the state of the roads and the fair's possible time of arrival. Next morning, a sizeable contingent of locals went to the bar where the bus stopped and organised a card school to help time pass. Parker was delighted to be part of that.

When the bus didn't come, one group started looking for the most sheltered spot, moving slowly like water diviners, and prepared a fire on the street for the roast. Other passers-by joined in and brought extra meat and drink. They ate and boozed the whole afternoon, swapping anecdotes and laughing, guffaws that echoed across the town, until jamboree gave way to lethargy. People had found a fresh worry to obsess about. Where had the bus got to? What if it had lost its way in some gulch, meeting the same fate as the caravan of fairground folk? The police were informed, but the few officers snoozing at the station were trying to recover from the effects of their big meal, and did not seem overly concerned by the mystery of the vanishing bus. A web of conjectures began to settle around this shocking occurrence: some asserted they had seen strange lights furrowing the sky the previous night, others remembered anomalies in events that an hour before had been normal. Parker understood how that scenario, a spontaneous, collective creation forged by inhabitants of a locality where nothing ever happened, restored those men's sense of being alive, or at least the memory of having been so once. The general conclusion was that the bus must have been hijacked by a vessel from outer space, but when the bus finally rumbled down one of the town's streets in a cloud of dust, nobody seemed surprised, rather they greeted it with blank indifference. Except for the relatives of passengers, everyone present made a slow, dejected journey home and never again mentioned the kerfuffle. The possibility of something extraordinary had hovered over their lives for a few hours, and now things had returned to everyday, drab normality. Parker enquired of the passengers, but nobody had heard of any fair, and he was advised to stay in town and be patient: if the caravan was in that neck of the woods, it would surface sooner or later. He decided to camp on one of the byways around Colonia Desesperación that marked out the boundary with the rest of the universe. He needed to rest a while, think about his future and plan out his next steps, so he made the most of the good weather to set up camp as comfortably as possible. He pulleyed down armchairs, table and chairs, double bed and carpet and bedside table. When he had finished organising what would be his home for several days, now immersed in the dark of night, he busied himself preparing a copious supper.

He spent the first few days doing maintenance work on his campsite and jotting down his experience with Maytén in his travel diary, though any certainty about what happened in the ghost train's shadowy passageways was fading. His memories were swathed in a thick fog where shadows, mysterious figures and silhouettes mingled. By the fourth day, Parker's scant patience had frayed, the hours he had spent stock-still set his nerves on edge and wasting time in the wrong place seemed intolerable. He needed to return to those byways and let his bloodhound instincts seek out scent of his prey. A blind impulse told him he should follow the parallel he was on already, towards the ranches where they would soon start shearing, or towards the coast, but logic suggested he ought to change parallel and continue southwards. Ground down by so many failures of instinct, he preferred to follow the dictates of reason: he struck camp and drove hell for leather to the port to deliver the cargo he had been carrying for weeks. Once he was freed from that task, he could venture to the ends of the continent. He travelled night and day, stopping only to sleep a few hours in his cabin, but when he reached the port, his boat had already sailed, and he had to wait for the next one. A week later the new cargo had been hoisted into his vehicle, a secretive dead-of-night operation. Parker knew the documentation relating to his cargo was often falsified to hide illegal merchandise, but that was none of his business. Smuggling networks controlled illegal trafficking in the region; some ports eluded the control of the authorities, and fake fishing boats often moored and were not logged in any register. Parker had stopped worrying about the world of humankind, and only wanted to live without bother or bothering others. When his truck was ready, he unfolded his map on the table, and traced a southwards itinerary across that expanse of vast skies and ocean horizons through which the fairground must be travelling towards an unknown destination. He would have to drive up the side of El Cangrejal to route 245 and then slip along a southern path like a tightrope walker, until he came down to earth again. Then he would decide what next. He opened a bottle of wine to toast his decision, and for the first time in his life felt driven by a force he could not tame. It was not only his attraction to Maytén, whom he hardly knew and from whom he could expect nothing very promising, but an impetus gathering strength within himself. He had become resigned to spending the final years of his life wandering alone across these vast flatlands, occasionally encountering other apparitions who also followed invisible itineraries, whose orbits crossed his once in a while. He prized his lonesome existence above all else, and did not need to share it with anybody, but something different was happening now, an obsession rather than an illusion of love. He would pursue her in order to measure the degree of reality present in that rather ridiculous scene in the ghost train, of which he could recall

128

only a few details. What if it had been one of those crazy dreams he often had when he slept in the open air, when the entire firmament pressed down on his body? As time passed, the words and glances they had exchanged became hazier and hazier. He wouldn't have minded if she had been an apparition or mirage, the product of a fantasy distorted by solitude. It was clear that the vicinity of that woman hid a marker and a boundary, a gateway to another stage in his life. Maytén was the oracle, the priestess officiating in the temple, the gatekeeper. Parker kept thinking that if fate had reserved another twist to his life, she was the one designated to lead him by the hand. It was impossible to know how far down the map he would have to go to find her and that's why he should call old Constanzo again, and invent a bigger excuse than his previous one to justify the enormous delay inherent in such a drastic change of direction.

O  O

Hours later, as he hovered between sleep and wakefulness in the parking lot of a roadside stop-off, mulling over his final thoughts for the day, he was disturbed by loud gabbling. Julio and Fat Juan, the two drivers he'd locked in a bathroom, had walked past his truck and recognised it. They were clinking bottles of beer, laughing and cavorting with two women in lurid outfits. Parker eyed them through his cabin curtain and readied himself for a confrontation, but a bottle smashed against the side of his vehicle.

"I know you're in there, you joker," Julio shouted, tottering as he threw with all his might another bottle that missed and smashed on the asphalt. One of the women managed to catch him just before he fell backwards. Sporting the inevitable leather jacket and ponytail, Fat Juan was dancing and opening a bottle of bubbly.

"We'll deal with you later, we're busy right now," he said, swallowing the foam spurting out. Parker listened for a while with a blank expression, convinced there was no point taking them on. He waited until he had forgotten him, then lolled back, put plugs in his ears and tried to sleep, but the vertigo induced by those heathlands, doorway to a world where sky, land and sea fused in a single level, prevented him from dozing off. As soon as they walked off, he left his truck and went for a stroll around the neighbourhood, avoiding the raucous groups laughing and singing under the luminous neon signs. He walked in circles, on the edge of the light glowing around the roadside stop and turning it into an island immersed in solitude. Every so often he came to a halt and peered at the dense chiaroscuro around him, watching the way light and shadow fed each other, energised by contrast. He concluded that his own nature belonged on that boundary, and that he needed to position himself in the world; then he returned to his cabin, started the engine, and freewheeled down the road, impelled by the force of gravity. Parker crossed the El Cangrejal wetlands, driven by an energy that prevented him from thinking about anything that did not involve that woman. He loaded up water and spare fuel, bought supplies and tried to catch up on his sleep at one of the last service stations, where drivers and travellers halted to stock up and exchange a few words before entering the desolate wastes. Days of driving across inhospitable terrain lay ahead: he had to traverse the gloomy canyons of Vallemustio, climb the heights of Chuiquiprén and make a gentle descent the other side of the mountains into the wetlands of Agua Sucia and San Sepulcro. After that, the world ended and nothingness began: expanses where a few clusters of houses arose and disappeared from one year to the next like visions or accidents of terrain, only to crop up in other places without their inhabitants even realising. Parker had several times crossed that imaginary line beyond which was a world that inspired fantastic visions and adventures – the route to the planet's southernmost regions, to vertiginous cliffs that fell sheer over crashing waves, fjords and narrows battered by raging winds and frenzied currents that connected one ocean to another. He had often driven along those coasts plagued by legends and shipwrecks, where the celestial vault was turned upside down, and above became below, where the continent was a prehistoric animal sinking its backbone under the ocean, and re-emerging in other geographies with other names and mythologies. He was very familiar with those terrains, but never before had he felt so deeply lost within his body.

The landscape was quiet and friendly on the first few days of his drive, but after a week, as he descended, the harsh climate began to throw up clouds of dust that started to affect his state of mind. He turned south-westwards for a day and a half, until he met the sixty-eighth meridian, along which he drove like someone slithering down a rope, and now and then he turned off it to avoid contingents of gendarmes, although these were only distant army patrols at the far end of the country, lethargic, empty-headed soldiers roaming the flatlands in search of a meaning to their lives. Several times a day he wondered why he was doing that, and each time he came up with a different answer. But they were trite responses, arguments that served only to fill the huge voids created by uncertainty and solitude. His firm resolve to persevere was the single element that gave any sense to that lunacy. He was abandoning a futile existence and deadening routine, a previous life he preferred to forget until it was buried by time.

His truck made slow, mechanical progress along roads that deteriorated by the kilometre and sometimes came to an abrupt end, forcing him to go back and change route. He crossed plateaux and depressions, chains of gentle hills that seemed to caress the back of the extraordinary, prostrate beast that was Patagonia. Nights fell with a strange heaviness, dissolving the long evening shadows, but Parker struggled to sleep, wracked by a vertigo that spread through his arteries; then he steered beneath the stars, feeling he was following mysterious lines, that he too was but one more speck on the firmament.

The last gypsy colonies that had ventured that far south, camping along roadsides, welcomed him like a family member. Parker drove across their encampments, and boisterous children greeted the arrival of that relative from afar as if they had been expecting him. They were never in the same place, finding them was a challenge that might or might not come off; they moved from one end of the continent to the other, taking their livestock with them. Every so often they vanished for long periods: their caravans crossed from coast to cordillera guided by opaque intuitions, and when the wind dropped and deflated their sails, they would set up by crossroads and barter goods with other groups. Parker's appearance was the perfect excuse to organise a big banquet and all-night party in his honour. On that occasion, the moment they learned of Parker's haphazard quest for an amusement park that seemed to slip away like water, they greeted him with cries of delight, but he extracted no precise information: nobody knew anything about the fair, or everyone had seen it drive by, but always in different directions. Youngsters lit big bonfires by their tents and roasted chickens and pigs on spits, while grown-ups smoked and drank liquor on the floor of the main tent that acted as a meeting point. Sprawling back on cushions and carpets, they talked business, while the women whispered and served food on ornate trays. Guests were always present at those get-togethers: members of other clans, people passing by who dealt in all manner of merchandise, from cars and spare parts to food and animals.

After a couple of days of almost nonstop partying, Parker concluded several deals and continued on the road with a cabin full of useless items. He drove through more towns and hamlets, and stopped at road-menders' shacks inhabited by hard men who came from every corner of the country, whose poverty forced them to subsist on precarious work on ranches and trading posts. He also spent several days with them, but gleaned no news of Maytén's caravan.

Five days later he made a halt at another encampment, this time of miners and oil-rig workers, a long line of huts straggling along the roadside, buried under dust and surrounded by huge mechanical contraptions and dumps in the crannies of which the wind seemed to linger and play a tune. He was intrigued as he contemplated these men with chapped faces and watery eyes, who walked slowly, smiled dimly, held out calloused hands and invited him to eat fritters and drink maté. They had no useful leads for him and he had to continue his journey guided by premonitions. When they said goodbye, the settlers hugged him, they were so grateful for his presence – the only link connecting them to the outside world – that he gave them all the items he had exchanged with the gypsies.

The further Parker wandered down the map, the gloomier he found the locals and the more austere their resignation. Those beings at the end of their tether, who slept in their work clothes, whose leathery faces mirrored the rugged terrain, welcomed him with a fatalism quite different from the din and uproar of the nomads. Two weeks later, after he had climbed a hill, a military barracks appeared in his sights, like an oasis in the middle of the desert with its red-roofed blocks and a parade ground marked out by dozens of whitewashed stones. Parker went over to the duty guard, spoke to the officer in charge and asked if anyone had seen an amusement park drive by. The officer ordered the troops to be asked, and while waiting, Parker reviewed the line of buildings constructed over desert pebbles, and the pole where a tattered flag was flapping. Young soldiers with Indian features, come from the north, wearing cracked leather boots and uniforms too big for their bodies, were smoking in silence, waiting for grub to be up. Leaning on barracks walls, they looked like languid lizards sunning themselves and contemplating Parker's presence with jaded eyes. The officer reported back that nobody and nothing had passed by the barracks over the last month, and that came as no surprise to Parker. Before leaving, he noticed that the officer was staring at him, as if expecting him to say something. They faced up to each other for a second, then a couple of glances were enough to seal a deal; they went down to the sentry box and conversed for a few minutes while a soldier served them maté. Parker placed a wad of banknotes on the desk, and the officer gave an immediate order to his subordinate, who, following the chain of command, passed it on to a subaltern. A cart soon arrived with a couple of soldiers and several drums of petrol that they loaded onto his truck. As stubborn and obsessed as ever, Parker kept asking any recruits he met about the fairground, but that only made things worse: one pointed one way, another then pointed in the opposite direction, and then another, and another, adding useless detail. They were not trying to trick him to gain a reward, but could see he was distressed and felt it would be impolite to say they knew nothing. Parker gave effusive thanks, and, just as he was about to depart, other soldiers appeared with parcels and messages to send from the nearest post office, in some cases for him to deliver personally. A few officers on leave asked to be driven to the nearest train station. Parker could not bear to see his cabin invaded by strangers and refused several such requests, but when he left, he did so with half the artillery section on the roof of his trailer.

After freeing himself from the army, Parker drove south for several days, and his spirits began to slump as the days became shorter and the temperature rawer. Animals of the steppe appeared less often, had almost disappeared; he could no longer orient himself using the location and movements of birds, guanacos, foxes and ostriches, but had to trust solely in the stars and his instinct, which were light years apart. He took advantage of a night-time stop to study the firmament and confirm that things functioned much better up above, but he had never seen the Southern Cross tilt so much, almost rest on the horizon, and felt suspicious. Orion's belt was flattened and he looked fearfully at Aldebaran. The sextant the journalist had lent him at their last rendezvous was no longer much help: on clear nights in the southern-most hemisphere capricious stars changed position, moved by the wind; constellations hid between the folds of a universe as wrinkled as a toffee wrapper.

Night-time dreams in those vertiginous regions were so intense and real they left you distraught for days, and beset by an inner restlessness that sent the senses out of kilter. However, there was no word or trace of Maytén and the fairground in those latitudes, and his own memories of furtive kisses and caresses in the ghost train's meandering passageways soon began to fade. Alongside the dummies and figures watching from the tunnels' shadows, with every day that passed Maytén was turning into a fantasy. The many maps spread around his cabin were of little help: he needed to improvise and use his instinct in order to go he didn't know where. If he hoped to find anything in those wastelands scattered at the foot of the hemisphere, he first had to lose *his* way. For that reason he turned off at each turning or crossroads, surrendering to an impulse or the hint of a hunch. The impact of distance meant reality kept fluctuating for Parker. His distant past remained solid and compact, but his recent past was a series of confused glimmers that flickered along the constant line of the road.

One afternoon he recalled that old Constanzo existed. He had given him no signs of life for two weeks – or three, he could not say for sure – and thought he ought to justify his disappearance from the map, though it did not overly concern him.

One morning Parker realised he'd driven through the same place time and again and had been going in circles for days. Those dizzying distances thrived on darkness and silence, and spawned peculiar thoughts. The night before he had dreamed that he was clinging to a web of parallels and meridians in order not to fall off the globe and be lost in the void. That abyss was guarded by two giants support-ing the world, surrounded by a whirlpool of raging waters the current of which pulled him into an eternal fall. He was woken by an unusual, suspicious silence that was not a simple absence of sound. He jumped to his feet, head spinning, unable to tell above from below, and saw moonlight flooding his cabin with spectacular phosphorescent brightness. Parker felt like a blissful astronaut gazing at the planet from his orbiting spaceship. Everything out there, below or above, seemed frozen, spattered with a magic substance secreted by the Milky Way. He assumed the milky landscape was the first, early snowfall in the area that year. On several occasions a vehicle had been buried by a snowstorm in less than a night. He decided to move on as soon as possible and seek refuge in a settlement, because if he lost his way in that remote wilderness, if snow rendered the roads unpassable, they would find his frozen corpse at the start of spring.

He waited for the light of dawn, put on the first clothes he found, and made a quick calculation: he had enough food supplies for a month and the fuel he had bought from the army guaranteed sufficient warmth. If he stayed put, he could happily hibernate under the thick layer of ice that would soon form on top. He'd spend hours and hours in the total silence of icy nights and days, under a mantle of frost like an Inuit in an igloo. He could listen to music and read, and wouldn't need to call Constanzo and fabricate new lies. He imagined himself being more out of this world than he already was, ignored by everyone, as rescue helicopters whirred overhead, unable to distinguish his vehicle in the infinite whiteness covering the steppe. He was delighted by the idea of erasing his existence, engulfed by the planet, and decided such a holiday from the universe would be a joy. Apart from old Constanzo worrying about his cargo, nobody would notice he had disappeared.

Parker opened the cabin door and encountered a strange smell of burning that irritated his nostrils. A forest in flames first came to mind, until he was startled by the supernatural silence floating in the air, a forewarning that something exceptional was afoot. The singular luminosity that had stuck to the filth on the windows, and to the moonlight gleaming on the snow, was still there, but thick phosphorescence now also stuck to his boots and face. He shut the door behind him, astonished by that apocalyptic landscape, as a cloud of fine dust detached from the roof and floated over his head like a thought bubble. He noticed that the wind was no longer whipping across the plateau. He picked up a fistful of snow from the ground that wasn't snow, but light dust that stained his fingers grey. Behind him, his vehicle looked like a piece of cake coated in icing sugar, and his footprints reminded him of the ones left by the first men on the moon: heaven and earth dusted with a light layer of talcum several centimetres thick. Parker ran back to his truck and shut himself in his cabin, as if demons were chasing him. He switched on the radio and waited for the news, but wait he didn't: every station was talking about the same event. The Lonkomollo volcano had erupted the day before, and a tall column of smoke and ash was spewing from its vent and had settled over the landscape. Parker sighed in relief, but was soon more worried than ever: he would not be discovered frozen, but unearthed centuries later by archaeologists, immobilised in flight like the remains of the inhabitants of Pompeii. He felt that intangible dust penetrating his pores and clogging his throat with every breath he took. He was afraid an element might be toxic, that any minute he'd be writhing on the floor with swollen lungs, so he wrapped a towel around his head, improvised filters that he placed in the engine's air vents, and told himself that enough was enough. It made no sense continuing that descent into remote regions inhabited by spectres incarcerated by the geography of that corner of the universe. His obsessive search for Maytén did not prevent him understanding that if he kept driving down, he too might be transformed into one of those beings that gawped when he passed by, that never returned his wave, beings whose brains had been hollowed out by their remoteness. They were like zombies; if you returned to the same spot days later, they stood in that same spot, their gaze lost in the distance.

"I reckon it's time to turn back," Parker shouted. He needed to get back on the road for his own salvation, although he wasn't at all sure where he would find that.

o  o

Parker followed the radio news on the erupting ash that had covered a large part of the territory, and headed north-east along roads that had not been blocked. Downpours of rain on subsequent days cleaned up the atmosphere, leaving a limpid sky that allowed sight, over the mountains, of a dark column of smoke, gases and volcanic detritus shooting upwards like an atomic mushroom. But if those heights were transparent, the earth was a swamp of ash turned to sticky mud. As he approached an expanse of large ranches, the fields by the road were littered with dead animals: rain that had fallen on the volcanic ash had accumulated on the sheep's wool and congealed into a thick, heavy paste. Unable to sustain such a burden, the animals, starved of food, had collapsed on the ground and died a slow death. Birds of prey circled above the carcasses waiting for the right moment to begin their work. The endless barbed-wire fences dividing properties had also yielded to the weight of terrified animals who perished on the wire, hooked when they tried to jump over in search of food or water. Parker drove across that desolate landscape of skins and bones, and journeyed back up country for days, without taking a break, until he was on familiar roads. In fertile valleys he loaded up a consignment of fruit to embark in La Guakolda, a port of little importance, on the same parallel where he was driving now, but half a meridian away. Although he had found no news of the fairground, Maytén was still at the centre of his thoughts for most of the day, and, though he could be sure of nothing else, he was sure they would meet up at any moment. He interrogated every human being he encountered on the road, and one day discovered someone who had heard of an amusement park heading towards Vinchucas across the arid central mesa, and another fellow who had seen a similar fair travelling between La Trocha and Puesto Viejo.

Parker decided to try his luck farther west, straining his itinerary with big ellipses, weaving a complex skein of bends and reverse bends to join up two dots.

"Drive to Cabo Albarracín, sooner or later all fair-grounds end up there," advised an old local he gave a lift to one afternoon. Parker had found him in the middle of an isolated track, lost between one void and the next, far from any settlement, and had pulled up, thinking he must need help.

"What makes you think I need help?" the old man had asked as he made an effort to hoist himself into the cabin.

"I thought it looked that way."

"You thought? I think you're the one who needs help."

"Where are you going?" Parker said, changing tack, used to the coarse nature of the terrain and its inhabitants.

"Can't you see I'm going nowhere?"

Parker shrugged and re-engaged with his own thoughts, ignoring him, but the old man was relentless.

"Do I really look as if I'm going somewhere?"

"No, you look as if you're just around and about."

"And if I did want to go somewhere, where the fuck would I go?" he retorted, pointing into the landscape.

They travelled several hours in silence, occasionally exchanging a monosyllable, and that was when Parker asked him if he had come across an amusement park.

"Cabo Albarracín is the nearest you'll get to an elephants' graveyard, and it's where all fairgrounds go to die in Patagonia."

"The one I'm looking for is still alive."

"That's what you think, there has to be a reason why you can't find it."

"And why's that?"

"And why's that?" the man parroted. He stared at the road for a while and then continued in the same grumpy vein.

"You *porteños* have got bad habits, and expect other people to solve your problems. Do you really believe things are that easy?"

"I'm not a *porteño* . . ."

"I'm not a *porteño*," the old guy parroted again, effeminately now. "You all say the same, you'll never accept that—"

"I was born in—"

"I couldn't care less where you were born. Listen to me, because I won't repeat myself. Drive towards the cordillera

141

for half a week over the forty-sixth parallel, and you'll find it opposite you."

"A cape near the cordillera? That can't be right," Parker challenged him, bent on antagonising his insufferable passenger.

The old man shuffled in his seat, affronted.

"And why not? Come on, tell me why that's odd," he said.

"Capes are on the coast, where there are peninsulas, bays, beaches . . ."

"I got you, no need to go on. Or do you reckon I'm backward?"

"Well then?" Parker persisted, now concerned about how to rid himself of that old man without becoming responsible for his death from starvation after he abandoned him on the next bend.

"Find out yourself, since you reckon you're so clever, it makes no odds to me."

"Is it a cape on the banks of a lake?" Parker followed up.

"No, there's no coast or lake. Forget it," the old man declared, staring at the road, unwilling to prolong the conversation. After another half-hour of driving in silence, Parker decided to assume responsibility for his death, simply to get him off his back.

"Where should I drop you?"

"Did I ask you to drive me anywhere? No, I didn't! You told me to get in, so you sort it, it's no business of mine."

"Fine then, get out here," Parker threatened, slamming on the brakes, expecting him to stop being so arrogant and apologise.

"Go to hell!" exclaimed the old man, as he got down, slamming the door behind him.

"You should find out what a cape is, you old idiot!" Parker snarled through the window, as he drove off. He could see the old guy in his side mirror signalling him to stop and he began to savour victory. He stopped the truck and waited for the rude fellow to plead to be driven somewhere.

"A *cabo* is a corporal who's not yet made it to sergeant. And what the hell does that have to do with water, you arrogant *porteño*!" the old man exclaimed, as he hit the window with his stick, turned round, crossed the barbed wire and went on walking until his figure disappeared into the empty steppe.

Parker stayed there for a while with his engine turning, waiting for something to happen, but, engulfed by the same void from which he had emerged, the man did not reappear. He drove on with a sense of discomfort that lasted the rest of the day. He decided to ignore that spectre's lunatic advice, but that wasn't to be his last surprise. The following day, when he was driving, a beer in one hand, listening to a radio that leapt from one wavelength to another, from one end of the dial to the other, he saw a car in his mirror flashing its lights at him. It caught up, and an individual in a threadbare overcoat stuck his top half out of his window and indicated to him to stop. He didn't immediately recognise his friend the journalist, then recalled that at some point in the recent past they had agreed to meet at Cuestal del Huemul. He had forgotten that rendezvous after what had happened with Maytén. Parker stopped at the roadside, but the car drove slowly for a good stretch, until the journalist succeeded in bringing it to a complete halt by throwing rocks tied to the chassis onto the road like anchors.

"Still not got your brakes repaired? You'll kill yourself one of these days."

"I've still got some brake capacity left, but I don't want to use it up, I'm keeping it for an emergency," the journalist explained as they greeted each other with the usual hugs. An hour later the encampment was up and running, between the truck and a large rocky tump that sheltered them from the weather, and they were breakfasting around the table.

"I couldn't make it to Cuestal del Huemul," Parker apologised.

"No worries, I didn't either. I had much more important business to see to. I was visiting the coast, making the most of the low tides."

"Hunting for clams?"

"My job is the pursuit of rarer species. I prefer submarines, but if they're clams, they'll do too."

"I see you've not improved since we last met."

"Where've you come from? The ash got to you, I reckon. Your truck looks like a sweet pastry. Was it Lonkomollo?"

"I was lucky to escape. Did you track down your Nazis or that U-boat number whatever?"

"I'm not looking for the 745 any longer, I'm after the 518, which set out stealthily at night on April 5, 1945 from the port of Kristiansand."

"Leave that for another night."

"You seem quite down, Parker. Anything wrong?"

"What could ever go wrong in a remote spot like this? Nothing, journo."

The journalist kept eating, eyes down, then he jumped up, took out a folder full of paper and maps from his bag and laid it on the table.

"Look how weighty my research has become."

Parker weighed the folder in his hand.

"How much do they pay you per kilo? I bet it's more than I get for a ton."

The journalist stopped chewing and stared at the horizon, his eyes sparkling with excitement. When he spoke next, his voice sounded hoarse and trembling.

"What's a kilo of pure history worth, Parker? It's priceless, but people don't understand that. And nobody is paying me, these are my savings, my retirement pot. In the meantime, I have to get by with this," he said, extracting from his bag a handful of documents, identity cards and fake certificates. He admired them one by one, and went on: "They're perfect, you can't tell the difference. I've got some new identities, if you're interested. I've got this doctor's card, and this is a judge's, and that one's a member of parliament's, and they'll get you through any police roadblock. Hey, try one, come on, I'll give you a special price."

Parker reviewed each document, shook his head, returned them, and thanked him.

"I've already got mine, and it's as well faked as any of those."

"Sometimes fake IDs are more convincing than real ones."

"Do you think I'm a fugitive like the Nazis you're looking for?"

"You always seem a quasi-ghost, hiding away, so I presume your ID isn't so terrific. If you like, I can sort the documentation for your truck as well."

"I don't know which of us is the more ghostly."

"Parker, you win that one. In my humble opinion."

"How much would it cost to whitewash this vehicle and get a decent driving licence?"

145

"I'll give you a licence for free. As for the truck, I'd have to consult some acquaintances."

"Will you get me clean, up-to-date papers for the truck? All in order?"

"And for yourself too, if you want to invest a bit more . . ."

The journalist looked at Parker's shabby appearance, then picked up his pencil and notebook.

"What name do you want?"

"You choose one."

The journalist jotted down a few facts, then shut his notebook decisively, like someone sealing a deal.

"Not even your mother will recognise you," he said.

Then they both said nothing. The journalist was deep in thought as he stared at the other end of the road.

"We are so alike."

"That's all I needed," Parker said.

"There's one big difference: you don't know what you're looking for, and I do."

"So, extra-terrestrials, lost submarines, Nazi leaders . . ."

"Don't laugh, one day I'll find proof and I'll be famous."

"And if you don't, you'll invent them," Parker parried, pointing to the fake documents spread around like playing cards, but the journalist was no longer listening. He was raising a glass and warmly toasting the friendship that united them. Parker followed suit without a word and calculated the risk of following that fellow's lead, his only friend in those lonely times, although, in fact, he didn't trust him at all. He too was excited, but he made sure he didn't show it.

"So what are you looking for, if I might be so bold?"

"I've lost an amusement park. I've been following it for weeks, but I've lost all trace . . ."

"An amusement park? Bad luck binds people more than good luck. You and I are soulmates!" he said, after pausing to reflect.

Parker frowned.

"You are not going to compare a merry-go-round to a submarine."

"There can be treasure inside a submarine."

"In a fairground, too."

The astonished journalist opened his eyes wide, leaned his glass on the table and grabbed Parker by the lapel of his coat.

"Are you serious?"

"A woman," Parker clarified, not flinching.

"Don't be stupid, a woman and treasure aren't the same, such comparisons can be dangerous," the journalist said: "If you want a good time, look for women on the road, they aren't in short supply."

"That's something else."

The journalist sighed and filled his wine glass.

"It takes all sorts, you yourself said as much last time."

"I got as far as Vallemustio, I drove through Agua Sucia and San Sepulcro, then I got caught when Lonkomollo erupted, and I lost all enthusiasm for driving farther south, even the stars looked peculiar, and, by the way, your astrolabe was no use whatsoever."

"Sextant, not astrolabe."

The journalist continued eating and reporting on naval action and submarines during the war, then he asked Parker, out of curiosity: "How can you lose an amusement park? It's like letting a tortoise escape, if not worse."

"I was careless, I looked the other way, and it was gone."

"Taking the woman with it! You're irresponsible. Now I get why you look so down."

The men said nothing for a good while, gazing into the sky, wracked by similar feelings.

"Wait a minute!" the journalist said with a glint in his eyes. "Four weeks ago I passed a caravan on the 196 going north, before the bridge. They were heading north-east."

Parker felt his heart race and fixed his eyes on his friend.

"Tell me what you saw – I'm in no mood for joking."

"A truck with monsters drawn on its sides, several trailers and caravans."

Parker got up, spread the map over the table and started to trace possible itineraries.

"It's them, I bet they were heading to Tambo Seco for the sheep shearing. They must be in La Conquistada by now," Parker calculated, peering at the small detail on the map. "If I go via Río Minas I'll be there in under three days, before the campaign's over," he said, and immediately began dismantling his camp. He came and went in a frenzy, driven by an impulse that had taken possession of his limbs. The journalist followed his every step, trying to help, then realised there was nothing more he could do there. He took his calendar from his coat and unrolled it next to his own map.

"Won't you get there quicker via Valle Alegre? The 124 is a better road, or the 170? Don't the rivers flood at this time of year?"

Parker thought aloud. "We can meet up in Montechato next month."

"I'll be busy, I can't guarantee anything." The journalist paused, then said: "Where there's a woman, more often than not there's a husband. Do you want me to come with you?"

Parker went on collecting up his things, not listening.

"If I go up as far as Punta Guanaco and take the 86 I'll gain half a day," he said. The journalist stared at him incredulously.

"Where there's a husband, there's usually trouble too."

Parker ignored him and hoisted up the last piece of furniture with the pulley, started the engine and prepared to drive off.

"Where there's trouble, there are casualties," the other persisted.

"Don't you worry, I can look after myself. And we'll meet up thereabouts. If the world is small, Patagonia is even smaller."

"The more I hear you, the more worried I am. Only people in love spout such nonsense."

The journalist went over to his car, took an item wrapped in a cloth from the glove compartment and handed it to him. Parker opened it cautiously and found a bright, shiny pistol.

"I don't like killing people."

"Don't be silly, it's so they don't kill *you*."

"Thanks, but I don't use weapons."

"It's not a weapon, it's a flare gun. When you need help, you shoot a flare into the sky. Best if it's night-time," the journalist advised him when they shook hands. "Then pray that someone will see it."

o  o

Five days later, he parked in a La Conquistada side street and walked off towards the main avenue. Parker knew for sure that Maytén was there even before he saw posters on walls and in shop windows advertising the visit by the amusement park. He spotted the fairground on terrain adjacent to the square, and was shocked because he was expecting something much bigger. As he drew close to the entrance, he saw that was all there was, and reckoned it had been reduced by half. The fairground was still closed to the public, but Parker could not wait any longer, and slipped between the empty attractions. His heart thudded as he reached the bar and hid among piles of crates of beer from where he spied on what was happening all around. Big empty spaces between one attraction and the next reinforced the feeling of neglect and decay. The Flying Saucers had no doubt decided to try their luck in other galaxies, and the dodgem cars were motionless and dodging nobody. There was also no sign of the Wriggly Worm, Flying Chairs and other minor attractions whose owners had preferred to find richer pastures. Something had changed in the layout of the stalls that stopped him from reaching his goal, but he soon spotted the Bear Hunt with the prizes hanging from the ceiling, and the mummies, vampires and skulls that still adorned the ghost train's awnings. The old lady's pond was there with its plastic fish; beyond that loomed the Big Wheel, whose orbit was drastically diminished, and finally the merry-go-round. The Bolivians were busy beneath the huge mouth, its fangs still dripping blood, carrying out the orders of Bruno, who he now thought seemed bigger and more dangerous. Eber and Fredy were pushing the cars, and their figures blended in with the motifs of terror daubed on their sides. Maytén was nowhere to be seen, and his brow darkened as he reflected that she too might have abandoned ship. Parker stooped and walked towards one of the caravans and on tiptoe looked through a window. His heartbeat accelerated, almost stampeded: a scantily clad young woman came into sight. He continued spying on Maytén until she finished getting dressed, when he felt a kind of dagger thrust in his calves. Treacherous cramp forced him to collapse on the ground, and his feet felt like blocks of marble. He waited, paralysed and ever fascinated by that spectacle, until his muscles stopped twitching and he could get up and limp off through the wings, first across the outer rim of the fair, and then the town's outskirts.

He returned to the fairground a few hours later. Now he was wearing flared trousers, dark spectacles, a spotless shirt whose wrinkles lent a trendy casual touch, and a worn jacket he had dusted down from the rigours of his wardrobe a while before. He crossed the park dodging children and families who were crawling along, walked past the firing range now being looked after by Eber, and sat down at the table in the bar feeling a tightness in his chest he had never experienced before. He stuck a cigarette between his lips, and while looking in vain for his lighter, he caught sight of Maytén, enclosed within the ticket booth's narrow walls, where she was cutting tickets from the stub and arranging wads of notes. No longer an oriental goddess, more like a Virgin in her niche. When she spotted him and the extinguished cigarette hanging from his lips, she did not look at all surprised. A faint tremor of resignation darkened her gaze, her expression changed and she smiled and gestured in a way he found hypnotic, then averted her gaze, embarrassed. Parker was about to spring to his feet, but a hand came to a halt inches from his face. The flame from a lighter flickered in the dark glass of his spectacles. Parker looked down and saw a pair of boots, and when he looked back up he was confronted by a gold ring and a huge watch that resembled a prize from the Bear Hunt. Then two brawny

151

arms appeared tattooed with hearts, knives and skulls, and a gold crucifix that nestled on a soft bed of curly hair. Parker brought his cigarette closer to the flame and inhaled until his mouth was filled with smoke.

"Thanks," he said, releasing a puff of smoke.

"Would you like anything else, apart from a light?" Maytén's husband enquired with one of the foulest smiles Parker had ever seen.

"A beer," he said, staring him out.

"Haven't we met before? You aren't from these parts."

"No, and I'm not *porteño* either."

"That's all to the good, one less problem," said the husband, patting him on the shoulder and laughing in a way that exposed his rotten teeth. A minute later he was back with the bottle of beer.

"Welcome to the fair, this is on me," he said, pouring the beer into his glass, before he returned to the kiosk and started bawling at groups as they arrived.

"Come on in, señores, step inside, the fair is open. Come and try your aim!"

Parker downed that beer and several more, focusing his attention on the young woman shut inside her display cabinet. He tried to be discreet, but the attraction he felt displaced all other thoughts. Veiled complicity existed: she looked at him without looking, and his whole body tingled.

Bruno was used to his wife attracting admiring gazes and fantasies that increased the number of customers, and he kept a watch on everything that happened around her.

"Come on, come on, time to have a good time, señores!" he repeated while he turned the stick under a blue flame and gathered the sugary filaments floating in the air into a head of candyfloss.

When she left her little office and handed him the cash box, Bruno attempted to caress her in his coarse but tender manner. He was trying to make his peace with her after their squabble, and his only language was the language of his hands. She sidestepped him, smiling uncomfortably, and walked away towards her sideshow. She strode on a few metres more, past Parker, looking in his direction but not at him, so he would register her fleeting eyes. Parker watched her disappear into the crowd, and thought all that must be happening in another dimension.

"So what's up now?" Bruno barked, seeing Fredy coming towards him.

"The main power supply has gone again."

"Can't you two sort it out? Don't you spend all day seeing divine light?" he grunted, laughing at his own joke.

"Don't make fun of our little god, boss, or something nasty might happen," the Bolivian warned as he headed towards the main fuse box.

Parker took out his wallet and left a banknote under a glass. He looked around, got up, rattling the bottles on the tin table, and staggered off towards the Bear Hunt. Maytén watched him coming with a smile that a shadow soon wiped from her face.

"Hello, remember me?" Parker said, but Maytén had climbed on the dais and only caught a glimpse of him. He tiptoed so as not to feel dwarfed, though a stab of pain in his legs told him that was not a good idea. He repeated his hello, he wasn't worried about looking stupid, because alcohol had long since washed any inhibitions away and he felt strong and animated, ready to sweep aside everything in his path.

"Of course I do. We met in . . ."

Maytén frowned, trying to remember.

"I forget the name, you know, all these towns are the same."

"Well, that's nothing to worry about now," he responded.

Maytén kept staring at him, until a complicit smile ended that first round of conversation. From then onwards, Parker was at a loss for words.

"This is a great set of attractions," came to mind.

She smiled shyly and looked at him out of the corner of her eye, wondering how far she dared go. He was still down there, uneasy, not sure what to do next. He had evoked Maytén's last appearance in the ghost train so often that he'd exhausted any real-life content, and that vision was now veiled by a subtle film of unreality. Which explained why he didn't have the courage to refer back to that encounter. Although he could still feel the texture of her lips, he wasn't sure that *she* remembered. He looked into her eyes as if to say, "It's me," but she seemed oblivious to the memory of that fleeting embrace in the shadows.

Sticky sweat began trickling down Parker's skin. He couldn't tell how long he had been standing in front of the ticket box, but he did know he had managed only a couple of sentences and a few disconnected words before abandoning his position and retreating to drown his failure in beer.

At that precise moment Maytén left the booth, signalled to him to follow her and headed towards the Bear Hunt, which was now less in demand. Parker caught up with her in a matter of seconds.

"Want to have a few throws?" she said with a wink and a knowing smile, as she handed over three rag balls. Parker had several shots, all unsuccessful, as he was unable to concentrate.

Eber, who had appeared from nowhere, shook his head after each failed attempt.

"You again, bro. Concentrate, look in front!" he said, his reproach prompting a rush of anger in Parker.

"I'll look where I want to," he replied between gritted teeth, as the balls rebounded and scattered without felling a single enemy.

"If you looked towards God, you'd see the light, bro."

Maytén ordered the handyman to take charge of the ticket booth.

"That bastard's always sticking his nose where it's not wanted. That must be the story of his life."

Eber went off with his hands in his pockets.

Parker was about to go after him, but Maytén's gentle voice brought him back.

"I'll show you how to throw," she said, standing beside him, gripping his arm gently. Parker quivered, and followed her instructions to the letter. He aimed, shot several times with one eye shut and soon several soft toys were heaped on the floor.

"You've won a special prize. Choose what most takes your fancy."

"What most takes my fancy? You being serious?"

Parker understood that was a turning point: he was being offered the tray and all he had to do was hold out a hand and take the fruit. There was only one possible response, and he wasn't going to waste the opportunity. Saying anything else at that point would have been absurd, and he would spend the rest of his days, wherever life took him, regretting not saying it. He could not care less if anyone heard.

"*You* included?"

Maytén ignored him and went back up into the stall, with a sashay that revealed all her sensuality. Parker pointed to one of the items on the top shelves.

"For the moment that prize will do me."

Maytén clambered onto a bench, stretching to unhook the prize he had chosen, her skirt lifting to expose her legs. She climbed down with a plastic stag's head wrapped in cellophane and handed it to Parker.

"I've been chasing after you for weeks," he whispered, his voice trembling, as he looked around.

She was in a state of shock for a moment.

"And I thought you'd never come," she whispered, reproach deep in her eyes.

"I looked for you in Colonia Desesperación, then I went halfway round the world."

"We changed our route at the last moment, there was no way I could let you know," she lamented. Parker seemed a changed man, not what he was weeks ago on the ghost train.

"Let's stop it here, it's dangerous," she said, framing her words with an uneasy smile, and looking nervously around.

"It's too late now, we can't. Let's leave together," Parker muttered, though his words rang with the intense, resonant tone of a jury delivering its verdict.

"This is madness. Whatever are we going to do?"

Where can we talk by ourselves, she wondered several times, and both realised there was only one place in the whole universe where they could see each other without being seen. Parker tried to caress her again, not so much in a show of tenderness as to confirm that he was talking to a creature made of flesh and blood.

o  o

Bruno and Eber were repairing a fuse box at one end of the fairground and it demanded their full concentration. Maytén and Parker were still face to face in the sideshow, their eyes locked into each other's, hesitating, waiting for something to happen, to decide their fates. In truth, Parker's fate had been decided long ago, and now she was the one who had to take the initiative. Maytén was no longer looking at Parker or the fair but within herself, reviewing her whole life, what she had lived and what lay ahead. Her hands gripped a book of tickets tight, afraid destiny would steal it away with a gust of wind. Parker tried to say something, but she gestured to him to shush, and closed her eyes for what he felt was an eternity. When she reopened them, a new world began to take shape around her. She tore off a ticket, handed it to Parker and pointed him to the ghost train. Parker went off holding the ticket between his fingers and the stag's head under his arm. The Bolivian attendant, in his old uniform and stationmaster's cap, welcomed him all matter of fact.

"At least you won't have to worry about your aim here, bro."

"Don't try it on with me, Eber? Get me?"

"No."

Parker turned violent.

"No what?"

"I'm not Eber, I'm Fredy," the Bolivian said, taking his ticket and returning half. Parker jumped into a car, settled himself comfortably in the seat and gripped the bar with both hands, knowing full well a deadly jolt could come any second.

Fredy activated the lever that set the cars in motion, then walked away, obeying a signal from Maytén, who was watching from the ticket booth as if it were an airport control tower. A gloomy, cavernous welcome wailed from the loudspeaker to a chorus of shrieking laughter. The train trundled off, and in a few seconds Parker, the only passenger, vanished through the entrance curtains. The cars accelerated round bends, brushed against monsters who threatened the passing train with axes and cudgels. Howls and shouts of terror echoed down the tunnels. Holding the bar tight to keep his balance, Parker's head bobbed from side to side. The car reduced speed, then progressed slowly through the pitch-black. When his sight had adjusted to the darkness, a cautious Parker stood up and got out. Guided by his instincts he walked down one side and stopped by a skeleton holding a scythe. He waited, crouching down, fists at the ready, listening to the procession of cars squeaking past. A silhouette loomed, penetrated the shadows, dodging hooded figures as it approached. He soon recognised the shapely form of his beloved Maytén and both held out their hands. When she was by his side, he pulled her towards his chest, saying nothing, until their bodies were a single silhouette surrounded by motionless witnesses. They kissed and lost all notion of time, uttering promises and words of love to each other as empty cars paraded by. Parker tried to caress Maytén beneath her blouse, but she pushed his hand away.

"No more hiding, let's go somewhere together," he whispered.

"We hardly know each other."

"We'll have time for all that. Anyway, there's not much to know, I am what you see."

"No, Parker, the ticket is valid for only one journey."

Maytén had never retraced her steps in life, but now, for the first time, she wanted to go back in time for a couple of seconds and give a different response. Here again was that blind intransigence, that enslavement to the things she said, that had transformed the fairground into an absurd, grotesque mausoleum for her when she was still so young. If the passage of time left a trail, like the tail of a comet, so you could catch it moments later, Maytén would have done just that. But if she gave it serious thought, it was all absurd: taking off with this stranger might turn out to be the most ludicrous act of her existence. You did not even have to reflect on what they would do and where they would go. They were two complete strangers standing opposite each other in the shadowy depths of an amusement park trying to determine their lives – one of the craziest things imaginable. All they achieved was to keep kissing with mounting passion.

Outside, at one end of the fairground, Bruno and Eber finished their repairs to the electrical fuse box and walked towards the caravans. Fredy was asleep on a chair in front of the shooting range, his head lolling back, giving the impression that he'd been decapitated. Bruno kicked the chair, making Fredy sit up in a state of alarm as his eagle eyes surveyed each installation. He watched the ghost train's empty cars going in and out, and his senses told him something was amiss though he did not know what. Slowly he put his tools on the ground, like a hunter afraid of frightening his prey, and let himself be swayed by a vague intuition.

Meanwhile, in the winding tunnel, the desperate lovers hugged and let go, sighing nervously. Maytén thought she heard a noise and moved away from him, listening hard, though, in fact, that sound was inside her head.

"That's enough, don't come back," she implored.

Parker caressed her hair, held her chin and sought out her eyes in the darkness. He had only a few seconds and could find few words to persuade her to leave with him, and he was not to know that, three bends in the track away, the burlap curtain was opening and silhouetting a muscular figure against the outside light. Both already realised, as they touched each other, resigned to being separated for-ever, that these were the last moments in their short-lived love story, before each returned to the world they had come from. Maytén would vanish into the same shadows from which she had emerged, like an early-morning dream, and Parker would leap on the train, emerge in the light of day and disappear down a La Conquistada side street. They had reached that point of inner anguish and tremulous mut-terings when one of the monsters in the labyrinth seemed to come to life. A chubby, tattooed hand snatched a scythe from the bony hands of the Grim Reaper and tiptoed to the source of all the mumbling. Maytén and Parker were about to say goodbye when Maytén heard another unusual movement, stayed quiet and waited. She caught sight of the scythe rising above monsters and humans about to deliver its blow. Unaware of the danger, distraught, surrendering to incipient love-struck melancholy, Parker was looking for a car to take him from there forever.

"Help!" screamed Maytén as she jumped, grabbed Parker's hand and pulled him stumbling along the passage-way. The scythe's violent swipe missed him, beheaded a Dracula with bleeding fangs and caught on a flock of bats that were hanging from the roof. Immediately there was a short circuit up above and a skein of cables coiled like snakes spat out lightning sparks. Maytén and Parker managed to jump into one of the cars, which were now beginning to gallop like wild horses. The entire ghost train structure shook and shivered as if hit by an earthquake, while her husband knocked down dummies and slashed the metal and card-board décor. Skeletons' tibias and ribs littered the floor like sets of chopsticks, and skulls rebounded from one wall to another. Fredy woke up when he heard the din, ran towards the entrance and met Eber, staring at him, aghast, terror in his eyes.

"There's witchcraft afoot inside, you know," he stammered, and crossed himself.

A moment later they both watched the tunnel exit in amazement: a demonic wind seemed to be blasting the burlap curtains. Parker and Maytén's car, decorated with splashes of red paint and a vampire's face, spewed out of the entrails of the ghost train. Parker was on his feet, twisting backwards, one hand gripping the bar, the other wielding an axe he had grabbed from the executioner.

"Help!" Maytén was still shouting, panic-stricken, holding him round his waist so that she wasn't tipped out on the next bend. Bruno loomed behind, out of his mind, flourishing his scythe and in a flash they all disappeared back behind the curtains. Eber and Fredy watched the scene unfolding before their eyes like a biblical cataclysm, and couldn't think what to do. The howling continued inside, the structure shook and electricity discharged; there was an explosion. The electric current failed and the din stopped. For a moment the only sound was the hum of the cars still moving along the rails, buffeting, insulting and wheezing, footsteps coming and going, sobs and heavy objects collapsing, until the depths of the ghost train went deathly silent. The terrified attendants approached the exit and saw Maytén and Parker run out, hand in hand; Parker was now flourishing the cellophane-wrapped stag's head rather than the axe. Fredy and Eber moved aside to let

161

them pass and looked on as they disappeared between the caravans. Moments later the curtains parted to let through a car that was decorated with the face of Frankenstein; it was transporting the body of an unconscious Bruno, his bleeding head rocking backwards. The car came slowly to a halt opposite his handymen, who were frightened by the spectacle and ran to take shelter in the ticket booth.

"You've got to help the boss, you know," Fredy said.

"The devil's abroad in there, and we'd better stay here until he's gone," was Eber's response.

Maytén and Parker reached the fairground exit, but before that she had walked back to her caravan. He stood guard while she went in and stuffed clothes and various belongings in a bag, took a tin from a cupboard, extracted a wad of banknotes, split it in two without counting, returned one half to the tin and left the caravan. Before leaving forever what had been her home for years, she pondered for a moment, walked back to the cupboard and replaced the banknotes in the tin. Meanwhile, in the ghost-train entrance, Eber and Fredy were walking towards the car where their boss was holding his head between his hands and firing curses in every direction.

Hours later Parker's truck was driving along the main road beneath large yellow and orange twilight clouds, speeding up and down undulating flatlands. Serious and focused, Parker checked his mirror every thirty seconds. Maytén was sobbing beside him, sitting with her bag between her knees. The cellophane-wrapped stag's head was the third passenger on the seat, silent like them, the only one managing an occasional smile. At that exact moment, in the deserted fairground, the two attendants were tidying up, pretending to work, not so much to deceive their boss who, still sprawled

162

in the car, was blubbing and howling to the heavens like a wounded animal, but to put the uncertain future awaiting them out of their minds. Colleagues from other attractions came over to offer help, but Bruno, finding strength in humiliation, sent them away with a wave of his scythe.

Hours later, Eber and Fredy were resting, prey to dark premonitions. Every now and then they went over to the car where Bruno was recovering from his injuries and checked that he was still breathing. The sun was setting behind the western hills, and a mass of low clouds floated over the fairground, which lay in a sepulchral silence, silhouetted against the last glimmers of light on the horizon.

○  ○

The truck's route drew a line that divided the plain in two: in one half, to the west, was Parker and the past, in the other, to the east, was Maytén and the future, but it needed only a slight bend for the two halves to come together like a pack of cards. Then on one side stood Maytén, the past and the ocean, and on the other, the mountains, Parker and the future.

The vehicle skidded a couple of times over the asphalt, then slithered like a stealthy serpent slipping between the folds of the hills. Parker had been driving for days, his gaze flitting from the landscape that was opening before him like a stage set to the side mirrors that provided a constant view of the road travelled so far, and proof that nobody was in pursuit. Maytén travelled with her bag still beside her, a Kleenex between her fingers, her gaze lost in the monotonous spectacle beyond the window. Now on top of the dashboard, the stag's forehead looked like the figurehead on the prow of a ghost ship, and at times was the only one of that trio with a clear idea of where they were destined.

The afternoon sun flooded the cabin and they were soon back on the plains. The truck seemed to stretch along the road and progress in a straight line, pursuing the horizon like an arrow whistling towards its target. Worried by the remorse on Maytén's face, Parker caressed her hair, a gesture she accepted in a routine, aloof manner. Then he focused back on the road, until he hit a crossroads. He hesitated, looked both ways, turned right, then left, and only at the last moment did he see a sign that said: "Beware Dangerous Road Drive Carefully". The truck opted for a track full of bends and potholes, dodging all the obstacles, as a rainbow fan of sunbeams filtered through the clouds. Parker kept glancing at his companion, fearing she might metamorphose into someone else at any moment. He eased the tissue from her hands, threw it on the floor of the cabin and gave her another.

"When tears dry, they're no longer of any use," he said, words that seemed more clichéd than when they'd come to mind. She stopped looking at the landscape and stared at him. When she grasped what the words meant, she picked up the screwed-up paper scattered around the cabin and threw them out of the truck. The wind over the plain tried to swallow them in one gulp, but the handful of balls flew straight back in. She had to make several attempts before she watched them in the mirror spinning through the air, falling despondently on the asphalt and snagging on yellow bushes by the road. That was when Parker noticed the bruises on Maytén's arms, but he looked away, not wishing to pry. He tried encouraging her with a few sweet words. She attempted a smile and her face relaxed, although she said nothing and kept looking out of the window. Hours later they traversed the heart of night drinking coffee and chatting in warm darkness that favoured cuddles and intimate exchanges. That solace was disturbed for a few seconds when the headlights of oncoming vehicles flooded the cabin and revealed faces wearied by so many hours on the road. They drove past a number of sleepy hamlets, then a service station and nightspot illuminated by red neon hearts and spectacles, in the entrance to which men and women laughed and drank under garish neon signs until dawn broke.

That morning Parker was startled to see the flashing lights of a lorry overtaking them at speed, and honking in short, sharp bursts. He tried to remember where he'd put the pistol the journalist had given him, but he didn't need it. "El Turco," he thought when he recognised the truck of an old colleague he had not seen for ages. His presence dispelled the anxiety he felt whenever he imagined Bruno was hot on his heels. They progressed side by side, without stopping, occupying the endless straight road along which they sped as if it belonged to them; then they slowed down and started a conversation, shouting at each other out of their respective windows. When El Turco noticed Maytén, he was surprised, greeted her and looked to his friend to offer an explanation. Parker expedited formal introductions from lorry to lorry, without entering into detail, and waited for the other driver to overtake so they could end the encounter, but El Turco wanted to celebrate with a toast, and chucked a bottle of beer through the window that Parker caught like an ace. In turn, Parker sliced a chunk off the salami hanging from the cabin ceiling and dispatched it in a similar manner, much to Maytén's astonishment. They drove like that for a time, the trucks almost touching, as they ate and chatted excitedly.

"Why don't you stop by the roadside?" Maytén said, unable to believe her eyes.

"What on earth for?" Parker said, shocked by her question.

They carried on that conversation for ten to fifteen kilometres, until the alcohol and arguments ran out. Before saying goodbye they engineered a final exchange of bottles of wine, cheese and fruit, then El Turco accelerated, honked farewell and disappeared into the distance. Parker and Maytén pursued their journey in the intimacy of the truck's cabin until she bedded down next to him, her dark tresses spread over the seat, and soon fell asleep. Looking at her, Parker felt an intense desire he hadn't experienced in years, and it no longer mattered on which side of a bend the past and the future, the two of them, east and west, or hope and disillusion, might be. He decided to drive on for a few more hours, and that afternoon, as the weather was fine and the danger from Bruno seemed remote, he sought out a suitable spot where Maytén, who was not used to such long trips, could land on terra firma. He stopped the lorry and began unloading his furniture, trying not to make any noise. He went to the cabin where Maytén was curled up asleep on the seat, took her in his arms and carried her to the bed as she muttered incomprehensibly. He made a fire with sufficient wood to keep the plains animals at bay, switched off the bedside lamp and got into bed next to her. Before closing his eyes, Parker looked at the canopy of starry sky above his encampment, and became engrossed in the constellations. Something had changed up above; again he thought he noted a variation in the design of the universe. That last thought skewered his consciousness, bewildering him. In the end he fell asleep as well, exhausted after so many lengthy days on the road.

Next morning Maytén started to wake with the first rays of the sun, and felt a cold breeze on her face. She yawned, tossed and turned in bed, and when she opened her eyes, everything was imbued with the sepia light of an old photograph. The first thing she saw as she stretched were the bushes and dry branches the wind had piled up around them in the night. Then she noticed the undulating hills. She looked around several times, at the truck, the smoke from the fire and the furniture scattered over the ground, and couldn't fathom how she could have ended up in such a place. Her incredulous eyes spotted Parker asleep by her side, and she felt she had only just woken up. Her whole body trembled; it was the dawn of the first day of a new life, she was being reborn and her gaze was rediscovering the world. The events in the fairground and their escape came to her in quick bursts, explaining her situation, but still she did not know one vital thing. Where the hell was she now? What was that kind of house without a roof? She sat up and saw she was in a bed on a carpet in the middle of a desert, next to a lorry by a roadside. Could that be a new kind of sophisticated hotel? A mirage, a dream? Parker, the only one with any answers, was still sleeping soundly. Her fingers brushed against his shoulder to check he was for real rather than to wake him up. Parker opened his eyes, turned towards her; he too needed a second or two to remember what he was doing there and why. He tried to kiss her, but she was still in a state of shock.

"Where are we?" she asked, finding it hard to believe they had slept in the middle of open country.

"Welcome to my home," Parker replied, getting up, his naked body wrapped in a thick blanket. Maytén studied him as he revived the fire and opened an icebox that looked like a monolith in the middle of the steppe. Was *any* of this possible?

"Is this where you live?" she said.

"Until we resume our journey, then I don't."

"I don't understand."

"You will after you've eaten your breakfast."

Maytén opened her eyes wider.

"Breakfast?"

"Breakfast in bed!"

She looked around again, more at a loss than ever.

"Your place is on the cold side," she said, pulling the blanket up to her neck.

Maytén fought off the frown that had beset her face for years, although she continued to be bemused.

"I can't believe I'm here," she said, as her sadness evaporated beyond the boundaries of that landscape.

"It's not a bad view," he said.

Moments later, they were breakfasting in bed, holding cups of steaming coffee, enveloped in the sharp, pristine morning air.

"How did you think of this?"

"I didn't. It just happened. It's a long story, I can't even say when it began."

"I never thought it might end up like this," she remarked, looking down. Parker glanced at her gravely.

"This is only the beginning," he said, but she kept her head bowed.

"I got you into trouble."

"If only all my troubles were of this kind."

"You hardly know me.'"

"In the worst-case scenario, you might be a vampire that escaped from the ghost train."

"I might be something even worse, extra cargo you won't be paid for."

"I could unload you in the first port."

She reflected for a moment, then said: "You seem like a good person."

"Don't you believe it. I was going to kidnap you."

"And where would you have taken me?"

"Right here," he confessed.

"I don't want to be a deadweight. As soon as I can, I'll go and leave you in peace."

"At the fairground I asked you to come with me, but I forgot to tell you where we were going. This is my habitat. I'm more at ease away from the world. Here you can forget your name and your past."

"I'd rather forget my past, but not my name. Why should anyone have to forget their name?" Maytén said, after a pause.

"It's a manner of speech. Here you are nobody, yet everyone."

Maytén gave him a surprised, rather suspicious glance.

"You're an oddball, sometimes I don't get you."

Parker jumped up and went into the pantry, grabbed a bottle of cognac and came back to the bed with two glasses.

"Not at this time of day," she said.

Parker stared at her for a second, trying to understand how time of day and cognac were connected. She looked away, then turned round to say something before having second thoughts. Parker grasped the situation, looked at the glasses and put them on the bedside table.

"All this is rather isolated, don't you think?" she asked.

"No harm will come to you here."

"You might get kidnapped. That's what you said you were about to do," Maytén retorted, and started to laugh. "I've always lived here, the south is a sad place, people are lonesome and mean, and alcohol is their only company."

"Loneliness is worse in the city."

"Are you happy here?"

"Well, you know, it depends, sometimes I am, sometimes I'm not."

Maytén sat up and looked sceptical.

"Do you have a home, or anything like, anywhere in the world?"

"I used to own a house. And have a car, a dog, and a wife."

"In that order?"

"No, the reverse, first my wife left, then my dog abandoned me, then my car was stolen."

"And was your house stolen too?"

"I had to sell it to the people who stole my car. Debts and suchlike."

"And did you have to sell your wife too?" she said, amused, though then regretted saying that. Parker smiled at her remark.

"She left of her own accord, before I could."

"Was she bad?"

"She did right. I was the baddy."

Parker got out of bed again, picked up a log, put it on the fire and stood looking at the embers while she peered at his saxophone case on the armchair.

"And I also had a band," he added, returning to her side.

"I love music. What did you play?"

"Jazz and blues, and a bit of country, but that all stopped."

Maytén looked at him mournfully, not knowing what kind of songs they might be. He went on talking, digging out memories.

"I've never told anybody about all that, and years have gone by. I'm afraid if I start, I may never stop talking."

"We have more than enough time, look how much time is out there," she said, pointing to the empty landscape.

Parker thought for a moment. He liked that comment: imagining that immense expanse was time rather than space. He decided she was a woman he could live with, and said: "The drummer and I were business partners, we had premises where we played every night. You know what that kind of life is like."

"How could I, if I've always lived in the middle of nowhere?"

"Nightlife, women, drugs . . . My wife was pregnant, and didn't want her child to have a father like me. When he was born, she got custody and left. Do you want me to continue?"

"I'm free for the day," she said, shrugging. He looked at her again and realised he was beginning to like something else about this woman as he got to know her.

"I've talked too much. Your turn now."

"There's not much to tell. I always wanted to live in a big city, in a house, like every other mortal, but never got that far. My family was horrible, I married the first guy who dropped by. I hate this land, this landscape, these people. Everything is unpleasant, sad and mean here."

Parker hung on her every word.

"My grandfather came from Italy, I don't know why he didn't stay there, you would have to be mad to come to a place like this. He was a smuggler and gold prospector, and a lot more besides I never found out about. He sired children all around, but stuck with only one, my father. He found refuge with Indians and took my father with him to their camps. Do you want me to continue?"

"We've plenty of time," Parker said, echoing her words, while he reflected that those stories would be good material to sell to the journalist.

"That bag there is all I own. My mother died years ago, and I'd rather not imagine what paths my sisters have wandered down."

"Now you're with me, this is your home," Parker consoled her. Doom-laden, she surveyed the scene and thought he must be joking.

"Well, thanks a lot," she drawled before carrying on. "Bruno worked in a factory until they sacked him, he had a gymnasium, but that didn't work out, then he bought part of the fairground. He became a violent, embittered individual. Perhaps he was always like that, and I'd not realised."

Maytén felt a tear roll down her cheek, and asked Parker for a tissue, but they had run out.

"I suppose men don't cry."

"I cry inside, dry tears. It's not good for the system, tears help lubricate your eyes," Parker said, going into the cabin and returning with a plastic drum he showed Maytén as if it were holy water.

"When I need to, I use these tears, they're fresh. I collect them in the Laguna del Salar salt flat. They're also used as disinfectant and natural antibiotics," he explained before pouring a few drops in a spoon and putting it on each eye.

"Now we can both cry for a while. Would you like some?" he asked, his eyes watering.

"No, I've got my own," she replied, trying a couple of drops on her tongue.

"We can also use them to boil potatoes and noodles," Parker said. Soon after that they were kissing and caressing under the blankets, then making love.

"What if we have a visitor?" she asked, looking down the road.

"I've locked the door," he said, continuing to caress her dark, lithe body.

○  ○

Parker and Maytén drove for several weeks from agricultural settlements in the valleys to solitary Atlantic coasts, where boats from overseas waited by the anchorage for the moment to moor. Day after day they were pushing to the backs of their minds Bruno and the circumstances forcing them to live that life on the road. Between station services, faraway settlements and quaysides, Maytén began to forget most of the years she had spent on the fairground, even though the future was still uncertain territory that sooner or later they would have to face head on, depending on the routes Parker took. She lived in a kind of cloud, distanced from her frustrations, but also from her hopes and desires. She felt suspended in time, lost in the remoteness, anaesthetised by a strange substance starting to circulate around her body, and for the first time ever, the discomforts of the nomadic life were outweighed by an unusual kind of happiness.

That stage in the life she was starting to experience with Parker brought huge pleasure and a feeling of well-being, devoid of anxiety or pressing tasks, a simple, sweet swaying between isolation and loneliness. She often wondered how she could now stand a routine she had always hated, and yet she felt fine. She had no answers, but didn't let it worry her: swept along by Parker, her surroundings became secondary, and she started to float outside the world. She began to understand why her companion had chosen that way of life; what at first seemed outlandish and absurd she now thought to be an original way of life, and she had adapted to its pace. A kind of general calm suffused things, a distinct cadence in everyday movements following a rhythm inscribed in the bare, empty countryside. Maytén didn't worry whether that serenity was or wasn't happiness; it sufficed for it to seem as if it were, with no greater expectations. Nor did she worry about being suspended in time to achieve that sense of serenity, because she had nothing to lose. They had been establishing a specific routine, each individual moment fitted into moments in the other's life, and that lent continuity to their existence. Their activities kept in step with the cycles of nature: after a long day on the road, when the sun dipped to return to the earth's entrails, they sought out a space protected from the gales and set up camp. There were corridors where the wind gusted in all its fury, but just metres away it changed direction and intensity. Frenzied whiplashes and whirlwinds vying over rights of transit transformed in a few metres into steady, gentle breezes. Maytén had grown up in those lands and learned from childhood how to tame a gale. You had to move around, using your intuition, observing the variety and nature of the vegetation, the way dust accumulated, the subtle lines the wind traced on the surface of the land. At each stop they looked together for those zones of calm, and thanks to her Parker learned the secret art of taming nature that his outsider status denied him. Then, while she prepared supper, he fine-tuned the detail to make the encampment more comfortable. They ate by the fireside or by candlelight, and stayed talking late until the night cooled, when they got into bed, pulled the blankets up to their heads and warmed each other's bodies. If it rained, Parker covered the encampment with canvas and plastic awnings; if the weather became too wild, they lodged in the truck's cabin. Sometimes, depending on his mood, Parker went off and improvised a few riffs on his sax, which he could only manage for half an hour because those strident sounds and impenetrable harmonies irritated Maytén and gave her headaches.

Parker kept to his routines with very few changes, and she adapted to his rhythm. If they didn't feel like travelling, they stayed in bed reading books or old magazines until it was time to eat lunch, and spent the rest of the day on maintenance tasks. At such times Parker hauled down a metal bath he had bartered from the gypsies, filled it with water from his tank and heated it with embers so he could then spend hour after hour soaking in warm water. That's how their days passed, threaded together like the beads of a necklace, with occasional stops in a village to buy supplies and load up water and fuel. She longed for the time when they reached such places, however poor and insignificant, in order to see houses and lights, and meet people to talk to and exchange opinions with. While he always wanted to leave as soon as possible, Maytén enjoyed those conversations, although they were short and with people not fond of conversing: swapping greetings, predictions or opinions made her profoundly happy.

One warm, sunny morning, after days of driving in bad weather, Parker was fixing a few problems with the truck and Maytén was washing her hair, up to her breasts in the bath's foamy water. Around them, blankets and sheets drying in the sun flapped like flags in the wind. Then Parker heard the noise of an engine and that set off an alarm signal in his brain: any of those vehicles might be Bruno hunting them down. Sometimes someone would stop and spend the night next to them; Parker would get up without alarming his companion, take the pistol the journalist had given him and crouch in a corner to ensure there were no surprises. This time he waited for the engine noise to vanish into the distance, but at once realised that one car was reducing speed and coming to a halt a few metres away. He stopped what he was doing, picked up the pistol and crawled towards the vehicle. He reached the back end of his truck and peered round, but didn't see the silhouette of a man who had circled round and now approached from the other side as if preparing an ambush. Oblivious to all that, Maytén was lathering her hair with her eyes closed. When the individual spotted her, he hesitated, changed direction, then resumed his walk. Parker's nerves felt raw; he heard pebbles crunching and turned round. He raised the pistol and took aim, but his body froze in that stance, and he panted, out of breath, on the point of collapse.

"Hey, steady there, I only wanted to give you a surprise," the intruder said, wrapped in his thick, dusty overcoat, carrying a bag of food and several bottles under his arm.

"And you sure did that, you fucking pen-pusher," Parker said, lowering his arm. "You're mad, I almost killed you," he added, while the other man put the victuals on the ground and hugged him for longer than Parker could tolerate, from a woman or a man. As far as he was concerned, a hug was a chin brushing against a shoulder, and two rapid pats on the back. He found kissing and fingering unnerving and clammy, preferring to leave his shows of effusion for more private moments.

"You don't half look rattled. Didn't you recognise my car?"

"I did the car, but not the way you braked."

"I keep my brakes for special occasions. We agreed to meet in Montechato a week ago."

"I told you I couldn't guarantee anything, I've been pretty busy of late."

The journalist listened, but his eyes were drawn over Parker's shoulders to where Maytén was finishing rinsing herself: he needed to be sure that, in a land of prodigies, he was not hallucinating. Maytén emerged naked from the foam, unaware he was there, and, without a care in the world, walked towards a towel hanging from a hook. The journalist looked at her in astonishment, convinced he really was delirious. When she saw him, she ran to hide in the cabin, leaping over pebbles as if they were burning coals. The journalist looked back at the foaming bath, now a lonely silhouette against the line of the horizon, and imagined that another woman would appear at any moment.

"Don't get your hopes up, there are no more where she came from," Parker said.

"Now I know why you're so moody," the journalist said, surveying the scene, before he hung up his overcoat and made himself at home by the table.

"What are you doing here? Weren't you going to the

coast to look for U-boat number whatever?" Parker asked, as Maytén emerged from the cabin, scented and smartly dressed, walked over to the table and apologised for the previous scene.

"You don't see too many flowers in this neck of the woods," the newcomer greeted her, his eyes glued on her.

"Journos gabble too much, and this guy even more so. What's more, he spends his time fishing for submarines," Parker warned, lighting the fire.

"True enough, I'm now investigating the whereabouts of U-boat 986 that disappeared in November 1944, but which I suspect continued on secret operations along these shores."

An intrigued Maytén observed him as he extracted more folders from his bag. Parker stared at him, revolving his index finger by his temples, but she remained intrigued, hoping he would take out a real magician's box of tricks, something she had never seen before.

"So what *exactly* do you do?" she said, confused.

"I research strange things, I'm a historian. German submarines at the end of the war—"

"Don't be frightened, he's not dangerous," Parker interrupted but Maytén was fascinated by his patter. From a distance, Parker sighed and looked up to the heavens.

"But that's a closely guarded secret, don't tell anyone, it could be dangerous," the journalist said, lowering his voice. "Is the young lady from these parts?" Before she could answer, Parker sat between them.

"No, the young lady is from over there," he said, pointing vaguely around. Then he changed the subject.

"So what are you thinking of doing now, journo?" The other man looked at him, taken aback.

"Continue my search, the usual."

"I meant, what do you intend doing this very minute?"

"Celebrate the publication of my book. I've brought meat and wine."

In due course Parker roasted the meat while the journalist disclosed to an enraptured Maytén his amazing research, most of which was quite detached from reality.

"You know so much!" she said as she served them. "You're so lucky!"

"I know lots more, but it's all pointless knowledge that takes up a lot of space."

"I'd like to know all that, even if it's pointless."

"You'd need an ocean of knowledge, but an ocean a centimetre deep. On the other hand, by way of example, I do know the name of the man who assassinated Archduke Ferdinand although I'd find it more useful to know how to fix the brakes of a car."

"Don't play the know-all. What *was* the name of that duke's assassin?" Parker challenged him.

"I'm not going to tell you. Go to a library, look it up, you won't learn a thing roasting meat."

"Your lies are a filthy puddle a thousand metres deep."

"I also happen to know the name of the Romanian archer who contested the world championship in 1930, and I'm not going to tell you his name either."

"I can live perfectly well without knowing those things, though you don't know them either."

Maytén felt uneasy and gestured to Parker to stop bickering, but the two men went on arguing and vying until they had finished their third bottle. A bored, silent Maytén listened to that idiotic squabble, which was really a kind of knightly duel over her. Every so often, one or other of the adversaries appealed to her to act as judge and mediator in their conflict. She intuited that she was the root cause of the contest and it flattered her, made her feel included, but she soon felt only contempt for what was fast becoming a drunkards' quarrel.

"No, thank you," she answered tetchily, when they refilled her glass, and made an excuse to retire to her bed.

Parker looked the other man in the eye and pointed at her, as if to warn him off.

"I don't think she'll be any use for your book, too dark-skinned to be German, just drop it, and stop looking at her."

The journo raised his glass in a toast.

"Your health."

"To yours, journo."

"Hers, I meant. I'm not too worried about your health. That young woman is wonderful. You're right to take good care of her, this place is full of vultures, you can't trust a soul. It's not easy finding a girl like that around here."

"If you want to learn, do your research and find out. Drinking wine will teach you nothing," Parker said.

"I'll give you one piece of advice: take her a long way away from here, get her out of these shitholes, go elsewhere. There's a fiesta not far from here in the town of Barranca Los Monos—"

"I don't need any advice from you."

"There are dances and suchlike. Entertain her, or she'll leave you. She'll thank you, and you'll thank me."

"I said, I don't need your advice," Parker repeated firmly, then he reflected for a moment.

"Barranca Los Monos? On the coast?"

The journo pointed to a spot on the horizon and gestured to the effect that it would be a long haul.

"Go straight along the national highway, turn left the day after tomorrow, on Monday turn right and drive on. It's the only ocean there is, you can't get lost."

"Is there any another route?"

"You prefer minor roads?"

"I don't prefer them, I need them. I see you forgot to bring what you promised me."

The journalist tried to remember, then hit his forehead with the palm of his hand.

"Brand new papers! I forgot, I'll bring them next time. Take the 210 until you come to a fallen tree. If you are still driving after three days, come back, because you must have missed it. At the crossroads turn left, it's a good day and a half – two days if it rains – and there are no police blocks. They know me well in Barranca Los Monos, so tell them I sent you."

The two men spent the rest of the night drinking and walking under the stars, talking about topics they'd forgotten a few minutes later. In the morning Maytén found them spreadeagled on the steppe, empty bottles at their sides, like soldiers fallen on the field of battle. The three were soon eating breakfast around the table: tortilla, fried eggs and coffee under a tentative sun.

"Can I ask you something?" asked a bewildered Maytén, who was holding a cup and surveying the landscape.

"Only if it's personal," the journo stipulated, smirking.

"Where are you off to now?"

"To Buenos Aires, for the publication of my book."

She sighed, with a distant gaze and touch of nostalgia.

"I'd so much like to be in Buenos Aires! People, bars, pavements, shops and cars!"

"If you want to, come with me . . ." he suggested, staggering to his feet and collecting up the scattered papers.

"But I want to go with Parker. Do you think he's fit to drive?" Maytén said, seeing the state of his friend. The journalist slurred his reply.

"No need t' drive, ther road takesh yer, like a faithful horsh."

Later Parker dragged his feet as he helped his friend to his car. On both sides, the road was an infinite line dividing the planet in two. They were hard put to coordinate the movements necessary for a goodbye hug, which on this occasion was short-lived. The journalist stopped in the middle of the road, looked both ways, stumbled, turned right, Parker let him walk for a stretch, then whistled after him.

"You're forgetting something," he told him, pointing to his car.

The journalist half turned and came back.

"Too true, thanks," he said, as he lifted a thumb, closed an eye and took aim. Then he switched eye and hand, and took aim again. "If I could only find out which of these routes is the right one."

"That's quite impossible."

"This road is too straight for someone who has twisted vision," the other remarked, still taking aim with one eye, then the other. "I mean life, not the road," he spelt out.

Parker watched him for several minutes until he was in his car. As he drove slowly by, the journalist lowered his window and peered out.

"Princip, Gavrilo Princip. I gift him to you," he said solemnly.

"The Hungarian archer?"

"No, the archduke's assassin. I could never have imagined that his name would resonate at this end of the planet. That, in itself, is noteworthy."

○  ○

The white blades of the truck's headlights sliced through the night, leaving a milky wake that dissolved in the darkness. On each side, night was a black rush of air sweeping the countryside, and nocturnal animals' eyes were like stars that had fallen across the middle of the plain. Inside, comforted by the cabin's warm shadows, Maytén and Parker floated in amniotic tranquillity, their faces barely lit up by the dashboard lights. They had chatted throughout the day, and now, exhausted by all those words, they let themselves be swayed by the silence of the drive and withdrew from each other. They shared only sounds from the radio and the few frequencies that leapt from the dial: distant, remote, archaic voices and tunes, as if issuing from another time zone enmeshed in a ball of electrical crackles. Parker felt that the constantly changing sounds from those faint waves were fingers that smeared the cabin silver, but for her they were simply a nuisance. Maytén suddenly heard a voice speak clearly of horoscopes and signs of the zodiac, and before it disappeared she fixed the signal on the dial. Parker was worried, a steady wavelength indicated something was amiss in the well-oiled mechanism regulating his hours on the road. He could not conceive of another way of listening to the radio than constantly jumping from one frequency to another, never sticking with a single one. He began to frown at the radio, then pressed a button and the wavelengths began to hop about the dial like young guanacos.

A miffed Maytén crossed her arms, looked out of the window and asked why they couldn't listen to the radio like normal people. Parker explained the unique feeling you got from station hopping and flying over tangos, cumbias and classical music. Five seconds, and then another jump to an evangelical's fanatical sermons, and five seconds later to the publicity ads, the weather forecast, and then a recipe, the news, the banal exchanges of anchormen with nothing to say, the grotesque guffaws of comedians cracking jokes, and radio soaps. The entire human realm was contained in those few radio stations, as they elbowed their way into the ether and revolved on his dashboard like a fairground carousel. That was how the human species paraded past him with their manias, preening and pretentious hollowness. He could only grant each specimen five seconds; any more was a waste of time.

"An ocean of wavelengths, but a depth of only five seconds," Parker said, mimicking the journalist.

"And do you find that fun?" she said, before glancing back at the void outside the cabin, but her companion, now inspired, told her in detail of the pleasures of driving through towns and settlements where others were destined to reside and die, and abandoning them to their fate.

"They must say exactly that when they see you drive past," she said, and Parker liked that remark, and was about to add something when a metallic voice started reading out messages. Those were the only programmes that deserved his time: messages for a family in Palo Mocho to go and get a parcel left by cousins in the police station; a message from So-and-So to his brother-in-law to warn he wouldn't be able to visit on Sunday; invitations to relatives to the party for

184

Evaristo Calfulén's fifteen-year-old daughter, which would be held in the club and not the parish church because the priest would not give permission, or the condolences from the community of Los Arbustos on the occasion of the death of Don Panguilef.

An incredulous Maytén listened to Parker, then stared at him for a while to check he was being serious.

"You're not right in the head," she said, looking back at the landscape.

They drove silently that night, cradled by the road's gentle curves. She leaned her head against the window and glanced at the outside world feeling gloomy. That hostile space held a veiled threat that reinforced her feeling of ease and safety by Parker's side. She liked that haven, the protection against all adversity that the cabin had become. It was one more element of the small routine in the aimless life she had learned to value thanks to him: arriving somewhere, setting up camp, sharing the night at his side, then leaving the next day. Maytén wondered if she had yet developed any deep, lasting feeling for this strange man who had come into her life. Something had changed, for the past weeks she had been living in a state of perpetual serenity that helped her to think. Although the new routine with Parker was far from being her ideal, a new way to see the future was developing within her as the hours and kilometres sped by. These thoughts suffused her with tremendous optimism, while radio stations lurched by and things around her assumed a luminous colour that contrasted with the chiaroscuro of night-time. In one such lurch, the radio spoke of the climatic conditions and unusual winds in the west that would provoke low tides in the months to come, but the minutiae

185

of the forecast were lost when another voice chimed in, hysterically heralding the imminent arrival of the angel of the Apocalypse foretelling plagues and catastrophes.

"Even the sea wants to leave here," she said as the melody of a popular tune rang out and disturbed their silent drive. Maytén's body, swept up by that wave of life, began to sway gracefully. A moment before the notes disappeared, she fixed the wavelength and upped the volume. Parker felt those strident sounds were perforating his eardrums, and was about to change the station and restore the established order but was stopped by Maytén's icy stare. He let a moment pass, looked her in the eye, and, somehow or other, her instant smile relaxed his expression. Their bodies started to move slowly, then quicker and quicker, shaking their shoulders and heads, until they surrendered to the music's tempo. They spent the rest of the night chorusing the songs she tuned into, off-beat and hoarse. When they began to feel hungry, she cut strips of meat from the previous day's roast and he opened two bottles with the opener dangling from the dashboard. They ate permeated by a sense of well-being, an acute contrast to the rough night and hostile steppe. Something had unjammed between them for the first time in all those weeks since their great escape. A now optimistic Parker recalled the journalist's advice, took out a map, unfolded it over the seat and pointed a finger.

"Would you like to go to a city? We have to unload here in Puerto Encarnación, a god-awful place, and the following week here, but we could take two days out and drive here," he asked, not expecting a reply.

"Barranca Los Monos? What on earth is that? A ravine full of monkeys?"

"A city," he said, feigning enthusiasm.

"With a name like that, it sounds more like a zoo to me and I hate monkeys,"

"No monkeys, but around this time it's their annual fiesta and there'll be dancing."

Maytén jumped with joy in her seat. Parker handed her a travel guide, and she started looking through its pages until she found what she was after.

"Barranca Los Monos, coastal spot, blah blah blah, located in blah blah blah, population . . ." Maytén broke off as if disappointed. "Five hundred inhabitants. It's hardly a city."

"That's an old guide. There must be more now. There's not much to do, people have lots of children, the population grows fast," he improvised.

That night they slept in the truck because the forecast was gales and showers, and they woke to light drizzle and lightning flashing in the cabin. They listened to thunderclaps resounding but not echoing across the empty landscape. When the sun came out, Parker suggested they go for a walk. Maytén liked the idea, but after studying the terrain, she thought he must be joking: her idea of going for a walk was not a random stroll in the countryside.

"Going where?"

Parker shrugged and with a sweep of his arm encompassed the whole space around them.

"I also hate foxes and ostriches," she said.

They prepared a picnic basket and coats, filled a thermos with hot water and left, prepared for a long odyssey. They dissected the steppe in a straight line until they became two small dots that had melded into the terrain, a luminous expanse beneath the midday sun.

"Where are we off to?" she asked after the first hour of

187

walking, seeing that the landscape never changed and the ground only offered thorn bushes, isolated shrubs and rocks. Parker did not respond, engrossed in strange thoughts. His truck also became a blotch on the far horizon.

"We've covered two kilometres, we must now change our direction ninety degrees," Parker said. Maytén stared at him and was amused; she could not think why she found his eccentric behaviour so entertaining.

"Are we heading anywhere in particular?"

"We must keep walking around the truck, but always the same distance away. It's the journalist's trick to avoid getting lost on the steppe."

"I should have suspected as much. How much farther must we walk?"

"A two-kilometre radius multiplied by pi, 3.1416, supposes a circuit of roughly twelve and a half kilometres. If we maintain speed and the distance from the centre, we'll cross this road twice and be back here in two hours."

Maytén sighed, resigned, as they started walking on the imaginary line around the vehicle.

"The total surface of the area we are walking, according to my calculations, is some twelve square kilometres," Parker said, sensing that space defined the exact spot they occupied as well as the precise moment in time. Then he added that there were pumas and guanacos outside the circle who jumped over the barbed-wire fences so they too stood out against the cosmic void where they lived and died.

"Pumas?" Maytén shouted, not grasping his drift.

"I was being metaphorical."

Maytén did not know whether to stick with the puma or the metaphor, one inspired fear, the other provoked that disquiet technical words arouse when you don't know the meaning. They walked on until Parker started to hop as he looked for the road, as if he wanted to look over a wall, and from that moment Maytén started to be afraid of the puma again. After a while they completed the semicircle and the roadway reappeared in front of them like a river. They sat on a rock and watched the dark asphalt flow by, that slow, imperceptible current separating them from the other shore. Parker suggested that was a good spot to have a bite to eat, or they could walk on, and picnic in the antipodes. Maytén preferred to go on, though the word "antipodes" sent shivers down her spine.

"Ready to cross?" said Parker, gravely.

"I can't swim," she lied, embracing the universe of Parker, who now picked her up in his arms and carried her over the bitumen river. Two hours later, after circumnavigating the truck, they returned exhausted to their departure point. That night, while they ate supper, Maytén discovered a different person from the one she had met inside the ghost train several months ago, which felt like years now. I swapped one lunatic for another, I must be the problem, she thought as her companion detailed all the geometrical figures one could trace by walking on the blank pages of the steppe, but she said nothing and listened intrigued. She watched Parker extract that kind of deformed trumpet from its case, the lamentations from which drilled holes in her eardrums, and she told herself it was far too much for one day; she fell asleep, exhausted. Parker covered her with a blanket and went off to improvise, trusting that now, thanks to Maytén's company and the full moon, he might be able to revisit old times and produce a decent sound. He started playing with great energy but after a few virtuoso riffs the music petered out, and the scant remaining chords flitted over the ground and faded into the darkness.

○  ○

The prow of Parker's juddering vehicle cleaved through the air, and the tarpaulins covering the trailer ballooned as if whipped up by an invisible hand. After half a day's drive, the flatlands they were crossing suddenly ended and transmuted into a high cliff from the high ridges of which they could see the ocean, an immense carpet of dark blue filigreed with fine lines of white foam. Towards one side of the cliff, endless kilometres of stony ravines and hazy beaches; towards the other, an expanse of sand dunes that curled in imitation of the waves and shifted at an elemental rate imperceptible to the human eye.

Maytén and Parker could hear the onslaught of the sand gusting against the window and the agitated flapping of tarpaulins. They halted on one of the cliff's balconies to survey the other liquid plain roiling beneath. The temperature had dropped and the wind from the sea had veered into what was now a headwind. They approached the edge of the precipice and felt it heaving, as if it were trapped between the rocks and the bushes. The infinite vistas aroused a feeling of anguish in Maytén, her eyes rushed frantically towards the horizon, then she closed them as she trembled, afraid of being swallowed up by that vastness. She hated the flat expanse of plain, now powered by an ocean, and sensed that all her being was disintegrating in the limpid air. Her impulse was to go along the cliff and seek refuge

190

in one of the caves or behind a salient, simply to feel something solid against her back. They walked along the edge wrapped in blankets, crouching in order to offer less resistance, and immediately discovered a huge bay opening up at their feet. At first they did not grasp that something weird was happening: the water had retreated from the coast and the beach was expanding towards the high seas, searching for part of the horizon that was not its preserve. The season's unusual winds had combined with the cycle of tides to create low tides that now laid bare large areas of reefs and the sea floor. They admired the spectacle of an ocean in flight for a while, then had to return to the cabin and continue driving.

A while later, as the truck descended the cliff towards the beach, the landscape quietened and the gale turned into a gentle sea breeze that drenched in brine everything it touched. The truck straightened its back and they drove for hours along the coast between huge blocks of rock that seemed to have dropped from the sky, as the line of cliff lost strength and height and started to touch the beach. Dunes appeared half an hour later, ranging over the asphalt in search of the coast, and soon a cluster of shacks surged out of the void, some abandoned, with brick-sealed doors and windows, others with a functioning store, a small oil tank and rooms to rent. They were rectangular, bare-brick houses, linked by paths dotted with pools of sea water.

"Shall we?" asked the trucker, as he parked, excited by the rare opportunity to walk along the bottom of a retreating ocean. She looked around, seeking an escape route she could not find, before agreeing with a shrug; they broke into a barefoot gallop along the infinite stretch of damp, dark sand the beach had become. The waves, kilometres across the sea, crashed down as if alien to that landscape. Parker used his thumb, his navigational tool, to measure distances and track the route along which the ocean might have fled, but as they moved away from land, they began to lose terrestrial reference points, and with them their sense of orientation. Their only guide was the distant bellow of waves and the silhouettes of vehicles racing down the beach. Very soon they were marooned, as after a shipwreck, and Maytén felt that she was falling apart.

"Please can we go back?"

Parker took her hand and looked for the way back to the coast, but realised it would not be easy; they were lost in a kind of flat labyrinth. Rivers of torrential water prevented them from walking back and forced them to change direction every second. Fear that the restless tide might cut off their retreat, even drag them out to sea, intensified, even though Parker knew it was several hours to high tide. A dark blotch indicating the outline of a vehicle appeared to his right and passed by in the direction of the sea without noticing them jumping, gesticulating and shouting, then vanished back into the distance. Parker decided to follow its tracks, and, after walking for a while, dodging puddles of sea water, they managed to reach reefs which offered a more elevated view of their location. Quite close, to the south-west, they spotted the hulks and masts of a number of wrecks sticking out of the sand. They ran over to them and, to their relief, discovered several vehicles and families camped out, eating and sunbathing between the rusty wrecks, sunken poops and prows sticking up their noses. Maytén and Parker were invited at once to join that strange picnic on the emergent sand.

"How far do we have to go to see the sea! I've never seen anything like it in my lifetime," complained the oldest man there.

"We used to have proper tides," said a woman who seemed to be his wife.

"It's the Arabs, on the other side of the world. They're siphoning off ocean and changing it into drinking water," another man commented.

"They'll end up drying it out," another said, as he offered the newcomers glasses of fizzy water. The oldest man nodded, very sure of himself.

"Those reefs are treacherous for fishing boats, and that's why there've been so many shipwrecks in this bay," he explained to Maytén, pointing to the wrecks and razor-edged rocks. "You never used to see the remains, but now they appear at low tide. It must be the devil's doing."

Close by, young kids and teenagers were playing football on a pitch marked out on the sand by strips of seaweed and tree trunks, with goalposts fashioned from the rusty tubes and metal sticking out from the sea floor. A group of eight- or nine-year-olds ran across the playing field carrying plastic buckets and spades, and began digging around the posts, until the angry goalkeeper chased them off, shouting and threatening. The gang stayed nearby, plotting, and waiting for the game to finish so they could dig some more, but then they had to stop their game. Small streams started seeping over the sand from every direction, forming bigger and bigger channels: the tide was rising. The adults got up quickly, issuing the order to leave, and a non-stop mobilisation kicked off. They soon loaded up their belongings, checked they had left nobody behind and started their cars. Parker and Maytén piled into the cabin of a van with other people. The caravan of vehicles began to drive back to dry land, taking long, sinuous detours to avoid the tentacles of water extending over the sand.

"It's dangerous to go so far into the sea; the treacherous tide comes at you from every direction. Years ago a whole family was marooned and their car was buried," their driver announced, dodging puddles.

"So how did they get back?" Maytén asked anxiously.

"They didn't, they're still here somewhere," the man replied.

Parker wanted to intervene, but could not. The man frowned and continued.

"On nights when the sea is calm, you can hear their lamentations as they call for help."

Maytén was frightened and sought confirmation on the other passengers' tense faces, but they were all looking ahead, and unwilling to speak up. Parker whispered to her to ignore all that, but she was intrigued and wanted to find out more.

"You can hear their voices out to sea at night?" she asked, ignoring her companion's elbows gently digging her in the ribs. The driver paused a moment before responding.

"Yes, and much else besides."

Parker sighed; absurd fantasies like these put him in the worst of moods. The tedium of life in these latitudes forced locals to live on such myths in order to have something to talk about at night. He had heard the stories in different shapes and hues on his stop-offs in small settlements; they formed part of their threadbare folklore, collective tales where each added individual detail, modifying the original versions. People had heard and repeated them so often that they had ended up believing them: shipwrecked Spanish galleons stuffed with treasure, accursed vessels that had been drifting aimlessly for centuries, buffeted this way and that by tempests.

"Have you heard of the Trinitarians?"

A shocked Maytén looked at the man, all set to hear the next story, but the driver went quiet. "Your friend doesn't seem very interested; he must be a *porteño*," he added suspiciously.

Parker felt insulted and was about to object when she stopped him with a dig to *his* ribs.

"He seems *porteño*, but isn't. And he's very interested, aren't you?" she replied, staring at him hard.

"Please do continue," Parker said, pretending to sound interested.

The other man waited for a moment, then went on.

"The *Santísima Trinidad* was a Spanish ship that sank off this coast during a storm."

Maytén seemed worried about the fate of those on board, as if it had happened yesterday.

"Were there any survivors?"

The man fell silent again, wanting to ramp up the suspense.

"The crew managed to reach land."

"Thankfully!"

"Where the Indians ate them."

Maytén grimaced.

"Those sailors were already condemned to hell and the Indians were possessed by souls that were damned."

"What happened next?"

"The descendants of those Indians were born for centuries carrying that curse: they have the same faces as the sailors. Indians with Spanish faces, it's ghastly. Patagonia

195

is full of these beings and they hide in the most surprising places."

"What do they do?"

"They do evil, and are always hungry. They hunt wild animals, roam across ranch land and steal livestock that they eat raw. They're called 'Trinitarians' after the boat."

Parker tried to change the subject by asking about the weather forecast, but Maytén was not ready to give up on one of the most interesting conversations she had had in recent years.

"Even if you kill them, they always resurrect. They're half-human and half-phantom."

"Have you ever seen one?"

"One? I've seen lots! They speak an ancient version of Castilian you wouldn't understand. Even the Indians are afraid of them, and that's why they banished those so possessed from their tribes. They had to hide on the salt flats, in caves or in abandoned mines, which is where they still hide."

"Don't take any notice. It's a pack of lies," Parker whispered in her ear. The other man lowered his voice and continued talking, almost whispering, so Parker could barely hear.

"They eat our sheep. We sometimes raid the mines and take them captive."

"And do *you* kill them?"

"I told you that they never die. There is only one way to eliminate them," the man went on, leaving that sentence hanging in the air.

"You have to eat them, so they can never come back to life," he said, "but it must be on Easter Sunday. If not, your soul is infected and you become as sick as they are."

Maytén opened her eyes and lifted both hands to her cheeks. She stayed like that until the line of dry land and clump of houses emerged in front of the caravan of vehicles. They drove the last few metres in silence.

"Have you ever heard of 'the disembarked'? They came to this bay during the Second World War . . ." the driver began. Parker took Maytén's arm, they exited quickly without offering a word of thanks.

"Why couldn't we listen to a bit more?" she snapped, pulling herself free from his grasp.

"I couldn't stand any more of those stories. Those guys were laughing at us, yet you were lapping it up! Besides, tonight is party night in Barranca Los Monos and it's getting late."

Maytén remained annoyed by Parker's scepticism for the rest of the afternoon. They returned to the truck and drove off. They crossed the expanse of reefs and bays that lead to Barranca Los Monos. Only proximity to a city could restore her good spirits. Before arriving, they drove past another of those sanctuaries decorated with pennants and faded red flags. Statues, candelabra and remains of fires surrounded various religious figures, and the chapels were still lit by red candles, miraculously, wax streaming down like volcanic lava. Maytén decided that she wanted to stop and make an offering to the deities of the road, to ask them for protection against the Trinitarians, and Parker had no option but to stop. While they mingled with other groups of pilgrims, they came across a huge poster welcoming visitors to the town's annual fiesta. Parker stared at it in disbelief for a few seconds, shut his eyes, took his head in both hands and unleashed a torrent of curses at one particular target: the contemptible journalist who had deceived him. Ahead of them, people on ladders were working on a large structure supporting a poster which proclaimed in large Gothic script: "Welcome to the National German Submarine Fiesta". Once they were back by his truck, he started punching a mudguard, wondering how on earth he could have followed the scribbler's advice. Maytén took a bit longer to grasp what was happening.

○ ○

By the entrance to Barranca Los Monos they confronted a black-brick monument representing the silhouette of a submarine complete with turret and periscope, in the shadows of which a band of shepherds were preparing a big pot of stew on a fire. A flock of sheep skittered around them, waiting for someone to lead them somewhere. Parker parked at the town entrance, near to where the fair started. A collection of small, white buildings lay before them, between dirt streets decorated with bunting, coloured ribbons, lights and stalls.

"This is better than nothing," Maytén sighed. Unlike Parker, she preferred to stay and see what it was all about; at least she could meet people, hear live music, eat something different in the restaurant and join in the fun and games. She felt at ease in that spot with its pleasant, boisterous atmosphere, so different from the sad, languid mood in Bruno's fairground. She insisted they stayed and Parker had no choice but to agree, though being in that place only made him feel anxious and wanting out: a strange vertigo had struck his back and he felt the presence of the cliffs throughout his body. Accustomed to the steppe where his eyes could wander untrammelled, that vast wall of rock was more than a threat: there was the possibility it would crash down and bury them forever. He was terrified by the idea that, in a few hours, once the sun had set, that grey mass would hide its last rays and sentence him to a darkness that had been forewarned. The line of shadow would run over them, sweep away the remains of the day, and that perpetual wall would prevent him from sleeping peacefully. It was a gloomy premonition. Parker suggested to Maytén that they should at least retreat to the higher part of the cliff, although it would take time, then rest on the high plain, beyond that sandy pit. She let him talk, nodding, unable to understand the subtle stress that staying there caused her companion, and assumed it must be another of his loner's whims. She begged Parker to let them stay the night and spend the next day in the fiesta, then they could continue their journey to wherever he wanted.

"Mountains don't fall on people, it's people who fall off mountains," Maytén told him and Parker had to agree, defeated by her ruthless logic. He would later work out how to overcome the weight of a cliff on his shoulders.

The annual submarine fiesta was a unique event in Barranca Los Monos and vicinity. Very few people visited that small fishermen's quayside in the rest of the year, since the majority of its inhabitants had emigrated and transformed it into a half-empty town that struggled to survive. Parker and Maytén were soon walking its streets dressed for a party. He was quiet and thoughtful, looking this way and that, as if afraid of an ambush; she bounced along, capturing every detail with a gaze heightened by the shadow around her eyes. Like a couple of villagers in their Sunday best from way back, they walked arm in arm and greeted passers-by. They went down a main street draped with German flags

199

between rows of handicraft and souvenir stalls. Stallholders in sailor attire sold chocolate submarines and torpedoes, cakes decorated with nautical motifs, paintings of scenes from naval battles, coins and medals, uniforms, history books and would-be war antiques. As they walked farther into the fair they mingled with visitors from neighbouring towns and a few European tourists, then they visited stalls selling local dishes and pastries before reaching the central square. The base of the monument in the centre seemed to be decorated by rectangular lines left by missing commemorative plaques that had been stolen over the years until that pillar of society had become anonymous, and the town had lost all memory of its past. Near the flagpole, which sported the national coat of arms and flag, they met two couples of young, fair-haired adventurers exploring the continent, in cycling gear and helmets, surprised by the unexpected fame they had found as blond foreigners. They held their bicycles laden with rucksacks, tents and sleeping bags with one hand, while the other signed autographs for children fighting to get a place in the queue. Now and then they broke off to take photographs, but quickly had to get back to signing autographs, because the people waiting became impatient, convinced that exotic foursome formed part of the festive attractions. Parker was curious and tried to ask them about their journey, but people in the queue were furious and let him know he should wait his turn.

"Don't cheat, *porteño*!" they shouted. Parker watched that small, restless crowd waiting with their pieces of paper. That minimal distraction was enough for him to lose sight of his companion and he failed to find her on the edge of town. He walked back along the main street and there she was in the next block, engrossed by a handicraft stall run by a pair of aging hippies. She was holding a small submarine made from painted bread while the old couple spoke an English Maytén could barely understand. One way or another, in a more or less dignified fashion, she discovered that they were Swiss, and had been touring that part of the world for years in their caravan. Maytén was fascinated by that encounter, and it ended with an invitation for her to dine that evening in the hippies' trailer, but Parker politely declined. She hounded him, annoyed by his arbitrary decision.

"We'd be closeted in a caravan, uncomfortable, and not knowing what to do," he said. Maytén stood in front of him.

"You seem scared of other people."

"What if they are a couple of murderers? There's a lot of strange people roaming around. You can never be too careful," Parker said.

"I wanted to get to know them."

"In which language?" asked Parker.

"We could have communicated in gestures."

"My vocab in gestures is much less than in words. I can make five or six, then they're only monkey signs."

"That's how normal people have fun. You're terrified of people, you must have an inferiority complex," she concluded, walking off in a furious temper. Parker continued through the fair, quickening his pace, forcing Maytén to hurry to keep up. Her reaction had really upset him.

"On the other hand, you must have a *superiority* complex. What do you know about me?" he said, without looking at her, thinking that she was ill-educated, had spent her life outside the real world, in isolated backwaters, influenced by television soaps or second-rate lyrics, and could have no deep understanding of people's behaviour. He decided to tell her what he was thinking; he looked for the right way and words to show her she was being arrogant, but she had read his mind and took the initiative.

"You don't need to know so much to understand people, just observe. You don't feel able to mix with other people, and that's why you shut yourself up in your truck. You use your past as a pretext, but you've always been like this. You've lost something, you don't even know what, and you'll spend your whole life looking for it," Maytén told him, blocking his way once again.

"I'm free and I do what I want, I couldn't care less about other people," Parker said, for his own benefit rather than hers, trying to elude not only her body but also her presence that was beginning to pall. She spoke to him calmly, turning his truisms into platitudes voiced by someone else. His usual flow of words now sounded like mere excuses and he missed the long conversations in the mirror of his cabin where every utterance rang out like a perfect argument to sum up the world, truths nobody could refute. He needed to return to his truck as soon as possible and grip the steering wheel, feel the gentle pressure of his foot accelerating or halting a weight thousands of times greater than his own. But that young woman was making life difficult for him, and he cursed the moment he had met her. He knew he could get rid of her that night in that town, but didn't know that her presence in the cabin, between him and the comforting image in the mirror, would be much harder to dislodge.

"Your manias and whims? You call that freedom? Listening to the radio like a zombie, going for walkies in a circle, like men in prison?"

"Shut up, I've had enough of the lot of you! People here talk for the sake of talking, prefer nonsense to silence,"

202

Parker said. It hurt Maytén to see him like that, but the situation seemed so ridiculous she soon burst out laughing.

"And you *porteños* prefer silence to truth."

"I told you I am not . . . !" he said, but he broke off when he saw Maytén laughing even more.

"You're so cute when you're in a temper. It makes up for your eccentricities, at least a teeny bit. If not, you'd be like those two trucker friends of yours . . ."

"They are *not* my friends!" Parker protested, on the point of asking her to leave him alone, but at that second a cog squeaked in some mechanism in his mind. As he observed Maytén's luminous, innocent face and the would-be seriousness with which she tried to repress a smile, he considered the possibility that there might be a scrap of truth in what that young lass from god knows where was saying. Parker sighed, lamenting that convictions, like so many other things in that accursed land, were as fickle as the climate and you only needed to turn round for them to be swept away by the wind.

"What could I find in a ghost train? A ghost . . ." Maytén lamented, resigning herself, and began to laugh again at the absurd situation.

"Two ghosts, not even one of which survives," Parker corrected her, mildly offended, as she took his arm and rested her sweet-scented hair on his shoulder. He felt the warmth from her body and presence beside him. He was flooded by feelings he had never experienced before. He felt quite silly as they walked past stalls hugging each other. They found a screen and several chairs at one end of the street where they were about to show a submarine film, but Maytén dragged him away before he had another of his bright ideas.

"Where's the dance?" she asked, looking around. Parker shrugged his shoulders and, dutifully, pretended to look for one. The last thing he wanted right then was a dance floor, but he was feeling guilty about his childish behaviour. He asked a local, and was soon back.

"There's no dance, but there is a play."

Maytén had already anticipated she wouldn't find what she wanted in that place, but she liked the idea of a theatre.

"What's the play about?"

"It's a reconstruction of the life of sailors inside a submarine."

"No, I'd rather find a bite to eat," she replied. She felt like buying or eating something, though she didn't know what. Just as long as it wasn't boat-shaped.

They walked on, absorbed in their own thoughts, until they realised that there was nothing in that town to justify them being there. They bought chocolate torpedoes and other supplies for the journey, and Maytén felt a little happier, after being entertained by something different, and they wearily retraced their steps to the truck. Once again they walked past the low houses on the outskirts, between waste and barren land. Parker whistled as he walked, hands in pockets, eyes blank, as if the conversation they'd just had had never taken place. He had to decide what to do with her, but baulked at the idea of separation.

Maytén had also forgotten their argument, and walked along hugging him, head down and sad, wondering how she could have lived so long in that kind of place, wasting the best years of her life for nothing. Her face grew sombre. Over the last few months, living with Parker, she had begun to evaluate what she had done with her life, or rather, what she had not. Ever since she could remember, she'd had very few options, and most had been worthless. Everything had just come her way, by dint of allowing herself to be swept along by the everyday, which offered few surprises in places like that. It was not as if she had taken a decision to leave her husband and the fairground and all her previous life: everything had happened randomly, or was some kind of joke played by fate. Something of herself had perished in those tunnels, in that sad, abandoned amusement park, like the dry skins reptiles shed among the rocks on the steppe. Even though she thought it was late to begin a new life, she too was changing her skin, a new existence was growing around her and starting to cover her naked body. Everything struck her as being so self-evident and immediate as she walked around that absurd, anonymous town that her previous life seemed like a clichéd story, like those she saw as a child when a strolling theatre company passed by her home.

"This land kills you slowly, and by the time you realise, it's too late," she said, thinking aloud. He replied in similar vein.

"It's dusk, the whole world feels sad at this time of day."

"My dreams died on me, by the day. I don't even remember what they were like," she went on, as she moved away from Parker and walked down the middle of the empty street.

"You've got lots of lives ahead of you. More than I have, that's for sure."

Parker caught a hint of a smile on Maytén's face between her moist eyes and runny makeup as she looked over her shoulder and her gaze was lost in the distance. Both were locked in a short silence that made them feel closer, until they suddenly caught sight of a spectacle that blocked out all thought. That land could be barren and miserly at times, but it was also prodigal when it came to portents: four massive skinheads with tattooed faces, sporting black leather biker jackets, studs and chains, were arguing heatedly, shoving and pushing each other. Iron crosses, fasteners, skulls and satanic motifs were spread medal-like across their chests. When they saw Parker and Maytén, they rushed threateningly towards them. Parker clenched his fists and calculated how long it would take him to reach his knife. He did not finish his calculation, his time ran out: one of the characters confronted them waving a bottle and they both could smell the reek of alcohol impregnating his clothes and body. The visible areas of his body were tattooed with dragons, eagles and Nazi symbols. He began gabbling in such a way that they could not tell whether he had a stammer or was speaking a foreign language, then he extracted a crumpled map from his leather jacket, while his quarrelling friends clambered into a vehicle parked nearby. When the man saw the vehicle move off, he broke into a run, afraid they were going to abandon him, and managed to open a door and jump in. A few seconds later the van, driven by a lunatic, zigzagged along the road into the distance. Maytén and Parker were bemused.

"It's time we left, this place is making me nervous," he whispered, remembering, after that scare was over, the oppressive presence of the cliff behind him. He needed to leave the coast and return to the drab, limitless altiplano in order to free himself of that inner tension that gave him nightmares, even when he was awake.

"I don't regret what I said. I can stay on here, if you want," Maytén made clear before getting into the truck.

"You must be mad," Parker said.

A while later the truck drove past the beach where the boys were still playing football, though now closer to the coast, on the rim of the new frontier marked out by high tide, while their old pitch framed by the remains of wrecks now lay kilometres out to sea, buried under the water. They were silhouetted against the evening light as the truck crawled up the slope that would take it back to the high ridges, where the last rays of sun still glimmered.

o  o

The days on the road were a novel experience for Maytén, and the hours she had passed in the truck were etched on her consciousness even more intensely. Every second reality changed with that constant motion, and time seemed to exist in an unstable realm. Maytén learned to perceive insignificant detail of the world around her: the changing aroma of the breeze, the different sounds depending on its direction, the infinite variety of tone a colour could have on the monochrome steppe, the harshness of the terrain and the speed with which clouds fell apart on mountain peaks. If that life initially threatened daily tedium, a new world was now revealed to Maytén thanks to the hours she spent observing – from the cabin. She needed the silence of frozen time to lean her head on the glass and let her eyes wander into the distance, roaming where her body could never go. She had adapted to almost every aspect of Parker's routine except one: the way his radio switched from one wavelength to another every few seconds. That craziness disturbed her peaceful reveries, and it felt like someone was dragging her along by her hair. She had even learned to tolerate the strident sounds from his saxophone, although she never came to like it. But most important of all she had started to dwell on happy moments from her childhood that were hidden deep in her memory so they wouldn't be infected by her subsequent life. Now as the days passed peacefully on the road, that danger retreated and the memories rushed back. She remembered playing with her friends, something that gave her a kind of retroactive happiness, even though she preferred not to know whether those scenes happened or she was imagining them. She had salvaged part of her life, and would not let it escape. Thanks to Parker she had learned how to lose herself in playfulness and deflect any residues of past reality that might spoil everything. Whenever they stopped to set up camp, weather permitting, they played hide-and-seek or blindman's bluff. Maytén jumped over the sofa and rushed off into the undergrowth, he moved like a wild animal on the alert, listened for the crackle of her footsteps, the rustle of her clothes, her breathless panting, until he had identified his prey, pounced and captured her. Then he carried her to bed and they got under the blankets and sheepskins, driven by the urgency of desire.

That night the truck's headlights lit up the dividing line of the road like a luminous ribbon issuing from the darkness. Maytén and Parker were serious and thoughtful, their faces dazzled now and then by the headlights of the few cars that came in the other direction. After long periods of silence, he looked at her to check she was still in her seat. She leaned forwards, resting her elbows on her knees, her hands on her cheeks and her eyes on the road. For some reason, she was in a bad mood that night; perhaps it was the long drive, or the moon and the dark night souring her soul, he could not tell. When the raucous music her companion had been listening to came to an end, she sighed in relief, but Parker rewound the tape with the end of a pencil and put it back in the player. Maytén waited a few seconds, then lowered the volume.

"How much longer do we have to listen to this? That cornet is drilling through my eardrums," she complained.

"That cornet is known as a saxophone," he corrected her, removing the tape and allowing the device to search the wavelengths by itself, but she wasn't mollified.

"Can't you tune into just one station?"

"They're all rubbish."

While they bickered, the radio, like an intrusive passenger, crept into their conversation and jumped from local adverts to weather reports. Between one jump and another they could hear electric crackles, snatches of conversation and music that never changed. That relentless babble, spewing through the ether, was an offence to the elemental silence of the universe. What he saw as blasphemies, she saw as the discovery of forms of life in a remote galaxy.

"Isn't it worse if you listen to them all at the same time?" she suggested mischievously.

"At some point one that's worthwhile will turn up."

"I know the radio stations in these parts, they're all the same. At some point, you have to select one and stick with it."

Parker sought out her eyes, though she looked in the other direction, and he let three or four stations pass until he found the one he thought most suitable, pressed a button and the radio obediently stopped there. The swinging beat of tropical music spread through the cabin like cheap perfume, and Parker made a huge effort and managed to turn a snarl of disgust into a faint smile. It was quite pointless, because she went on looking out of the window, and frowning.

"Is that an improvement?" he said in a conciliatory tone. An hour later, when they were driving along a section of gently sinuous road that rocked the cabin and their bodies this way and that, he got a positive response. The road straightened and the truck stabilised, but her body still moved to the rhythm of the music. Thirty minutes later came the first smile, almost accidentally, when he was spying on her in the mirror: he liked entering her silences when she was asleep or engrossed in thought. A couple of hours went by like that, until they opened a bottle of wine and spread food items they had bought in the last town across the top of the dashboard. They drove the rest of the night without a care in the world, the music on full volume as they sang, danced and jumped in their seats.

The next morning they stopped at the first service station, which would be the only stop that day, packed with trucks and bustling customers. Maytén was delighted by that unexpected encounter with civilisation and changed into more elegant attire, tidied her hair and made up her face. While she waited for a table to come free, she mingled and bought cigarettes and magazines from a kiosk. Parker was waiting his turn in the queue by the telephone booth, holding his old diary, looking at his companion out of the corner of his eye and observing the people coming in and out. He ran his finger through the dog-eared pages over names and numbers scrawled, crossed out, corrected and written over like an ancient palimpsest. He made several calls, some of which were now wrong numbers and others that no longer existed at all. He dialled the last number left, as a queue of impatient people formed behind him. He let it ring several times, and, to his huge surprise, a voice at the other end not only replied but even recognised his name. Maytén, who had grabbed a table near the window, watched him, intrigued by a conversation she could not decipher. Parker returned to the table and moved her magazines aside; she waited for an explanation she did not dare demand. They ate breakfast to the clamour of televisions rehearsing the day's news. Parker glanced around, never staring, but began to feel uncomfortable in that throng from the moment he spotted a group of truckers he knew sitting around a nearby table. Someone greeted him from afar, but he looked down and pretended he hadn't heard. Maytén was curious and asked whether he had spoken to old Constanzo.

"No, I talked to someone else," he said tersely, making no attempt to sound convincing. "I'd like us to leave this place as soon as possible."

She looked around, and was about to react angrily, but then managed a smile.

"I'd like to stay a bit longer," she said. "Why don't you wait for me in the truck?" She wasn't interested in making friends or meeting people, but wanted company and some lively background noise to make up for the days she had spent seeing only guanacos and ostriches. Parker nodded uneasily, and made for the door, but when he walked past the truckers, he noticed them leering at Maytén and talking loudly about her. He came back and sat down next to her, determined not to leave her alone in that place.

"See how you can't live without me?" she joked as she got up to get some more coffee. Parker glanced out of the window, worried, vaguely looking for something: a moment earlier he thought he had recognised a truck and when he saw the two truckers he had locked in the service station bathroom at Teniente Primero López walk through the door, his worst fears were confirmed. Fat Juan walked in first, wearing the inevitable shabby leather fringe jacket, which made him look like a cowboy movie actor, his fingers and neck festooned with rings and necklaces and his long hair tied behind him. He was followed by his thin, tattooed friend, Julio, a lugubrious, scar-faced spectre. The newcomers greeted the other truckers with waves and over-the-top hugs and wandered about looking for an empty table. Parker picked up one of the magazines and pretended to read, hiding his face, making himself even more conspicuous. Fat Juan spotted him at once, and tapped the back of his shoulder.

"There's room here, Julio," he shouted to his buddy, in a way that prompted many of the people there to turn round and look. Parker held out his hand and greeted him, feigning cordiality, while the other squeezed hard, not allowing Parker to retract his hand.

"You're not going to believe who I've found," Juan said, wagging his finger, and when he finally released Parker's hand, he burst into loud guffaws that ended in a coughing fit.

Julio walked over and nodded, staring defiantly at Parker.

"Our mate the practical joker! The south is such a small world!" he declared, while a curious smile spread over his face, revealing a toothless mouth. Both sat down next to Parker without waiting for him to invite them.

"What's happened to the service here? We're starving!" Juan exclaimed impatiently, straining his neck towards the counter, looking for a waitress.

"You think you're such a smart-ass," he spat into Parker's face, raising his forefinger a second time. Parker threw his magazine onto the table and stared at him. Julio, who seemed less affronted, intervened to stop the situation reaching boiling point, but failed.

"I didn't find your jape in the service station bathroom at all amusing," Juan said.

"It was a joke among friends," Parker countered.

"You're not getting away with it," Juan said, increasingly annoyed, leaning his voluminous body threateningly into Parker.

Julio tried to cool things with a change of subject.

"Juan is off to Río Turbio to look for coal, I took on a load of fish the day before yesterday in Puerto Chico. Are you still doing fruit? Those trips pay so poorly, it's better to carry merchandise," he said to calm down the atmosphere. Juan was getting more and more impatient as he looked at the counter for a waitress, summoning one at the top of his voice.

"So you like reading women's mags? It must be true what they say about you being a bit odd," he said when he saw the magazines. Julio burst out laughing, but soon went on to other things.

"How's trade? People say you live on the road and never come near cities."

"I'm always on long hauls."

"You must be up to no good, dodging the police and transporting contraband," Juan said, provocatively, slapping him on the back.

"That's my business," Parker retorted, but he broke off when he saw Maytén approaching the table with a tray and two cups. Several men looked her up and down and made comments. Maytén put the tray down next to Parker, and the two truckers broke into applause.

"You finally put in an appearance, kid. We've been

waiting for you for some time. What's on the menu?" Julio asked, keeping his eyes on her body.

"Something's telling me the meat's tasty here," Juan said, elbowing his friend. Parker interjected abruptly.

"She's a friend and she was sitting here with me."

Julio and Fat Juan shut up immediately, astonished, then they stood up and greeted Maytén with effusive kisses. Julio gave her back her chair, took one from an adjacent table and ogled the young woman.

"I know your face. Haven't we met somewhere?"

"Maybe," she said, without giving him a glance.

"You should have told us you had company, particularly such a pretty girl. You always were the silent type, and look at this lovely little friend of yours," Juan said, winking at Maytén. Parker gulped his coffee down and looked at his watch.

"Time for us to go," he added.

"Off already? Do stay and have a bite, it's on us," Julio said.

"Persuade him to stay," Juan said. "It's obvious he takes notice of you."

While they talked, Julio observed Maytén, who was looking quietly down at the table, and tried to remember where he might have seen her before. Parker collected his things, took her arm and they both stood up, said a hurried good-bye and headed towards the exit to whistles and innuendo from all sides. Still struggling to associate that woman's image with Parker, Juan remarked enviously: "I don't reckon a woman like that will stick by him long."

Julio was still looking at her, scouring his memory, even after she had left. He tried to locate her face among the women in the bars and clubs in towns and service stations

214

he had driven through over recent months, but Maytén did not match any. The wily Parker had removed her from their sight as soon as he could, so he had had no chance to put the question to her.

"Who is that gal?" he asked, his eyes closed.

"Doesn't she work in that fair that's usually around Teniente Primero?" Julio said, and hit the palm of his hand with his fist. "That's it! The ticket seller! She's the wife of the owner of that amusement park, the guy who used to be a boxer."

"We'll soon find out what happened, nothing's secret here," Juan said, as he read the dishes of the day on the menu.

"He owed us one and now he owes us two," Julio said, watching her svelte silhouette disappear between the bulky trucks. He started peering at the dishes of the day, unable to imagine that Parker would soon owe them three.

They had only just left the service station when Parker asked Maytén to wait for him in the cabin so he could furtively look out Juan's truck, parked next to Julio's. He walked over to the drinking-water tank, unscrewed the lid and pissed into it, looking this way and that. Then he screwed the lid back on and rejoined Maytén, now ready to leave.

o  o

That morning Parker had woken up in an ebullient mood; the previous night they had cooked a big supper and made plans to enjoy the life ahead of them. They had celebrated with a bottle of champagne cooled in one of the rivers by which they had stopped, then made love under the stars, until the first dawn light rose above the hills to the east. A lazy sun spread an orangey glow above the encampment and traced an elongated shadow that shrank as midday approached. Parker made the most of the fact that Maytén was fast asleep under a thick layer of blankets and hides to do something he had been postponing for some time. He got out of bed, naked, and felt the cold morning air scrape his chest like a knife blade. He took a few unsteady steps on the rough ground strewn with pebbles and thorns. Arms crossed, he hopped onto the asphalt, walked to the white line in the middle and started running faster and faster. The lengthy shadow that appeared next to him looked like a dislocated puppet about to fall apart. He ran at top speed, waving his arms, absorbing the morning sun and limpid breeze through every pore of his skin. The energy from the earth that Parker felt through his bare feet was like a ground connection through which he shed his demons. Shouting manically to refresh his oxygen, he jumped and howled into the sky. He cavorted like a ram, lay on his back and rolled over the dark layer of tar, possessed by invisible lymph from the planet. He returned to the truck an hour later, hoarse and exhausted; inside the cabin Maytén was waiting, worried and wrapped in blankets. She thought something horrible had happened to her companion, but when he drew closer and she saw he was naked, worse things came to mind: an attack of madness or black magic. Parker came over, relaxed and smiling, having shed the tension from hours of driving.

"My hour of gymnastics," he told her, but she didn't appreciate that. She had woken up feeling anxious and stressed out by the wind. Whenever she drank half a glass too much she felt her head was about to explode. Stringent acidity upset her insides, rose from her stomach to her face. Her method to restore her good spirits was cleaning and tidying; that way everything not working properly in her life calmed down.

"The fire went out, we've got no wood, the cabin is caked in dust, and you go running like a madman."

"Cleaning is a waste of time, dust disappears by itself, the same way it comes. In nature, nothing is ever definitive or lasting."

Maytén stared at him, half bemused, half angry.

"Dust passes through our truck and goes on its way, it doesn't stay forever. Nor do we: sooner or later we'll leave this place," he said, intoxicated by the fresh morning air.

"Do smells go by themselves too?"

"No, smells change, they never disappear."

Maytén stared at him for a few seconds, finding no sense in the conversation, and repeated her observations word for word. As Parker didn't seem to understand her arguments, she picked up the clothes littering the cabin, and the blankets and sheets, and made a heap in the open air.

"All this needs washing," she said, and armed with a broom and a brush, she set about sweeping everything she could, from drawers to the cabin's smallest nooks and crannies.

"So dust disappears by itself, does it? And towels clean themselves too?" she said, while he breathed in the morning breeze.

"A towel serves to dry what has just been washed, which is technically clean already. There's no reason it should get dirty."

Maytén sent a thunderous look in his direction and asked him if those brainwaves were his or if he had read them somewhere. She couldn't understand the way he saw the world; for her there were no halfway houses: things were clean or dirty, people were good or bad, police, police, and thieves, thieves.

"You complained about work at the fairground, and you're at it again. Everyone has his hobby horse, cleaning is one," he said, walking between the hillocks of dirty washing.

"On the contrary, you have a mania about dirt."

"I don't waste time dirtying things, I let them get dirty by themselves."

"And you don't waste time thinking that others might be right."

Parker was annoyed, lit a cigarette with an ember from the fire, walked away from the truck and urinated in the open, a cigarette between his lips as he stared into the distance.

"You're a brute, and don't realise it," she told him.

When he returned, he halted in that immense chaos of objects scattered around him and reflected for a few moments. It all seemed so normal that Maytén's words lost any meaning. Mess? You could find mess in a house, in a place with roof and walls, but not in the middle of those flatlands, where things enjoyed complete freedom to be anywhere, without seeming out of place.

Once they had finished squabbling, he remembered the previous evening when they had eaten to the crackle of camp-fire flames under a starry vault, and the moments of making love with Maytén.

"Do you think this is how brutes live? There is harmony in the way we live. I can't understand your grumbles, and your obsession with order."

"Is the idea of having a bath so hard to grasp?"

"Not in a city, but it's different here," he said, with a broad sweep of his hand.

"It's true, this is *your* house and *your* life, and I'm invading *your* space."

Parker sprang to his feet, gripped her shoulders and spoke softly.

"This isn't *my* house, it's not even *a* house. We're on a road."

"I don't want to invade your house or your road; the problem is I'm already inside," she said, removing Parker's hands.

Parker let time pass, washed using cold water from the tank, put on clean clothes and started to look for wood, then he washed the dishes and tidied, with the single aim of making Maytén happy. She joined in, although she knew only too well that it was an absurd task: no clear boundary existed between what must and must not be cleaned in a house with no walls. Besides, from childhood, her idea of cleaning was associated with buckets of soapy water sloshing across floor tiles. She slumped down on the sofa, defeated. She surveyed that indefinite spot where she had been living for weeks, weeks that now seemed like centuries, and wondered how long she could continue with Parker. What about when winter came? She had never felt so downcast since she had freed herself from Bruno, and wondered whether she did not prefer her old life on the amusement park. She could not explore those dark simmering tribulations that, given the tiniest space in your head, nested, reproduced and stayed embedded beyond any rational control. She tried to clear her head and forget all that lack of comfort which, even though it might not last forever, now seemed unending. She wondered if she should wait before venturing off on her own, things might change with the weather, and the possibility remained that she might find a way to lead a normal existence, life as it ought to be lived. Meanwhile, Parker had moved away from the truck, a spade over his shoulder, and was starting to dig out a pit from the stony terrain. Stooped over a container, Maytén began to wash clothes, and every now and then she looked around out of curiosity.

"What do you reckon?" asked Parker proudly after the last thrust of the spade, brimming with enthusiasm. Maytén stopped hanging out clothes, walked over and observed the fruit of his labour.

"It looks like a hole in the ground," she said, as if she were attending the burial of a relative and waiting for the last flurry of earth to hit the grave.

"If we find oil, we could build a service station and settle our roots," Parker said. He busied himself constructing a four-sided structure with sticks and bushes he strapped down, and then improvised a curtain over the opening from several blankets. Maytén had tried to dissuade him several times, but he took no notice. Parker worked with blind determination that shut out words he did not hear. Maytén's suspicions were confirmed.

"A bath, I imagine. A brilliant idea."

Parker missed her irony; he was too busy admiring his work. That pit represented his compromise with the territory, a new way to bond with the land he travelled every day, leaving only the stones around the fire, blackened by flames and ash. He had never before interacted with the ground, and was now leaving a trace behind after moving on, his contribution to the planet's surface.

"Yes, it is a bath," he declared proudly. A downhearted

Maytén observed the semblance of an awning tilting over on the steppe, covered with undergrowth, and looking more like a bomb shelter. Half-naked, the spade over his shoulder, Parker seemed convinced his construction was one of humanity's great leaps forward, that roadsters would die of envy if they could see it. Maytén listened to him, resigned, her burning desire to sob her heart out growing with the absurdity of the situation. Parker put down the spade and tried to console her anguish, which lost all meaning now they had a bath like everyone else. Maytén thanked him with a gentle wave and lowered her eyes to avoid the fatal embrace with which the boundless steppe was beginning to overwhelm her.

"What *will* become of me?" she said, her face downcast, and then she stopped. She did not want to be like those little women who spent their lives sighing and blubbing. She had steeled herself in desert flatlands as she had in life, defying the isolation, snowstorms and gales, but something strange was happening to her now. She had rarely been able to communicate her feelings; not to her father, in the little time she'd spent with him, nor to her mother, a woman toughened by the struggle to survive. She had only ever had emotional ties to her sisters, which time and distance had erased. She had hated dusks from the moment she started having memories; when night descended in those parts, something died within her, a wound in her breast grew as the world faded and darkness engulfed everything. Whenever the afternoon breeze blew – and it could last for weeks – that sense of abandonment turned her heart to ice. Her childhood had been lived in transit from towns to ranches, anonymous places where people moved in herds, following the same cycles of survival as the animals on the steppe. The only antidote to sadness had been the walls of a temporary bedroom, the place most like a house she had ever known, with its smell of burning wood and freshly cooked food, where she played with her sisters in bed while outside it rained and was cold and the world was boundless. That was why when she was in a throng everything seemed more cheerful and relaxed; she liked to be in places with new people who had come from distant places, who chatted and bought things and told stories. Inside packed bars and brightly lit shops she felt protected and accompanied, sure she was safe from all evil.

Parker listened, not saying a word, and now grasped what she was feeling, but out of contrariness, not empathy: he felt quite the opposite. Maytén and he were two halves that were almost a perfect fit, although one was the total negation of the other, its shadow and its reverse.

Maytén paused to allow a moment of mutual silence while he stayed still and looked this way and that.

"This is taking us nowhere. Best if I leave in the next car that comes along. The quicker it happens, the better for both of us," she concluded, scarcely hiding her sadness. Parker felt these exchanges bound them tighter and tighter, even if they had come late in the day when they no longer needed them. He could not find anywhere on the landscape to rest his gaze that was not her, as she collected up her belongings in the cabin. In a few minutes Maytén sorted her scant baggage into a couple of bundles that hung from her shoulders like saddle bags, and walked off along the road. Parker stood next to her, cursing his own stupidity, regretting his sad, petulant comments, which now seemed more absurd than ever. By way of an apology, he explained that it was his only way to fight loneliness in these remote places; one became used to a mechanical existence, clinging to rituals and manias. She regarded him with a mixture of boredom and resignation, never stopping, although she did not know where her footsteps were taking her. There were two options, one way or the other, up or down that road. Parker asked her several times to wait before they separated, and promised to avoid any more outlandish behaviour. Maytén strode along, not prepared to give way. Then she stopped and walked in the opposite direction. Overhead the clouds had coalesced and were no longer a herd running amok. The bushes that had been shaking restlessly were now still, watching what was happening.

"Which way is the nearest town?" she asked out of the blue, gesturing to the far ends of the road that disappeared between bends and hills. Parker sat down, his head between his hands, and looked around several times to get his bearings.

"Everything here is far away."

"This way or that?" Maytén insisted.

"It makes no odds, you'll get nowhere walking. We could drive to a train station tomorrow," Parker suggested, and his words had never seemed more unreal.

"Best to end this once and for all," she said, feeling that her body was being torn apart, as she dropped her bags on the verge and sat down to wait for something to happen; if it was a passing car, better still. Parker approached from the opposite side, his hands clasping the nape of his neck. Something was beginning to break within him too, though he was unaware of it.

Two hours later both adopted the same motionless stance; a flock of birds and a herd of ostriches had been the only signs of movement. Parker said nothing, but he knew nobody was going to drive by now. He got up and went to cross the road to sit next to her, and she waved to him to stop.

"Let's talk," he said.

"Let's talk, but you stay on that side and me on this."

They repeated the same things they had been saying all day while the sun passed overhead and the shadows of their bodies lengthened on that strip of roadway. Everything looked frozen in the landscape, except for the two dark shapes on the road that shifted as the landscape turned around them. Parker felt crushed when he realised that words not only did not help the situation, but made it even more problematic, and he sat back on the verge and continued to look at the sky. The late afternoon wind slackened into a breeze until it stopped altogether; birds disappeared from the sky; an unreal calm descended over them. He closed his eyes for a long time, and when he opened them, Maytén was still sitting where she had been sitting before. The capricious weather was now a thin, marble-like drizzle that fell on them, turning them into statues.

"It's difficult to separate in this kind of place; you wait and wait, and nothing ever happens," Parker said.

"Let's keep trying," she said, yawning, wishing that a giant hand would come down from the sky and send each of them on their way. They were stuck in a puddle of stagnant time. The slightest movement required maximum concentration, and their thoughts snagged on a corner of their brains. Nothing moved and nothing breathed. They remained silent for a while, lit up by the sun of the steppe, until Maytén galvanised herself, stood up, picked up her bags and headed back towards the truck.

"Please, Parker, let's go to that train station," she begged,

convinced at last that eking out the agony was far too painful. Parker caught her up, made no response and they were
soon back in the truck and driving off.

o  o

The train station was a mere whistle stop consisting of
an ancient, solitary stone house on the bare steppe, built
a century ago by the English, plus a long, open wooden
gallery that served as a platform. There were several dilap-
idated sheds and three sidings where coaches and engines,
abandoned to the elements, were dying a slow death. The
level-crossing barrier was raised while the rails were escape
routes to a perspective that was vanishing over the horizon.
A post leaning at an angle was home to an alarm bell, a red
light and a sign warning: TRAINS PASSING. STOP, LOOK
AND LISTEN. There was not a single animal or human to be
seen on that becalmed landscape.

Parker stopped the truck opposite the station, and while
Maytén waited in the cabin, he walked around trying to find
out when the next train was due. He called the stationmaster
several times, knocked on doors and clapped, but nobody
replied. An old, wobbly notice that must have been years
old, announced that trains had been suspended until further
notice. He looked around the empty offices, and found an
old man dozing in a rocking chair in the signals room.

"Are you in charge of this station?"

"No, I'm Little Red Riding Hood," the sleepy-eyed man
replied robotically.

"Didn't you hear me shouting?"

"I heard you perfectly, but the station is shut at this time
of day."

"So why didn't you respond?"

"What was the point? You were going to find me anyway."

Parker counted to ten before he continued.

"When is the next train due?"

"I already told you that the station is shut and there's no customer service. You'll find a notice with the railway times outside."

"It says the service is suspended until further notice."

"So why bother asking, then? You *porteños* think the world has to wait upon you."

Parker tried again to count to ten, but only made it to three.

"And who the fuck told you I'm a *porteño*?"

"And who told you I'm the stationmaster?"

Parker walked out, cursing the fellow under his breath, but happy to know that there were no trains for Maytén to catch.

"Wait, come here! The day before yesterday a telegram arrived with the latest information, and it might be of interest to you," the stationmaster called out, picking up a sheet of paper from his desk. Parker turned round and walked back reluctantly, now that the prospect of separation was once more on the cards.

"So what does it say?"

"That the train service is still suspended."

"Are you all idiots around here?" Parker exploded.

"I couldn't say, I'm not a local."

"So where are you from, if it's not a rude question?" Parker said, to find out what his response would be, but the man did not seem willing to comply.

The stationmaster stretched out his feet, crossed his arms over his chest and shut his eyes. He nodded towards a dot on the horizon, beyond the dead rail tracks and this side of the horizon.

"I'm from over there, but I don't think that is of any interest to you."

"Beware of the wolf, Little Red Riding Hood," Parker said, but the man had already fallen asleep and was snoring loudly. Parker walked back to the truck.

"There are no more trains; the service has been suspended for years," he informed Maytén.

"Are you sure?"

"We're going to have to stick together, for the moment," Parker said.

Several hours later, as they waited in the silence of the quiet cabin for some idea or act to arouse them from their paralysis, alarm bells began ringing over the level crossing and a red light lit up and went out.

"A train's coming!" Maytén cried out.

Parker stared in disbelief at the barrier, which was descending from the heights, squeaking and settling into a horizontal position.

"Are you up to your tricks trying to keep hold of me?" she said bitterly. "I didn't think you were capable of such a thing."

"I swear I'm not," he shouted, then leapt down from the cabin, ran to the level crossing, stopped in the middle of the track and looked several times one way and the other. Apart from the noise of the bells and the whistle of the wind, it was as silent as ever for kilometres around: the train was still a long way away. Maytén picked up her bags, walked to the platform and sat on a seat to wait, while Parker left for the operations room to seek explanations from the sta-tionmaster, or whatever he was.

"Why didn't you tell me there were more trains? One is on its way!" Parker cried, storming into the office like a whirlwind. The man was still dozing on his chair, his feet up on the desk and his arms folded over his chest. When he spotted Parker, he sat up, looked at his watch, stretched and got to his feet. He went over to the operations board, activated a lever and the level-crossing alarm immediately stopped ringing.

"It's not on its way anymore," he said.

Parker ran out onto the platform and looked both ways again, as the barrier squeaked its way upwards, shuddered and pointed back at the sky. The landscape sank into an even deeper silence. He went back into the office, not really knowing why, but he needed to. The man had now put on a railway worker's cap and was sitting at his desk holding a clipboard. He anticipated anything Parker might have been about to say.

"It wasn't a train, if that's what you wanted to know. It's my alarm clock, my nap's over and it's time to open the station."

"An alarm clock?" Parker muttered to himself.

"In what way can I be of help, my friend?" the man said, with a warm smile.

"If there are no trains, what on earth are you doing here?"

"What business of yours is that? Do I meddle in your life?"

"Don't you think it's a rather futile job?" Parker said.

"You never know what might happen here. You might always get an intruder asking if a train's due."

Parker turned and sat dejectedly next to Maytén. Both understood that their only choice was to continue the way they had come, making the most of the energy that was left from their escape. That barrier lifting was a message to them, she liked to think. They should go on, there was no other solution, the only way out was forward. They decided to contrive a possible form of coexistence, and over the next few days a truce was established during which they fetched and carried various cargos as if nothing had happened. Things improved after Parker's change of attitude. She put her anguish to one side, and the discomforts of life on the road and camping out, now alternating with hotel stops, were relegated to the background.

One afternoon, intrigued by Parker's frequent, mysterious telephone calls, Maytén decided to find out who he was talking to. He always answered evasively and gave the impression he was hiding something, but on that occasion she had him cornered. Parker relinquished his surprise element, and told her he was in conversation with a friend in Buenos Aires who could lend them a flat in the city centre for a few days. Maytén sat up with a start, moved by news she welcomed with a prolonged hug. She immediately wanted to know when and how, but Parker had details to finalise and preferred to wait. Both knew that this would not resolve their differences but it would buy them time and allow them to act as if they were on holiday. Then, who knows what might ensue?

"We'll find a solution, it's nothing serious," Parker assured her in a tone that tried to be confident and sure, although he thought the situation was very delicate. He had been turning it over in his mind for days, and not found a hint of compromise or a way out. He was not prepared to change his life and freedom for a city existence, doing jobs he loathed. However, he could not renounce her, or the new person he was through her eyes. In any case, thinking about that no longer made sense. If he succeeded in borrowing his old friend's flat for a few days – his only remaining friend! – it would be a glorious goodbye present for Maytén. He hated the turmoil of city life, people bustling down streets, packed shops and buses, but a change of air wouldn't be a bad idea. At least to refresh his memory of why he rejected cities and valued the empty landscape that was *his* from the smallest pebble or shrub to the remotest cloud on the horizon.

Maytén was won over by Parker's suggestion, and from that night onwards her every gesture showed her enthusiasm. The longed-for dream had seen off the big clouds darkening her days, and she licked her lips thinking of the days to come. The next evening, seated in front of the fire, lit up by the flames, they felt that warmth was inviting them to open their hearts to each other. Parker opened another bottle of wine and recounted one of the many chapters from his past. Staring into the embers, he told her how the music bar he had set up with other members of the group had begun to lose money, as a result of slipshod accounting. Their deficit had multiplied so fast it was already too late when they decided to address it. They had to resort to dodgy loans and be in hock to sinister characters who hovered over nightspots like scavengers, offering help that led to enforced partnerships and signing of documents. Parker and his group were left at the mercy of unscrupulous individuals who used their premises as a cover for drug trafficking, something that generated a higher income than music. Now they were securely located on the other side of

230

the law, money flowed generously enough and the conflicts seemed to have been resolved. A criminal gang associated with a group of musicians who gave a unique shine to the premises guaranteed good business, and it was so good that one night the group's drummer took the opportunity to run off with a huge sum of money, thus achieving one of his most fruitful drum rolls ever. As the one responsible to the traffickers for that money, Parker was called to account the next morning, and no holds were barred.

Maytén was frightened as she listened to that amazing story. It was like watching a film. Her dark eyes opened wide; she had little understanding of the detail, but was aware of how serious it was.

"Couldn't you call the police?" Maytén said.

"That wasn't necessary, they *were* police."

Maytén stared at him, in awe for a few seconds, expecting an explanation that was not forthcoming. If she was not sure who were the goodies and who the baddies, she could not follow the plot, and if they turned out to be one and the same, it was even worse.

It was the first time, and perhaps the last, that Parker was able to relate those incidents which filled him with shame. He discussed the tiniest ins and outs, feeling something stirring within; it was also the first time he had recounted to himself episodes that, after making his escape, he had buried in the remotest corners of his mind. He had been forced to sell his house at a loss, and that sum, several times less than was due, allowed his wife and their newly born son to reach safety and live a new life away from there. The hoodlums informed on him, and his face was splashed over several front pages. After all that, Parker had no option but to vanish.

"I had my moment of fame, and look at me now, hiding on the road. My life was hardly a success, but at least I have the consolation that I got out."

Listening to his voice recounting those events after such a long time lifted a huge burden from his conscience. Now he had shared part of his life with Maytén, his memories seemed a little less grim.

"Don't start being nostalgic, Parker. Someone may be hunting for you this very minute."

"They'll never find me here . . ."

"I was referring to my husband."

"Naturally, that seems to be my fate. But he can't find us either, you never find what you're looking for down here. This is the land of the unexpected."

They enjoyed a siesta after lunch, and that afternoon Parker heated some water and sank mounds of clothes, towels and yellowed sheets into the soapy water. They allowed the dry weather and intense light to purify the vehicle's dank zones. They washed the curtains, scrubbed the dashboard and windows, shook the carpet, and emptied wardrobe drawers. Parker's elemental chaos was yielding to her hands, which folded, scented and tidied everything that passed under her gaze; the world immediately became brighter and more luminous in Parker's eyes. Thanks to that simple miracle, the landscape, the clouds, the very air of the flatlands became so limpid and close you could touch them. Parker now drove with an unaccustomed feeling of fulfilment suffused with power, and the desire to imagine plans and projects. He had recovered something akin to enthusiasm.

At the next stop, a battered service station with two ancient pumps that looked like a woman with arms akimbo,

Parker went to the bar-cum-office, dodging muddy puddles and pools of oil. The man in charge, a tiny Indian with a resolute expression, eyed him as he opened the cracked, dirty glass door.

"Does the telephone work?" Parker asked, pointing to a booth with a seat, a table and a telephone directory that might have been open at that same page for centuries. The employee observed him with contempt.

"It used to."

Parker lifted the receiver, but there was no tone.

"Does it work or doesn't it?"

"'It used to work' means last month, but not now."

Parker cursed under his breath. He needed to make two calls, one to old Constanzo and another to his Buenos Aires friend.

"Is the nearest telephone in Puesto La Chueca?" he said.

"No, sir, you've got that wrong," the man replied.

"How come? La Chueca is the nearest service station going north."

"I know, but the nearest telephone is this one, señor," the attendant answered, taking a telephone blackened by use out of the drawer. Parker walked to the booth, plugged in the telephone and dialled his friend's number, but nobody replied. Then he rang his boss. He knew he'd find him in his office, a glass of whisky in his trembling hand, surrounded by empty bottles, buckets of ice transformed into water, and calendars of naked women. When Parker heard his growl, he poured out what he had to say: pay in arrears, the need for an increase, working conditions that had never been respected, and a request for holidays. He also told Constanzo that the vehicle needed a good service, and demanded his driving expenses be updated.

"Who's that?" the old man asked again.

Parker unleashed a stream of curses that echoed around the narrow booth. He reiterated his complaints, exaggerating each demand in order to penetrate the wall of alcoholic haze surrounding old Constanzo.

"You've turned up! They've been expecting you in Colonia Prometida for years!" he shouted in a fury. For a while they argued, neither listening to the other.

Before slamming the telephone down, Parker reminded him to look for a replacement, otherwise he would abandon the truck and go on holiday anyway.

"Alright then," his boss finally granted, promising to replace him himself. Parker left the cabin feeling calmer and happier.

Maytén was sipping coffee and eagerly turning the pages of the magazines she had bought in the kiosk; they gleamed with glossy colour photographs and advertisements that gave her the everyday sensation of belonging to the human species.

"Any news?" she said. But Parker did not reply. He chewed on his thoughts. He recalled the journalist's advice, that he needed to amuse Maytén if he wanted to keep her.

"We could go to the sea and have a swim," he said after a while, recognising that things were taking a turn for the worse. Maytén looked dubious, but imagined a sunny day on the beach, lying on warm sand, and dozing off to the vague sound of breaking waves.

"We have to drop off a load in Puerto Médanos, and there's a beach just before you get there."

"A day by the seaside tomorrow!" Maytén chirruped.

"Not tomorrow, next week," he corrected her, adding, with the air of someone who had just had a vision: "I know where else we can go too! The National Fiesta of Patagonian Dinosaurs is about to begin."

"Is there really a fiesta for dinosaurs?"

"They serve fantastic meat too," Parker said.

○  ○

The vehicle stuttered to a halt by sandbanks behind which the Atlantic Ocean raged with all its fury. Waves of salt water and foam sprayed over the dunes and dissolved in the wind. Parker and Maytén hunched over as they walked in an attempt to deflect the gusts, while a river of sand snaked under their feet in pale filaments that stuck to the rocks and the wheels of the truck. Parker tried to speak, but the wind snatched the words away. They continued to crouch, dodging the thorny scrub they walked by. They climbed the dunes carrying baskets of food, two folding chairs on their backs and a sunshade Parker thrust into the sand to help him progress, like an oar. After reaching the top they made their descent to the beach and found shelter on a promontory that at last permitted them to exchange a few words. They flattened out their canvas sheets and fixed them so they wouldn't fly off, but they couldn't stretch out because the sand was whipping against their faces. Parker unfurled the sunshade so it acted as a screen, and they snuggled up against it, feeling triumphant and contented. They hugged and kissed for a while under that protective shield, enjoying the powerful energy emanating from the sea. The beach was a huge, blurry expanse flooded with salt water and pounded by waves. Amid the haze and jetsam dragged along by the tide were bones of sea lions scattered across the strand and flocks of seagulls floating motionless on the turbulent water. They had done the hardest part of their trek. Now it only remained to pluck up courage, strip off and run into the sea. They went in, holding hands, until the water reached their knees, but before they could swim a wave crashed them to the sand. They tried again, and when they managed eventually to float in the cauldron of foam spinning them round and pushing them into each other, they felt the current pulling them every which way towards the coast, preventing them from entering the water. Maytén was familiar with those stormy seas. She took Parker by the hand and led him into the sea, making the most of the gaps between the breaking waves. Once they overcame that barrier, they were able to float in relative calm, swaying on the back of the waves, still holding hands. They did not need to swim; the ocean swept their bodies backwards and forwards, lifting them above the foam and depositing them on the seabed. Maytén recognised both the areas of flatlands the gales avoided, and the areas of sea where the currents cancelled each other out and created placid zones. They could thus relax for half an hour, until they were frozen and decided that the best place to spend the rest of the day was behind the windows of the truck's cabin. They collected up their belongings, wrapped themselves in canvas sheeting up to the neck and walked back like a couple of spectres. They shivered as they entered the cabin between the whirlwinds of sand and bracken clattering against the side of the truck. Parker boiled water for tea while Maytén put on warm clothes and energetically dried her dark hair, which was full of sand, then switched on the radio and looked for a station that was broadcasting music. An announcer's voice erupted, announcing the weekend's events, but when she tried to keep that station, the dial moved on to the next.

"Parker, I'll go mad! This radio never stays put!" she shouted in a daze, turning the knob to try to get back to that voice. The announcer immediately reappeared: ". . . the best music in the south with La Puñalada Quartet next Friday and Saturday in Pueblo Seco, Sunday in Barranca Los Monos . . ." but he was again lost in a flurry of blurred noise and electrical interference. Maytén fiddled with the knob. Other voices, sounds and music appeared before that voice resurfaced. ". . . a big tropical fiesta and dance tomorrow in Puerto Médanos, an exclusive ambience to welcome in the summer, a Caribbean atmosphere with La Pedregosa orchestra in Los Médanos restaurant hosted by its owners, opposite the square tomorrow, nine o'clock, don't miss it, señoras y señores . . ."

Parker poured the tea into two steaming mugs and they snacked and sneezed. She had been wanting to go to a tropical fiesta for years and told Parker what she had just heard. Parker assured her that they could sleep in Puerto Médanos that night, and she felt a wave of ecstasy surge through her body. They hadn't finished getting dressed and now they began to strip off again, slipping between the fresh, clean blankets to frolic for a good long time.

They had to take a side road to reach Puerto Médanos and drive along a broad avenue blasted by the gale crossing the cliffs. The town comprised a square, at the centre of which a dune had formed, half burying a monument to mariners, covering the sailor up to his waist. His torso emerged from the sand like a desert creature; in one hand he held the rudder and in the other a mast where a faded coloured flag flapped. The square was surrounded by a service station, a bar, a hotel and two restaurants where stevedores, customs officials, sailors and truckers congregated every night. There was also a bank, a church, council offices and other lesser concerns. The town had thrived thanks to the port, where several ships from overseas docked every week. One avenue left the square and led to the quayside, built on a long cement breakwater that acted like a marine parade, until it sank its spine and disappeared among the dunes like a prehistoric animal. A line of sheds and warehouses were arrayed opposite the docks, whose cranes were the town's highest point. On Sundays, entire families climbed there to set up in the empty cabins so they could survey the landscape when the weather was grim, or to sit on the outside platforms when it was warmer, and they'd spend the afternoon in those heights drinking maté and listening to the radio until nightfall.

The following day Parker left Maytén in a clothes store in the square and drove along the quayside and put himself in the long queue of trucks awaiting their turn to unload their cargoes into the ships. Parker had to unload pears and apples he had brought from the valleys and then load up tropical fruit from overseas. He let the stevedores do their work, shut his cabin doors, and went back to the store where Maytén was waiting. He found she was more upbeat and enthusiastic than ever, trying on brightly coloured clothes in front of a changing-room mirror, while a shop assistant kept bringing her more hangers and dresses.

"What about this one? Does it look tropical?" she asked Parker, flaunting her sheathed body.

"Something hotter would be better, with palm trees, flowers and a blue sea, plus the odd banana," he told her.

When the shop assistant brought the latest design, Maytén accepted she would have to make do with something subtropical, which, in any case, would seem exotic enough in the context of the Patagonian steppes. She spent

238

the rest of that afternoon closeted in the cabin of the truck, her hair in curlers, trying out in the wing mirror makeup for that evening from the box of cosmetics Parker had given her at the fairground. For his part, Parker had found the lost suitcase where he kept the few dressy clothes he had salvaged from his previous life. His trousseau comprised a shabby suit he would wear when playing in the club, a few shirts and a tie that still had its knot from the last time he had worn it. He had had to rummage a lot, since the new order presiding over the truck, a product of Maytén's mindset, represented for him disorder in which he easily lost his bearings. He found it at last, covered in dust and tucked away in one of the remotest crannies, and began extracting its contents as if he were exhuming a corpse. The suit stiffened by time, still preserved its human shape and gradually came back to life as he spread it over the dashboard. He shook off the dust, patted it, stirring it from its forlorn state, though he was fearful it might fall apart at any second.

The moment they had longed for came and they walked down the town's empty streets in their finest attire. Radiant and flushed, she tottered on high heels arm in arm with Parker, covering her head so as not to ruffle her hair. A tight miniskirt struggled to rein in her curvaceous hips, emphasising her figure and revealing lots of leg. By her side, Parker seemed less in party mood, straitjacketed in a rigid, angular suit. He had had to wriggle inside and adapt to its shape. His tense, smartly shaved face rose up proudly from the collar of his starched white shirt. A few magical twirls and he had managed to hide the creased sleeves poking out of his jacket cuffs by rolling them up to look like biceps. When they reached the square, they entered the restaurant and crossed the dance floor where several couples, lit by coloured lights and lamps, were dancing to the mournful music coming from the loudspeakers. As they adapted to the gloom, a trashy décor on the walls emerged: ribbons, plastic flowers and palm trees. An usher accompanied them to a candlelit table, the flames of which combined with the torches on the walls to project restless shadows. Parker thought it was more of a Gothic soirée than a tropical event, which he associated with cheerful music and bright colours. On the other hand, Maytén was as happy and optimistic as ever, the venue met all her expectations, especially when the spotlights were switched on and a stage set appeared with suns and skies painted above a glittering sea. A presenter in Bermuda shorts and a flowery shirt welcomed the "very special clientele" and celebrated the event by cracking jokes and doing imitations. The Pedregosa orchestra launched off with a sequence of popular tunes greeted by the audience with applause and approving whistles. Some musicians were disguised as lifesavers, others as bathers, and the rest wore colourful outfits that fused Hawaiian and Mapuche motifs.

Maytén and Parker ordered bottles of bubbly and dined by candlelight, until the orchestra struck up the notes of what was hoping to sound like a bolero. Several couples got up and started dancing. Parker took Maytén's hand and swept her into the middle of the dance floor, where their bodies swayed in perfect harmony. Maytén lowered her head, rested it on Parker's shoulder and closed her eyes.

"Thanks, but don't fall in love with me," she warned. Parker used only two or three muscles to dance. He had to use one more to reply.

"It's too late."

"Let's not go to Buenos Aires, it's too dangerous."

Parker assured her that things would turn out fine, he had planned almost everything. She leaned her head on his shoulder again, smiled with watery eyes and her sad gaze wandered around the other couples. They danced with their eyes shut, isolated in their own universe, until the tempo changed and a tide of raucous, frenzied bodies swarmed onto the floor ready to strut their stuff until dawn. Parker wanted to flee that place, but it was too late; the only option was to dance on. Resigned, he took Maytén by the waist and began to swing his hips. Both were soon draped in coloured garlands and streamers, and balloons and confetti that looked like snowflakes. They spent the whole night dancing to the sound of cumbias and merengues that alternated with other rhythms they couldn't pin down. Maytén stopped first, then had to drag Parker away, tottering and weaving between the tables. At the end of the night they raffled bottles of bubbly, two maracas and a couple of congas. Slow, smoochy music flooded the room by way of an adieu as the partygoers began to disperse. Parker and Maytén danced with a few other resolute couples, lulled by languid, yawn-inducing notes. When dawn light filtered through the windows, the last dancers and the orchestra withdrew, and they were left on the empty dance floor, drifting to a rhythm no longer created by the musicians but by their own lethargy. Attendants began to sweep the floor and pile up chairs and tables and one came over and tapped Parker on the shoulder.

"The party's over, señor," he said, apologising for his interruption. Maytén and Parker opened their eyes and separated, as if they had been caught doing something indecent. They looked at the empty venue, lit up by the

241

bright glow of dawn, in the doorway of which musicians and employees were awaiting the moment to go home. They returned to their table, collected their things and went out into a morning that was beginning to reveal the silhouettes of buildings. As the marine sun appeared, they walked towards the port, leaning into each other, stumbling, trying to find their bearings between identical, symmetrical edifices. Maytén immediately realised she must take charge of the situation, and took the bottle Parker was carrying, so gently he didn't notice, then deposited it on the pavement. It was no mean feat to reach the quayside and find their truck, hidden behind walls of stacked boxes of fruit. Once in the cabin, as she helped Parker undress, a stevedore came over holding a folder full of documentation. Parker slipped out, his torso half naked.

"There's been a hitch and we can't unload your cargo," the man said. Parker tried staring him in the eye to work out what he meant, but failed. The man repeated himself several times.

"Why not? Are you work-shy or what in this town?" Parker said.

"Your ship set sail last month, señor."

"But there will be others, won't there? The ocean's full of ships . . ." he said, stumbling and pointing to the sea.

"Documents relating to the shipment, the declaration of contents and permissions are missing," the worker went on.

"Jussht unload the cargo, I want to get some shshut-eye," Parker hissed, annoyed, hearing the words slur in his mouth. The man went back to the office, consulted invoices and shipments, and returned with bad news, by which time Parker had already retired to his cabin and was slumped over his bunk asleep. Maytén looked for the money she had stashed among her things, separated out a wad of banknotes and handed it to the stevedore, begging him to resolve the issue as best he could.

"Very well, you're the ones taking a risk," the man warned as he grabbed the banknotes. Maytén clambered back into the cabin, covered Parker with several sheepskins, removed her makeup, settled down next to him, and closed the curtains. A gang of stevedores immediately arrived and began unloading the cargo; several hours later they had reloaded the truck with a consignment of tropical fruit.

○   ○

A week later, Parker and Maytén had bid goodbye to the ocean and were slithering down side roads into the hinterland. They crossed arid mesas and drove up and down undulating steppes. After the fiesta in Puerto Médanos they deferred decisions on their future. Prickly arguments and thoughts faded from their lives and they established a truce.

"What will we do with the cargo if it's not been declared?" Maytén asked.

"We'll sell it on the cheap somewhere, I have my contacts, and then we'll pocket the money. As an advance on what Constanzo owes me."

Maytén was not so sure; people around there were not keen on mangos and papayas, but no more was said. A relaxed sense of well-being permeated the cabin as they watched the landscape rush by and the sun veer westwards. That afternoon Parker smiled as he drove and tapped out on the dashboard the rhythm of the music. Maytén stared at the road. Sometimes she leaned into him and took his arm, then withdrew to lean her forehead on her window.

She was wondering whether the future was not perhaps about drifting across the countryside, a way of being suspended above everything and everywhere. But she wasn't going to give up her dreams and ambitions for so little, and wouldn't allow herself to be duped by that artificial peace. There was an almost imperceptible crease on her forehead, created by the web of tangled thoughts burrowing into her mind. Why didn't she let herself be cradled by the truck's movement, by the shifting weight of her body as she swayed from one side to the other as the road sloped and curved round? Something suddenly snapped inside her, shattering that passivity. No, that could not be, she couldn't possibly continue like this, a strange voice insisted. Maytén shifted uneasily in her seat, she wanted Parker to stop, so she could walk on soil, take a few steps and feel the solid substance of the planet under her feet, touch the stones, dust and earth on the dirt road. She was about to tell him to stop, but a sudden feeling that it was all meaningless intervened, it was Parker's fault, he was so languid and laidback, always indulging his demons, subdued and trapped like sheep in a corral. *Her* demons were on the loose, cavorting round her mind: impressions she found unsettling; emotions she must rein in.

On the days that followed, Maytén chose the music they would listen to and Parker had to bite his lip and respect her choices, however much those cloying harmonies jarred his nerves. An unexpected encounter with some crossroads posed a dilemma that could be decisive in these latitudes: should they continue to Sierra Cantera via Cuchilla del Señor, where they couldn't be sure they would find fuel, or head to Vuelta del Sapo Norte, where there were no guarantees that they would either, but at least the drive was short and they'd manage to avoid the gendarmerie, people who weren't renowned for their spirit of compromise? They went for the second alternative, which would also enable them to find a telephone to call Buenos Aires.

Parker felt bad about the precarious living conditions he was offering his companion, who was increasingly weary of the solitary life, and he thought holidays might be a solution. They needed to abandon their itinerary for a time, then they would see. The next morning they reached Vuelta del Sapo Norte, another abandoned train station, all that remained of which were a few sheds, a water tank, a yellowing house, a warehouse and a service station. The lorry turned round a couple of times, like a dog before it goes to sleep, and came to a halt opposite a pump.

"I'd not get out here even if I were completely crazy," Maytén said.

Parker jumped down, ordered the attendant, a boy wearing a poncho over his grey overalls, to fill the tank, and headed towards a telephone cabin with his telephone book. Half an hour later, when he emerged, the attendant was waiting for him, hose in one hand and the cap to the tank in the other.

"How much do I owe you?" Parker said, taking out his wallet.

The attendant looked at him blankly, and Parker had to repeat the question.

"Nothing," the answer came.

"You did fill the tank, didn't you?"

"No."

Parker tried repeatedly to get an explanation out of the boy but failed. He observed him blankly, as if he reckoned that Parker should be the one doing the explaining.

"There is no petrol," he announced after considering his response. Parker snatched the hose from him.

"So where can I find some in this shithole?"

"Over there," the attendant replied, all calm and collected, pointing to a pump a few metres away.

Maytén's presence ensured that Parker didn't lambast the youngster.

"Did you get through?" she asked him.

"My friend will lend us his place, we're off to the capital!"

Maytén was happy. They ate lunch and celebrated the news, made and remade their plans, then laid out a map and worked out possible itineraries. Parker pointed to a few places, indicating the roads with least traffic.

"This will be the only tricky stretch, but we can drive by night."

Maytén jotted down in her diary everything she wanted to see in the capital, day by day. She studied sights to see in the guide and noted them in an exercise book. The days to come took shape, mutated into names and places crammed between its lines. Parker got goosebumps as he visualised whole families walking like cattle, vacantly chewing the cud. People out on Sunday queueing to visit tourist traps, bottlenecks from one end of the city to the other – the thought of it induced in him a sudden depression. He tried to think of other things to avoid this anxiety that might threaten his companion's bliss, but he could not exorcise his own panic attacks. He preferred to keep quiet, hide his state of mind and give himself up to the music, the only thing that could distract him from that incipient nightmare.

Maytén soon closed her notebook contentedly, stared at the road that the truck's maw swallowed voraciously, then fell asleep. They drove through the night until dawn's pristine light began to shape the sinuous line of the horizon. They made short work of breakfast, preparing for an exhausting day, and drove off in a nervy mood: she because she was about to fulfil some of her dreams, and he because he did not know how long it would take to get through that business and return to his nomadic life. Quite unawares, Parker had been infected by Maytén's fervour, and after years of internal exile his fear of the city receded. He trusted that once she had indulged her wilful desire to see Buenos Aires, they would resume life together on lonesome roads and landscapes. He even thought they might settle down somewhere and build a shared space, but it was too early for ideas of that kind; first they had to resolve immediate obstacles. Around midday an alarmed Maytén gave a start and screamed. Parker, who was driving half-asleep, suddenly opened his eyes thinking a demon had appeared, rapidly turned the steering wheel, and put the truck into a couple of skids. There was a mobile control post a hundred metres away that comprised two battered, mud-spattered patrol cars and several shabby-looking police. Maytén tensed as one of the police stood in the middle of the road and energetically indicated to Parker to stop.

"I knew they'd catch us and it would be my fault," muttered a disconsolate Maytén, her hands on her head. Parker waved out of the window, stopped in the middle of the road and greeted the policeman with gestures she thought were quite inappropriate.

"Parker, long time no see! What have you been up to? Will you stop for a maté?" asked the policeman, pointing to a verge. A few metres away two police were heating up a sooty kettle by hanging it from a gun barrel over the flames of a fire.

"I can't, I'm on my way to Buenos Aires."

Saying you were heading to the capital granted kudos, and the intrigued policeman stood on the running board to get a better glimpse inside the cabin.

"Ah, now I get it," he said the moment he spotted Maytén, who stammered a greeting.

"Señorita, wouldn't you like to share a maté with us?" the officer insisted, sounding very keen, but she said nothing, unable to decide whether or not he was being serious.

"Next time have a roast ready and we'll stop," Parker said. The policeman bade him farewell with a handshake, gestured in the direction of her body and winked.

"I'm carrying several tons of mangos and papayas going cheap. Know anyone who might be interested?" Parker said. The police consulted each other.

"What is a mango?" asked the one holding the kettle on the end of his gun barrel. Parker explained gravely.

"They are like apples, but different," he explained and the policeman shook his finger at him.

"And papayas?"

"Papayas too, but even more so."

"I don't reckon . . . People here don't eat peculiar things, they don't trust them. They're even wary of bananas," said the second officer, keeping his eyes fixed on Maytén. Parker waved and drove on.

"You're going to be eating fruit for years, Parker. But at least you've got someone to help you," they shouted, as he moved away.

"They're friends of mine," Parker told an intrigued Maytén.

"Why didn't we stop?"

"In these parts it's best to be friends with everyone and nobody, never taking it too far."

"Friendship is something else."

"The rules are different for life on the road and for a sedentary existence. You're always alone and in transit here, and all of a sudden you might need help."

"That means you are using people."

"Precisely, you're beginning to grasp how to live this kind of life."

Upset by his tone, Maytén said: "I'm better equipped than you to live around here, people make friends and commit themselves, even if they don't need to. I'm referring to normal people, not those who live outside the world, going this way and that, because they've no idea where to go."

"Harping on about that again! This is *my* world!" Parker shouted, pointing to the landscape, "and I'm inside it much more than you are in yours, if you even know what that is."

"My world is everyone else too, and I belong to them."

"Words are all very well. Tell me, do you have any actual friends?"

"No, but I want to get to know people and make friends."

"I'm too grown-up for that kind of thing."

"You're not grown-up, you're old. Did *you* ever have any real friends?"

Parker could not think what to say. This was like a squabble from a bad TV soap.

"I'm not sure. Maybe."

"You did or you didn't. Real friends, not people you meet up with every now and then, and eat, sing and get drunk with, and say goodbye to next morning."

"In that case, I don't."

"If you don't sow, you won't reap. Why bother, if every-one is always in transit? People here turn as barren as the landscape."

"Do you think it's any better in cities?"

"Nothing could be worse than this, loneliness kills peo-ple's ability to feel."

"Everything is simpler and more basic here, feelings are what you see. When people live on top of each other, the best and worst feelings proliferate like weeds, mingling and mixing . . ." Parker could not elaborate, another crossroads without signposts was forcing him to slow down. He tried to get his bearings from the line of mountains, then asked Maytén how far it was to the main road. She picked up a large map, unfolded it with difficulty, twisted it round sev-eral times and ran a finger over it. Parker held out an arm, took the map and turned it round. Maytén started looking for the number of the road, trailing her finger over the end of the map.

"It says Paraguay here."

"Down, the south is farther down," Parker explained patiently, while she looked from the map to the landscape, hoping for a clue.

"The map's got it wrong. Which province are we in?"

"The one where we've been all week," he said, looking for their location on the map. He put his finger on a place and returned it to Maytén so she could get her bearings, but she was only interested in tangible data: when and where they would arrive, not how. *That* was a man thing.

"We'll go east, straight on at the next crossroads, then take that direction and get back on a minor road via the shortcut you can see here to the right of the mountains, before we get to the bridge past the bend."

"And in a few days . . . Buenos Aires!" Maytén sang out, clapping her hands, before turning serious. How many would "a few days" be? Speed was a very approximate concept, a combination of space and time, allied always to other phenomena. Around there you could travel at the speed of three rivers a day, two provinces a month, five towns a week.

"What's our speed?" she asked Parker, who was briefly contemplating the countryside.

"Eight guanacos an hour," he concluded, knowing full well what he meant.

For the rest of the journey Parker drove wondering what it would be like to return after so many years to the city where he had experienced the worst in life. He felt something begin to stir in his memory, a dormant area of his existence that was waking up. His ex and their son must live somewhere in that city and that thought prompted several questions. Should he call her and talk? To say what? He had little hope of finding her. Their ties had been severed abruptly and he had never heard a word from them. He could ask her relatives, ask acquaintances; the task of tracking her down seemed as difficult as confronting her in person. The details of his escape from the city turned into an avalanche of ugly memories crushing him. The image of his former partner, the treacherous drummer, resurfaced alongside one of the gang leader to whom he still owed money, a murderous policeman who was perhaps still looking for him. Maybe it was time to settle accounts with the drummer; it would not be so difficult to track him down in the world of nightclubs, he must be around, playing in some band. Parker had not had the courage to hunt him down at the time and remind him of his betrayal of a long-standing friendship traded for financial gain. He would ask after him, any of his old acquaintances could give him clues, and then turn up one night out of the blue and tell him everything he had been unable to say years ago. Parker imagined himself entering a gig at a packed club, discovering his prey poised over drums and cymbals. He would launch himself at him and hit him with all his might. Those thoughts of revenge rekindled his subdued demons and aroused an unexpected fury, a part of himself he did not recognise. He saw himself kicking the guy on the floor, in front of an audience that would not know how to react. Once the bloodied drummer started to beg for forgiveness, he'd tell him he could keep the money, that he had only come to tell him how low he had sunk. And the murderous policeman? That was more difficult, but he would find a way.

"What are you thinking?" Maytén said when she saw his opaque, hazy expression. Parker's hands gripped the steering wheel and he did not answer. He knew he would never do anything like that, and that the past was well and truly buried. After a lengthy silence, Parker looked away from the road and at his companion, who was staring at him, oblivious to the emotions churning within him.

"I was thinking that we are going to have such a good time," he lied, smiling broadly, as he started sketching out elements of a new life they would both share: they would ask for a loan, buy the business from old Constanzo, alternate life between the road and a city, even if it was not huge, at least a city with asphalted roads and high buildings, a centre with shops and people walking on pavements, and a bus terminal where buses from all over the country stopped. Maytén listened, and felt a wave of happiness course through her veins, although she had long ago learned to steel herself against empty words and promises.

The truck followed the road across barren heaths and anonymous settlements as the sun set behind the clouds on the horizon. All of a sudden, as darkness fell, after going round a bend, Parker gave a start. A peculiar mixture of blinking lights and silhouettes giving off phosphorescent glints came into view. His first thought was that a vessel from outer space had landed in front of his vehicle, but he never got to rehearse his words of welcome to those extra-terrestrials: the sad reality was soon only too apparent. He hastily hid the bottle of wine under the seat, gestured to Maytén to remove plates and leftover food from the dashboard, turned down the music, settled back in his seat and placed both hands on the steering wheel. Some two hundred metres ahead, at a mobile control point, two gendarmes were standing in the centre of the road, their phosphorescent jackets lit up by the flashing light of sirens; they shone their torches at the lorry to indicate it should stop at the side of the road.

"Are these guys friends of yours too?"

"I don't think so," said a worried Parker.

○  ○

In all that time the amusement park had languished like a vessel drifting on the high seas, pummelled by the waves and buffeted by the wind. It had slid from village to village across the gentle slopes of the steppe, and what was left was now stranded on a hilltop outside a town that did not even warrant a name. When the sun dipped and its rays ran sheer with the ground, the moribund structure of the Big Wheel, which was big no more, a flattened oval fallen on its side, etched an arabesque on the line of the horizon.

Next to it, the skeleton of the Figure Eight leaned on the point of collapse.

The path into town, a dry, yellow dirt track, passed it by, meandered towards the first houses and came to an end opposite a large, crumbling wall. On that hilltop, exposed to the elements and the gales, the remnants of the amusement park had become part of the landscape. Rusty metal, upside down dodgems, tin ponies, tanks of war and carriages were piled on top of each other. Next to what was left of the ghost train, a nervous Fredy looked towards the town every now and then while he stood guard at the tunnel entrance, a black hole in the noonday sun. All of a sudden he decided to approach the tunnel's mouth, flourishing a stick. He measured every step, strained his neck to peer into its depths, but the tattered burlap curtain did not allow him to see inside. All he could hear was the noise of tin-plates that had been clattering with the same frenzied rhythm for months. Fredy shivered, almost laid low by a breath of stinking air from the labyrinth's entrails, whose passageways now displayed cracks and crevices that let in the powerful bright light from the steppe. A violent gust shook the structure with the force of an earthquake, Fredy retreated without turning round and sought refuge under the fallen arch that had marked the entrance to the park back in its glory days. An hour later Eber's silhouette appeared walking along the path, a bag over his shoulder and two hens hanging by their feet from a pole. When he arrived, he went over to the old ghost-train ticket booth, opened the door and released the hens inside.

Fredy stared at the bag.

"What else have you managed?" he said, as Eber showed him his meagre haul, in which bottles of coloured fizzy pop held pride of place.

"That was all you got for Dracula's cloak?"

"It was moth-eaten, and they've given me a lot for a collection of holes," Eber said, starting to revive the embers of a melancholy fire dying between the twisted metal sides of a kiosk. He added the remains of an old chair and blew until the first flames flickered. He placed a big pot on them, then the two men sat down to play cards on the tops of crates. From time to time they sipped long and hard on their huge bottles of fizzy pop, wiped their mouths on their overcoat sleeves, and concentrated on the cards that were held down with stones to prevent them flying away.

Scattered around, the dummies that had fallen off the ghost train looked like the dead on a battlefield in their dingy, dusty, mangy uniforms. The bulging eye sockets of various decapitated heads stared at the sky, recalling past glories. Frankenstein lay hunched between sacks of detritus, grimly surveying the horizon, while Dracula, who had tumbled among twisted skeins of cables, was taking a rest without his cloak but with broken canines, longing for the shadows of the labyrinth.

"That's it, I've won, and now *you* can go and wake up the boss," Eber said, laying his last card on the crate. His voice momentarily melted into the wind whistling between the metal attractions, bringing with it bracken, pieces of plastic and pebbles.

"I went last week. It's your turn now," Fredy said.

"No, it's yours. I can't, you can see I'm cooking," Eber said, looking for a packet of rice, the contents of which he poured into the steaming pot.

"You know it's not, bro."

"You know it is, my friend," Eber said, extracting from the bag a few vegetables and a chunk of bleeding meat wrapped in newspaper. This too he threw into the pot, then he stirred the stew using a table leg as a spoon. Fredy nodded, resigned, pulled himself up, and stood for a while watching the noisy bubbles of steam rising from the simmering stew.

"I suppose it is," he conceded.

They had eaten nothing for days, and the simple act of watching something cooking brought relief to the stomach, like a kind of aperitif. Fredy picked up the stick and walked gingerly towards the entrance to the ghost train, gripping the crucifix around his neck and using the stick to open the burlap curtain. He peered inside and started shouting, ready for any devilry that might emerge from the shadows.

"Hey, boss!" he shouted a couple of times, but nothing and nobody responded. "Hey, dinner's ready, boss!"

Eber stopped stirring the stew and went over to join his friend.

"You're going to have to go in," he told him.

"Are you an idiot or what? I'm not going in, you can if you want."

"You lost at cards, bro, it's your turn."

Eber and Fredy stood there for several minutes, staring into the tunnel, hoping something would spare them from having to penetrate the ominous darkness.

"Hey, boss, dinner's ready!" they both kept shouting, although their words vanished into dark crannies and everything went silent again.

Fredy entered the ticket booth and opened the door, there was a flurry of feathers and the two hens escaped, desperately flapping their wings between the remains of the fairground. He took the key to the switch from a box and walked to the panel that controlled the ghost train's movements.

"What are you doing, you fool?" Eber asked, as his eyes tracked him.

Fredy activated the levers several times and said nothing, listening hard for sounds from inside the labyrinth still immersed in silence save for the wind gusting through the structure.

"We've not had electricity for months, how on earth do you expect anything to move?"

"You never know, our Lord might work miracles," Fredy said, lifting and lowering levers.

"Hey, nothing for it but to go in," Eber concluded, picking up a scythe cast aside by a skeleton dying his second death.

After preparing for battle like two medieval knights, they opened the entrance curtain and went in through the mouth of the tunnel, shaking with fear. They walked along the rails until they were engulfed by shadows, keeping a wary eye on the mannequins still erect as the den's last sentinels. Several cars appeared around them, some on their side, others on the rails, expressions of pride on their battered snouts. They reached a half-dark zone, the area where Maytén and Parker had had their first rendezvous. It was not hard to find the car they were looking for: Bruno's sleeping bulk was sprawled out, a bottle of whisky by his side, his hands hanging down. The boss's presence steadied their spirits and they moved forward, tripping over bottles scattered all about. Eber held out a hand and touched him repeatedly, reminding him that a meal, the first in several days, was ready, but still Bruno gave no sign of life. Fredy cleared bits of masonry and dismembered dummies from the rails, positioned himself behind the car and slowly pushed, afraid that one of the sentinels would realise they were liberating

257

a prisoner. Eber covered their retreat by holding the scythe aloft, prepared to slice off the first head that crossed his path. As they withdrew, the screech of the rails became more and more strident and they were panic-stricken as they pushed the car whose face had become unhinged. Their screams combined with the creaking structure blasted by the gale and the screeching wagon to create a proper ghost-train pandemonium. Bruno's trembling, gelatinous hulk shook on each bend, giving the impression that the car would leave the rails at any moment. Whenever they passed by a figure that threatened to obstruct their exit, Fredy threw himself at it, kicking and punching.

Disturbed by this sudden racket, Bruno began to emerge from the alcoholic haze in which he had been living for weeks, opening and closing his eyes to focus on what was happening. He was amazed to see powerful darts of light flying through the cracks, as the out-of-control car hurtled towards the exit. Finally the enormous maw spewed out those interlopers, who shot out as if they had been ejected by the tunnel's innards. Blinded, Bruno twisted and turned in his seat, trying to get back to sleep. But now the nightmare seemed over and, with half a right eye open, he began to grasp the situation. He got up with difficulty, shouting and swearing at them to push him back into the shadows where he had sought refuge from life's misfortunes.

"Hey, boss, the food's getting cold," chorused Eber and Fredy, happy to have escaped unhurt from that evil place, though their hearts still thudded in their chests.

Bruno opened the other half of his right eye and came face to face with reality; he gazed at his handymen and his memory began to reconstruct recent days, weeks and months. At last he realised that this desolate place, full of abandoned remnants and scrap iron, was all that was left of his old fairground, and that befuddled, puffy human mass was all that was left of his own person, and he threw his head back and threateningly demanded to be pushed back into the tunnels. He wanted to forget all that, he bawled, and they should let him die in peace. Fredy and Eber pushed the carriage towards the entrance, its monstrous face now leering at them with renewed relish, but a second before returning to that gloom, Bruno opened part of his left eye and his nostrils caught a whiff of stew wafting towards them from the campfire.

"Stop!" he shouted, and his handymen braked abruptly.

"What have you cooked?" he roared, his eyes now wide open.

"Hey, boss, the usual, potatoes and rice," Fredy said, while Eber took Bruno by the arm and helped him out of the car.

"*Yet again?*" he said, as he stretched his numb legs, and made his bones crack, preferring death by starvation to a repeat of the Bolivians' stew.

"No, boss, the last time was rice and potato, and we've now got meat from the village."

The word "meat" delighted him, and all three were soon slurping loudly, holding their plates in one hand while protecting their food from whirling dust with the other.

"What are we going to do now, boss? Nobody comes here anymore," Eber said.

"Who the hell's ever going to come? Look how dead and buried it all looks! You spend the whole day doing nothing."

"And what are we supposed to be doing? I mean, we've no electricity, no money, no food, nothing, boss," Fredy lamented.

"Clear off if you want. To hell with it all. I couldn't care less."

"We've nowhere to go, boss. At least here we have a roof over our heads," Eber said, pointing to the caravans that had survived in a state of disrepair.

"We won't abandon you. The ghosts in there will swallow you up."

"I mean, you live in the dark, if you moved closer to God, you'd see the light, boss," Eber advised.

"Enough of that! The only light I need is the one that moves the attractions. I'm not interested in any other."

"That's the only one we don't have."

"You must seek out the light of the Saviour, you can't see it just like that. We carry it within us."

"Where's my chessboard?" Bruno shouted as he wolfed down the last mouthfuls of stew. Eber went to the caravan and soon appeared with a dust-covered crate. Bruno took it as if it contained something fragile; it was all he had of Maytén, the only material trace her presence had left after the years they had shared. He opened it thinking a little of her would linger on the shiny pieces he took out one at a time, seeking memories that had clung to their surface; there was the gentle touch of her fingers as she slid them from one square to another. He removed plates, cards and bottles from the crate and began to place the pieces on the board, following his own fancies: rooks in the centre, pawns in vertical lines, and the tall statues that Maytén insisted on calling kings alternating with knights and bishops. That was what he liked best about that game: positioning the pieces capriciously, moving them as he wanted, with nobody telling him how he should do it. He was not worried by worldwide rules; his own were the only code he respected.

Now Maytén had gone, he could play without having to explain himself to anyone, but he did need someone on the opposite side, and only the Bolivians were available.

"Play at little statues? Of course, we know how to, boss," Eber told him.

"It's called Qhapaq Chunkana, it's like a gringo game, but isn't. You've not put them in the right places, this is where Inka goes and his Warmi, and the two Pukaras here, over there the Kawallus, and Piyun right here," Fredy said, but he was not allowed to finish.

"I'm not interested in how the Incas play, this is the south, and down here we play the way we want to."

"It will be hard to play if we can't agree the basics. Kawallu's little statue takes two squares forward and then one to the side. Pukara always goes to one side or the other, but never diagonally," Eber instructed him.

"You're worse than Maytén, you agree because you want to beat me," Bruno shouted, upset by their rudeness, but after a long haggle, he relented. They played the game following official rules, although Eber and Fredy sometimes let their boss have his own way, so great was the respect they felt for him. Which was even greater after the poor man had been betrayed by his wife. They played the same game the whole day long, simply to cheer him up and see some hope radiate from his face. Nonetheless, Bruno seemed despondent, and at times lost his concentration, as his eyes wandered off into the distance. Tired of a game that no longer gave him pleasure, he returned to the little hut marooned by what remained of the carousel and opened the door. Two hens flew out flapping their wings. Bruno ran after them, kicking out, and then spent time rummaging among his possessions for a bottle of whisky. He soon emerged empty-handed, cursing everything that existed. Fredy picked up the bag he had brought from the town, took out a bottle and handed it to him.

"Here you are, boss, but think about what you're planning to do from now on, or those evil spirits in the ghost train will eat up your soul," Eber suggested humbly, his small frame a shadow of his stout employer's. Bruno growled his thanks and at once drank from the bottle.

"I mean, if you sought out the light of our Saviour, everything would be much easier. Before winter comes and we're buried under snow . . ." Fredy said.

Bruno took another swig and gave his handymen a look of contempt.

"I don't have many ideas left. Just one, my last," Bruno said and started walking. Every two steps he stopped and looked into the distance, then changed position and carried on at the same pace, followed by his handymen, who looked like his bodyguards. The three of them processed between the remains of the fair.

"What happened to my motorbike?" Bruno suddenly said.

"I don't think it's working. Why do you want that, boss?"

"Look for it and get it to work, I'm off for a few days, you can stay behind and look after things until I get back," Bruno ordered, saying no more, and returning to the hut. Eber and Fredy glanced at each other as they followed him.

"Where are you going?" they chorused, but Bruno shut himself in his little house without further explanation and spent the night there.

In the morning he breakfasted on the previous day's leftovers, threw the plate to one side and walked towards the spot where his aides were polishing and giving the last touches to the motorbike they had found among piles of dodgems and remnants of attractions.

"We've got it looking like new, but don't reckon it will work," Fredy said.

Bruno went over to the bike and inspected it for a second, shaking his head.

"That's not my bike, you idiots. That was the bike from the carousel, together with the ambulance, the tank and the fire engine," he pointed out, unusually phlegmatic.

"Find my bike and I want it working before noon," he thundered as he returned to his hut, where he filled two bags with his scant belongings. Eber and Fredy took the whole morning to unearth Bruno's bike from under tarpaulins and plastic sheeting at the other end of the fairground. It still had some petrol in its tank, and when Bruno reappeared a couple of hours later, he found it ready to go.

"Won't you tell us where you're going, boss?" Eber implored, but Bruno strapped his luggage on in silence.

"Better forget Maytén, she'll be far away, don't make problems for yourself," Fredy advised, but Bruno was obsessed by his idea, and wouldn't listen, let alone follow advice.

"What shall we do with all this if you don't come back?"

"If I'm not back in a month, do whatever you want. It's a present from me, just go where the wind doesn't blow," Bruno said, taking a wad of banknotes from a pocket.

"Here you are, I only need enough for a week on the road," he concluded, putting his foot violently down on the starting pedal, which, as was to be expected, didn't kickstart. They had to push him to the incline of a hill, down which Bruno rode off in fits and starts until the engine started to shake and splutter.

"Wait!" shouted Eber, as he looked for the Grim Reaper's scythe he'd used to defend himself against vampires and werewolves.

"Take this, but only use it when necessary, and, you know, look after yourself," the Bolivians said, waving emotionally as Bruno stuck the scythe in his belt, tied the helmet strap under his chin and accelerated away, leaving his assistants commiserating behind a cloud of dust.

○ ○

Parker slowed down and stopped his truck at the side of the road, amid glints from the flashing lights of patrol cars and signs that, in the darkness, created a scene from an old sci-fi movie. Silhouettes with luminous jackets immediately surrounded the vehicle, while white torch beams inspected the truck's every corner.

"Are they police?" Maytén said.

"I'm hoping they're beings from another planet disguised as police," Parker said, as the intrusive lights swept the cabin's dark interior, and his belongings looked for crannies to creep into.

Parker peered out of the window, a gendarme greeted him martially and began interrogating him in a stern if cordial tone, still shining his torch inside. Maytén felt humiliated by those eyes prying rudely into their home and personal space.

"Where are you headed?"

Parker tried to smile, but couldn't, his haggard face bristling with stubble and his wrinkles heightened by the merciless light that made him look like a police mugshot.

"To Buenos Aires, we decided to spend a few days and . . ."

"Are you carrying anything?" the soldier interrupted, still peering inside.

Parker was hesitant, first saying he was, then that he wasn't, and finally yes, just a little bit, but they didn't let him finish.

"Driving licence, papers, insurance, passenger and cargo documentation, please."

Parker stammered, "OK," and pretended to look for what they had requested, when he was in fact looking for an excuse to get them out of that jam.

"How many people are travelling?" the other man asked, while Parker fiddled with papers in an envelope, finding no inspiration, let alone any valid documents.

"Me and her, the people you see," he said, handing him a sheaf of dog-eared papers. The torchlight turned to focus on their faces.

"Is that all you have for me?" the gendarme said after checking the contents.

"I could add a few minor papers I've got to hand," Parker said casually, opening his wallet, but the officer hardened his attitude and advised him not to aggravate the situation.

"These don't give you the right to drive a commercial truck," he barked, flourishing an old, crumpled driving licence in one hand and several yellowing, scarcely legible forms in the other. Maytén smiled and leaned over Parker and handed the soldier her own papers, but he did not give them a glance.

"There's more than one irregularity. Where are you from?"

Parker did not manage to answer that question either. Where did he come from? He'd been driving in circles at that end of the continent for years, turning this way and that, with no fixed point of departure or arrival. Parker's trajectory over recent years had been a mess.

"Say something, anything," Maytén whispered, but Parker had fallen silent unable to think in the practical language of the man questioning him. How could anyone who navigated by the stars and let himself be guided by nature's whims answer that question?

"Give him an answer!" she insisted, as the tongue-tied Parker looked at the military policeman without a single word coming to his rescue.

"What can I say, if I don't even know where I come from?" he whispered. The gendarme gave him a cold, professional look and gestured to one of his colleagues.

"Get out and come over to the unit," he ordered civilly enough.

The mobile unit comprised several vans and caravans that acted as an office and communications centre, with an array of aerials and radar antennae on the roof. At one side was a parking space where several customs officials were inspecting vehicles. Parker and Maytén walked around the verge towards the main office, still lit up by red and blue flashing lights.

"Where on earth did these guys come from? It's the first time I've seen anything of the sort," he muttered.

"I'm scared," she said, clinging to his side, then whispered, "I hope this lot also invite us to a roast, but I doubt they will."

Maytén changed her tone and told him to hurry up and

invent something though Parker knew there was little they could do.

"Are we carrying anything illegal?" she said. Parker hesitated for a moment.

"I don't think so . . . Mangos and papayas. I don't know which is worse."

An officer invited them to sit down at a desk, while an operator typed in Parker's and the lorry's data. The sounds of the transmitter filled the air with a harsh clatter that put Parker on edge, especially when he heard the metallic voices with his personal data going in and out of the device. In the meantime, outside, other military police were inspecting his cargo and opening boxes they selected at random. Parker shuddered when he saw dogs eagerly sniffing every corner of the truck. Things were rapidly going downhill and he realised he would not survive the situation unscathed. He watched them examining his domestic items and furniture, those gloved hands exploring his drawers, between sheets, inside cupboards, checking books, writing and photographs. The luminous beams from their torches pried into the private entries in his diaries, and the soft, warm space of the cabin – hitherto the amorous universe he had shared with Maytén – collapsed in seconds. Humiliated as never before, Parker felt dejected, lacking the strength to attempt to explain himself. When she saw that, Maytén decided to intervene; she stood up and explained their situation in detail, in a gentle, pleasant voice. If initially the officer, concentrating on the task in hand, seemed unmovable, he soon became more understanding. Maytén felt the weight of what had happened rested on her shoulders, and was determined to do whatever she could to save Parker from that crisis. Her friendly manner mellowed the man's aloof, bureaucratic stance and he concluded by saying he would do whatever he could to help them.

They sat in silence, smoking, until the gendarme returned with their papers. He explained the issues one by one and how they could not continue their journey for the time being. Under his breath Parker cursed every generation of these military police, but they both listened, heads bowed and humble, nodding at every word the officer said, as if it were the verdict of a jury. Their fates depended on the sympathy they could arouse in their executioner. Parker kept calm and said that if they let them drive on his boss would resolve the problem in twenty-four hours. The soldier lifted up the folder and waved it in the air, saying that was impossible, because they could not find any records relating to a transport firm, let alone its owner. Vehicle and cargo could not be allowed to continue, and must be impounded.

"My boss *is* on the careless side," Parker acknowledged, trying to justify himself.

"Not only your boss, you as well: your permit does not allow you to drive trucks, not to mention the fact that it ran out years ago. And it's best if I do not probe any further," he said, brusquely closing the folder.

Maytén intervened, speaking straight from the heart. "It was all my fault, this gentleman was only helping me get out of a difficult situation."

The military policeman looked at her hard, and compared Maytén's face to the one in her document.

"It looks as if you've now got yourselves into a worse one. If it depended on me, I'd let you drive off, but I can't. The truck must be impounded until the case is taken before a magistrate. Ring your boss and tell him to come ASAP," the soldier advised, and walked back to his office. Just before opening the door, he turned round, looked at Parker and asked him if he was also transporting a house move.

"That is *my* house. It's where I live."

The soldier looked at them askance, and after a moment's hesitation he added he would make an exception and allow them to stay in the truck. Parker and Maytén went back to the cabin, silently wrapped a blanket around themselves and stretched out to sleep. They woke up as the dawn light was casting a yellow tinge on that strange spectacle of the truck and the unit's mobile installations, where the military policemen were drinking maté and warming themselves around a circular campfire. Parker immediately began to set up *their* encampment on the side of the road facing the flatlands; they tied down the canvas awning, and arranged all the furniture available, under the perplexed gaze of the military policemen. Several came over, smiling and making comments, asking questions that Parker sidestepped without even turning round, then they moved away, shaking their heads and concluding hell knows what. Oblivious to their surroundings, Parker and Maytén finished setting up camp with all the comforts at hand, imagining they were in for a long stay, and cooked a sumptuous lunch. Parker ate, his eyes riveted on the vast expanse of steppe, hoping for an answer; Maytén put her knife and fork on the table and shook her head.

"I got you into this mess and I must get you out of it," she said.

"There's nothing you can do. The only really guilty party is wretched old Constanzo. When I see him, I will give him an earful."

"No, Parker, you knew what your situation was, you've been living like this for years, and sooner or later this was bound to happen. And you've been lucky, they might have caught you with a cargo of contraband. You'd have acted the fool again and taken the can for everyone else. Your history is repeating itself," she said. Parker ate, saying nothing, chewing steadily, his eyes lowered.

"Maybe, maybe," he said between mouthfuls. She tried to add something, but he interrupted. He stood up and walked through the encampment looking for inspiration.

"You must carry on to Buenos Aires all the same. I'll stay here," he told Maytén.

"I'm not going to abandon you, and that's not up for discussion."

"In any case, your husband is probably looking for you, it's dangerous to stay marooned here."

"Bruno will have forgotten me and he'll have found someone else by now. Let's work out how we're going to get out of this pickle," she went on, positioning herself behind him. Parker stopped, caressed her hair and suggested they take a walk to clear their heads and sort out their ideas They walked several kilometres along the road, but were soon bored: walking across the steppe made no sense, for the moment. In the afternoon they got into bed, short on ideas, and pulled the blankets over themselves. The wind was getting colder by the day as the sun dipped down. They spent the rest of the day there, whetting the curiosity of the soldiers who made fun of them from a distance.

Next morning Parker had no need to wake up; he'd had a sleepless night. Wrapped in several blankets poncho-style, only his hand with a cigarette visible, he had walked in circles around the encampment, lit up by the ashen moon.

Every so often he walked through the unit and stopped to warm his hands by the fire where the duty guards gathered. They had now accepted the truck as part of the landscape. He took the maté and advice on offer, extracted information about the weather and the state of the roads and joined in their conversations in an attempt to gain their trust: the men might have their uses, and it was not sensible to rub them up the wrong way.

He waited for the sun to appear on the horizon, cooked breakfast and got into bed next to Maytén, warming up his body that had been chilled by the early morning cold. He asked her to wait while he found a way to communicate with old Constanzo and tell him to get them out of this mess. Maytén looked at Parker for a few seconds and repeated that wherever he went, she would follow, even if they had to walk deep into the night and come back whatever the time, whatever the weather. They got a bag ready, secured their encampment, and asked the military police if there was a car that could take them to the next village.

An hour later Maytén and Parker reached a dubious stop-off point in Llanura de los Muertos, where a store and a bar were open. Customers were conversing in low voices and drinking gin at tables and the bar. One of them, an old fellow of indeterminate age sporting a beret on the tilt, pointed to a telephone, half hidden between sacks of rice and yerba maté.

On this occasion, Constanzo seemed sober and lucid.

"I didn't find a replacement, and I don't have time to hit the road, so your holidays will have to wait," he announced when he heard his employee's voice. Parker interrupted before he started to hear whinging he might have to endure for an hour.

"We've got another problem, the military police stopped me," he said, and a stream of coughs and spits echoed in his ear as he gave a brief account of what had happened. Old Constanzo kept coughing, but this time it was simply his way to gain time. Parker repeated his message, exaggerating causes and effects, in case alcohol was befuddling Constanzo's brain. But, for some mysterious reason, his boss was sober, and his voice sounded lucid and sharp.

"I don't believe a single word you are saying," he said in an overbearing, suspicious tone. "The last time you invented some mechanical problem to go somewhere or other with a woman you had picked up. All your problems are excuses to get out of working," the old man told him with another bout of coughs and throat-clearing. When Parker started insulting him, the locals stopped chatting and looked scared, and the bar owner came over to see what was wrong. Maytén tried to calm him down, but he pushed her to one side. That shouting match lasted a few minutes more until Parker ended it with a blow that made the shelves shake.

"You're a bastard," he thundered before hanging up, then remained silent, contemplating the void. The locals resumed their conversations and the bar returned to normal. Parker ordered a slug of gin and downed it in one, then asked for another. They decided to leave as soon as they could to avoid being caught there at nightfall. They paid their bill and went out to face the elements; the blasts of wind almost swept them off their feet. They waited for a car to drive by and take them back to the truck.

"I need to go home," Maytén muttered. Parker looked at her, astonished.

"We no longer have one!"

Maytén took a few steps ahead, stood in front of him, and blocked his way.

"Yes, we do, for the moment."

"But we're stuck there, we can't move."

"Houses don't normally move."

"Do you want us to stay on there, with those extra-terrestrials as our neighbours?"

"You and I are home, not the truck. It's known as home sweet home."

That made Parker think and he gave her an odd look.

"I've never used that expression, 'home sweet home'."

She stared deep into his eyes, reinforcing her presence not only on those byways, but in his life.

"You'll get used to it," she said, and then they walked along the asphalt until the silhouette of the stop-off point disappeared into the distance. After they'd been waiting for an hour, Parker heard the sound of an engine behind him and stopped in the middle of the road, holding his hands up. A car travelling at some speed missed him with a last-minute swerve, honked, then vanished over the horizon. They were still walking an hour later: she, wearily in a straight line, a headscarf around her head, he, sideways or with his back to her, turning backwards and forwards, an unlit cigarette between his lips and his coat collar pulled up.

"I've never walked so far to find a telephone," Maytén said, staring at the horizon, for the sake of saying something, not meaning it as a joke. Parker sighed.

"By now we should be strolling through the city centre," he said.

"Let's forget Buenos Aires and think what we're going to do tomorrow," she said without looking up, walking along, balancing on the tightrope the line along the middle of the road had become.

"Let's forget tomorrow and think where we're going to spend tonight if nobody gives us a lift," he said.

○  ○

Bruno flew across the plains as swiftly as an arrow, leaning over the handlebars to stop the wind hitting him in the face, funnelling it backwards. He was riding with no particular destination in mind, like an animal pursuing its prey. He ignored signposts, and could not have cared less about north or south, the shortcuts or byways, lakes or deserts that were ahead. His engine stuttered when he climbed undulating terrain or hit an invisible wall of wind. He was carrying two drums of fuel that hung down the sides of his bike, a big bottle of drinking water and a bag, and a bundle of blankets and coverlets arranged like a saddle on his seat. His body was sheathed in a cracked leather jacket with a compass and a telescope strapped to it; over one shoulder a haversack, over the other, the Grim Reaper's scythe. Bruno only halted that blind chase to buy supplies or ask for information. Whenever he found trucks parked by hostelries, he left the road and paid a visit, using his bloodhound's nose to sniff out the scent he was after. He whirled in ever tighter circles, like a bird of prey, and peered into each cabin with caution. If truckers reacted aggressively and rebuffed his intrusion with stones and threats, Bruno returned straight-faced to the asphalt and continued his drive to nowhere in particular; if, on the other hand, they were hospitable, he braked and jumped off so his motorbike could recover from all those leagues on the road, as if it were his loyal horse. He walked to stretch his stiff limbs, joined the groups around campfires and enquired if anyone had seen his Maytén. The men looked at him askance, imagining the dramas lurking behind his questions, but his spartan, solitary, fierce aspect inspired respect. That was how Bruno gathered intelligence, some true, some false, but all given in good faith with the aim of pleasing him and sowing seeds of hope in a wandering figure whose face was etched with sadness. One morning he stopped at an encampment of gypsies who, as a result of their nomadic life, knew everything that happened on the steppes. And that was how he discovered that a lorry with a beautiful female passenger had been seen in Sierra Turbia driving towards the coast, and that they had been hauled up in Confluencia for days. Bruno suspected the fugitives were heading for the capital, and realised he had no time to lose if he wanted to catch them before they disappeared into that labyrinth. They told him he should first go to Salina Desolación, two days by motorbike, and then continue along the edge of the salt flats for another, cross the river, climb Sierra Turbia from the south to Pampa del Infierno and then go down to the coast. Bruno added up the days on his fingers and decided he did not have enough time.

"Unless I fly through the sky," he said.

The gypsies felt his unhappiness, and without asking too many questions, because they had already grasped his predicament, they told him that there *was* a way to fly. Bruno looked at them one by one, and believed.

"Crossing the salt flat, though I would not do it. It's very dangerous," an old gypsy said, drawing a map on the ground with his walking stick.

"I'm dead already," Bruno said, and they believed him. They wasted no time and revealed the secret trails across the vast salt lake that they'd used for generations to carry their merchandise before roads existed. It was an immense, white, flat, treacherous area where the sky touched the earth, where there were no paths or tracks or any other form of life except for saltwater geysers. The old gypsy spoke up and began drawing an itinerary on the ground, indicating dry and flooded zones, crossing points between islands, hollows where the stagnant air was polluted and brought on dizziness and mirages.

"If you cross the salt flat this way, you avoid the wet part, but you'll go through the accursed zone and arrive in no time; if you take this other route, you avoid the accursed zone but take much longer; if you get lost, you'll never arrive or return, and I do not intend to come looking," the old man said, pointing his walking stick into his face. Bruno was more determined than ever to defy any danger now only a few hours separated him from Maytén.

"The accursed zone?" he said, but the men glanced at each other and walked away. Only the old man was left.

"The Indians tell a tale I'd better not tell you, because you would not go. They say strange people inhabit that part of the salt flat, and when an outsider shows up, their mouths water. And it's not because of the salt."

"The Trinitarians?" said Bruno, who was familiar with those tales, but the old man raised his chin and threw his head back, completely unmoved.

"I don't know what you're talking about, I'm saying you should avoid the old salt mill, and if someone walks across the salt flat towards you, run in the other direction."

Nonsense, thought Bruno, and refused to listen to any more. He copied the map drawn by the old man onto a sheet of paper, stocked up on water and food, jumped on his bike and set off. He followed a dirt track to the shore of that dead sea, gateway to an immense whiteness you could intuit from afar because it diluted the sky's deep blue into a pale blue. The grey trail he was driving along faded, and Bruno and his bike were a tiny dark dot within absolute emptiness. He consulted his compass and oriented it, following the old gypsy's map; he looked for south-south-west and plunged into the void. He had to follow a straight line, maintain a steady speed, and never veer; the slightest bend might be fatal because there were no points of reference in the depths of Salina Desolación. At any moment, after the first hour, a small grey blotch should appear on the horizon that would eventually become the peak of a remote promontory: the Sierra Turbia. He had to keep to that trajectory, even though compasses, clouds or instinct told him differently. The salt flat finished by the old salt mill on the opposite shore, and the trail that led to Pampa del Infierno would reappear; then he could say he had been lucky. Later, at last, would come Confluencia, and Maytén sequestered in a castle turret.

Bruno straightened his dark goggles and wrapped his whole body so not a single centimetre of skin was exposed to the dart-like rays of the sun. All went smoothly for half an hour, until the first mishap occurred: for a moment he felt his bike was flying through clouds and cumulus. The line of the horizon had disappeared and been replaced by a confused mass of thunder clouds that were reflected on the ground. Clouds and sky above, clouds and sky below and all around, in line with the tales that spoke of potent, evil mirages. He stopped, feeling queasy and dazed – dizziness's dagger stabbing his chest – and that was his first mistake. He realised at that precise moment that he was in the middle of water a few centimetres deep. The up and down sides of the world had transformed into a mirror image, and looking one way or another made no difference. He dismounted, feeling topsy-turvy, and began walking over that distorted mirror. Surrounded by water and sky, up to his ankles in brine, he walked fearfully back to his bike and sat down in an attempt to recover his balance. The world seemed to stabilise, and he felt a kind of relief, his bike was the single fixed point in that vast, shapeless, horizonless expanse that was enveloping and choking him. Although he had lived his entire existence on flatlands, that blind expanse of distance-less space was crushing him underfoot like an insect and shattering all his certainties. No longer sure of his destination, he was forced to continue very slowly, until the deep water compelled him to take to higher ground. And this was his second mistake. He soon realised he was going round in circles, or another fanciful, geometric pattern, and hours later he grasped that they were not circles but spheres: in that hell without up or down, the circular became the spherical, and the whims of geometry, laws. He consulted his compass again, and the grey blotch that should herald Sierra Turbia failed to appear in any direction. He resumed his original orientation, the water still up to his ankles and the sun blistering down, but the horizon continued to be a dead line. Like a car headlight in the night, or rather its opposite, a dark blotch stood out in the midst of total brightness. Sierra Turbia at last, thought a relieved Bruno, turning towards the salvation of a silhouette that had just appeared on the horizon. After pursuing it at length, he realised something was wrong: that faint blotch was taking too long to turn into a crag. He stopped again and surveyed each millimetre of the sphere his blinded eyes allowed him to see. Nothing showed up then or later; the dark shape of Sierra Turbia remained a blotch. An endless amount of time passed, and he soon understood that the shape was narrowing at the bottom, was becoming round and separating out from the horizon before soaring into the heights like a bubble. Sierra Turbia, his only fixed point of reference in three hundred and sixty degrees, was taking to the sky! He shivered when he realised that the promontory he had been chasing for hours was a mere cloud, a mass of volatile gases that now assumed strange shapes, joining other clouds and departing, leaving him alone. He rested his head on his handlebars, and cried for the first time in his life, beside himself, so much so that the water of the salt flat seemed sweet compared to his tears. "It was a cloud, a shitty cloud," he growled, hitting his forehead against the handlebars. He recalled the warm shadows of the ghost train and the protection afforded by its tunnels, the friendly presence of its monsters, its Draculas and Frankensteins, even the Bolivians. He cursed himself for abandoning those certainties and felt the weight of an infinite universe pressing his being into the void. And what if I am dead, he thought, and, still crying, he removed his poncho and the rest of his clothes, which the water of the salt flat swept away. He stood naked under the merciless sun and stumbled towards a dry area, where he stretched out on the rough surface and waited for his body to dissolve into the salt. A supernatural glow surrounded him.

"The Bolivians were right! The light!" he whispered, his strength gone. "I saw the light!" he repeated, crying and laughing, in a sliver of voice that soon vanished into silence.

○ ○

While Bruno liquefied in the light of the salt flat, many kilometres away among the half-buried remnants of the amusement park on the edge of an anonymous hamlet, Eber and Fredy were playing cards in the leaning caravan where they spent their days and nights.

"It's a month since the boss left. What are we going to do now?" Eber bemoaned. Fredy left the caravan, walked between the scattered dummies, walked past the mouth of the tunnel without turning his back on it and headed to the ticket booth that had become a chicken coop. He collected two freshly laid eggs with one hand, and with the other activated the lever that in another era had ignited the ghost train. He knew nothing would happen, but repeated the gesture every day hoping for heavenly help.

"Our Señor has not given us any light today either," he announced.

"Are you an idiot or what?" Eber said, as he did whenever he saw the other Bolivian trying those ridiculous manoeuvres.

"Nothing left to eat either, two eggs today and that's it. We must do something."

Fredy crossed the fairground towards the path leading to the hamlet and disappeared among the houses that looked over the plain. Eber remained, watching him for a good while until he was gone, then he climbed into one of the cars littering the hillside, like salvage boats at the ready before a shipwreck, and sat down to review the panorama. Three days later, while he was dozing on one of the carousel ponies, a strange elongated shape crawled across the hills. Eber opened his eyes and instinctively spurred on his mount: a gypsy caravan comprising an old Fifties truck, several battered vans and ox-drawn carts were approaching the village and climbing the hill where the fairground was marooned. Fredy was travelling in one of the carts with the head of the clan, one of the many that peopled the flatlands. A swarm of men of every age, equipped with the necessary tools, began dismantling every part of the fair, bit by bit. They worked slowly and steadily, carrying things here and there, loading their vehicles with anything they could use – and what they could not, as well. In a few hours the oval Big Wheel was compressed and the Bear Hunt and ghost-train tunnels were reduced to piles of beams, with planks and scrap metal spread all over the ground. Monsters, mummies and dummies lined up on the terrain like fallen soldiers with no names or country. Eber and Fredy took responsibility for loading the corpses into carts and giving them an honourable farewell. They had shared part of their lives with them on the ghost train, from the heyday of the fairground to its decline. The carousel's ambulances, fire engines, tanks of war, pairs of horses, flying saucers, patrol cars and tractors were chained together and dragged off down the hill. Eber and Fredy watched in silence, clutching wads of banknotes as the caravan disappeared across the flatlands. They put all their belongings in the only remaining ghost-train car, walked downhill towards the road, then started walking aimlessly, pulling the car behind them like beasts of burden.

"Hey, what are we going to do with all this?" Eber asked, pointing to the money crammed into their pockets.

"We'll give it to the boss. We'll find him, God willing," Fredy said, panting and pulling the car, from which a forlorn dismembered Frankenstein was watching. They crossed the plains for days without exchanging a single word.

○  ○

"Let's go back to the bar and ask them to let us bed down somewhere," Parker suggested to Maytén when he determined that no vehicle would be passing through there anytime soon. They sat silently on the verge, they had no words left for that day and were only hoping it would end one way or the other, that it would end, for heaven's sake. Parker caressed Maytén's hair and looked at her lingeringly. She stayed still, her eyes closed.

"Someone will help us, good-natured people attract their like," she said ingenuously, and moments later they heard the sound of an engine. The outline of a car coming towards them appeared out of the hills and then, equally quickly, disappeared.

"They won't stop, don't let's waste any more time," Parker said. Maytén sprang to her feet and started gesticulating in the middle of the road. A dingy transit van, decorated with strange signs and symbols, drove slowly by, as stealthily as a ghost ship, and juddered to a halt.

"I told you good people still existed!" Maytén shouted, jumping for joy. The mysterious transit van stopped a few metres in front and stayed put, as they tried to get an idea of the interior and its occupants, but curtains were pulled over the windows. A second later a door opened and a brawny, tattooed hand beckoned them in. They picked up their things and sat side by side on the middle row of seats. The stench of alcohol and ill-digested food hit them. Two massive, ferocious-looking individuals sat in front, and the back row was occupied by two men of similar ilk, who would have been blond if they hadn't been skinheads.

"I've seen this lot before," Parker whispered to a startled Maytén. The transit drove off straightaway, and, as they

282

managed a closer look at their travelling companions, their smiles of gratitude began to fade. Their greetings met with grunts and comments that sounded like dogs barking. Encased in a black T-shirt emblazoned with a Gothic *Deutschland uber alles* gripped by the talons of a two-headed eagle, the driver turned round and studied them, grimacing darkly. A rank belch found its way as best it could between his yellow teeth and combined with other vapours. His companion, another huge guy, his ears dangling hoops and Celtic crosses, did likewise a moment later, and Parker decided that, if this was the welcome cry in the language of these barbarians, he ought to reply in one way or another so as not to seem impolite.

"I don't feel these guys are what you'd call good-natured," Parker whispered in Maytén's ear. She shut him up with an elbow to the ribs and tried to conceal how scared she was. Clad in leather jackets adorned with iron crosses, sharp-pointed studs and death's heads, the four men soon forgot them and went on arguing in a language that had to be German or something similar. They circulated a tattered map that soon made the journey from one end of the van to the other. Each pointed to a spot, then another would snatch it from him and point to somewhere else, and ditto with the next guy. Maytén and Parker watched the map pass under their noses, glanced at each other perplexed, and wondered how they would escape without taking a leap through a window.

"I know where we saw them before!" Parker suddenly remembered, a tad relieved, though not overly so.

"In that horrible town with the submarines?" she asked, amazed anyone could come from so far away to such an insignificant place.

"Barranca Los Monos. They looked lost even then, it must be worse now."

"The journalist won't believe this when I tell him!" Parker said, getting another elbow. Bawling what were no doubt curses, the driver crumpled the map into a ball and threw it out of the window. The four argued at length over places, times and directions in which to head. His companion in the front suddenly turned to Parker, stared at him suspiciously, then uttered a few incomprehensible words that aspired to be Spanish. Parker did not want to seem rude and gesticulated to make it clear he did not understand. The other guy repeated the same words in a sinister tone, ramping up the volume.

"They're lost and want to know where they are," Maytén explained, appealing to common sense rather than her ears. Her words met another flurry of shouts, when one of the guys in the back roared violently at the others. The phrase *Sieg Heil*, tattooed on his forehead, flapped like a flag.

"*Verstanden, verstanden*?" shouted the guy in front.

"What do they mean by that?" she asked anxiously.

"They want to go to Verstanden, it must be one of those German settlements on the cordillera," Parker said.

Parker addressed the two in front by repeating, "*Verstanden, verstanden*," then indicated in a series of gestures that they should keep on as far as Comandante Sagastume, turn right and continue for two and a half days to Verstanden. It was not a genuine route, even if Verstanden existed, but it would mean going past his impounded truck. When the neo-Nazis realised it would be a lengthy drive, they started squabbling, shouting and threatening again. Parker tried to calm tempers, but the guy behind, apparently a Dietrich, pushed him violently back in his seat.

284

"The cordillera's in the other direction," Maytén said, making no sense. "Did you send them this way on purpose, so they would take us to the truck? Knowing it might cost us our lives?"

"They've been lost for weeks, I don't think they'll get their bearings any time soon," he said. Just in case they saw through his lies, he warned Maytén to be prepared to jump ship, but tempers rose and dipped with no logic in that peculiar transit van, and all of a sudden they went quiet. The van drove across the steppe in the last light of dusk, until darkness fell.

"A few more kilometres, and we'll be safe and sound," Parker said, when he noticed that those in the front were commenting suspiciously on what they saw on signposts, but without the map they could not work out where they were heading or discover his deceit. When they were finally approaching the police unit, the arguments resumed, but the sour looks and gestures were now aimed at Parker. At one point, the second guy in the front turned to Parker, looking furious and sounding threatening, but one of those in the back row, the would-be Dietrich, hurled a can of beer that smashed against the windscreen, spilling its contents. The driver braked, throwing everyone forward. Maytén and Parker leapt onto the road like parachutists abandoning an aeroplane in flames, and watched the fisticuffs from a prudent distance, not understanding what it was all about or who was on which side. Punches rained down aimlessly, but concentrated on one man in particular.

"The guy with the tattooed forehead is defending us, the other three want to kill us," Maytén intuited. They would very soon bring him to heel, so they cantered off in the direction of the truck, still several kilometres away. They looked over their shoulders as they ran in case they needed to gallop or dodge a projectile. After a while, the shouting stopped and the transit van drove away into the distance.

"Home at last!" sighed Maytén, as they reached the military police unit and stopped in front of the truck.

"The little we have left," Parker grunted.

"Home is where we are, and as houses do not move, this is more our home than ever," she said as she cooked supper.

The next morning, Parker woke up early after another sleepless night and sat on his armchair to contemplate the dawn, while Maytén slept on under several layers of blanket. He smoked as he focused his thoughts, which had not allowed him a moment's respite the whole night. He went back to bed, tossed and turned, thinking how they might free themselves from the net in which they were trapped. Countless images from the road came to mind, of dying animals hooked on barbed-wire fences, transformed into hides by the dry climate of the steppe. He got up again and walked around the encampment to chase those ominous visions from his mind. He gathered up things scattered by the night winds, and woke up his companion with breakfast ready. While they chatted casually around the table, they failed to notice a human form moving under the truck. Between one sip of coffee and the next, Parker spotted an unusual bulk out of the corner of his eye, and, not saying a thing to Maytén, he calculated where the nearest weapon was. He thought of his pistol, prayed that the military had not requisitioned it, but it was too far away, like his baseball bat, and all he could find to hand was a heavy rock. He put his cup on the table, lifted the stone with both hands, and approached the side of the vehicle, ready to bring it down

286

on the intruder. Maytén saw her companion in that strange stance and sat up, alarmed. Parker gestured to her to keep quiet. He mouthed, "Your husband." She raised a hand to her lips in terror, while he waited with the rock held aloft, but nothing seemed to move under the truck. He waited a few seconds, crouched down and discovered a human body wrapped in a sleeping bag.

"Who goes there?" Parker asked repeatedly. The bulk wriggled out like a worm, and a huge skinhead with a tattoo on his brow drowsily emerged. Parker lowered his weapon, while she tried to decide if she preferred that scary character or Bruno to make an appearance.

"Careful, this guy doesn't like being woken up," advised a tense Maytén. The German opened his eyes, and once he had got used to the daylight, he looked at them and attempted a friendly salute to compensate for his appearance. Then they saw his bruised and battered face.

"*Schlaffen*," he exclaimed from the ground, yawning grossly and contorting his forehead, converting his tattoos' Gothic script into Arabic. *Now he wants to go to Schlaffen*, Parker thought, indicating he should come out from under the truck, and kept hold of his rock. The German emerged with a struggle, dragging a green rucksack behind him. He stood up, shaking off the dust. Parker invited him to sit down at their table, where breakfast leftovers still lay. Maytén followed the scene warily, trying to discover what Parker was up to.

"Won't it be dangerous to eat breakfast with this guy?" she said matter-of-factly.

"He's an unhappy lad who needs some tender loving care."

"If he needs TLC, you're the one to give it," she said, as she boiled up more coffee. Parker did the introductions, while the ravenous German devoured with both hands the slices of bread she served him.

"Dietrich, from Germany," the neo-Nazi said through a stuffed mouth. He stood up, clicked his heels and raised his right arm.

"I've got another idea," Parker said.

She observed him suspiciously.

"I hope it's better than your previous one."

"We're going to adopt this troglodyte, he's exactly what we need," Parker explained, as he shook his hand. She tensed.

"I'd prefer a dog for a pet."

"That is what he is, a guard dog. And a butler."

Dietrich recounted his story, using clumsy gestures and a mixture of English and Spanish. From what they gathered, he and his friends had come from Germany, where they'd been made redundant from an engineering factory. They had decided to use their redundancy pay to buy a transit van and tour this remote part of the planet. They had been driving down to the Strait of Magellan for weeks, but fraudulent handling of the joint fund which paid their expenses had created problems. His comrades had swindled him and wanted to get rid of him, which was why they'd parted ways on a vague pretext, with a beating, leaving him flat broke. Parker said he could stay with them and help them in exchange for meals and a roof over his head. Dietrich's face lit up, and he signed the deal by violently slapping Parker on his back three times with a smile that revealed how many teeth he had lost in fist fights.

"House where?" the neo-Nazi asked, looking around.

"This house," Parker said, pointing to the truck. A disheartened Dietrich contemplated the encampment; it did not fit his idea of a house, and he imagined there must be a misunderstanding.

"You see I'm not the only one?" Maytén said.

She was not convinced by this arrangement. Sharing their table with this man did not appeal at all. She resolved to give him Spanish classes, convinced that words bring people together.

"He's more intelligent than he seems," she said after the first lesson. Parker installed their new helping hand in the back of the vehicle, in a spare bed with a cupboard covered by a tarpaulin and plastic sheeting; later he instructed him to collect firewood and light a fire so Maytén could cook lunch. Then he pointed him to a toolbox and they both worked on top of the lorry for the rest of the morning, under the soldiers' watchful gaze.

They dismantled wooden panels and other parts of the trailer, with which they built a shelter, a table to act as a counter and several shelves, until they had created a roadside stall. An officer soon ambled over, intrigued. Parker was ready for that conversation, he knew the head honcho would appear at any moment to find out what they were plotting. The soldier walked around their construction, his thumbs hooked in his belt, clicking his heels whenever he stopped to inspect a particular detail. Parker invited him to sit down at the table.

"I'd like to remind you that your lorry and cargo are impounded," the man said gruffly, rejecting his invitation. Parker led him to one side and they began walking around the area by the stall, out of sight.

"Officer, they're tropical fruit, mangos and papayas."

"Mangos and . . . ?"

". . . papayas."

"Mangos and papayas . . . Are they edible?"

"Would you like to try one?"

"No, thanks, I'll take your word for it."

"They won't last much longer," Parker said, almost as an oversight.

"It would be a pity if they rotted," the military man agreed, putting a cigarette between his lips and surveying the area. Parker provided a screen with his hand and it lit. As they walked back to the stall, they compared calculations; Maytén observed them from a distance, realising that more numbers than words were tripping out of their mouths. They soon agreed an amount, and sealed their deal with a handshake.

"We can start," Parker said to his companion after a while, when they were eating a stew the German was devouring with relish. That same afternoon, to make the most of the increase in traffic at weekends, Parker and his assistant unloaded boxes of fruit and arranged them tidily on the counter. Then they put up very visible signs advertising the items and their prices, and secured them with sacks of sand. Maytén cut the mangos and papayas in half, emptied out the seeds and stones, sliced them, then filled the fruit again in the style of a tropical platter. By dusk the stall was ready to go. The first three vehicles stopped in front and several people came over, intrigued by that unusual spectacle in the middle of the desert.

"What can you do with that?" they asked, but Parker's spiel did not suffice and he had to give several demonstrations. The sceptical crowd watched him eat slices of fruit, laughed, then turned and walked away.

"Let me do it," Maytén said, and she started to demonstrate, clad in a tight-fitting dress that in its own sweet way underlined the qualities of the tropical fruit.

The following day sales rocketed thanks to truckers and a number of families heading to the coast for the weekend. From then on their business prospered beyond belief, since word went round towns and villages where they had never seen a mango, a papaya or a young woman like Maytén, except in magazines and on TV. Every afternoon, as shadows spread over the unit and the truck, Maytén, Parker and Dietrich, exhausted, raised their glasses around a huge campfire. After midnight, the gendarmes brought along guitars and demijohns of wine, and they ate and sang into the early hours. Dietrich, who contemplated these peculiar rituals attentively, sat on a crate, far from the circle, and tried to assimilate the sounds and gestures he was witnessing, convinced they might be his salvation. Stimulated by the abundant food and alcohol on offer, he soon joined the choir, imitating their songs by using the few words available to him.

Owing to the mysterious whims of the roads that regulated the movement of men and animals, the unusual traffic kept increasing, forcing the gendarmerie to double shifts and controls. Dozens of cars and trucks parked on either side of the road waiting for permission to leave. Documentation and merchandise were inspected as if it was an international crossing, even though it was only a provisional, internal frontier, a division that divided nothing, a transition point between two areas that were exactly the same. That absurd boundary obeyed a caprice of nature and pushed human fauna from one side to the other of its simple existence.

A week later, Parker, Dietrich and Maytén had sold every single box of fruit. A new officer in charge of the detachment banned partying, in order to preserve an appearance of seriousness, although Parker continued to hand over the agreed amount, which was then shared out between the rest of the squadron. The night-time gatherings fell off until they disappeared altogether. After the tropical fruit, Parker began to sell everything he had accumulated over the years in the truck's vast hold, mainly the old things: antiques and objects he no longer used. News soon spread across the steppe, and the fame of that itinerant roadside stall spread far and wide. Weeks later the moribund truck had been transformed into an open-air market selling baubles and curiosities. Tourists, idlers and collectors kept coming, drawn by word of mouth. Parker and Maytén toiled from dawn till dusk with Dietrich, who removed the earth and sand that threatened to bury the encampment, now that autumn winds were gusting and the weather was becoming increasingly severe. Parker knew that unexpected renown would be short-lived, and might bring an unwelcome surprise; it was no longer a safe place for Maytén, however close they were to law and order.

Everything that moved in those barren wastes obeyed a pre-set rhythm, the might of an earth that was impossible to control. The animals of the steppe, the birds and the gendarmes followed their own migratory patterns, like labourers, gypsies and commercial reps. Some routes were mysteriously abandoned from one day to the next; human and animal currents changed direction and aimed for other latitudes. All that was easy to register, but impossible to forecast: when those mutations happened, they just happened, end of story. The winds went crazy. The north wind, carrying earth and hot dust, spread into the domain of the wind from the pampas, which defended its territory by generating areas of low pressure that changed the mood of everything moving on the plains; then hurricanes arrived with oceanic rage from the high seas, turning on themselves, generating spirals of water that hit dry land with the full force of their weight. Soon, nothing and nobody would travel those heaths; a freezing night would descend as easily as frost, and even the military detachment would be transferred to other districts. Even so, they still could not imagine what would become of them, what surprises that joker nature held in store.

o   o

Parker's encampment gradually degenerated into a precarious slum, covered with tarpaulins, shiny plastic sheets and wooden panels that shook and rattled. Sand had piled up against the sides of the truck and empty fruit boxes that had not been hacked into firewood were scattered all around. On one of those mornings when gales pounded relentlessly, several trucks waited their turn opposite the detachment, their sidelights flashing. While the military controlled the traffic, Dietrich and Parker nailed down panels that were threatening to blow away. They protected their eyes with spectacles they had improvised from bits of plastic, or by putting canvas bags over their heads. A blurred silhouette emerged from the dust cloud, crossed the road, circled the truck and walked slowly towards them, carrying a heavy sack on its shoulders. Maytén was the first to see that stranger approaching, and felt paralysed for a second. That was one way Bruno might appear. It wasn't the first time she had imagined a similar situation, and of all the reactions she had rehearsed, a cry of alarm was the only one she could manage. This time her scream froze in her throat as the silhouette closed in on Parker from behind. When she got over her shock and let out a cry it was too late, the intruder was practically on top of Parker, who could only swing round. The silhouette fell on him, arms spread-eagled as if taking a dive. Parker stepped back as fast as a bolt of lightning, and his hands searched for a stick he'd seen a moment before, but they found nothing. He could only turn and jump on his aggressor and try to neutralise the onslaught, and both men rolled on the ground while Maytén screamed a second time.

"What are you doing, you pesky so-and-so? Are you mad?" panted the silhouette breathlessly, as they rolled over the sharp pebbles. Parker immediately recognised the journalist's voice, helped him to his feet and justified his reaction.

"Is that any way to show your face? I mistook you for someone else, and that's the second time," he said.

The journalist replied gruffly, as he shook the dust from his overcoat, "I only wanted to give you a surprise. I was going to ask you how things are, but no need to do that now."

Maytén was still petrified, about to emit her third scream, her hands over her mouth. When she saw it was the journalist, she waved to him, and both were soon chatting on the settee.

"I see you are prospering. This time it was easy to track you down, everyone everywhere is talking about this place, but nobody mentions you, it's all about this young lady," the journalist said, raising his glass. Parker poured out a round of wine and let a few minutes pass before continuing, then nodded towards the gendarmes.

"It looks as though we'll be staying here a while."

"Don't be so cruel. You're surely not going to let such a flower wither in this cruel desert?" the journalist said, his eyes glued to Maytén.

"These guys won't let me go."

"This lot? I know them to a man. If you like, I can talk to their chief."

Dietrich appeared carrying a large platter of fried eggs and roast meat he put down clumsily on the table. The journalist eyed him up.

"This is Dietrich, my assistant. I think he might be of interest to you."

"So you've got yourself a butler?" he said as Dietrich set the table and served the food.

"Pleased to meet you," the neo-Nazi stammered. The journalist greeted him with a firm handshake, trying to guess how this character had landed there. Then he stood up and studied the Gothic letters on his forehead.

"A real Nazi, like the ones you're always hunting," Parker said proudly. The journalist sat down again, disappointed, and they started eating.

"These are the new Nazis! Things have really gone downhill. They only dress like that to frighten off blacks. Did you buy him as a memento of those submarine celebrations?"

"We found him abandoned on the roadside. Now there's a good story, I'll lend it you for a news scoop. In exchange you must help me out."

The journalist put down his glass of wine and looked at the German, who was now stuffing in one mouthful after another, seated on an empty crate.

"I've lost interest in submarine stories, they're invented by people with nothing better to do," the journalist said as he extracted several folders crammed with manuscripts from his bag.

"Years of research dumped in the rubbish, so someone can come along and make a film or write an absurd novel about Nazis in Patagonia," he snarled, launching the folders into the sky, sending sheets of paper flying everywhere.

"Nobody ever came to the south, and now it's full of tourists. German submarines! You have to be deluded!" he added.

"So what are you going to do now?" Maytén asked, tying a scarf around her head to keep the dust at bay.

"Writing's a tricky illness. Do you know what the only cure is?"

Parker and Maytén said nothing, anticipating his reply, but the journalist paused for effect.

"The only cure is to keep writing."

"There you go, more senseless word games! Keep trying the Martians," Parker said.

"That's a fool's game. Have you heard of the sea monster living in a lake in the cordillera?" he mumbled, making sure no-one else could hear.

"A sea monster?" she exclaimed, enthused and leaning over the better to follow the story. Parker sighed when he saw how easily the unworldly Maytén was attracted by such madness. He tried to return to the previous subject, but she would not give up.

"So what did you discover?"

"That you are more beautiful by the day."

"Hey, don't you start," Parker warned, but Maytén shut him up.

"I can't reveal any of my findings, but the moment I publish my book, I'll give you a copy, signed and dedicated."

She was discouraged for a moment, but was excited by the idea that someone might give her a book with a personal dedication.

"By the way . . ." the journalist said, taking a sheaf of papers and identity cards from his bag and offering them to Parker.

"They came too late, journo, I don't need them anymore."

"They're no use in your present life, but in your next one, which may be tomorrow, you'll need them."

Parker took the documents and spread them out like a fan. Maytén wanted to know where the journalist was heading.

"I never know where I am going, but it's very likely I'll want to shake off the dust from these byways in Buenos Aires. Not this dust, but the dust that sticks inside you. It would be my pleasure if you consented to accompany me."

"I told you not to start on that," Parker warned him again. Maytén leaned back in her chair, and murmured: "I'm going nowhere without Parker."

"That's what you call love, quite the best disease to catch."

"Love can never be a disease," she said sternly, challenging him with an icy gaze.

The journalist talked, eating all the while. "If it's not a disease, it's not love. Do you know what the only cure is? To keep loving."

"Now he's starting to try his hand as a poet. Take no notice," Parker said.

"Poetry is the worst of all evils."

"Do they pay you to pen these clichés, or do you do it gratis?"

"Don't argue!" she shouted, as she went off to boil up some coffee. Parker took the opportunity to whisper to his friend.

"I need a favour, you can have the German in exchange. He's good at pushing vehicles, if you have a breakdown."

"That grotesque guy? No, thanks. He doesn't seem at all reliable."

"He's tame and doesn't bite, he can fish too, and might help you catch that monster you're looking for."

"I'll help in any way I can, but you keep him, you need a bodyguard. On the road they say the girl's husband is driving around."

Parker was about to divulge what the favour was, but Maytén's footsteps forced him to break off.

"What secrets are you telling each other?" she said.

The journalist said: "We were talking about how beautiful you are."

Maytén glanced at them suspiciously, making it clear she was not going to be put off so easily. She decided not to ask for explanations, as she'd seen a stream of vehicles pull up by the stall. Traffic had increased that afternoon, and it was a chance they could not miss, so they went back to sell off the few remaining items. Having got their permission, the journalist went to talk to the man responsible for the soldiers, his old acquaintance, to find out Parker's exact situation. He soon returned and took his friend for a walk far from the truck, where they could converse without being interrupted. Distant thunderclaps from over the horizon resounded like the fury of a battle. Both stood and watched the black clouds stampeding across the sky, a deluge in the making. The journalist waited for a second, then continued talking.

"The head honcho told me there's nothing he can do. The problem's not just the truck, it's you as well. There's a warrant out for your arrest."

"Things are getting interesting," a pensive Parker replied. Part of him was expecting that piece of news. In the distance, the truck's motionless silhouette disappeared and reappeared under the hurricane gusts of dust and bracken. While they chatted, sheets of paper from the folders flew by like butterflies before fluttering out of sight. The journalist was untroubled by that paper chase, in fact, he seemed to enjoy it.

Parker went on: "I can't even escape in one of your submarines."

"Those soldiers owe me a few favours, and I did a deal with them. They will act as if they've not seen you, but you'll have to leave anyway, they're soon going to up and off, and this place will be snowed under in a few weeks."

"I've got to move on yet again?"

"That way you'll keep fit," the journalist said, animated by a breeze no longer laden with dust, but with shafts of icy cold that bit deep into his body. "Would you let me write your story?"

"I'm the only one who writes my story."

"I don't think you've got time, even if you knew how to. You have to escape her husband's clutches, he's dangerous."

"Another one looking for tender loving care," Parker said.

"Your truck and mobile greengrocer's have attracted people's attention."

"The flatlands are massive."

"They may be massive, but there are very few humans, and the winds impel them into the most unexpected places."

"Will you or won't you help me?"

"My only weapons are words, and her husband's armour will be sturdy enough to withstand that kind of weapon."

"That's why I have my bodyguard. But it's about her, I don't want her to continue living this kind of life."

"Are you making me a present of her? I would prefer her to the German."

Parker and the journalist went on conversing, head to head, in the open with the elements, against a backdrop of clouds shifting over the undulating plain. They agreed and disagreed through signs and gestures, and when their plan was fully fledged they returned to the encampment where Maytén was anxiously waiting.

"You two still plotting?" she said suspiciously, intuiting mischief afoot, and without waiting for an answer, she handed Parker a wad of banknotes she had extracted from her overcoat. Parker took the money and put it with the rest of the takings from those days, a big unwieldy bundle of dog-eared notes he kept in a cardboard box. The journalist reacted to a gesture from Parker and made an excuse to leave, so they could be alone. Parker and Maytén now faced up to each other.

"I don't think I can go back to the capital, and I no longer have the little I had to offer you. You ought to go your own way. You're under no obligation to stay with me," Parker said, trying to close the box. She looked at him, understood nothing, and could not take what he was saying seriously.

"Let's abandon all this and go anywhere. This isn't the only life there is, there are many more."

"I think I've used them all up."

"Let's stay here then. Let's convert the truck into a food stall, we've done very well so far," she said, pointing to their money box. Parker sensed he was at a crossroads in life where there were no correct or incorrect decisions. He was sure of this much: he had never become the source of Maytén's frustration, nor would he allow her to sacrifice her own ambitions to the little he had to offer.

"Take a look, you're surrounded by wretched poverty you don't deserve. This is *my* territory, but it's a living death for you, it makes no sense for your youth to wither here, you should go to Buenos Aires and wait for me there."

"I no longer hanker after that. I'm going nowhere without you, these separations always end badly. There'll be time to go to the capital, if not this winter, then the next, when everything's sorted," she replied, as the storm approached and the sunbeams disappeared behind the clouds.

Parker looked at her for several minutes. He could wait no longer; time was pressing and they had to reach an agreement now. He could not be sincere: any sincerity would degenerate into deception. Maytén could ruin her own future by clinging to blind conviction, and to avoid that, he must lie, even though he would regret it for the rest of his days. He found it hard to look her in the eye as he spoke; it was a real struggle. He realised that moment was the end of that phase in their lives; it was almost a stroke of good fortune they had been brought to a halt there, but they could not continue like that. The illusion of bliss they had concocted might be a delusion to overcome the lack of horizons that lay beyond the truck. Immobilised in the middle of the steppe, ambushed by gale-force winds piling sand along its sides, that vehicle was already a rigid dividing line.

Parker plucked up courage and suggested she take advantage of the journalist's trip to the capital; he was someone she could trust and he could drop her at the house of his friends, who were still expecting them. He assured her she would be able to stay there as long as necessary until they could meet up and continue their life together, wherever. A stab of pain in his throat made him wince when he saw her so silent and submissive, alone in the middle of that accursed landscape that swallowed people up and spat them out like figures without substance. Maytén looked blankly at him, as she listened with resignation to his words that were like prison sentences.

"No, no," she whispered.

Parker pointed to the leaden sky where clouds were running amok like an unleashed flock of sheep; he reminded her that very soon snow and the cold would make those heaths uninhabitable, and the wind would be a razor slicing through everything that got in its way. Half of the roads would be rendered impassable by rivers bursting their banks, the terrain would become a constant stream of mud that would fissure under the frost, days would shorten and they would be living in the pitch-black for months. But Maytén knew such times better than anybody; she had been born and bred there. She was not frightened by the climate, the solitude or the penury caused by that merciless life, and even less by the idea of renouncing what she had wanted all her life, her childhood dream: to live in a real city. The only thing tearing *her* heart to shreds was the idea that she would never see Parker again.

"No, no," she said several times, on the verge of tears, but Parker was unmoved.

"When will we meet again?" she said.

"Soon," Parker replied. Reluctantly Maytén accepted Parker's arguments and his suggestion that they should separate for a while. She told him she trusted his word, that she would look for work and wait for him as long as was necessary. Parker saw his mean lies had hit the bullseye, and felt a second stab of pain in his chest. He started collecting the banknotes piled inside the box, made a wad and handed it to her, but she refused it, not giving it a second thought.

"You'll need it more than I ever will," she said. She knew what her companion was like; if she accepted that money, she ran the risk of never seeing him again.

While they planned their future, a violent curtain of wind lashed them, and from then on their main worry was securing the tarpaulins, plastic sheeting and panels, which looked like the sails of a ship gone crazy. Dietrich and the journalist held down the structure of the camp with huge rocks as rainwater cascaded from every direction, sluicing down and forming puddles. Maytén was shivering from the cold and wrapped Parker's overcoat around her while the journalist collected up some manuscripts and tossed others into the rain.

"I must leave before we sink into the mud and the roads are flooded, this downpour augurs nothing good for the next few days," he said, collecting up his things. He looked at Parker questioningly, as if awaiting his orders.

"Can you take Maytén to the capital?" he said, a question he had formulated several hours earlier. A silent Maytén hid her tears with a smile, went to the cabin and began to pack her bag. Once again she must place all her life in a tiny space. Once she was ready, she and Parker embraced at length; each felt the other's body tremble. At the moment of separation, Maytén and Parker were no longer the same people; nobody could imagine what would happen from then on. Whatever that was no longer depended on them; the shadow of destiny had come between them. What remained to be done took a few minutes that seemed like hours: Parker and the journalist shared a goodbye hand-shake and a vague promise that they would meet up again in a specific location between two dots on a map. Maytén and Parker moved like a single body as he loaded her baggage. She made herself comfortable in her seat, smiled transparently, and the car slid off into the distance along the shiny ribbon of asphalt and vanished behind curtains of water. Parker observed that final scene from the middle of the road as rainwater streamed down his hair, hoping there would be some other outcome, but the dice were cast and nothing else could happen now. After a while he started to walk around the truck in circles, increasing the radius each time. A growing spiral was pushing him into the dark heart of those elements; water poured off him. He imagined he was crying, but couldn't be sure whether it was tears or rain cascading down his cheeks.

○  ○

Bruno heard voices around him that sounded like angels or celestial beings. His whole existence was swathed in blinding light. He tried to open his eyes, but was stopped by sudden fear. Where was he? Was that famous death, without monsters, skulls or scythes? In his delirium all he could remember was a white cloud engulfing and liquefying him in a state of serenity he had never before experienced. He feared he might be in the same supernatural kingdom that was home to the inhabitants of the ghost train. When he succeeded in opening his eyes, they met the muted glow of the salt flat, that ocean of life where he had lost his way because of the gypsies. Those voices rang out ever more clearly, but he could not understand what they were saying. "The light!" he recalled. That, whatever *that* was, involved God, perhaps the Bolivians weren't so wrong. He had finally found it! He had lived his whole life in darkness! He pinched his body to check he was physically there and saw he was stretched out on a bed under a straw roof, being observed by two peculiar characters who wore dark glasses, whose heads and bodies were clothed in rags.

"Who art thou and what dost thou in these parts, stranger?" said one of those individuals with an accent that was new to Bruno. It was like another language, but one pronounced in such a way that he understood every word. He sat up in a state of wonder; only God could speak like that.

"My Lord, I am Bruno, your son. Finally, I can see You," he said, tears in his eyes, while those uncouth creatures walked around him and eyed him sceptically.

"Thou shouldst know a miracle has spared thee from death. We found thee and have returned thee to the kingdom of the living," said one, slavering and relishing the fleshiest parts of his body.

"Thank You, my Lord!" said Bruno, bringing together the palms of his hands.

The second individual, who was heating water via a set of mirrors that multiplied the impact of the sun's rays on a huge cooking pot, told the first: "You see, my liege, this man is mad; he's had so much sun it has fried his brains."

"Offer him a maté while we wait for the water to boil, and see if he recovers his reason," he ordered, then he directed some ancient prayers to the heavens, and added: "Providence has remembered us and sent us our daily bread. Blessed be our forebears!"

When they offered him a maté and a handful of fried patties, Bruno sucked hard on the tube and his body shook nauseously. He spat out several times, but he could not get rid of the foul taste of brine burning his mouth: the maté was made with water from the salt flat.

"It grieves me that it is not to thy liking, for it is all we have," the man apologised, helping him to his feet. Bruno saw he was inside a hut with walls of salt and a thatched roof of sorts. On one side were small mounds, blocks and sacks of salt, on the other several symmetrical rows of bowls of blue crystalline water. He realised he was on one of the shores of Salar Desesperación, in a shelter used by workers from the old salt mill, who had found him half-dead after he had lain unconscious for a couple of days.

Bruno began to remember who he was, what he was doing there, and, most importantly, what his destination had been. His bike and baggage were leaning intact against a wall. He threw himself on his bag and looked desperately for the bottle of fresh water, which he drank breathlessly, under the astonished gaze of the men. The image of Maytén appeared like a flash of lightning, rather blurry now, without the sharp outline he recalled from the moment when she left him. The dark mass of Sierra Turbia finally rose up before him in the midst of all that light. The memory of his mission and his rage at the humiliation he had suffered restored his lucidity and the strength necessary to continue. He thanked his saviours as he revved his bike, and they watched him prepare to depart, hugely disappointed.

306

"Stay with us, good sir, we are honest folk and will keep thee company. Thou can trust in our good selves," one of them said forthrightly, but Bruno was no longer listening.

"God speed, and may good fortune go with thee," said one of the miners, resigned, his eyes watering as he waved goodbye. Then he went over to the cooking pot where the water was beginning to boil and poured it out, letting it melt back into the salt. They no longer needed it.

"May thou reach the heights of good fortune in thy expedition," said the other man, and both stood and watched Bruno's motorbike fragment in a series of reflections and vanish in the pristine void of the salt flat.

"I swear to God we have let another prey escape, and my mouth was verily watering," said one, gloomily.

"Dost thou think we did what was right? We are not what we were, we should have forced him to stay."

"Heaven alone knows when we shall see human flesh again."

"If we abide by these codes of chivalry, we'll be damned to fasting for centuries to come," sighed the other, as he gulped down the maté Bruno had left half-drunk.

Weak, thin and haggard, his skin scorched by the sun, Bruno was back on the road in pursuit of his beloved. He had succeeded in escaping from Salar Desesperación and saved hours of biking by using his bloodhound scent as he traversed the steppe, looking for clues on every bend of the road. The following afternoon he found two trucks parked on the verge. He slowed down and drove around several times, sizing up the situation. Bemused, Julio and Juan watched him encircle them and recognised the owner of the amusement park, whose plight was now common knowledge throughout the region. They did not need that distraught spectre with a vacant gaze to tell them what he was looking for. Bruno stopped his bike and the two truckers smirked at each other and invited him to lunch: it was time to settle accounts with Parker. They could forgive him the number of times he'd made fun of them, when he had locked them in a service-station bathroom or peed in their drinking water, but not his outrageous conquest of Maytén's love. Gossip had informed them of the exact location of Parker and his vehicle, marooned in the neighbourhood of Confluencia or Cerro Caído, news that had spread through half of Patagonia; all they had to do now was tell distraught Bruno the quickest way to get there. To goad him on, they pretended to know nothing about his situation and told him Parker was living with a beautiful young woman, one of the prettiest in the south, by the name of Maytén, and then waited for Bruno's mouth to foam. But Bruno had lost the faith that ignited his longing for revenge, and nodded witlessly at whatever they said or advised. Every now and then, between one mouthful and the next, he grunted and dropped his jaw, deaf to the innuendo and double-entendres which they hoped would incite him. He stopped eating, put his goggles and helmet back on and disappeared into the distance on his motorbike.

After days of riding in the rain, enveloped in a cloud of water, Bruno zipped past the car in which Maytén and the journalist were driving towards the capital. His blurry eyes behind his goggles saw only dots and lines on the horizon.

She was travelling, mind in a distant place, leaning back on her seat, eyes closed, cast down by aching grief the promise of a future rendezvous could not heal. Even if the journalist had not previously seen the biker pass by, given the direction he was zooming, he imagined that relentless rocket had one goal in its sights and might very well be who he thought he was. He calculated it would take him a day to reach his target, and was minded to warn Maytén, but stopped himself in time. She opened her eyes and saw the journalist's startled expression as he looked in the mirror.

"What's wrong?" she said as she sat up, fearing the worst.

"Nothing, go back to sleep."

In the meantime, a day away, Parker and Dietrich were working nonstop selling off everything of any value. From the night after Maytén's departure, Parker had continued to walk in circles until the early morning, smoking and drinking whisky. He was mentally embroiled, wrapped in a shabby raincoat that made him look like a gumshoe out of a black and white noir. The military had been dismantling their unit for some days, and the contingent had been reduced to a few men under orders to close it down the moment the instruction came. The radio repeatedly forecast that the rains would continue and be more intense this year, so a large operation was underway to evacuate and assist the affected communities.

While Dietrich, his faithful pet, slept at the foot of his bed wrapped in blankets and strips of canvas, Parker checked the ropes and weights securing the awnings that sluiced off a steady waterfall. He got into bed, ignoring his butler's snores. Snug in his sleeping bag, he selected one of the many books abandoned in the cabin's crannies and tried to distract himself, but to no avail: the image of Maytén greeting him with a wave and saddened eyes blotted out everything else. He could still feel her trembling body from their last embrace. When Dietrich's snoring became unbearable,

309

however much he kicked the shapeless bulk at the end of his bed, bad temper flavoured the sadness of separation. Later on, while the German struggled with the puddles and streams of mud snaking across the encampment, Parker searched every corner of the lorry for his personal belongings, and everything he had salvaged from his previous life. He wanted to rid himself of those relics. Dietrich helped him arrange every item on the almost empty counter, then he set down his sax, the pistol the journalist had given him to defend himself, the sextants and astrolabe, a collection of long-forgotten pipes and all the books he could find. At some point Parker picked up the pistol, inspected it for a few seconds, assessing how useful it might be, and removed it from the counter. The old fruit stall had been transformed into an antique and second-hand goods market: suitcases of clothes, paintings, blankets, tools, the plastic stag's head – still wrapped in cellophane – that he had won on Maytén's stall, the remnants of a life he had lost that now seemed to be somebody else's. Dietrich had also put part of his life up for sale: his collection of war souvenirs, epaulettes with insignia of rank, imitation iron crosses, his passport and fascist organisation membership cards. On this occasion, their pop-up market was more successful: given the prospect of the imminent flooding of roads, the traffic of evacuees grew exponentially. Long queues of vehicles stopped to ask for information on the roads and before continuing their journey nosey passengers visited the market in search of bargains. Dietrich hawked his goods in his language, probably a pointless exercise, but it added an exotic touch to the proceedings. It took Parker very few days to rid himself of almost all his furniture, plus the crane he used to set up camp and his tools, and finally he gathered up the items

310

nobody would buy and threw them into a tin drum where bits of wood, paper and rags were already burning.

At that precise moment, only a few kilometres away, Bruno was bent over his bike, hurtling along, defying the wind, his baggage strapped down and the scythe over his back. He reached the vicinity of the military control point just before nightfall and spotted Parker's truck, barely lit up by the flames of a campfire. His legs shook at the prospect of an imminent encounter with the wayward Maytén, but before blindly rushing in, he accelerated to the max, climbed to the top of a nearby hill and studied all activity below through his telescope. He thought that the vehicle he had been chasing for so long, stripped of its wheels, half-dismantled, engine top and doors open, now seemed more like an animal's carcass being devoured by ants. When the cars that had stopped at the stall and the few remaining gendarmes had taken shelter in their caravans, Bruno left his baggage, grasped the scythe and strode downhill, half-hidden by the shadows. He felt no emotion, imagining he had already carried out several times what he was about to do, that turning up in that spot was a mere formality. As he approached, crouching like a wild animal, Parker and Dietrich were counting and sorting bundles of tattered banknotes by the light of the fire. Both heard steps on the stony ground, but the glare from the flames prevented them from seeing if it was a drunken gendarme who had lost his way, or a night-time animal looking for leftovers. Parker repeatedly asked who was there, lit a torch and held it aloft to light up the terrain. First he saw a stooped bulk moving forwards, then he recognised Bruno's thin, emaciated face furrowed by wrinkles and the cruel weather.

"Where's my wife?" Bruno said, flourishing his scythe.

Parker allowed him to come closer, and gestured to Dietrich not to intervene.

"You are too late, my friend, she's gone," he said casually, pitying that defeated, lonely man, then he looked away and continued feeding the fire in the drum. Bruno searched for a trace of Maytén, and for several minutes the three of them froze in the vastness of the Patagonian night. Dietrich, who did not really understand what was happening but sensed the threat, crossed his arms and puffed out his chest, defending his master with the zeal of a guard dog.

"What have you done with Maytén, you bastard? She's my wife and you stole her from me."

"Maytén's gone, and she's not coming back."

"It was all your fault," Bruno moaned, and his tears melted into the dust from the road on his face.

"She wasn't happy in that life. Maytén has gone, whether you like it or not," Parker said, throwing more items on the fire.

"You have to be an idiot to let a woman get away," Bruno shouted, and when he saw Parker was about to throw the mud-spattered teddy bear on the flames, he attacked him in a rage. He managed to land a punch on his nose before either he or Dietrich could react. The furry animal flew into the air, Bruno stretched out his hands to try to catch it, but couldn't stop it falling on the fire and going up in smoke in seconds. A brawny arm tattooed with Gothic script grabbed Bruno by the neck and knocked him to the ground, howling in a language that sounded like the devil's. After a brief skirmish, Dietrich disarmed the raving Bruno and easily brought him to heel, though he could not prevent him from grabbing Parker's pistol when he momentarily dropped his guard. Bruno examined it briefly, and, convinced that Providence

312

had placed it in his hand, he aimed at Parker's face. The three of them once again froze beneath the starry vault.

"I should have killed you before, it makes no sense now," Bruno said, pointing the pistol towards the sky and pulling the trigger. First came a boom, then a few seconds later there formed above them a huge halo of light that chased darkness away as the ground was illuminated by the bluish glow from the flare, which descended slowly like a supernatural force, projecting strange shadows over the steppe. Parker remembered that the journalist's weapon was not a firearm but a flares pistol, while Bruno observed the glow over his head in ecstasy.

"The light! I have seen the light again!" he said, falling to his knees. It was the second time this had happened in the space of a week, after a lifetime of living in the darkness of indifference. He imagined that divine brightness brought another message from heaven he could not continue to ignore. He forgot his humiliation, the disintegration of his life, and blessed the Bolivians, asking them to forgive him for not listening when they spoke. A wave of hope coursed through his body, lighting up every corner of his sombre consciousness. Dazed by that ecstatic epiphany, he let hallowed good fortune sweep him off his feet, and blacked out yet again.

Parker and Dietrich collected a series of ropes and tied Bruno, sunk in mystical ravings, tightly to the side of the truck. Hours later, the early morning found them roasting strips of flesh on a wire over the fire, while a bottle of wine passed from mouth to mouth. Parker untied Bruno, sure that he no longer presented a threat, and after a while the trio were drinking and eating in silence. When they finished the last strip of meat and there were no more bottles left to open, Parker climbed into the cabin with his sleeping bag. Dietrich and Bruno bedded down by the fire wrapped in canvas and blankets, protecting themselves with the little they had from the rain that was resuming its onslaught. The following day they heard on the radio that rivers in the region had broken their banks and flooded most roads. The military detachment had disappeared, the last soldiers had towed away the caravans, leaving in their place the smoking embers of their final campfires. Several signs in the middle of the road, now blocked by rocks, tree trunks and posts, warned travellers that they could not continue northwards. The whole region had been split down the middle, dramatically fissured from east to west. The few drivers that reached that place alighted, impotently waved their fists, surveyed the scene, and went back the way they had come.

○  ○

Maytén opened her eyes and the first thing she saw was the steamed-up, rain-spattered window. She sat up and tidied the stray hair from her face so she could see where she was. She had to lower the window, and the water blowing in created strange shapes from the layers of dust stuck to the seat that seemed to belong to different geological eras. Outside, the rain-soaked landscape spread towards the rest of the universe. She shifted in her seat and with each move dry dust flew up like a cloud of insects. By her side, the journalist hummed tangos in step with the rhythm of the windscreen wipers. Maytén yawned, discarded her blankets, and was greeted by the journalist whose bloodshot eyes betrayed hours of night-time driving. Maytén stared at him, at a loss to explain what she was doing in that vehicle with that man, and tried to find out the time and how long it would take to their destination, but he wouldn't give her a straight answer. She could only think about reaching the capital and counting the days to her reunion with Parker, whether it took weeks or months. However, that morning she had woken up thinking she was doing something ridiculous. It was possible Parker would keep his word and meet up with her as soon as he had resolved his issues, but he might also have just been easing her gently out of his life. There were moments in the day when she trusted him, and others when things lost all meaning. And what if it were a game both were playing, a deception both were complicit in, to end a situation that had no possible solution? The lines their destinies were following had touched for a moment, then ceased to follow the same signals. Words of love and promises no longer mattered; their lives were moving apart with every minute that went by. Maytén asked repeatedly where they were, moving anxiously in her seat, but was never satisfied by his evasive replies. It distressed her to hear him chattering about their progress, which he did only to distract her, and she soon stopped listening. According to the journalist, they might reach their destination in a few days if the state of the roads allowed them, but the radio kept warning of rivers overflowing their banks on all roads and they were forced to keep turning off and changing roads to make any headway. She listened to him attentively, though in her heart of hearts she was weighing up other options.

"What's the next town?" she said, gazing at the mud-spattered windows. The journalist's voice and presence seemed increasingly tedious.

"Maybe Salto Viejo, maybe Monte Colonia, maybe none in these barren wastes. We can take nothing for granted."

"Your jokes do not amuse me. Drop me off in the first place we come to."

"Who said I was joking?"

"I'm not going any further with you."

"I wouldn't advise that, there's no way back now, and if we don't cross the Río Grande in time, we could be trapped," the journalist told her, leaning towards the windscreen to get a better view of the road ahead.

"I'm not crossing any river. I want to go back to Parker's truck," she insisted. The journalist glanced at her, gravely.

"To do that you'd have to cross the Río Blanco, and it has just burst its banks. The Blanco is worse than the Grande when it loses its temper."

Maytén gathered up her belongings and said nothing, holding her bag, ready to jump off at any moment. After they'd driven through a small cluster of houses, she lowered her window to examine the place, but a watery gust forced her to shut it.

"Please leave me here. There's bound to be a bus."

"There's nothing here."

"A place to eat then."

"I told you, there's nothing here. Further down the road we have to fill up with petrol, and there might be food as well," the journalist said, turning the steering wheel sharply to avoid a puddle. Every so often the vehicle lost speed, held back by the force of the water; it would take off from the ground for a few seconds and seem lighter. Then it slid slightly to the side before stabilising. Maytén was terrified and gripped the dashboard while the journalist tried to recover control. They drove for several hours along roads that were filling up with vehicles heading in the same direction.

"There must be a reason why people are going this way. In these situations you go where others are going, or put your life at risk," the journalist said. Maytén inexplicably resented this man. She suspected that she had fallen into a trap in which he'd played a part. She suspected the abrupt way she had had to separate from Parker was proof of a plot.

"I've been driving through these areas for years, and it can take the rivers weeks to return to normal and months for the roads to be repaired."

"Don't think you're such an expert," she said in irritation, and turned to look out of the window. The temperature seemed to lower from one minute to the next, a cold draught invaded the cabin, and the journalist, who was shivering, moved the heating lever several times, but a cloud of dust came out of the vents and triggered a coughing fit. She looked for an overcoat on the back seat, and, as she moved folders, papers and piles of clothes and blankets, she glimpsed the box where Parker kept the money they'd earned. What was that money doing in the hands of the journalist?

Maytén asked for an explanation, but he was taken by surprise, stammered and could not find the words to explain. She stared at him, waiting for a response, but she'd guessed it all, before one came.

"Parker asked me to give you that box once we reached the capital, and not before. But you may as well take it, now you've seen it."

Maytén looked at him suspiciously.

"And why would he do that?"

"I wouldn't have any idea."

"Don't play the innocent. Someone's playing tricks, and it's probably you."

"The money is for you."

"That money isn't mine, it belongs to Parker."

As she spoke, Maytén felt a surge of anger that soon turned to frustration. Parker was deceiving her and had no intention of meeting her in the capital. The box with all their takings was ample proof of that.

"So you've been told to remove me from the scene?"

"I'm only carrying out my orders."

"I now see why you were always muttering together," she sighed, feeling betrayed.

"It's for your own good," the journalist said.

"I'm the one who will decide what's for my own good! Parker owes me an explanation."

The hazy outline of a service station appeared on one side of the road, and the journalist was forced to stop. To their mutual surprise, a real exodus of people and vehicles was underway, with all the elements of a biblical disaster. There were army trucks, private cars, vans belonging to mining and oil companies, minibuses and buses packed with passengers. Labourers, miners and whole families, their belongings over their shoulders, were trying to make it to the nearest cities in the north, located behind the ramparts of water the rivers were building. Maytén was struck by the feeling that these human beings were escaping from a catastrophe, and while the journalist drove around the crammed area looking for somewhere to park, she observed in amazement the crowds getting on and off, unloading bundles and bags in the teeth of horizontal sheets of rain. She had never witnessed such a spectacle, not even when the Tres Bocas volcano spat out clouds of ash over an entire winter. Several rows of soldiers in plastic ponchos were passing crates of food for isolated settlements down a long line that seemed to have no beginning or end.

"We've got another problem now," the journalist remarked anxiously. A never-ending queue of vehicles snaked chaotically round, waiting to refuel. Nervous drivers argued at the tops of their voices defending their place in the line, while rumours circulated, each one spiced with its individual fears and fantasies.

"You still want to go back to the truck? You ought to be thankful if we can drive on," the alarmed journalist said, squabbling with other drivers over his place in the queue and praying that fuel would be available when finally he reached a pump. Maytén no longer trusted anything he said, and suspected all manner of intrigue. She felt she was a mere object the two men were transporting here and there, as if she were a cargo they had to deliver. She felt a desperate desire to rebel and retaliate, and swore she would make Parker pay for this.

"I'm going to look for something to eat," she exclaimed moodily, then got out and disappeared into the turbulent throng. When she walked past the bathrooms and was about to walk inside, a heavy hand descended on her shoulder: an employee pointed to the long queue of women waiting in the rain. When her turn finally came, the mirror revealed to Maytén a face lashed by rainwater and worn out by hours on the road. She rubbed her bloodshot eyes, tidied her hair and tried to repair the ravages of exhaustion, ignoring the shouting and knocking on the door of women complaining about their long wait. She had to join yet another queue in the restaurant, but when the moment of truth came, she was no longer hungry; she could not eat until she had sorted out her situation. She emerged from those premises sadder and more disillusioned than ever. A sudden blackout triggered by a thick layer of clouds led to the lights and neon signs being switched on. She was stunned by that premature night in the middle of the day, that artificial climate, like a pretend cheerfulness, created by the colourful lights. In any case, she had already decided on her next step: she would go against the flow, go back to where her companion had stayed, to a period of her life she had no wish to abandon. Whatever the cost, she needed to speak to Parker and ask him to explain himself, then she could get back on track with her own life, in the place where it had come to a halt. Those days were crucial, each hour that passed locked them in different territories; other rivers overflowed and shut off roads, other currents pushed and pulled, and there was little one could do. To make her voice audible over the noise from the tempest, she had to shout at each driver who was arriving or leaving, and ask if anyone could take her. Their replies confirmed what the journalist was saying: nobody was going back, they were all in flight. Maytén suddenly noticed army transport, tall vehicles that went everywhere, through water, snow, sand or whatever, and she had a brainwave: she walked back across the parking lot, dodged the torrents of water gushing off shiny tarpaulins and approached a group of soldiers who were inspecting a convoy.

"I must get to Confluencia, kilometre 560 on route 203, near Pampa del Infierno," she told one who seemed a higher rank. The man, a young officer clad in a plastic poncho that made him look like a warrior from a bygone age, invited Maytén to get into one of the vehicles. There he consulted a map for several minutes, looking for the place Maytén had mentioned.

"Access is blocked. Why on earth do you want to go there?" he asked, staring at her. Maytén did not have the will to respond, and said something hesitantly, gazing hard at that spot on the map.

"We have to drive that way to evacuate various settlements. If we can't get through in Santa Pérfidas, we'll have to find another point of access," he said. Maytén's gloomy face was vaguely lit up by a distant glow.

"So I can go with you?"

"It's not advisable to go to the central region, people are seeking safe havens on the coast or the cordillera."

"I'm not looking for a safe haven, I'm looking for something else," Maytén told the soldier with a determined gaze. The soldier hesitated briefly and jumped out to consult with other colleagues who were organising the convoy. The officers talked among themselves, their eyes converging on her. The man came back and sat next to her.

"I should warn you it could take a day or a month, and there's no guarantee we'll ever get there."

"That's fine," she said, and the man looked at her for a moment, surprised by her determination. Maytén felt relieved for the first time in a long while, as if she had fulfilled part of her mission. A uniformed woman appeared soon after, handed her a raincoat and warm clothing; the convoy was almost ready and they might leave at any moment. Maytén spent ages searching for the journalist's car, and finally found it in the middle of the bottleneck of straggling vehicles.

"Where did you get to? I've been waiting for you for over an hour," he said furiously. She had never seen him so angry. At that point several cars began to move off as the queue advanced. Maytén sat next to him and gathered up her belongings so quickly she surprised the journalist, since there was nothing to excuse such haste.

"What are you doing?" he shouted. After taking a few steps, Maytén returned to the car, took the money box and tucked it under her arm.

"I'm going to return this to its rightful owner," she said.

The journalist started to say something, but had to break off. In that chaos the line of cars moved a few metres forwards, and those behind him started honking their horns to get him to move on. Maytén vanished into the crowd, and the journalist tried to follow her despite the insults from other drivers who accelerated, overtook him and argued over the empty space. He ran through the throng after her, but then had to go back to his car and recover his place.

"Wait a minute, don't go yet, I've something I must give you!" he shouted desperately, but she was wrapped in her raincoat and couldn't hear a word. Another driver agreed to move his car on as the line advanced, then he grabbed a bundle of handwritten papers he was carrying among his documents. It was the letter Parker had written to his companion, saying he should hand it over together with the money box as soon as they reached their destination. He gripped the sheets of paper and shouted out her name as he ran from one end of the service station to the other, but he couldn't spot Maytén in the jostling crowd.

"Wait, I've got something I must give you!" he bellowed, holding the letter aloft, hoping she would see it.

"Maytén!" he kept shouting as the rain sluiced down, while everyone looked at him as if he had gone mad. Several bystanders decided he must be a postman and started to whirl around him, shouting out their names and asking if they too did not have a letter. Others asked for news of friends and relatives and some handed him envelopes and messages to deliver in different places in the region. A small crowd surrounded the exhausted journalist, hysterical men and women bawling out their names or demanding items. He had to elbow his way through the throng around him, then slip away and return to his car. When he had filled his tank, he parked his car in a safe place and resumed his search, calling out Maytén's name, still holding on to the letter. As night fell, the area emptied out, and a long caravan of red lights disappeared into the pitch-black steppe. The empty petrol pumps, their long hoses crossed and dangling in front and behind, looked like sentries from a sci-fi movie set.

"Maytén, Maytén!" he repeated to the benefit of no-one, hoarse, soaked and shivering with cold, until the whole area was deserted. Downcast, he got into his car, where his travelling companion's fragrant scent still lingered, and put the sheaf of papers inscribed by Parker on the dashboard. Outside, the last remaining employees were sealing installations with wooden boards and constructing trenches with sacks of sand to hold off the waters that would shortly flood the area. He switched on the engine and heating, tapped the car dashboard repeatedly until tepid air started to circulate, then drove off. Before reaching the main road, he passed a long line of military vehicles parked to one side, waiting like an obedient animal for the signal to depart, their engines purring, their headlights raking the darkness. He lowered the side window the better to see if Maytén was inside one, and could not stop a gust of wind blowing the letter away, scattering the sheets over the asphalt. He stopped to collect them, but the water had already smudged the ink and Parker's scrawl was now a dark blotchy mess the mud soon swallowed up. The journalist drove out onto the main road and immediately became yet another red light adorning it like a Christmas tree.

○  ○

Parker, Dietrich and Bruno spent the entire time the rains lasted – day after day, week after week – sheltering under the awnings and tarpaulins tied to what remained of the truck. They'd collected enough wood to keep warm and cook the pitiful food supplies they had left, mostly army campaign rations they had negotiated with the departing gendarmes: green cardboard boxes containing cigarettes, chocolate, biscuits, powdered milk, tinned goods, matches and small bottles of liquor. Familiar with the climate in those barren wastes, Parker had ensured they had guaranteed food stocks for the difficult days ahead, not only until the rain stopped, but also for when they had to abandon the remnants of the truck and go elsewhere. With these military rations, plus a plentiful supply of wine, they could take refuge for weeks in what was left of the encampment, like wild animals in their burrows. They spent hours playing cards, struggling to maintain their battered refuge and fighting the water coming at them from above and below. Stinking of smoke and alcohol, dishevelled and mud-splattered, the trio lived cheek by jowl in the most absolute of silences, avoiding words, exchanging the minimal gestures and grunts necessary to coordinate joint actions, like handing round a bottle or a piece of firewood. At night they wrapped themselves in blankets, canvas or anything else that wasn't wet, but sometimes their timetables were reversed, they slept by day and spent nights awake around a campfire that stubbornly resisted the rain. Its flames highlighted their delirious, bearded faces, their unkempt hair and their smoke-reddened eyes that made them resemble sailors marooned on a desert island. They finally lost all idea of time, and, abandoned to their own devices, they waited for something to happen, although they could not imagine what it might be.

One morning, which might just as well have been midday or afternoon, Parker woke up and realised something unusual was afoot. There had not been an extraordinary snowstorm, no active volcanos were spewing ash over the valleys, dense banks of fog were not settling in for days, none of that was happening, but something much simpler: the rain pouring down from the awnings had mysteriously stopped. A spectral silence had detached itself from the firmament and was now slipping over the remnants of the encampment. Bright sunlight penetrated the cracks and they would have heard birdsong, had a single tree existed in the thousands of kilometres around them. Their three heads peered between the folds of the canvas, lit up by the rays of a timid sun. They should make the most of that truce to take their next step. They explored the vicinity, as if they had just disembarked on a strange land, while icy gusts lashed their bodies, dispelling any false hopes of spring. A single shiver shook all three. Taking advantage of the dry weather, they put out their clothes to air, collected up their belongings and readied themselves for an immediate departure. Dietrich followed suit, though he could not guess what his fate would be; he had learned what life was like in those latitudes and allowed himself to be dragged along by whatever came his way. He had forgotten the few words of Spanish learned in the silence of that enforced cohabitation, where one gesture sufficed to say the little there was to say.

Parker distributed rations and got ready the bicycle he had negotiated on the stall. Bruno readied his motorbike by connecting and disconnecting tubes, massaging cables and adjusting valves. Standing bereft, the tearful, anxious Dietrich gazed at his companions, who failed to notice, so busy were they preparing their departure. He went over to one, then the other, like a tame, timid dog in search of a master, wanting to know whom he could stick with, but it was futile: Bruno and Parker were preparing to leave at any moment without even a farewell wave, and he would be abandoned in the midst of the flatlands. Resigned to his lonesome fate, Dietrich traipsed towards the void, sat down on a rock and turned his back on them. He sat, head down, drawing shapes in the mud with a stick, looking forlorn, and swore he would not turn round until his two friends had ridden off into the distance. His melancholic pose contrasted with the phrase tattooed in Gothic script on his furrowed forehead, which now seemed a salute to defeat rather than victory. He did not realise his fate had yet to be decided.

As the motorbike revved, Bruno approached Parker, looking like an astronaut on the launch pad in his full garb with the Grim Reaper's scythe strapped on his shoulder.

"Let me have him, he's no use to you anymore."

Parker looked at him blankly.

"The gringo, I mean. You stole Maytén from me, now give me the gringo and we're quits."

Parker hadn't considered his own fate, let alone his butler's. He imagined he would go his own way, now he had a little money, but was not thrilled by the idea of surrendering him like that, let alone to Bruno.

"And why would *you* want him?"

"I had this idea, but I won't tell *you* what it is."

Parker remained lost in thought for a second, then stared at Dietrich, who was still saying nothing, aware his future depended on these men.

"Alright, we're quits," Parker said. Bruno grunted to the German to get on the bike. Dietrich mumbled, picked up his bundles and jumped nimbly aboard, his heart brimming with joy. A moment later they both climbed onto the strip of asphalt, then slipped and stumbled down the middle of the road heading south until they had gathered sufficient speed. At times the motorbike seemed nailed to the landscape. Parker observed them as they rode away, fighting the ups and the downs, until they vanished from sight among the undulating hills.

Parker walked back. Not wasting any time, he salvaged some wooden staves that had supported the awning and tied them with wire to the frame of the bike so they acted like masts, then made up a couple of sails from the canvas and fixed them to the main mast. That took him a couple of hours, but he was happy with the result, and when his rigging was ready, he tied on his luggage. He loaded it up like saddlebags, and steadied his sails for the off. At first light he studied the direction of the wind, the position of the sun and the movement of the clouds from one quadrant to the other, then gave that place one last glance. The truck was resting with its muzzle buried in the ground, empty, half-dismantled and wheel-less, doors and engine cover open. He found it an effort to push his heavy bicycle up to the asphalt, then he jumped on and waited for the signal to ride off, his forehead close to the handlebars, his feet pressing on the ground. When he thought the moment was right, he pulled a rope hard, the two huge sails unfurled with a snap and swelled out like a dark stain on the limpid air. He didn't even have time to glance back at what had been his home for years: the bicycle shot off and for a few moments he was almost swept away. Parker leaned his body forward first to one side, then to the other, vying with the capricious gusts and adjusting his handlebars to correct the zigzag threatening to push him off the road. He was forced to fight the wind in almost hand-to-hand combat to find the direction he wanted, until the bicycle stabilised. He soon vanished over the horizon, flying down that dark ribbon of road, and travelled the whole day with muscles tensed as hard as rock. He sometimes thought of stopping to rest, but had to make the most of the tailwind. Without mishap he crossed humps over gently flowing streams and a number of bridges that had just been freed. Furling and unfurling sails during the day, and folding them in order to sleep at the roadside by night, Parker cycled for several days lashed by memories of Maytén. At each stop he rolled up the canvas sheets and tied them to the masts, placed rocks on the bike so that it was not blown away by the wind, snuggled into his sleeping bag and fed on military rations. He heated tins of canned food by using alcohol tablets, then consumed the rest of his provisions, including the small bottle of whisky and cigarettes. He did not really know where he was heading, nor did he want to know; it was better that way, because he had no options or preferences, and that spared him the effort of having to choose. He often came to forking roads, but the speed he was cycling at did not allow him to read the signs. That was all for the better too; he wouldn't have had time to change direction.

For the moment, he simply had to profit from the fair wind which could change at any moment. Nevertheless, he had a vague notion of where he was drifting, and his orientation indicated he would soon cross a railway track, something that never guaranteed a train, but did promise the possibility of houses where he could beg shelter in order to recover his strength. One afternoon when his muscles were creased by searing pains and he let himself be carried along by a starboard breeze, Parker spotted a dark stripe amid the grazing lands: a huge goods train chugging in the same direction as himself. Freezing cold, a mass of sores and cramp, he could not miss such an opportunity. He calculated that at some point, kilometres ahead, their paths would cross. Parker adjusted his sails to catch the biggest volume of wind and reach the level crossing before the goods train, which disappeared every now and then into the undulating countryside. After one bend he heard a hum of engines and there it was less than a hundred metres away, juddering across the level crossing. He calculated he had little time to board, and no option but to throw his bags over his shoulders and leap from his bike as if he was abandoning a ship. The moment his feet hit the ground, he felt a hand push him forwards, the bike veered and fell over, carrying its sails along the verge. Parker ran along the road driven by that impetus, almost stumbling, at a speed that was more than his legs could stand. When his body finally reasserted control, he reached the tracks, where the last wagons were rolling by. With one last effort he grabbed a rail and leapt into an open truck transporting mineral ore. Once aboard he collapsed, exhausted, staying like that until he recovered his breath. It was no use peering at the surrounding landscape to find out where they were heading. He was still lost, although that was no longer his problem, but the one facing the men who, twenty or thirty trucks on, were driving the train. He lay on his back, staring at the vast vault of sky, while the regular beat of the wheels cradled his body. A fresh sense of freedom gripped him as he crossed the undulating steppe. A strange current was pulling him into the deepest recesses of his being, and he was happy for that to happen.

○ ○

The ramshackle bus, its roof laden with bags, suitcases and boxes, went up and down white-frosted hills, its moribund engine wheezing and clouds of black smoke pouring from the exhaust with every change of gear. Huddled together in the dank warmth, several families of labourers and miners were returning to their abodes after the floods, now that rivers were returning to their normal channels. Although most roads were still blocked, many corridors had been opened up thanks to the intervention of military engineers. The passengers, men and women with weathered hands and faces, looked robust enough with their peasant smiles. They travelled taciturn in their seats, wrapped in ponchos and overcoats, staring out of steamed-up, dusty windows. They shared their provisions as if words no longer had any meaning and real communication resided in that division of goods, a gulp of wine, a round of maté, a piece of bread, even the monotonous silence of their journey. They were the implicit rules of coexistence that prevailed in the precarious life of the steppe.

Maytén was in the back seat, surrounded by the children she had played with on the drive. A small community had developed among the passengers in the bus, who had adopted her as soon as they left one of the evacuee camps.

That pleasant young woman, travelling alone in search of something she could not describe, appealed to people's sense of solidarity.

Maytén stood up and tried to find her bearings in a familiar feature of the terrain, but the rains had changed the entire topography of the region. She asked her fellow travellers for indications. Up until then they had been very supportive, but were now responding reluctantly and evasively. She noted that something strange was happening; they now seemed anxious and worried about something they had in common. They kept looking at their watches, asking each other the time every five minutes, until they all nodded simultaneously. One of the women, the oldest, got up and solemnly addressed the sleepy-eyed driver, patted him on the back and returned to her seat. The driver with a bored expression on his face switched on the radio, and the voice of a presenter announcing the start of the radio serial immediately spread down the bus. The passengers sat comfortably back in their seats and prepared to listen to the next episode of the story. Maytén felt she was in a cinema and that the lights would be switched off at any moment. For an hour her attention was held by the voices of the goodies and the baddies, those suffering and those losing hope, scorned lovers and traitors, heroes and losers, the passionate and the tepid. Each passenger was riveted to the plot of that soap opera that, twice a day, every afternoon and evening, reached the most distant boundaries of the territory, bringing life to the empty desolation of the steppe. Whenever the signal weakened on a bend or slope and the narrative was interrupted, the listeners engaged in debate about the dialogues or sections lost in the ether, empty spaces they filled with their own fantasies, until a few kilometres on the signal returned and the radio serial pursued its natural course.

Maytén had lost count of the time that had gone by since she last saw Parker, and of the weeks she had travelled these byways to reach where she had been when weather and floodwater swept away that part of her life. She knew only too well that what she was doing was ridiculous, but, whatever the cost, she needed to return to that place; she had set herself that goal the day after they separated. She sensed that that spot where they had left each other was also the only point of departure from which she could reshape her future life, the final hemisphere, a wound she must heal in order to bury it and the remains of the past in boundaries set by the wind. She had had little time to sob and lament in the midst of the chaos ruling the region, where a mass of aimless humans moved blindly within a maze of blocked roads and isolated settlements. Parker must still be there; he could not have moved on until water levels went down; it was a matter of days. As time passed, the distance increased, and little by little turned into an absence; every day she took to reach one of those clusters of houses, cross a stream or reach a crossroads, was one more day destiny placed between them. In any case, she would persevere, even if it took months to find that spot under that sky at the end of the world. Parker was her small victory over life, the one brief moment she had shared something like love, before the steppe had engulfed them. Life wouldn't give her another opportunity like that, even if they did eventually chance to meet. That territory could be so vast they might never see each other again, but a paradox of geography meant those same features sometimes brought people together, and who was she to say their paths might not cross? But those thoughts were not enough, she must find Parker and look him in the eye for a few seconds without the mediation of words. If he had planned to offload her in order to recover his life and freedom, Maytén would be the first to understand, but she needed to confront him, so their story together could have an ending and they could each continue on their own path, wherever that might be leading. It was the only thing she could hope for; she was not impelled by any optimism about reuniting with him or resuming a life they had abandoned on the verge of a road, but simply wanted to discern in his gaze something that still remained blurred. Then she would leave forever, however whimsical and unpredictable the roads might be at that far end of the continent.

When the radio serial was about to conclude, the signal weakened and the device went dead, denying them the end of the plot. Maytén remembered Parker's cabin and the lunatic frequencies that kept jumping like animals over barbed-wire fences, and had to exorcise the memory with more pleasant recollections. Impatient passengers began blaming the deadpan driver for the sudden interruption to the soap opera.

"It's not my fault," the man apologised, but tempers flared and a kind of mutiny started. Several men and women stood up and surrounded the driver, asking him to stop the bus and recover the lost signal as soon as possible, but that did not suffice. The man had to go back, then drive on, leave the main road, trace circles and effect different manoeuvres over the steppe until he found the exact spot where the plot thread had been interrupted by the side of a hill. The vehicle was on an incline, its snout looking up at the sky. When they heard the actors' voices again, the driver braked and got off to look for rocks to put behind the wheels, then the passengers could return to their seats and give themselves up to what remained of the story. A while later, the radio serial concluded and the vehicle drove off. As her travelling companions argued heatedly about what had happened, Maytén leaned towards one of the windows and looked around her. It was difficult to identify terrain in a land where everything seemed identical, could have the same features over hundreds of kilometres. She was searching for any reference point that might indicate the place, a sign or detail, and asked the driver to let her get off. She was hoping that outside, standing in the middle of the road, she would be able to find a clue to lead her to her goal. The icy wind blasted her body. While she walked around and examined the landscape inch by inch, the passengers peered at her through the grimy windows.

"So where *exactly* do you need to get to, señorita?" the driver asked out of his window.

"I need to get to Confluencia."

"Which Confluencia?"

"Near Pampa del Infierno, kilometre 560, route 203."

The driver shook his head several times, he had never heard of those names or numbers. He consulted some of his passengers, convinced the place did not exist, but then it struck a possible chord.

"And why do you want to go there? If that place exists, nothing was ever there," he said, but as Maytén did not reply, he shrugged and lost interest in the subject.

"I'm looking for a truck parked by a unit of gendarmes," she explained. At once the other passengers got off and went into a huddle to discuss the matter and offer their opinions. Most mentioned different places, some thought it was up north, others down south. As a result of that conference, where no two answers were the same, the spot she was hunting became a chimera, until one woman remembered the location of "that truck where things were sold". Maytén had told some of her female travelling companions about her affair with Parker, and the gossip soon spread throughout the bus. People felt sympathetic towards her and started offering her advice and a range of opinions on the possible outcomes from that business, just as in their radio drama.

The driver was uneasy and hooted to reassemble that scattered flock, and once they were all back in their seats, he asked if they all agreed to extend their journey by several hours in order to take Maytén to "the truck where things were sold". Everyone raised their hands to vote, and the verdict was unanimously in favour. The vehicle carried out a couple more manoeuvres, turned around and drove back to the crossroads, then took the turning to Sauce Muerto, from where there was a shortcut to Confluencia.

The wooden sign with faded letters where you could still read CAREFUL ROAD CLOSED came into view, knocked to one side of the road, next to several upended drums, remains of campfires and scar-like marks in the mud. Maytén knew at once they had arrived, although that was all that was left of the military detachment. The driver stopped the bus. She got off and walked along the frost-covered road while expectant faces followed the scene through steamed-up windows, though nobody said a word. Seconds after she had jumped out, the driver turned his bus round and parked his vehicle, ready to resume his original itinerary. Maytén took several steps, and struggled to recognise the place. The truck was in the same spot, on the verge, now a skeleton half covered by sand and bushes, its chassis dismantled and a constellation of parts littered around. She walked between unused firewood, broken crates, empty bottles, ropes and canvas sheets coiled between axles, and reached what was once the centre of the encampment. She stood absorbed in that scene for an instant, but it brought back no memories. And then she felt a presence behind her; the sound of steps suggested she was not alone. Maytén's instinct was to run towards the bus, which was waiting idly on a slope, but she decided to find out who or what was there. She walked to the back of the site and met a huge pair of eyes looking at her suspiciously, questioning her: it was a young guanaco that had strayed from its herd. Maytén gave a start, but was soothed by the animal's serene gaze. Both stood there, confronted each other, rooted to the spot for what seemed an endless period of time, and the only movement giving any life to that scene was the steam issuing from the guanaco's snout with each breath. The image of one was reflected in the eyes of the other, until the animal looked elsewhere on the steppe, searching for its herd. It began to canter with surprising grace, then broke into a run, taking short jumps, until it built up momentum. Maytén saw the barbed wire ahead and shuddered. She shut her eyes tight as the guanaco prepared to take that decisive leap, then reopened them. The animal seemed to hesitate before making the final effort, calculating the distance, but the youthful muscles of its rear legs lifted it over the sharp barbs with a feral elegance. Maytén stood and watched the ochre back of the guanaco bob up and down between the bushes as it ran towards its herd. Once it had disappeared over the horizon, she started to walk back to the road without turning round, until the remnants of the truck became one more blotch on the plain. Still not turning round, she walked back over the double yellow line to the bus that was waiting with its engine purring. The passengers were sitting inside, still and serious, their blank faces feigning a lack of concern. Maytén got in, said nothing, then the driver shut the door by activating a lever, and juddered off towards the road he had come along, leaving a trail of black smoke in his wake.

o  o

"Gold, did you say, or didn't I hear you a-right?" Parker asked incredulously.

"Gold, I said, you heard me a-right," the journalist said, taking nervous drags on his cigarette, the smoke from which twisted around the car before being sucked out of the window. The car was crossing one of the mesas on which the steppe rested in order to contemplate the ocean. Pale spring flowers peeked shyly out from among the bushes on the plain. Parker was travelling by his side, in dark glasses, his long, sparse wisps of hair ruffled by the warm breeze. The noonday sun blistered down on the asphalt, granting no shadow beyond that thin dark outline.

"I always thought you were mad, journo, but now I'm not so sure: madmen don't persevere in their lunacy, at some point they have their doubts," Parker said, surveying the load of spades, picks, sieves and other items in the back seat that he imagined, without too much effort, were digging tools. He took a final gulp of beer and threw the bottle out of the window.

"The only gold I ever had was in a tooth, and I lost that. I must have swallowed it at some point," Parker said.

"Now's your chance to get it back."

"I don't mind at all that *you* want to prospect for gold, what worries me is that I'm here by your side."

"Trust me, I have intel that will make us famous. Have you ever heard of La Podrida and Santo Diablo?"

"They don't sound at all promising. A putrefied woman and an evil devil?"

"They're mines that have been abandoned for decades. Very few people know of their existence, and nobody living knows their location. Treasure is waiting for us there, I found references in old documents that I checked out in the capital."

"I can imagine how this will finish: papers blowing in the wind."

The journalist looked at him a couple of times and accelerated, ignoring Parker's complaints. They drove towards the coast for several hours, helped by a luminous breeze that swept across the dry steppe heated by the sun, making it dry and warm again. Parker was dozing, every pore of his pale cheeks enjoying the sun's rays, when a sudden manoeuvre made him jump out of his seat. The journalist violently jerked the steering wheel and the car swerved.

"What's getting you now?" he asked, annoyed rather than intrigued, while his companion turned the car around without as much as a glance at his mirrors.

"That road will take us to Salar Desesperación in a matter of days," he said, pointing to a turning that was barely visible. Parker searched his memory, that name meant something, but he could not think what, and then he recalled the story of the Trinitarian cannibals and was startled.

"You can forget that nonsense!" he shouted, as he grabbed the wheel, as they dug each other in the ribs, turning the car 180 degrees round until it was facing the direction from which it had come. They struggled for a while over who was in control of the car. It zigzagged from one side of the empty road to the other, as driver and companion shouted at each other.

"I'm sick to death of your fantasies! Let's go and prospect for gold, if you must, but I'm not going to let you chase the story of Indian souls possessed by Spanish sailors."

"Hey, take it steady, we'll kill each other! Don't force me to wear out the few brakes I've got left," the journalist said.

"I'm not moving from here," Parker threatened, opening his door.

"I never imagined you could be such a coward. We'll cross the Strait of Magellan in a week, and in a few days will reach La Podrida, when water from the melting snow will have restored crystalline purity to the streams," the journalist said, but Parker had lolled back in his seat enjoying the sun on his face and pretending to be asleep.

The tailwind kept driving the vehicle forward at unthinkable speeds for its old engine, which shook, vibrated and squealed anxiously, unaccustomed to such feats. They soon reached the end of the mesa and parked at an angle so the doors could open without being wrenched off their hinges by a gust. They walked to the brink of the precipice to contemplate the deep blue ocean and the wild white horses spreading out beneath them, but they were stunned. The ocean had receded and was barely visible: a distant luminous strip tucked away on the horizon. A vast stretch of wet sand had taken its place. Once again the low tide and the wind from land had driven the seawater far into the distance, creating an endless plain dotted with rivulets and pools. Down below they could see a small cluster of fishermen's cottages that survived the gale-force winds thanks to the shelter afforded by the cliffs. Parker recognised the spot at once; it was where he and Maytén had walked into the water coming over the sand and been surrounded by the treacherous tentacles of high tide.

"Something odd's happening in the village," the journalist said, seeing an unusual buzz of activity in the settlement, a kind of meeting or spectacle. He grabbed his binoculars and saw all manner of vehicles, carts, cars, horses, vans and trucks parked around a huge stage where a small crowd had gathered.

"I can't believe my eyes, Parker," he said incredulously. Parker stretched his hand out to take the binoculars so he could see with his own eyes, but his companion returned them to their case.

"We have to see this in person," he said. They returned to the car, astounded by that desolate panorama of an ocean defeated by a beach, and drove down the slope to the centre of the hamlet. They walked past the first houses, following the sound of strident music. As they drew nearer, they spotted a box where a theatre performance was in progress. They could see very little over the heads straining to watch the spectacle. Parker and the journalist made themselves comfortable in a corner and to their amazement discovered a wooden stage set up like a boxing ring, decorated with paintings and drawings of monsters that were very familiar to Parker. A huge sign with fluorescent letters announced: DEBUT THE NEW INTERNATIONAL WRESTLING CIRCUS.

Bruno was standing inside the ring in military dress uniform, his broad shoulders decorated with lurid sea lions that made him look like an operetta general. He announced through a microphone: ". . . for the very first time in

Patagonia and the surrounding territory, straight from Japan, the champion brothers of the martial arts, Hiroshima and Nagasaki, will now step up to fight."

Wearing kimonos, Eber and Fredy jumped onto the stage imitating karate chops and war cries. Whitened faces and eye shadow emphasised their Altiplano features. A timid ovation grew and exploded into applause and whistles that echoed down the hamlet's narrow streets. Bruno called for silence by gesturing wildly to a crowd that was becoming frenzied.

". . . they will fight the ghastly murderer just arrived from Germany, Adolf Killer . . ." Bruno concluded as another round of clapping greeted the unrecognisable Dietrich wearing a flimsy military uniform. He jumped into the ring, shouting and barking orders in German, intimidating the expectant audience with his ferocious gaze. Acclaimed by the crowd, he took off his jacket and revealed the eagles, swastikas and Celtic crosses tattooed on his body. Bruno's Bolivian handymen approached stealthily from behind, ready to ambush him, while Bruno put the microphone to one side, took off his fancy outfit and joined the group of wrestlers. There followed a fierce burst of wrestling – threats, punches and kicks, flights and falls – that brought the fascinated audience to the point of delirium.

Parker and the journalist were immersed in the shouting, and before the fight finished, they headed silently to their car.

"Let's drive on before it gets dark," Parker said in a monotone voice. The journalist nodded and then halted.

"Don't you want to stay? I'm sure they'd find a role for you."

Parker took hold of the journalist by the shoulder and pushed him into the car. They drove south, following the sinuous coastline; several weeks on the road lay ahead. The car crossed the dunes – the broad sweep of the bay was now dry because of the retreating low tide – and they followed the tracks of vehicles that had ventured over the sand towards the distant ocean, to the site of the wrecks. The journalist reduced speed and looked for a place that would enable him to leave the road.

"Do you want to go down to the beach now that it's low tide? I'm sure we'll find remains of galleons, and some treasure or other."

Parker grabbed the steering wheel and with another abrupt jerk pointed the car back on course. They tussled for a few seconds.

"Hey, journo, stop all this fantasising. Get back to reality, grow up, it's about time. How long are you going to keep on like this?"

The journalist looked at him and acquiesced without protest, then drove back to the road, accelerating as much as the moribund engine would allow.

The car very quickly melted into the distance.

At that precise moment, deep in the ocean bay, level with the reefs, several families were picnicking in their cars as their youngsters played football on a field they had improvised on the sand. They had set up one goal by using rusty metal pipes, remnants of a wreck that had surfaced. When their game was over, a group of kids building sandcastles began to excavate around the pipes. They used spades, buckets, hands and fingernails to remove sand and make a large circular pit. Like a line of disciplined little ants, those kids came and went, carrying sand to complete their castle before the waters rose and they would have to go back to the coast.

All at once one of them stopped and pointed at something inside the pit; then he told everyone else and all the kids gathered around to take a look at the huge iron carcass, the source of the pipes they'd used for goal posts. They went on digging and removing water nonstop, ignoring the shouts of the adults, until a dark turret emerged with old numbers covered in rust that were difficult to decipher. The threat of the rising tide and the adults' shouts compelled the group to go back to their vehicles before the area was covered in water again. One of the last children stopped and observed the large "U" that had appeared on one side of the turret, followed by several numbers. "Seven, four and five," he read, staring at that inscription for a few seconds, strangely fascinated. Then he shrugged, turned his back on that strange structure being engulfed by the incoming tide, and ran and jumped between pools of water until he was back with the rest of the gang.

*Buenos Aires, 2017*